M000202431

Summoning is all I know . . . but I don't know it well enough.

I have powers I don't fully understand. And my lack of knowledge is putting everyone I love in danger. Unfortunately, my teacher disappeared long ago.

So I'm stumbling along trying to figure things out on my own, making more than my share of mistakes. And now, a few powerful magical beings have started keeping tabs on me. Which makes me wonder . . .

Why are Faerie and Hell suddenly so interested in an untrained summoner? And why did my sexy-as-sin sorta boyfriend leave after a single night of passion?

I'm almost afraid to find out. . . .

Books by J. D. Blackrose

The Summoner's Mark series

Demon Kissed
Fae Crossed
Hellbound (coming soon)

Fae Crossed

Book 2 in the Summoner's Mark Series

by

J. D. Blackrose

Bell Bridge Books

This is a work of fiction. Names, characters, places and incidents are either the products of the author's imagination or are used fictitiously. Any resemblance to actual persons (living or dead), events or locations is entirely coincidental.

Bell Bridge Books
PO BOX 300921
Memphis, TN 38130
Print ISBN: 978-1-61026-175-3

Bell Bridge Books is an Imprint of BelleBooks, Inc.

Copyright © 2022 by J. D. Blackrose

Published in the United States of America.

All rights reserved. No part of this book may be reproduced in any form or by any electronic or mechanical means, including information storage and retrieval systems, without permission in writing from the publisher, except by a reviewer, who may quote brief passages in a review.

We at BelleBooks enjoy hearing from readers.
Visit our websites
BelleBooks.com
Bell Bridge Books.com
ImaJinn Books.com

10 9 8 7 6 5 4 3 2 1

Cover design: Debra Dixon
Interior design: JimandZetta.com
Photo/Art credits:
Man (manipulated) © Artofphoto | Dreamstime.com
Symbols (manipulated© Samiramay | Dreamstime.com

Dedication

This book is dedicated to my wonderful family.

Chapter 1

Jonah didn't like me very much.

I sat at my sister's table. Her husband, Jonah, sat across from me, and Ruthie, their daughter and my niece, was next to me in a high chair. The square table sported a white embroidered tablecloth, candlesticks, a wine glass, and a challah, a traditional bread for the Jewish sabbath. It not only tasted delicious fresh, it also made the best French toast the next morning. The setting made me nostalgic, and I fought back tears remembering those peaceful times when it was just my sister, my mom, and me.

Jonah glared at me, furrowed his brow, and stabbed a fork in the direction of my face. "What's wrong with you?" he snapped, his frustration at my presence overshadowing his manners. "Why are you crying? You should be happy to be here. You're lucky Mikayla is such a forgiving sister. I wouldn't have invited you."

Mickey shot him an irritated glance.

Though Jonah criticized me for being emotional, his aggression had nothing to do with my unshed tears and everything to do with how my summoning had placed his wife and daughter in danger. Though that demon situation had been resolved, he still didn't want me anywhere near his family. Mickey and I had made our peace, however, so Jonah suffered my presence, though not gracefully.

"This food smells so delicious. Exactly like Mom used to make. It brings back a lot of memories," I whispered, then bit my lip to keep from bawling. Mom had passed a while ago, and I couldn't recall my father's face. Mom had done her best to keep up with traditions, and Mickey had made the same recipes we'd eaten together as kids. Each bite was a trip down memory lane.

I stroked Ruthie's head as she shoved a fistful of mashed sweet potatoes in her mouth, grinning as orange goop oozed between her fingers and baby teeth. I vowed not to be like my father, whose disappearance still colored our lives. I swore I wouldn't miss any more important moments.

Mickey kissed me on the head. "I'm glad you're with us."

My midsection vibrated, and I couldn't tell if it was my phone buzzing or my stomach growling.

The reverberation at my middle occurred again. Definitely a muffled phone vibration.

I wondered if any other summoners had out-of-office messages saying they couldn't answer because they had Shabbat dinner plans?

Probably none, but how would I know? I'd only met one other summoner—Trace. After my summoner's mark, the Kiss, came in, my mom hired him to train me. I still didn't know how she'd found him. I'd gone through her things after she died and found nothing to indicate where he'd come from or how she'd reached him. Not a phone number, an email, or address.

To further complicate matters, he'd disappeared before completing my instruction. I wished there was a summoner convention where we could trade secrets or have seminars on "Demon Contracts and Loopholes" or "Tips for Dealing with Dragons" or "Best Incense for Removing Rakshasa Stank." For all I knew, there weren't enough summoners around to even have a convention.

Hell, there probably weren't enough for a picnic.

I had no right to a pity party. Due to my dealings with a demon, I'd messed up my relationship with my sister, and my brother-in-law still held it against me. Mickey had forgiven me, and that's why I was here, at her home, for Friday night dinner. Now that things were safe, I'd eat this amazing food, hug Ruthie, ignore my phone, and be grateful.

My younger sister was five-three, dark haired and had warm, chocolate eyes. I was five-ten, dirty blond and green-eyed, so we didn't look alike, and I'd bet money that no one would describe my eyes as "warm." At best, I'd probably get "guarded," "apprehensive," or "wary." I'd place money that the word "crabby" would sneak in as well.

Mickey studied me across the table. "Why didn't you bring Asher to dinner? I told you to invite him."

I'd wanted to avoid this conversation, but Mickey had our mom's knack for pinpointing uncomfortable topics and forcing me to face them.

"He . . . uhm, left town."

She paused with a potholder in her right hand and a spoon in the other. "When will he be back?"

I rubbed my forehead. That traitorous, skulking, love-'em-and-leave-'em, gorgeous bastard had left me after a single night of passion. I'd woken to find an origami bird on my pillow and no Asher. At least I thought it was a bird. While sleeping, I'd rolled over and smashed it with my forearm, and the mangled paper made it hard to tell. I could make out wings. Since he knew of my love for birds, that was my guess.

"Don't know. I've called his mobile, but there was no answer. He's not at work either. He disappeared without saying goodbye."

He'd surprised me by bugging out after our night together. I knew he had his secrets, but hey, so did I. There'd been no reason for him to run away.

Jonah fed Ruthie another spoonful of potatoes but gave me a sidelong glance. "Maybe he saw the weirdness in your life and decided he couldn't take it."

A cruel observation, but possible. Then, I remembered something. "He left six months' rent, cash."

Mickey fed Ruthie a spoonful of green beans, which my niece promptly spit out. "It sounds like a family emergency. He'll be back. His behavior was rude, but I'm sure there's a reason."

I shook my head and pushed my plate away although I'd only eaten only a few bites. "He doesn't have parents or siblings."

"Then there's no excuse, and he doesn't deserve you. Put him in your rearview mirror. You're too good for him."

I didn't feel "too good." I didn't feel good at all.

Chapter 2

If you want to hustle up money fast, bartending at a fae bar is a terrible way to do it.

Joey's bar door opened with a slam as two young men, drunk as skunks, pushed it with their feet.

"Canwegetadrinkaroundhere?" the first one said, sloshing his words together so I had to concentrate to understand what he was saying. They stumbled over one another and cut quite a profile in their rainbow shirts, cargo shorts, Vans, and wrists wrapped in coordinating pink and purple bandanas. They swayed on their feet, and the taller one propped his friend up on the wall, holding him there with a shoulder to protect him from falling. They giggled at some unspoken joke.

"They must have come from the Pride Parade downtown," I whispered to Joey, my half-gnome boss. I found their flamboyant entrance endearing, but by the tapping of her hairy foot, I could tell she wasn't impressed. "They like to hold it in early September."

I studied the two men and realized the problem. These guys were human. Utterly, completely, totally, adorably human.

I smacked my head with my palm. "Ah, right. They shouldn't be able to see this place."

An elf I didn't know stood and cast a glamour so smoothly, I would have missed it if I hadn't been watching. A gasp spread around the room.

"Hey now, chaps," he said, sounding and looking like a British pensioner. "How about I call you a taxi to take you two home, safe and sound? No time to be pissed in the streets these days. Not safe."

He stepped outside, leaving the door open and waved an arm. A cab appeared in seconds, faster than one ever came when I needed it, and he handed one of the guys a couple of twenties, whispering something in his ear. They thanked him with sloppy handshakes and back-pounding hugs, which he took with good cheer. He gave them a jaunty wave as they drove off.

The elf closed the door and returned to his true self. That's when I noticed he was extraordinarily tall, at least seven feet. He paused a moment, studying the crowd. Our patrons stayed preternaturally still in his presence as he approached the bar.

He tapped his lip as he looked at Joey. "I think," he said with a grin and an Irish lilt, "that those two lads drank so much, they slipped through the veil and mistook a *fae* bar for a *gay* bar."

Joey swallowed. "I'll strengthen the wards. I know it's important to keep humans out."

He didn't acknowledge her but turned to peer at me. "You're the one who helped Pinky, am I right?"

"Yes," I replied. "Can I pour you a drink?"

His eyes lit with pleasure. "I could use a wee dram."

I reached for a nice Glenfiddich 12-Year-Old, but Joey stayed my hand and pointed to a high cabinet I'd never opened. She handed me a key to unlock its glass door, and I stood on a stepladder to retrieve an unopened bottle.

"What's your name?" I asked the new elf.

He laughed. "I'da no sooner give you me real name than turn meself into a frog, lass. But ye can call me Liam."

"Okay, Liam, here's something I've never poured." I showed him the bottle, and his eyes widened.

"Redbreast 21-Year-Old Irish Whiskey? Oh, Joey, ye know the way to me heart. Be careful with that, Rebecca Naomi Greenblatt. Every drop is gold."

He used my full name. That bothered me. From everyone's reactions, I could tell he was someone of authority, so his use of my full name was a power play. I stifled my irritation and opened the bottle while he watched me like a hawk.

"Neat? Ice? Splash?"

"Splash, please."

I poured two ounces, added a touch of water, and handed it to him with the amount of reverence it appeared to deserve.

He accepted it with two hands, swirled it, and breathed it in.

"Spicy. Nectarine." He took a sip and chewed it, breathing through his nose. "Ah, Joey, you've done me good with this. Zesty, fruity. A touch of pepper, methinks. Wonderful."

"I'm happy you like it," she said, her voice low and quiet.

He sipped and asked me a question. "Why did you help Pinky?"

"No one else would."

"Yes, but he wasn't one of yours."

I had no idea what he meant. "He's my friend. No one else

protected him. He was lost and wanted to go home. Everyone here"—I gestured to the bar—"made fun of him."

"Aye. That they did." He growled at this, and I swore the fae in the bar, who'd been remarkably quiet, all winced.

A few more sips later, he finished his whiskey. He placed his glass on the counter and clapped his hands. "That's why we'll help strengthen the bar's wards."

The fae stiffened, and several grumbled.

"What about a favor imbalance?" asked another elf, while his friend pawed at his elbow, clearly not liking that his compatriot had asked this question. "What will they owe us in return?"

The elf's friend shook his head and slid his stool away from him as if to say, "I tried, but I'm not with stupid."

Liam glared at the elf, power crackling around him. I jumped back and noticed Joey's head bowed, eyes on the ground. What the hell was going on?

"This favor *will* balance the scales. We owe Rebecca for helping Pinky, since none of you saw fit to do it. You all left the poor boy over here to suffer, knowing his mother was begging for someone to find him." Liam shot a look at the pixies at the round tables and pointed to the one I privately called Gimlet girl, but whose real name was Laurel. "Even you and your sisters. On three."

On the count of three, every fae in the bar closed their eyes and did something magical. My hair blew back as a magical waft of glowing power pushed its way outward toward the walls. The air pressure increased so suddenly, I thought I'd pass out. My eyeballs pressed against my lids, my tongue against my lips, and my cheeks hollowed. I blinked against it and fought to stay upright.

And then, it dissipated, fading like it had never been.

Liam wiped his hands together. "Joey, the wards should hold now. Evans?" He addressed the elf who'd asked the question about favor imbalance. "You'll be bringin' Joey new crystals tomorrow to solidify the magic."

Evans croaked out a "Yes, my liege."

"I'll be takin' my leave, for now. Rebecca, save that bottle for me. We have further business."

Every fae in the room lay draped over their table or had their head in their hands. I'd made it to my feet but leaned on the bar top, so all I managed was a finger wave. Liam strode to the door, but instead of opening it, he walked *through* it, disappearing from sight.

"Was that who I think it was?" I asked.

"Shhh!" said Joey from where she lay on the floor.

Evans staggered to the bar and held up a finger, indicating I needed to wait, listening to something I couldn't hear. He hesitated a few more seconds, then nodded, visibly relaxing, as did the entire bar.

Evans rubbed his eyes with his knuckles. "Yes, Becs, that was Oberon, and I'm afraid he's taken an interest in you."

"Shhhh! Don't say his name again. He might come back," said Joey.

"His taking an interest is a bad thing?" I asked.

Joey motioned for the bottle of super primo Redbreast. I handed it to her with a glass, and she poured herself a drink and slurped it down. "It's dangerous. The king's attention is rare and complicated, and always, always alarming."

Evans grimaced. "Not to mention Titania."

"Titania! The queen? I have to worry about her, too?"

He nodded. "Naturally. If her husband shows interest in a female, you can count on her wanting to know why."

"Oh, for Pete's sake." I rolled my neck and shoulders and got busy serving drinks to the suddenly parched crowd. Bolstering magical wards took a lot out of a person—or an elf, or a pixie, or a dwarf—as evidenced by the clamor for refills. Joey's bar was about to have a banner night. I hoped my tips would reflect it.

"Why is Ober—ah, the king, concerned with me?" I asked my boss as she dipped dirty glasses in a cleaning solution and then rinsed them in clean water.

"You helped Pinky, for starters."

I poured three drafts in a row, sliding them across the bar to a crew of elves, and opened a new bottle of chardonnay for the dwarves. I told everyone I'd be right back and hurried to the back rooms where Joey stored the extra liquor and supplies. We had to change out a keg.

"But I agree," Joey said when I returned, wiping her wet hands on a towel and picking up where we left off. "That's not enough to draw his eye."

"His words reminded me of a server who waited on me in Gregory's bar. Remember when I went with Laurel?" Laurel was a stuck-up pain-in-my ass pixie who only drank her gimlets with high-priced vodka. We didn't like each other, but she'd taken me to Gregory Adamos's bar when I was scoping him out. Gregory led a Greek mob syndicate and made bad choices. Of course, her helping me had a price. I now owed her a favor, and the weight of it pressed against my shoulder blades, itching and burning. I carried it all day, every day, heavy and burdensome. It slowed me down when I exercised and annoyed me while I slept. I couldn't wait to free myself of it.

Joey rubbed her hairy chin. "I recall. In what way?"

"The waiter spoke with an Irish accent and told me to 'stay interesting.' It struck me as odd, but there'd been so much going on, I blew it off."

Something niggled at the back of my brain, and I paused, thinking. I served a young dwarf a glass of merlot and didn't even remark on his choice of a red wine. I made a whiskey sour by rote and poured a shot of tequila, neat, without looking at the shot glass.

I was too preoccupied with letting this memory scratch its way to the surface.

When it came to me, I almost dropped the case of chardonnay I'd brought in from the back. I bobbled it, but didn't break it, and managed to place it on the floor so I could unload it. I stood and tapped Joey on the shoulder.

"You know," I said, my voice heating. "I bet he was also the elf who helped me dissipate the death magic. Remember the one with the Van Dyke beard? The time I almost lost control here in the bar?" I'd had death magic inside of me, and it had wanted out, so it had released harmful gray tendrils of magic into the bar. I'd reeled it back in, but it had been close. Ironically, that death magic had eventually morphed into a set of bow and arrows which I now had in my apartment. They'd allied themselves with me and had helped me kill a warlock.

Joey stopped drying a mug to contemplate my words. "Crud on a cracker. You're right. He's been watching you for a while."

I stored some of the wine but left out several bottles to chill. We were swimming with dwarves this evening, and they drank like fish. I grabbed a bottle opener and huffed out a peeved breath. "This can't be good. I feel violated."

A stout dwarf returned with the empty wine bottle and ordered two more. He paid for both and handed me a gold coin as a tip, whispering, "Good luck, girlie. I'd bet my beard that you'll see the king soon. Mark my words, he's wantin' something from you."

I leaned in closer and whispered back, "I can't imagine what, though."

He scratched his head. "Keep your head on your shoulders and remember that fae favors are double-edged. Whatever you think he's doing, he's really doing something else."

A frog leaped from his beard, startling me. He caught it with a nimble swipe and put it back in the gnarly mess. "Don't mind him. He's a flirt."

It was my turn to take a wee dram of whiskey. I poured it and shoved the gold coin in my bag, a knot of worry in my tummy that no alcohol could relieve.

Chapter 3

I lugged my battered old knapsack up the fire escape and unlocked the back sliding glass door, casting one last glance at what had been Asher's window. Still dark. I reminded myself that I didn't care and entered my apartment. I'd check the birdfeeders in the morning. The blue jays bullied the sparrows, but those little brown-and-white darlings darted in and out all day and chowed down on the feed I left for them, emptying it fast. Still, I refused to fill it more than once a day. They needed to learn how to forage, and my birdfeed habit emptied my wallet faster than anything else, even food.

My apartment above So Long Noodles wouldn't win any decorating awards, but it was home. Mr. and Mrs. Long had replaced my cracked Formica kitchen counter after I'd hustled up some tax-free help for their restaurant, which was nice. I'd recruited three wee fae, Trick, Rin, and Jimmy, to help organize their pantry and keep a detailed inventory list. In return, the four-inch-tall men slept in a luxury dollhouse condo, indoors, where it was always warm. They'd been freezing on the cold streets of Smokey Point, Ohio. Northeast Ohio had two seasons: winter and construction, and winter persisted for many months. The current September air swept warm through the city during the day, but at night, a chill crept in. It infiltrated my bones and made me want a cup of tea and a sweater.

With the counter repaired, the kitchen looked better, but otherwise, the apartment was the same—old-fashioned peach bathroom, puke-brown sofa, a few bright decorative pillows to distract visitors from the overall blah of the place, and a soft blanket or two. Plus, books. I'd collected quite a few of my own, but I'd also taken out a fair number from the library, with the help of my part-fae librarian friend, Timothy. They lay scattered everywhere.

I dug the gold coin out of my pocket and tossed it in my bag. I dropped the knapsack by the back door and patted the death magic bow and arrows that stood against the wall in the same corner. The arrows vibrated under my touch.

"Sorry fellas, no one to kill right now. But the fae king paid a visit to me today in the bar, so maybe your luck will change. I've been told it isn't a good sign. Awful things could happen any day now."

The arrows hummed.

I grabbed a glass from the kitchen and called out to them. "Don't get too excited. I'm trying not to annoy people these days. Simple summonings, bartending, and saving money. That's it. That's my focus. I've had enough danger to last me a lifetime."

The bow's string twanged in an obvious snort.

"Keep your opinions to yourself."

Filling my glass with water, I sat on the couch and stared at a pile of books stacked on my coffee table. The top one, a self-help book, entitled *You're Never Alone: Finding the Angels Within,* mocked me.

I'd picked it up thinking it might help me feel better. With my mom dead, my father God knows where, Pinky back in Faerie, and Asher now gone, my faith lay in tatters. On top of this, my dearth of formal summoning training bothered me. My piecemeal knowledge had more holes in it than a moth-eaten dress.

The Kiss marked the inside of my left wrist and resembled lips, hence the name. With a "seagull" swish on the top and a "V" underneath, the Kiss marked me as a summoner. It meant I could summon beings from another plane, or pantheon, even from Hell, and they'd appear when I called, with no danger to me. A demon couldn't take my soul. A dragon couldn't light me on fire. A goat god couldn't butt me to death.

Handy.

However, as with all things, there was a rub, and it was a considerable one. A demon couldn't take *my* soul, but he could make a deal with someone else to kill my sister or set fire to a flower shop that happened to be next to a Krav Maga studio I attended, harming my teacher inside.

As a couple of completely random examples.

I'd learned the loopholes the hard way, by trial and error. Trace, who'd taught me for two years, from ages thirteen to fifteen, left one day and never came back. Much like my father, who'd left me, my mom, and my sister when I was small. I didn't remember my dad, and my mother had removed all his photos from our house, so I didn't even know what he'd looked like. I'd tried to get Mom to talk about him, but she'd flatly refused.

I got up and washed my glass in the kitchen sink, staring out the window into the dark sky. Last week's summoning had involved a famous author who'd requested that I call a fictional vampire from her books. They'd been turned into movies seen the world over, plus a video game, tabletop game, and a new comic book series. The multiplicative belief system had made it possible for me to manifest the fictional character. I hadn't thought it would work at first, but I summoned him and to my complete surprise, he showed up. Despite his fictional origins, he was a vampire, so I kept him contained in a circle with my client safely on the other side of my office while she asked him questions relative to her upcoming novel. She wanted his opinion on the new plot.

It took some effort to get rid of him, and I warned her that the more she did that, the more real he'd become. If she wasn't careful, he'd be calling the shots and instead of the antagonist, he'd be the good guy.

My phone rang. I pulled it from my pocket and held it between two fingers as if it were a dead fish. Who called at three in the morning?

I checked the number, groaned, and let it go to voice mail.

I returned to the living room, flopped on the couch, leaned my head back and breathed.

The phone rang again. I ignored it.

It rang again. I finally answered. He'd keep calling until I picked up.

"Nick Adamos, what the hell do you want?" Nick was Gregory's younger brother.

"How do you know I want something?" Nick asked. "Maybe I was checking on your welfare."

"You could do that at lunchtime."

"Your lunchtime is seven p.m."

"Regardless, that's better than three in the morning."

"I knew you'd be up."

I sighed. "Nick, we're through with each other. Quits. Kaput. Done. Whatever we had is over."

"Don't make it sound like we broke up after going steady in high school. What we had was a summoning mishap, a duke of Hell, and a green troll."

Accurate. Valefar, Sixth Duke of Hell, had once held Nick under his thumb due to a summoning mistake on my part, plus a little of his own hubris. Perrick, a green-tinted plains troll, served Nick's mobster older brother, Gregory Adamos, and was Nick's best friend.

"Exactly right, so what's the deal with the early morning call?"

"I want to hire you."

I sat up straight. "To summon?" My voice must have risen a full octave. Hadn't he had enough?

I could hear Nick squirm. "Well, yes. But it's not what you think. No demons."

"Gee, that's a relief."

"No, really. I've learned my lesson."

"Who do you want me to summon?"

He hesitated.

I yawned. "Tell me, Nick, or I hang up."

Nick rushed his words together. "I wanttospeaktomymom." He blurted out the sentence, combining the words so that I had to think a moment to decipher it.

"Mimi Adamos is dead."

He continued, rushing as if the words would get away from him. "Yes, of course. But you could summon her ghost, her soul, whatever it is."

"It won't work, Nick, and it's probably a bad idea, even if it could. I don't know where her soul resides. We could open a door to something dangerous. Or profane. Or plain insulting, like from somewhere no one wants us to visit. What if she's in Hell? We can't risk that."

"She's in Hades."

I blinked. "I'm sorry, what?"

"She believed in the old gods. Greek gods. She loved the stories. She always told us about the Greek myths and how her great-great-grandmother made her promise to visit the Pergamon Altar and make a sacrifice to Athena and Zeus."

"Oh, so she traveled to Athens each year?"

"No. Berlin."

I put the phone on speaker and placed it on the table. "Start from the beginning."

"There's really nothing to explain. The Pergamon Altar is an enormous building that used to stand on the acropolis of Pergamon, an ancient Greek city on the border of Turkey. The altar and friezes were excavated and moved to a museum in Berlin. It tells the story of the Greek gods defeating the original Titans. My mother used to travel to Germany each year and write a check to support the maintenance of the ruins and the museum, which served as her annual offering."

I rubbed my eyes. "So, you think she's in Hades because she supported antiquities research?"

"You're belittling it."

"On the contrary, I'm fascinated. I've never summoned from the ancient Greek pantheon. But I'll tell you up front, this isn't going to work."

"Why not?"

"Because no one believes in that stuff anymore. Lack of belief equals lack of power. The faith system died with Constantine."

"*I* believe that's where she is."

"Sorry, Nick. I don't think you can pull someone from Hades in modern times." I yawned again, a big body yawn with a bellow like a moose. "I'm tired and need sleep. I'm not talking about this with you anymore. It's a myth with no power, Nick."

"Wait a minute."

"Sorry. Gotta go."

"But—"

"Hanging up now."

I hit my cell phone's *end* button and wandered into my room. I stripped out of my clothing, donned a nightshirt, and felt my way to the bathroom to wash my face and brush my teeth. Then I stumbled back to bed and fell face-first on the covers.

Mimi Adamos taught Nick's brother, Gregory, everything he knew about being a ruthless, son-of-a-bitch crime lord.

If she was in Hades, she could damn well stay there.

Chapter 4

I woke in the morning starving for real food, so I headed downstairs to the restaurant.

Kenneth Long, the owners' son, greeted me with his wide smile. "Becs! Hungry?"

"You bet. The usual, please?" I laughed at his T-shirt, which read, "I wonder if bacon thinks about me, too."

"On it," he replied, and started chopping vegetables for my egg foo young. The Longs were an interesting family. Mrs. Long was an herbalist, and Mr. Long a trained physician, but when they'd immigrated, they started the restaurant rather than pursuing medical licensure here. They'd helped me when I'd been infected with the death magic.

I sidled up to the counter to watch Kenneth work. He diced veggies like nobody's business. His mom and dad were talking in the back, something about finances and investments. "How's the restaurant doing?" I asked.

He blessed me with that megawatt smile again. "Great! And thanks to you. . . ." He winked and jerked his head toward the large built-in pantry and walk-in freezer. "We've been ordering just what we need. No over-ordering, no running out of key ingredients. My dad even taught the little guys to use a computer."

That boggled my brain. "How do they use a computer with their miniscule hands?"

He laughed, dumping my fixings into a hot pan. He knew I liked them softened prior to adding the egg. "They jump on the keys! It's hilarious, but they're efficient."

"How's Petal?" I asked. "Everything going well?"

Kenneth's new girlfriend, Petal, most likely had a dash of fae in her, but I didn't mention it to him. A stunning, delicate Chinese girl, her refined nose and dainty ears reminded me of those belonging to several elves I'd met.

My personal chef blushed, beating eggs with a practiced flick of his right hand. "She's good," he replied softly, as he added the egg to the pan. "We're taking two classes together, so we see each other quite a lot."

"Have you met her folks?" I asked and grabbed a plastic fork from the tray on the counter. Kenneth grimaced, snatched the fork out of my hands, and handed me a real one. "Not yet," he said. "That's a big step, and we're taking it slow."

"I approve. Take your time. There's no rush." He plated the egg foo young, no gravy as was my preference, and I took it to a table to eat. I added a few dollops of sesame oil and sat down for my feast.

Kenneth having a girlfriend made my life easier. He'd had a crush on me, but I'd hooked up with Asher, and the conflict between the two of them had gotten tiresome.

Besides, I liked seeing Kenneth happy.

I finished eating, placed my plate and fork in a plastic bin for dishes, and ran back up to my apartment. I had a few hours before going back to work, so I changed into workout clothes, filled my feeders, and hopped down the fire escape with my bag. I left the bow and arrows at home, and they sighed, unhappy at sitting for so long.

I, on the other hand, celebrated not having to kill anyone.

I drove to the one place that made me both happy and sad. Oded's newly restored studio had several security upgrades, including cameras at both entrances. Inside, a large, glowing sign at the back door said, "Fire Exit," and he'd installed a fire extinguisher in every room plus an automated external defibrillator in the primary practice area. Oded wasn't taking any chances. A fire had destroyed his studio in July.

A fire that was pretty much my fault.

The rebuild happened fast, thanks to the mobster insurance money paying for it, but the former money-laundering flower shop next door where the fire had started sat rebuilt but empty. The crime family involved was Gregory Adamos's competitors, the Andinos.

I surmised that Oded hid a gun near the check-out desk and probably had another in his office. Trained by both Israel and the United States, Oded had seen battle, and it showed in his eyes, even before the fire that had burned part of his right side.

"Rivka," he greeted me. He was the only person I allowed to use my Hebrew name.

"Oded." I rose to tiptoes and pecked him on the left cheek, avoiding the newly healed, sensitive skin on the right. The burns extended down his side, but his right forearm had taken the brunt, and he'd needed a skin graft, which didn't take, and he'd required a second. His girlfriend, Zara, had told me that he'd used the forearm to protect his face, which is why he'd only suffered a second-degree burn on his cheek. The smoke inhalation had been hell, though, damaging his airway and lungs.

He'd shaved his hair down to a buzz cut, and his usually dark, Mediterranean skin had paled. Now leaner, he looked meaner, with a more prominent jaw and cheekbones, and haunted brown eyes.

"How are you feeling?" I asked.

"Better every day," he said, his voice hoarse.

"You're lying."

Oded shrugged. "What do you want from me, Rivka? I have to clean, moisturize, and redress the burns constantly, not to mention keep an eye out for infection. The whole process is painful. I sound like a pack-a-day smoker, and I've never had a cigarette." He motioned for me to follow him into the main practice room.

I didn't know how to respond so I reached out and gently squeezed his hand.

He squeezed back but then shook me off and pointed to a corner. "Place your bag against the wall. We'll warm up together. It's important that I stretch."

"Where do you want to start?" I asked, after plopping my stuff down and removing my shoes.

"Mountain pose. Let's get centered."

"There's a lot of noise in here." People were chatting, hitting the mat, skipping rope, and practicing self-defense moves all around us, creating a cacophony of jumbled, distracting sound.

"All the more reason for you to focus," my trainer said, ever helpful. "Follow along."

We put our feet together, tucked in our hips, and lifted our shoulders. "Breathe," he said. "In for two, hold, then out for three. Repeat. Close your eyes."

Well, he closed his eyes. I closed them for a second and then peeked to watch him.

Truthfully, looking at him made me sick to my stomach.

While I hadn't done anything to trigger the fire, I still blamed myself. I'd been involved with the responsible parties—the mobster Gregory Adamos, the demon Valefar, and Perrick, Gregory's troll hit man.

But mostly, I blamed the dangerous organized Greek crime syndicates for their rivalry which had caused it all. The Andino and Adamos families could tear each other to pieces for all I cared, but their violence had spilled over to other people. People I cared about.

"Your eyes are open," said Oded.

"How could you know that? Yours are closed!"

"I can hear it in your breathing."

"That's bullshit, Darth Vader."

He opened his eyes and chuckled. It was the first time he'd laughed, and I loved it.

"I'm right, though," he said.

"Yes, you are." I watched him wince as he stretched an arm above his head. "Did the Andino Trading Company pay for your hospital bills?"

"Rivka, don't worry yourself about such things."

I put a hand on my hip. "Please answer me."

"Health insurance paid for most of that."

"Most? Not all?" I demanded.

Oded stopped me with a quick cut of his hand. "Enough. I don't want to talk about it. More work, less talk."

Several sun salutations later, we were both looser.

"Okay, Rivka, let's practice some basic self-defense moves."

"Like what?"

"Isaac, come on over, please?"

A man the size of an oak tree lumbered over and waved at me.

I waved back. "Uh. Hi. Nice to meet you."

"You too," said Isaac, in a disconcertingly high tenor.

"Isaac, attack Rivka please."

Isaac lunged and caught my wrist and pulled me toward him. I stepped into him, moving fast and brought my other hand down and around with an open palm, as if I intended to slap his balls, and followed up with an open hand to his face. He released me, and I ran a few steps as follow through. Incapacitate and escape, that was the mantra.

"Excellent, Rivka. Nicely done. But you aren't using your voice," said Oded.

"What?"

"You need to get loud. As loud as possible. Use your voice."

"What do you mean?"

"Isaac, please?"

Isaac gave him a thumbs-up, opened his mouth, and yelled, "Help! Help! Call the police!"

Not one person in the studio looked in our direction. I guessed they were used to it. I'd never focused on shouting for help before, choosing to concentrate on breathing and my opponent. Then again, any time I'd been accosted, it had involved a warlock or other magic user. I didn't want the human police to respond.

But, to please Oded, I'd try.

We repeated the move again, but as Isaac came at me, I shouted, "Stop! Stop! Call the police!"

"Better!" Oded said. "That's the way."

"I see you're using your voice," said a woman, from behind me. I looked to see who it was.

"Hey, Zara."

Zara gave me a brief hug, then walked over and kissed Oded on the lips. He rolled his eyes.

"Stop it, you big dummy," she said. "I'm not hiding our relationship anymore."

"Nor should you have to," I said.

"No, we don't." Oded took her hand. "I chose to disappoint my parents but live my life the way I want."

I thanked Isaac for his assistance, and he jogged off. Then I turned back to Oded and Zara. "Why are your parents disappointed?"

Zara's face darkened. "They weren't too thrilled at our relationship. They wanted him to go back to Israel, to return home to be closer to them."

Oded took her hand. "Love sometimes forces us to make hard choices. We can't please everyone." He chucked Zara under the chin. "My life is here."

"They'll come around, Zara," I said.

"Yes, they will. My family always does," said Oded.

I wasn't so sure, but I didn't rain on their parade.

Oded paired me with a woman about my age, and we practiced different techniques against wrist holds and forward and backward choke holds. I had to remind myself again and again to shout for help. It just felt silly.

"I've gotta go," I said, walking to the corner where I'd dropped my bag. "I've got a lunch date with my sister."

Right before I stepped out the door, Zara tapped me on the shoulder. "Becs?" I quirked my chin at her. "I'm not lecturing, but. . . ." She heaved a big breath. "Please remember that speaking up tells people what you need and how to assist."

I frowned. I'd never thought of it that way.

Chapter 5

Because I had to go to work at the bar later, I chose to meet Mickey at the Dapper Diner, a 24/7 joint near Joey's. I'd been there with Pinky before, and their homemade desserts were to die for.

Mickey stood outside the door waiting for me, thumbing through her phone. She didn't hear me approach until I was right on top of her.

"Hey!" She squeezed me tight, and I clutched her hard. We embraced a long time, grateful to be together. I let her go with a peck on her cheek.

"Shall we?" I asked and opened the door, sweeping my arm to usher her in with a bow and a flourish.

She batted her eyelashes at me. "Why, thank you."

The diner was the coolest. An old-fashioned white counter with red swivel stools occupied one length of the room, while booths lined the outer edges. Two-tops and four-tops took up the middle. Overhead, there were 1950s-retro deep-bowl pendant lights the color of ketchup. The obligatory aluminum napkin holders rested on each surface, flanked by small rectangles of jelly, marmalade, and honey. Cylindrical sugar containers took up additional space and sat next to containers of artificial sweeteners in pink, yellow, blue, and green. A dessert case showed off homemade pies, cakes, and pastries. White napkins wrapped around silverware lay ready for guests.

We took a booth by the back where we had privacy, and my former server waited on us again.

"Hey, Betsy. Good to see you."

She cocked her head at me, wondering how I knew her name, and then suddenly pointed her pen at me. "I remember you. How is that nice young man? Did he ever get adopted or placed permanently? He hasn't come back for food in a while." When Betsy had met Pinky, all she'd seen was a homeless boy. She couldn't see past the glamour to his true form.

"He actually made it back home, which is what he wanted. His mom missed him."

She clucked her tongue. "So many kids run away and don't know how to find their way back. Glad to hear it worked out for him."

Mickey's eyebrows shot up. She didn't know anything about Pinky.

"Whaddaya want to eat?" asked Betsy, flipping over a page on her ordering pad.

"I'll have the chicken salad sandwich," said Mickey, pointing to the blackboard listing the day's specials.

"Chips, pickle, come with. What to drink?"

Mickey ordered a lemonade, and I ordered a Caesar salad.

"That's all you want?" Betsy asked, writing down my order.

"Yup, saving room for dessert."

"Good plan. We have lemon meringue."

After Betsy left, Mickey showed me the pictures of Ruthie she'd taken that morning. My niece wore a white dress with little red hearts on it and was so freaking cute, I couldn't stand it.

"She's cruising around the room holding on to furniture," Mickey said. "It's fascinating to watch her progression, but we can't get things out of her way fast enough. She knocked over Jonah's old CDs. I've told him multiple times to put them away."

"I'm fairly sure you can give those away now," I said. "I mean, he has a phone with all the music he could want."

She giggled. "I boxed them up and put them in the attic. He won't let me get rid of them."

We hit a lull, and she played with her fork. I decided to broach a possibly touchy subject.

"Have you thought about going back to school?" I asked. Mickey had a college degree in psychology and had been training to be a social worker before she'd gotten married and decided starting a family meant more to her.

Mickey looked past me but shook her head. "Not now. Maybe when Ruthie is older, unless we have a second one."

"You want two?"

"We've talked about it."

I waited a beat, wondering if she'd say more. When she didn't, I reached over and patted the top of her hand. "Hey, I'm sorry I pried."

"It's okay. It's a hard topic though, ya know? Everyone says you can have a career *and* a family, but I'm not so sure. I see women who try to balance them, and they're constantly exhausted. They always feel like they're missing out—either on their children's milestones or advancement at work. I don't want to be pulled in both directions."

"I get it."

Our food arrived, and we dug in. Mickey took a big bite of her sandwich and changed topics, speaking between chews. "What was that about the boy? The one you discussed with our waitress?"

"Don't talk with your mouth full," I said, pouring the dressing on my salad.

She swallowed, then opened her jaws wide with an epic eye-roll to show me her empty mouth and asked about Pinky again.

"Real mature!" I said, crossing my eyes at her.

She giggled again, but her face grew serious. "But, for real, tell me."

This was also a tough subject. I bit my lip, considering what to tell her.

"He was a lost teenager. He'd been here a long time, sleeping in the park, and I helped him get home to his mom."

"That's it? That's all you're going to tell me?"

"He was sweet." I wiped my mouth with a napkin. "He just lost his way."

She held her pickle in her hand, her sandwich in the other like some delicatessen gladiator. "I can't imagine being on the street. Even at our worst, when Mom taught both high school and community college to pay the bills, we had a home. Running water. Electricity."

I snorted. "True, but you sure didn't like it then. You complained constantly that we had to share a bedroom, and you scolded me for leaving my sneakers in the room."

She waved the pickle at me. "You had bad foot funk." She took a bite and swallowed. "Yeah, it was tiny, and we shared a room—"

"And a bathroom," I reminded her. "Three females. One bathroom."

She laughed hard. "Yeah, that was terrible!" She sobered as she remembered. "But it was home. We made it that way, the three of us."

"I miss her."

Mickey sucked in air, a heavy inhalation, and then let out in one long breath.

"Me, too. Fuck cancer."

Mickey rarely cursed. I raised my water glass. "Damn right. Fuck cancer."

We'd lost her three years ago. It hurt like yesterday.

"Becs!" A lithe, gorgeous young man with wispy blond hair and fine features approached, a man I didn't recognize.

He held out his hand to my sister. "Evans. Evans Forrest."

Evans. The elf from Joey's but glamoured to look human. On second look, I recognized the light-green eyes.

Wary, I greeted him back. "Oh, hey, Evans. It's nice to see you." I had no idea what he wanted or why he'd greet me like this out in the open.

"Will you be at the bar tonight?" he asked.

I winced. I hated bringing up Joey's in front of my sister because she couldn't see it or go there. Especially after what happened with the parade guys and Ober—I meant, the fae king.

I schooled my features. "Yes, I'm working tonight."

"Excellent. I have those crystals for you."

Oh, that wanker. "That's great. Give them to Joey, though, okay? They're for her."

"Okay. Will do. See you later." He loped out, every eye on him.

Mickey's head swiveled back and forth between me and Evans's retreating backside. "Who. Is. That?"

I sipped my water. "Some guy from work I don't know very well."

"He's a little young for you, but hubba hubba. Those cheekbones!"

"Oh, stop it. He's a child."

Truthfully, he could have been a thousand years old or ten thousand years old. What did I know? Still, he had the judgment of an adolescent.

"I hear young is good." She winked at me.

"Mickey!"

"Fine. Whatever. Don't tell your sister. But answer this—when did you get into crystals? Are these healing crystals? Decorative?"

"They're for someone else. I bought two crystal geodes for my boss. She's into that kind of thing."

"Oooooh. What type of geodes?"

Shit. What kind? I said the first words that popped into my head. "Ah . . . quartz? I think?"

She held her hand to her heart. "That's so lovely. Quartz brings harmony. I have a quartz geode at home that I love. What a thoughtful gift. Do you know where he purchased them?"

Just then, Betsy came around and asked if we wanted pie. While I took a moment to respond that'd I'd changed my mind about dessert, I thought about my sister. I hadn't known that she liked crystals.

I hedged. "I don't know where he got them, no."

"Can you ask?"

"Um? Maybe?"

"Oh, forget it. I'm going to pop out and ask him. I know it's a little weird, but collectors like nothing more than to talk shop. I'm sure he won't mind." She finished her pickle and stood to follow him.

"Wait!"

She looked at me expectantly.

"He may not want to give up his source."

"Please, Becs. It's a harmless question. Come on."

No one could ever refuse Mickey anything when she looked at them like that. She'd been perfecting that big-eye, heartfelt, chin-quivering gaze since she was a toddler.

"Okay, we can try." I told Betsy that we'd be right back and motioned for Micks to follow.

When we walked outside, Evans was nowhere to be seen.

Mickey wrinkled her brow in disappointment. "Aw, darn it. We missed him."

"He must have moved quickly."

She put her hand to her forehead to block the sun and searched the street. "Where's the bar? Is it close by? Maybe we can stop in?"

I put my head in my hands. I'd tried this once before, but she hadn't believed me then and she wouldn't now. "Mickey, it's right over there." I pointed. "But remember I told you that you couldn't see it? It's glamoured to be invisible to nonmagical people."

Mickey's demeanor changed at the mention of glamours and magic. She'd always pushed back against the notion of a world that she couldn't sense, see, or touch. When we were younger, I thought maybe she'd been jealous—and perhaps she was once—but now she loved her life and her family and saw magic as either an illusion or a threat.

She placed her hands on her hips and gave me the beady eye. "You're at that again? An invisible, secret bar?"

"Well, it is. I'm sorry."

She shifted her eyes away from mine. "Really? You're still selling me that bag of goods?"

She stalked back into the diner and plopped in her seat. I joined her, squirming into the booth. She narrowed her eyes, and her look could have shattered marble.

I tried again. "You know how I can summon things? Entities?"

She gave me a grudging nod.

"Well, my ability to do that means I can see and enter the bar. You don't have those talents, so you can't."

She nodded, a slow up-and-down that told me she was barely holding on to her temper. She dabbed at her mouth with a napkin and then placed it on the table, ever so carefully.

"You're saying that I'm a plain, vanilla human being and you're Wonder Woman with an invisible airplane, I mean, bar."

"No! That's not it. I'm not trying to make myself out to be better than you. I'm saying that the Kiss makes me closer to the paranormal world. You know that it came in when I was a teenager. You were there. You lived through it."

Sorrow clouded her face. "Yeah, I did, and then your teacher vanished, and you were bereft. Nothing good has come of that Kiss."

I jerked back, shocked. "That's not true."

"That mark got you mixed up with bad people. People who threatened our lives."

"Yes, but—"

"And I thought you stopped doing it, but I see you haven't. Why? Because it makes you feel powerful?"

My jaw dropped, and it took a second for me to protest. "It's not that it makes me *feel* powerful. It *is* powerful, and I can use it, if I'm careful."

She flung her arms out to her sides. "If you're careful? This is so upsetting." She leaned forward. "Let me tell you what I know, in theory, because I've never witnessed you doing anything with the Kiss. The mark on your wrist allows you to do something I cannot, something hinky, called 'summoning,' and summoning involves ritual, and people's beliefs. I realize that there's power in that. Power that I can't necessarily explain, and that science can't explain, so we call it magic."

"Okay, that's a start."

She held up her hand to stop me. "However, I know for *certain* that your magic often gets people in more trouble than when they started. You summon whatever it is you summon because they're desperate to solve a problem or get information and you're their last-ditch effort."

"Not always, and I'm working hard to make sure my clients don't make bad deals or get hurt in the process," I said, but I could see my argument failed to reach my sister. Her eyes blazed with frustration and ire. I slumped in my seat and crossed my arms across my chest.

She clenched her hand into a fist and bumped it on the table. "You're missing the point!"

"No, *you're* missing the point. I was given this power—I didn't choose it. I used to hate it. I wanted nothing more than to give it back to whomever had bestowed it on me, but I can't."

My sister rapped the table with her knuckles. "You can choose to use it or not."

"I tried to quit, and it found me anyway. I got rid of the dangerous people. Now I only summon here and there to help make ends meet and help those who need it."

She looked down, hiding her face with her forearms, elbows on the table. She smoothed her eyebrows with her index fingers.

"Mickey. Mickey. Look at me."

She did.

"Summoning is a part of who I am. It's like having freckles or being right-handed. It's impossible to change it."

"Bull hockey. Jonah was right. You're like an addict who can't stop."

"It's not that. It's just. . . ."

She leaned in. "What? It's just what?"

"It's what I was born to do." I removed a leather bracelet imprinted with various protective symbols from my left wrist to show her the mark there. "Trace taught me to use it. Not completely, true, but a good amount. Why would I want to stop completely? I've got it in hand now, and if I'm careful and take the proper precautions, it's not a problem."

Mickey sat back, slowly shaking her head, lips pressed tight. "It's as if I'm talking to a junkie. That's what they say too, you know? That they can do a little. They've got it under control. It's all false."

"This isn't an addiction."

"Let's see," she said, holding up her hand and ticking things off with her other index finger. "You can't stop it. It hurts people you love when you use it. You can do a little if you're 'careful.' What about that is not addiction?"

I slumped in my seat. Was I addicted to summoning? I didn't think so. I also didn't think I *could* stop using my abilities. Even if I forced myself to, would my magic go away? Atrophy and die? Or would it burst forth from my skin like an alien in the movies? I didn't know how to describe it to my sister. She didn't believe in a literal Hell, much less Faerie, and had no magic of her own. Trying to explain it to her was like describing life beyond the pond to a tadpole.

Nevertheless, I had to try.

"Micks, it's not like that. Not using my magic would be like forcing me to only use one eye—without a patch. Imagine being asked to keep your right eye closed, on your own, and only use your left. Impossible."

Mickey grabbed her crossbody bag and slipped it on. "Creative analogy, but I don't buy it. 'Impossible,' is what every addict says."

"Using your innate abilities, including magical ones, isn't addiction. You wouldn't say a musician is addicted to playing the cello, or an artist is addicted to sketching."

"Your abilities have hurt you and endangered me and Ruthie. Cellos and sketches don't do that. You promised you'd end it, but you didn't. You need help or you, and your family, will never be safe."

She stood, and I reached across the table to grasp her wrist. "If this is about the invisible bar, I can't change that, but I can introduce you to some folks who will help you understand." Meeting the wee ones would blow her mind. I'd have to ask their permission first though.

She shook her head and glanced at my hand around her wrist. I released it.

"No, Becs. I don't think meeting any of your summoning groupies is going to help."

She left, and all I could do was watch her walk away, my breath heavy and my chest tight. I put my bracelet back on and composed myself. After I was certain she'd had enough time to drive away, I dropped cash on the table for the bill, added an extra twenty dollars for causing a scene, and walked out into the sunshine, unable to feel the warmth on my face. I slapped at a late-season mosquito and trudged toward the bar.

More dejected than ever, I kept my head low and avoided eye contact, so it took me a moment to notice the tingling on the back of my neck that told me someone was watching me. I put my back to a brick wall and took out my phone, pretending to answer it as I looked around for the source of my discomfort.

There she was. A woman hid behind the half-open door of a shop located between the sushi place and a new store advertising make-your-own-pottery parties. The narrow door made it look as if the shop stood sideways, in profile, so only those truly searching for it would find it.

The woman who peeked out was dressed in a long black skirt and blouse, her hair tied back in a severe bun. Her lined face indicated an age upwards of sixty, but her strong posture made me think she was younger. Her hands gripped the doorframe, holding the door in place so it wouldn't swing fully one way or the other.

She took a single step toward me, pushing the door wider, and held out a hand as if to issue a warning, or perhaps to call me to her.

"Becs! Your shift starts in five minutes. Get in here," Joey called out, beckoning me from the bar's front entrance. She must have been watching for me, which meant it was busy. I took one last look at the woman in black. She shrank back into the dim light of her shop.

"Who is that woman?" I turned to face Joey, pointing over my shoulder toward the storefront.

"What woman?"

"Standing in the doorway of that new shop across the street, next to the sushi place. Have you seen her before?"

"Becs, there's no shop, no woman. The only thing next to the sushi place is an alleyway I wouldn't set foot in after dark."

I looked again, and she was right. The shop and its door had disappeared.

As had the woman.

Chapter 6

Runes covered Joey's ceiling along with multiple fans that circled alternatively clockwise or counterclockwise to dissipate magical energy. Six new, white crystal geodes lined the external perimeter of the room pulsing shielding magic so strong, they gave me a headache when I walked through the door.

"Hard-hitting, isn't it?" commented a dwarf when he saw me stagger. "Don't worry," he continued, "if you drink enough chardonnay, you hardly notice!" He and his friends guffawed, toasting with their wine glasses.

I stumbled over to the bar and held myself upright by leaning on the wood countertop. As I swayed under the crystal's power and worked to steady myself, I noticed that Joey had scrubbed the place until it gleamed. The copper spouts and rivets glittered against the stools' leather tops and wooden legs. The tables glowed and smelled faintly of orange wood polish. Even the scuffed floor sparkled.

"The crystals wouldn't work properly until I cleaned the whole place," Joey said, motioning for me to take my place behind the bar. "They're sensitive and persnickety, but they're powerful, so I'm grateful. Sorry about the head rush. It should wane soon."

Joey had gathered her long white hair into a ponytail, but strands escaped and trailed down her back. Her muscular, hairy forearms flexed as she washed dishes with practiced expediency.

I motioned to her spotless, blue chambray work shirt. "That's your dress one, isn't it? What's the occasion?"

She grunted, a surprisingly deep sound for a four-foot-tall woman. "Got wood polish on my work shirts, and the brownies wouldn't come until I installed the crystals, so I'm behind in laundry. You know how it is. They're efficient, but they have rules of their own."

I did know. You couldn't acknowledge brownies or thank them in any way because they'd disappear and never clean for you again. But you could leave them a small item in trade.

"I'm assuming you left a suitable present for them?"

Joey's face brightened. "Popcorn! They love it."

A big pile of dirty glasses needed washing, and I passed them to her, one at a time. "What kind of popcorn? Anything specific?"

She hooted. "Any kind! I got a huge can of kettle corn this time."

I filed this knowledge away for future use. The crystals' effect on my head had already faded. I poured two fingers of Jack Daniel's Old No. 7, filled three glasses of chardonnay, and took an order for Laurel, my least favorite fae. Her pixie posse followed her every move, and with their perfect bodies, long, shiny tresses, and magnificent eyelashes, even in full-sized human form, they made a striking—albeit catty—Barbie-esque clique.

"Vodka gimlet, barkeep, and use Tito's this time," she said, tapping a long nail on the bar top.

"You know my name, Laurel," I said, getting ice for the shaker.

"I hate being too familiar with the help," she replied, flipping her blond hair over her shoulder.

"Oh, for heaven's sake," I muttered. I sloshed the Tito's over the ice, added the simple syrup and fresh lime juice, gave it all a good shake, and poured it into a martini glass. I even added a lime wheel as a garnish. I pushed it to her and said, "Take it and go."

"Tut, tut," she said, picking up the glass. "That's no way to speak to paying customers." She pivoted on her red-heeled foot and sashayed back to her fawning coterie. I caught a dwarf staring at her ass, salivating. I handed him a napkin. "Not a flattering look," I said with a wink. He blushed and tossed the rest of his wine down in one gulp.

"They're so pretty. So delicate," he said, motioning to his empty glass. "And they'd never accept a dwarf as a friend, much less a boyfriend."

"Then they're shortsighted and missing out," I said. "No charge for the refill."

He stood a tad taller, enough so I could see his nose over the bar. "Thanks, Becs. That's real nice of ya."

Joey hustled behind the bar carrying a huge tray full of glassware. "Still having trouble with Laurel, I see?"

"I can't believe I owe her a favor."

"She helped you out with that Gregory thing. You have to fix the imbalance." Fae survived on the concept of balance. If someone did something for you, you had to do something for them of equal value. That's why the favor I owed Laurel caused me so much discomfort. I needed to find a way to pay her back, pronto.

"Lemon drop martini, extra sugary rim!" I called and placed it out of the way at the very end of the bar. Three tiny fairies flew over and licked the sugar with long hummingbird tongues, chattering in their high-pitched voices.

"I miss Pinky," I said, watching the tiny fairies. Pinky hadn't come back after returning to Faerie, and I had no way to reach him except asking another fae for a favor, and that was out of the question. Laurel's favor itched between my shoulder blades, as it was. I couldn't wait to be rid of it, but she hadn't called in her chit yet.

"I do, too," Joey said, lifting yet another heavy tray over her head. "His mom probably won't let him return."

"Can't blame her." I wiped up wet glass rings from the bar top. Joey left to deliver drinks and nachos. I tossed two menus to a pair of elves wearing hunting gear. I didn't ask what they were hunting.

Joey returned with the tray now full of empty plates. "How's your sister?" she asked. "Didn't you have lunch with her today?"

I took the tray from her, so she could deal with the dirty dishes, then groaned. "Terrible. She accused me of being addicted to magic and said I couldn't keep my family safe until I got—" I held up my fingers in quote marks, "—help."

Joey wiped her hands on her apron. "She's not totally wrong."

"What do you mean?"

"Well, she's incorrect about the addiction part, although I can see why it looks like that for a nonmagical human. But, where she's right, is that you can't keep yourself or them, safe until you learn all the ins and outs of your power."

"Exactly how am I supposed to do that?"

"You need a teacher."

A let a mirthless snort fly. "My trainer left when I was fifteen and never came back. And I've never met another person with the Kiss. They don't offer classes like this at the YMCA."

"Well, duh, but, you have resources. Use them."

A selkie called for another Salty Dog. I made it and walked it over to the baby pool. A second selkie wanted one, and then the other three chimed in so I made four more, all of which I hand delivered because the selkies had trouble manifesting legs and only did it under duress. It smelled bad when they shed their seal skins, anyway. I preferred the half-shift. They looked like mermaids but without the cell phones.

One with long red locks stopped me before I left, grabbing my shirt sleeve. "Do you have any more sea salt?" she asked. "We're getting pruney."

"Coming right up."

While obliging the ladies, I pondered Joey's words. What or who could help me find a trainer? Kiss-wielding summoners didn't advertise.

The door leading outside opened, and a pale-green, awkward figure entered wearing an ill-fitting suit. Perrick was a plains troll, and it must have been difficult to find menswear that fit him correctly. And while I could sympathize with his wardrobe woes, it didn't mean I had to like him. Joey rolled her eyes and I scowled, turning my concentration to clearing tables at the far end of the room where a party of twelve elves, including Evans, discussed the stock market.

"Hey, doll," one of them said, obviously drunk. "We hear you have Oberon's attention."

The rest of the elves shushed him, and Evans smacked him on the shoulder. "What the hell are you doing, man? Wasn't one visit enough?"

"Yeah," I said, clearing a half-empty mug of draft beer "I'm already under his microscope. Don't make it worse."

The drunk elf snagged the half-empty glass and slugged it down in three gulps, wiped his mouth, and then handed it back to me with a belch. "Sorry, kitten."

"And what's with the 'doll,' and 'kitten,' stuff?" I asked. "Stop that. It's weird."

He shook his head as if to clear it. "Sorry. My last visit to the Slow World was in the 1950s. First time back. Guess times have changed."

"Guess so." I walked away, weaving my way back to the bar, avoiding a group of fae shooting darts. The fae called our realm—Earth, Midgard, whatever name you used—the Slow World, since time moved differently here. That's something the fairy tales got right.

With an enormous, full-belly sigh, I walked behind the bar and finally addressed the green guy. "Perrick, what do you want?"

"A beer?" He adjusted his hideous tie.

I poured a draft with a huge foamy head and plunked it down in front of him. "Here's a beer. Now what do you want?"

"Awww, Becky, don't be like that."

I picked up a sharp knife I used for slicing limes and slammed it down between his thumb and forefinger. "Call me Becky one more time and you lose a finger. It will take a lot of Kansas home soil to grow that back, and Asher isn't around to fetch it for you."

He swallowed and stepped back. "Sorry, Becs. I thought we were friends."

"We're not. I liked how you treated Nick, so I helped you get the dirt from your home patch to keep you healthy, but then you had to go and make a deal with Valefar, which resulted in the near death of my friend, who is still badly burned and suffering. Shimmy your bad self right out of here, please."

Perrick placed his full beer near me and looked down at his shoes. "You're right. I owe Valefar a favor now, and I'm lucky that's all it is and he didn't get my soul. Thank you for clarifying the contract. I'll do whatever I can to help Oded, if you tell me how."

"Pay for the balance of his medical bills. Insurance only covered a part of it, and he's still in a lot of pain."

He frowned. "I would have thought the Andinos' insurance would cover all of it."

"I don't know what happened, because Oded likes privacy and didn't share the details. He's paying for his care, not the Andino family, and this includes the treatment he got at the hospital plus ongoing doctor's visits."

"I'll look into it."

I gave him a curt nod, my expression unyielding. I'd believe it when I saw it.

Perrick withdrew a twenty from his wallet and placed it on the counter. "Listen. I know Nick called you with a request to summon Mimi."

"Yes. I told him no."

"That's why I'm here. I came to warn you that Gregory's bought into the idea."

I rubbed my temples as my headache roared back.

He sighed. "Anyway, expect a call."

I leaned my elbows on the counter. Gregory Adamos. Rich mobster. Callous scumbag. Also, looking for love. What a peach. I wondered when my phone would ring.

Chapter 7

I woke the next morning obsessed with finding a trainer. Joey's words reverberated in my head. I needed to understand the depth and limitations of my abilities, or I wouldn't be safe, nor could I protect my family.

I considered my next move while standing on my fire escape. The blue jays shrieked and flew from my railing to a nearby tree and back again, waiting for me to throw peanuts. The robins stalked the ground searching for insects, and a crow cawed at me from a tree branch. Our neighborhood woodpecker tapped the telephone pole near my bedroom window, a hard staccato rhythm as he searched for tasty treats. Many of the songbirds had already left, although they still trilled in the forests of southern Ohio. I vowed to get to the Lake Erie shoreline to catch the sandpipers and plovers before the end of the month.

A stray cat caught my eye, stalking a flock of starlings. It lunged in a black blur and came up empty as the starlings took to the sky, but the cat reminded me of something.

When in need of information, what better place than the library?

I threw on a cleanish T-shirt, grabbed my bag, shoved my feet into my sneakers, and clambered down the fire escape to my car. A beat-up red Prius on the outside, it ran like a sports car thanks to my magic mechanic, who'd souped the coupe and given me a way to outrun warlocks.

It took about twenty minutes for me to get to the library, thanks to some traffic. I parked in a pay lot and traversed Third Central Plaza, once owned by Third Central Bank. I didn't know what happened to the first and second banks.

The public library rose over the square, casting part of it in shadow. Made of red brick and guarded by two statue sentries, a dolphin and a ram, it also boasted a gorgeous stained-glass suncatcher in the entrance archway.

I always stopped to greet the statues, not quite convinced that they weren't alive. "Hello, Dolphin. Hello, Ram. Good to see you today. Thank you for guarding the library."

The first floor sounded like any library. Photocopiers ran papers, people lined up at the main reference desk, and book carts clacked on the linoleum floors between the bestseller displays. The magazine rack flaunted the latest issues of popular publications as well as the one major local paper, the *Smokey Point Sun*. Students sat hunched over computers they borrowed by the hour in the back, and their pens scratched over notepaper.

I rode the elevator to the third floor, which was usually almost empty. This level housed old encyclopedia collections, ancient dictionaries, foreign language reference books, and it smelled old and musty. Books, even those long abandoned, still held valuable information and taught us what was important in their time. It saddened me to see them unused and unattended. I walked the perimeter, touching the spines, murmuring reassurances that they still mattered.

After making my rounds, I climbed a circular staircase of thirteen steps, holding on to the shiny brass railing. The steps ended at a hole in the floor of the fourth level, which required that I hoist myself through like an eight-year-old climbs into a treehouse. Problem was, I'd passed age eight long ago. I placed my hands on the edge, jumped up, pulled myself through the hole, using only my upper body strength, and shoved my knee between my hands to brace myself. I brought the other knee up and balanced. Hard work, and worthy of a ten from the Russian judge, the effort left me breathless for a moment. I stood and dusted off my hands on my pants.

A rotund, orange cat meowed at me. "Hey, Stacks," I answered, giving the library cat a pet. "What's going on today? Have you seen Timothy?"

Stacks didn't tell me if the diminutive quarter-hob librarian was around, but he did encircle my legs, almost tripping me until I picked him up and rubbed him around the ears and under the chin. Given how tidy the fourth floor was, I guessed Timothy had been there recently. Hobs, like brownies, liked to keep house or tend fields. He indulged this instinct by reshelving.

I placed the cat on the ground, much to his displeasure, and wandered the room. "Where can I find new information on the Kiss, Stacks? I've never found anything before, but maybe there is something I missed. Or, perhaps I've been looking in the wrong places."

The fourth floor's filing system was unlike any other library I'd ever visited. Organized alphabetically by subject, it made searching nigh impossible, and it was a vast collection. Capriciously categorized, you could find books on the same topic in different areas.

The Dewey Decimal System was a thing of distant memory here, if it had ever applied at all.

I'd always searched in the "magic subjects" area, which kept information on various paranormal entities and their powers, but maybe I needed to look elsewhere. For example, if I wanted to find information on fairies, you'd think I search under Fairy, or Fae, but you'd be only partly right. Fairy information also fell under Britain, Celts, Mythology, Sidhe, Fair Folk, *Midsummer Night's Dream*, Tinkerbell, Underhill, Urchins, and Welsh, and that's just what I had personally located.

I'd found rules on summoning demons in the Demonology collection but nothing under "K" for Kiss.

There had to be something I'd missed.

Valefar and a warlock had called me Kiss Born so I checked the "B" section but found nothing relevant. I crisscrossed the aisles, wandering through alphabetically, Stacks winding around my legs, rubbing against me, purring.

I placed my knapsack next to the beanbag chair I used when visiting this floor. It was too heavy to carry around. Before I could go to the reading area, the cat flopped in front of me and turned on its back, demanding tummy rubs. I bent to pay His Highness his due, and that's when I saw it. Right at the edge of the "M" section was a slim volume bound in an unusual opalescent cover, entitled "Mark, Seals, Symbols, and Madness, Vol. 2." I slipped the slender book off the shelves, noting it was the only book of its kind. The books on either side were entitled "Marcus Antonius" and "Marketing Multi-Dimensions," a confusing title.

Giving Stacks one last tummy rub, I took the book to the beanbag chair and opened the cover, shocked to encounter printed pages of spidery handwriting in note form. The first one read: "Avatar: shape of animal" with no other information. I flipped through until I got to "Mage Mark: pentacle, five starts in circle, energies held together." That meant nothing to me, but the next entry did. "Mark, Summoner's, see Kiss, Volume 1." I flipped through looking for the Kiss section and found nothing. Vexed, I ran back to the shelf to double-check that Volume 1 wasn't mis-shelved, but no, I couldn't find it anywhere. I searched under "Summoner," again in vain.

"Ugh! This is insanity," I exclaimed, while Stacks licked his nether regions. "Don't you care, cat?" Stacks stretched, rolled over, and closed his eyes.

"Guess not," I grumbled.

"Becs? Is that you?"

"Timothy?"

I turned to see Timothy standing near the entrance to the fourth floor.

"Isn't it hard for you to hoist yourself up?" I asked.

Timothy crinkled his nose. "What do you mean?"

"It's difficult for me to heave myself through the entrance hole and climb up, and I'm much taller than you are. How do you do it?"

Timothy's bright-blue eyes blinked in confusion. "I'm not following. I walk up the stairs and open the door."

I got the feeling that this level was playing tricks on me. I eyed Stacks, who stretched again, nonchalant.

"Timothy, what's this level of the library?"

"The fourth."

"Tiiiimmmothy?"

"Fine! It's a pocket dimension. Only those who need to be here can enter." He turned and walked over to the reference desk. "And don't ask any more questions. I'm not answering."

"Why?"

"Because I've said too much already. Dig too hard and you'll be banned."

That made me shut up. I hesitated and met him at the reference desk. "Can you tell me about this book?" I held up the skinny handwritten volume. "I've never seen it before, and it appears to be Volume 2. I need Volume 1."

"Let me take a look." He climbed up onto a tall stool, so we looked at each other eye to eye, and I handed him the book. He flipped through it, face scrunched.

"This is new to me, too, and it appears quite old." He stroked the binding. "This cover is so unusual."

"Can that give us a hint about who wrote it?"

"Maybe? I'll ask around." He placed the book under the desk. "In the meantime, I was hoping you'd come in."

"Why? What do you need?"

Timothy squirmed on his stool. "I was hoping I could call in that favor and ask you to call Granny?"

I owed Timothy a favor, too. He'd tracked down some information for me, and my payment was one summons to his great-great-great-something grandmother.

"In fact," he added, sitting up straight. "She might know who wrote this book, or where to find the other volume."

"That's a great idea," I said, perking up. "She knows everything." I mentally started cataloguing my summoning supplies. "Do you need her for something in particular, or will this just be a social call?"

"She asked me to give each of my kids an item when they turned twenty-one. You know I have eight, right?"

I nodded. I couldn't even begin to imagine having eight kids.

"Anyway, my eldest is about to have her twenty-first birthday, and I'd like to know what the rings do before I gift the first one."

"She gave them each a ring?"

"Yes, braided sweetgrass rings. I feel the magic, and while I trust Granny, I'd like to ask her what happens when they put them on before I hand them over."

"You didn't ask before?"

He blushed. "I trusted more then. Now, not so much."

"I think that's prudent, Timothy. You have my number. We can do this tomorrow evening if that's good for you?"

"Perfect."

"I'll need to get a few things to prepare. And yes, if you don't mind, bring the book. We'll see if she can tell us anything about it."

I bade him farewell and descended the stairs, pondering what I'd learned. Someone, somewhere, had spent time cataloguing marks and symbols of power. Who the hell could that have been? And what might they know about my Kiss?

Chapter 8

I climbed into bed that night, wondering if the missing "Volume 1" contained any useful information. Part of me doubted it. It seemed like a big, fat tease, as if the library took pleasure in torturing me, batting me around like Stacks would play with a mouse.

And, *of course*, the fourth floor was a pocket dimension, not an actual part of the physical library.

I wondered who controlled it. I didn't know much about pocket dimensions, but someone had to have created it.

Ah well, that was a mystery for another day. I was too tired to think about it, and it wasn't like it mattered to me at the moment. My life was weird enough already.

I thrashed back and forth in my bed until sleep finally, *finally*, took me.

Soft lips on mine. Strong arms around me. I breathed in Asher's scent. Was I in a Dreamscape?

I didn't care if it meant I got to spend time with him.

Asher cradled my face in his hands and brushed his thumb over my lips. "I've missed you," he said.

I stroked his wrists, taking hold, trying to keep him right there. "Why did you leave?"

He kissed my cheeks, first one, then the other, then my eyelids. His dark-brown curls haloed his head, and I ran my fingers through them and down the nape of his neck.

"I didn't want to," he said, softly, on a sigh. "I didn't have a choice."

I stepped back to study him. "There's always a choice." He wore a white button-down shirt, sleeves rolled up to his elbows, displaying his sexy, strong forearms. His jeans fit him like a glove, his interest in me evident.

He pulled me back close, holding my body to his. His warmth sank into me, and for the first time since he'd left, I relaxed. I closed my eyes and pressed my cheek to his shoulder. We enjoyed the feel of one another, reveling in each other's touch, before it was his turn to step back. He teased his hands down my arms and held my hands.

"Becs, believe me, if I could have stayed, I would have."

I shook my head. "I don't understand."

"I'm stealing these moments, as it is," he said. He broke eye contact and stared down at his empty hands. "There's something important I have to tell you."

"I'm totally confused."

"I know but pay attention. You're being watched. Observed. You've become too interesting."

I now officially hated that word.

"Oberon already told me this. I know, but I don't know what to do about it. I don't even know what I did to garner his attention." I released his hands to cross my arms over my chest. It killed me to lose contact, but his words frustrated me.

Asher looked over his shoulder. "I have to go." He leaned in and kissed me, the pressure of his lips against mine hard, urgent.

"What aren't you telling me?" I demanded, breathless after his lips left mine.

"There's a prediction: 'The child of the changeling who isn't a changeling will upset the balance.' That's what's got everyone scared."

The Dreamscape cooled, chilling my skin. The surrounding nothingness grew dense, weighty, and the hairs on the back of my neck stood on end. What was he talking about? A prophecy? A divination? How absurd.

No, not absurd. How *cliché*.

I opened my mouth to say something but couldn't think of anything appropriate. Not a single suitable word or fitting sentence entered my brain. I considered multiple retorts and discarded them, one after the other. None sufficed. I eventually settled on the only thing that summed up my feelings.

"What the fuck does that mean?"

"A child of a changeling who isn't a changeling." He squeezed both my hands. "That's you, Becs."

"Look," I said, my jaw so tense I thought I'd crack my teeth. I focused on relaxing it before continuing. "My parents were both normal people, not changelings. So I can't be a child of one."

I paced away from him, out of his reach. "And, then there's the rest of this gibberish. How can a changeling not be a changeling? You are one, or you're not. It's black and white, plus or minus, yes or no. It's a binary kind of thing. There's no middle ground."

I stopped pacing and put my hands on my hips, spitting mad by this time. "And on top of all that, there's you and this visit. You come to me in my sleep, after being gone for weeks and drop pithy, mysterious omens that don't help me at all but just leave me more confused? This is your idea of a Dreamscape drive-by? Well, screw you, Yoda."

He pinched the bridge of his nose with a pained expression. "If you knew how much this is costing me. . . ."

"If you knew much it hurts to be abandoned! Discarded." Unasked-for tears leaked down my face. "You ditched me. Why?" Softer, under my breath, I asked, "Why does this keep happening to me?"

"I'm sorry, Becs. I'm so, so sorry. I didn't mean to hurt you."

"Well, you did." I swallowed the lump in my throat, pushed down my urge to weep, straightened my shoulders, and gave him a hard stare. "Make it up to me by explaining these spooky forewarnings."

"It has to do with your father." As soon as the words left his mouth, he doubled over, gasping.

I took hold of his shoulder, shaking him. "What's wrong? What do you mean my father? What about him? Where is he? Is he alive?"

"Stop—" He flew out of my grip, captured by an unseen force around the waist and yanked away, his arms stretching for me, until he was out of sight. He disappeared in a haze of gray and ivory, cream and alabaster, pink and ochre. As he vanished, a thick cloud rolled over me, and his memory faded as my brain crashed into a hard reboot.

I woke early in a haze, rubbing my face, anxious, without knowing why. I scratched at my skin, my arms and legs, as if I had a rash, but nothing was there. My back itched as well, and I struggled to reach the center with a pencil. My eyes watered, and I put drops in them, wondering if something new had bloomed and I was having an allergic reaction. Annoyed, I made coffee and drummed my fingers on the counter as my mind tried to figure out what was causing my discomfort.

I carried my coffee to the fire escape and stared at the birds dropping in for some seed. I placed my mug on a small round side table I had out there for that exact purpose and refilled the feeders, taking comfort in this familiar, meditative action. I added peanuts in the shell to a wreath feeder and birdseed with the raspberries in another. The blue jays loved it, of course, and I smiled when a nuthatch arrived, hanging head down to peck for his meal. The huge, red-bellied woodpecker landed on his favorite telephone pole and banged his head into the wood like a drummer in a hard rock band.

And that's when it came back to me. Asher. Something about my father. As the caffeine hit and the sun rose, bits and pieces fell into place and I became irritated again, but for a different reason. Could Asher dream walk? Had that truly been him? And if he couldn't, then dream Asher had been a stand-in for my subconscious, created to tell me something important. Something about my father and the end of the world as we knew it, yada, yada, yada.

Besides, how trite. Couldn't my imagination come up with something better?

I finished my coffee, enjoyed the company of the nuthatch for a moment, then went back inside to write down everything I remembered. I grabbed a small journal, scribbling "Asher" and "changeling." I wrote "Dad" in the middle and drew lines to the other words knowing that this was somehow connected to the father I didn't know. The one who'd never come to see me, hadn't been around to raise me, and to whom I owed nothing. I wanted to tear out the pages and forget the whole thing. He'd left when I was four. It had been too long.

Instead, I stuffed the small journal in my bag and went to the store.

I'd never summoned anyone from Faerie before Mildread Purplefeather Moonshine, Timothy's great-great-great-something grandmother. A hob, she hit my waist, if that, and wore pointy black shoes and a housecoat. Her nose overhung her chin, and she'd smelled like a horse. Hobs liked helping, keeping the ways of house, home, field, and stream, in working order. While brownies were solely domestic or small-business based, hobs enjoyed the outdoors as well. If you were so lucky as to have hobs assisting you on your property or in your home or business, ignore them. As I always reminded myself, you may leave an item in trade, but never, ever, thank them.

With the fae, it was about equilibrium. If you need a specific thing from them, say, information, then you must provide an object or information in kind. Timothy would bring something for his request, but I needed something for mine, and I found the perfect thing in the grocery store.

I bought two bouquets of flowers, a bottle of Manischewitz Concord grape wine, and a bag of Pink Lady apples. I visited a specialty store in the same shopping area and nabbed a few other items. I took my purchases home, dropped them on the kitchen counter, then dressed in running tights, a long-sleeved T-shirt, and strapped on my sneakers.

By habit, I ran toward the north part of the city, crossing the street and jogging through the basketball court, oddly unoccupied, with a sad, deflated ball lolling in the corner. I proceeded through a barrier of scrub grass, crossed a main street, and finally arrived in the nicer part of town. Moving at a moderate pace, I made it to the hospital area and the Winter Medical Park.

A sturdy man with graying hair, a goatee, green overalls, and worn work boots waved at me.

"Hey, Mr. Lincoln."

"Becs! I'm glad to see you. Do you know what happened to Pinky? I haven't seen him for a while."

"I helped him find his way home. He's safe now. With his mother."

"Very happy to hear that. You did right by him."

I wiped sweat from my brow, waved some gnats away, and glanced at the oak tree where Pinky used to sleep. "Yeah, but I miss him. I'd hoped he'd come back to visit."

The groundskeeper donned his gardening gloves. "Me too. Sweet kid. Glad he's not on the streets, though. Kid loved the trees, especially the apples. Probably good he's not here. He'd be upset." Mr. Lincoln pointed to a couple of apple trees in the distance. "They're not doing as well as they used to. A couple got cork spot. I'm adding lime to the soil and calcium spraying, but they don't look as nice as they did. They used to be our heartiest trees. Strange thing. Not sure why it happened."

I hummed my agreement. "I'm sure they'll bounce back."

He smiled. "It's under control." He winked at me. "I know what I'm doing."

"I have full faith in you, Mr. Lincoln."

"Have a good run."

"Thanks. See you soon."

I took off, knowing exactly why the apple trees got cork rot. Pinky used to take care of them, partial to the lovely fruit trees. His nature magic infused health and vitality. Without him, the trees' susceptibility to disease returned to that of any average tree.

If he came back, he'd get them fixed up. I wished he'd return soon. The trees weren't the only living things that needed him.

Chapter 9

I texted Timothy to meet me at seven thirty that evening because sunset was about eight p.m. I didn't know if you needed to summon fae after sunset, but if Mildread worked in the fields, she might appreciate the consideration.

Then again, she might sleep all day and work all night. What did I know? Last time, she came at sundown and that was the extent of my knowledge.

I arrived at the storage facility and opened the door to my office with the app on my smartphone. The steel curtain rolled up and out of the way, revealing the interior. Battery-operated lighting illuminated the space, and a cloud of gnats gathered at the ceiling. A divider separated the right side from the left. The right side was the client's half, the left was mine.

I'd divided the space in two because I needed to keep my clients safe if I summoned a baddie on their behalf. While my particular brand of magic protected me from direct harm, it didn't safeguard anyone else. Eating the summoning client was a great way to get out of a bargain, and I was unwilling to slap a dragon on the nose with a newspaper and yell, "Bad boy!"

The sparse right side hosted a chair for the client and a trash can. Summoning didn't create much garbage, but the stomach upset could get nasty. A handy waste receptacle took care of that problem.

My side included a comfy, oversized chair in a terrible floral pattern with a blue throw pillow and blanket, a microphone and speaker for talking to the client when necessary, and a colossal gunmetal-gray industrial desk loaded with books and bobbleheads. I foraged for furniture in the discard pile other tenants left behind when they vamoosed the storage facility concrete jungle. People did this often. The storage facility's utilitarian structure and unending rows of warehoused detritus sucked the joy out of everyone with a pulse.

But it was perfect for summoning. Many things didn't have pulses.

Using a stencil, I chalked a green circle onto the floor. Then, I opened a steamer trunk I kept in the far back corner next to my desk and placed five forest-green candles on the circle, equidistant from each other. I lit them with a long grilling lighter I'd picked up from a hardware store.

I placed the kosher sweet wine in the center of the circle, added all but two of the apples, the flowers, and what I hoped was the kicker item—a bag of good loose tobacco. A little extra sweetener for the pot.

My question involved the nature of the book I'd found in the library and my powers. A summoning such as this required specifics. To the perimeter of the circle, I added a book of Celtic fairy tales, an old quill pen, a notebook, a picture of my Kiss, and for the hell of it, the only photo I had of Trace, my trainer. In it, Trace stood next to me, looking into the camera with a face of grim determination. Maybe training me was harder than it should have been? Maybe that was why he left?

I picked the photo back up and studied it, for the millionth time. Tall, lean—rangy, really—with silver hair and green-gray eyes with little yellow flecks. They looked like fading storm clouds over the lake, just as the sun peeked out. I remembered him clearly, a figure of authority. Trace had filled the void my father's absence left in my life, and then he had left, too. No wonder I was so screwed up. I put the photo back down.

I swept the rest of the floor and was putting the broom away when Timothy arrived, carrying a small bag.

"Look what I brought!" he said, holding out his hand.

"What is it?"

He opened his bag and showed me a blue lapis oval the size of a robin's egg, dark blue with gold rivulets running through it.

"It's gorgeous. Is that actual gold?"

"Pyrite. Fool's Gold, but beautiful all the same. I think Granny will like it."

"She'd be crazy not to." I took it from him and placed it in the middle, next to the wine.

"Don't call her crazy," he said with a smirk. He crouched to look at the other items I'd placed in the center.

"Is that tobacco?" he asked, eyes wide. "She'll love that."

"I hope so. Let me get the contract." I extracted a blank contract from my desk and filled in the client's name, who we were summoning, the request, and then signed it. I pricked my finger and smeared a drop of blood next to my name. Timothy did the same, and the magic snapped into place with a high-pitched, piercing pop.

Timothy jumped. "Well, that's new."

I wrinkled my nose. "I don't know why that happened."

He turned from me, eyebrows together, a worried look on his face. "Maybe you're getting stronger?"

Or, maybe something was about to go wildly wrong.

I kept my concerns to myself but double checked my setup. Circle? Yes. Fairy tales? Check. Items for trade? Check. Contract completed properly and signed? Blood? Check and check.

Everything seemed proper.

"Did you bring the library book?" I asked.

"Yes." He patted his satchel.

"Thanks. Let's get started." I pointed to the client's half on the other side of the partition. "Go sit in the chair," I said.

"Why? I didn't actually need it last time, and I can't see Granny well."

"By the book, Timothy. By the book."

Grumbling, he walked to the other side of the divider and climbed into the chair.

"I still can't see," he said.

"Hold on." I gathered a few books and the throw pillow. "Let's see if we can get you situated more comfortably."

I went over to his side, and he clambered down. I used the books to increase the height of the seat, added the pillow on top, and motioned for him to get back on. He easily sat a foot higher.

He craned his neck to look over the divider and nodded. "Much better. Why'd you make the bottom part of the divider solid wood? Why not make the whole thing transparent?"

As I walked back to my side, I answered. "To minimize the visibility of blood spatter."

Timothy gulped. "Doesn't blood stain wood?"

"Oh, no. It's fake, not real lumber. Also, when you come back over to my side, you'll see I've added plexiglass over the wood."

He rubbed his chin. "Good to know. We're not expecting anything like that, are we?"

"Of course not. Everything will go smooth as silk, just like last time."

I hoped. That clanging pop echoed through my brain.

I closed the rolling door and stood next to the circle. "Mildread Purplefeather Moonshine, great-great-great grandmother of Timothy Moon, I summon thee as a bearer of the Kiss on behalf of your family member and myself. We seek information you may have and offer items in trade."

I held my breath and waited.

And waited.

Nothing.

I tried again. "Mildread Purplefeather Moonshine, great-great-great grandmother of Timothy Moon, I politely request your presence as a bearer of the Kiss. I'm asking on behalf of Timothy and myself, seeking your company and information. We offer wine, flowers, lapis, and tobacco in trade."

Total silence.

"What's wrong, Becs?" Timothy asked.

"I don't know."

"Try one more time? Maybe she's busy."

I removed my leather cuff, a bracelet I wore to cover my Kiss. It was encircled with protective symbols: a Solar Cross, a Star of David, the Eye of Horus, a Pentacle, and a Chamsa. Feeling naked as soon as I removed it, I nevertheless dropped the cuff on my chair. I took a breath and centered myself, pressing the Kiss with two fingers.

"Mildread Purplefeather Moonshine. We do not want to bother you if you are otherwise occupied, but your great-great-great-grandson, Timothy Moon, has an urgent question to ask you. I do have questions of my own, but I call on his behalf. I summon you by the power of the Kiss."

I hated giving up the opportunity to ask Mildread my questions, but I owed it to my client to get his answers.

A tiny sliver of light appeared over the circle. It widened an inch, then another, and a small, thin, brown, bespeckled hand reached through, followed by a skinny arm. The hand dropped a ragged square of paper, snatched up the tobacco, and withdrew, quick as a wink. The sliver of light twinkled once and slammed shut.

Unbelieving, his hands to his chest in utter surprise, Timothy leaned into the microphone and said, "Becs, what happened?"

Just as flummoxed, I sank into my chair. "I have no idea, Timothy. That was Granny's arm, wasn't it?"

"Looked like it, but I can't be sure. I suppose it was her, but it's hard to judge from one appendage."

I retrieved the paper and unfolded it.

"What's it say?" Timothy asked, leaning forward.

"The sweetgrass ring for night and day. To meet the clan, it finds the way." I opened the door for him, and he scampered over to my half of the room.

"What do you think this means?" I asked.

"I'm not sure. . . ." He trailed off. "I need to sleep on it, but it sounds as if the ring allows my kid to meet her Fae family for a day and night? Maybe? They meet somewhere here? In like a field or meadow and the ring leads the way?"

"Plausible."

Timothy rubbed his eyes. "Why didn't she come through?"

"I truly don't know. Maybe she's in the middle of something else? The shower?"

"Well, this is disappointing, but at least we got some kind of answer. There's only one problem."

I picked up a candle to clean up my floor. "What's that?"

"She took the tobacco, which is your trade offering."

I flapped my free hand. "That's no biggee."

He sighed, his little shoulders rising and falling together. "Yeah, it is. Now I owe *you* a favor, Becs."

A candle under one arm and a second in my hand, I thought about what he said. I closed my eyes and paid attention to the area between my shoulder blades. The imbalance with Laurel burned, and now, a small tingle existed alongside it.

"Huh. Well, we'll figure it out."

"I appreciate you doing this. I'm concerned about Granny, though."

I handed him the flowers. "Take these home to your wife, and don't fret about Granny. She's a hard-working hob with things to do. She probably couldn't step away."

Timothy pulled his keys out of his pocket. "You're probably right."

I squeezed his shoulder. "I know I'm right."

"See ya around." He got into his car and drove away, leaving me there by myself. I cleaned up the rest of the stuff, putting the wine and photos away for another time.

Timothy worried that something bad had happened to Granny.

I just wondered how Granny knew what question to answer.

Chapter 10

I drove out of the parking lot with Mildread on my mind. Distracted, I accepted the phone call before checking Caller ID.

"Ms. Greenblatt."

I hung up.

It rang again, and I answered it.

"No."

I hung up again.

Gregory Adamos should die and go to wherever his mother currently resided.

Immediately, remorse for wishing for someone's death crashed down on my head. *Loshen hara*, my mother's voice echoed in my head. Evil speech. In this case, evil thought, but my Jewish guilt didn't know the difference. Wishing ill on someone was plain rude, and also, it had a tendency to bounce back to you.

So when the phone rang again, I answered it in a civil manner.

"Rebecca Greenblatt."

"Are you going to hang up again?" Gregory asked.

I sighed. "Against my better judgment, no."

"I'm much obliged," he said, his voice dripping with sarcasm.

"Are you calling about summoning your mother?"

"I called to discuss the possibility."

I thought for a second. Gregory had resources I did not. Connections. Worldwide acquaintances. People who owed him favors. Maybe he could find Trace?

"Where are you?" I asked.

"At home."

"I'm not driving all the way out there. Meet me at the Dapper Diner. You know the place?"

"I'll find it."

"Good. We have things to discuss, and I think this conversation is best done in person. I'll be there in twenty minutes."

"It will take me longer."

"Hurry it up, then." I disconnected the call.

I drove to the diner, parked, and entered the cool restaurant.

I got a booth in the rear, near the emergency exit into the alley, kept my back to the wall, and watched the entrance.

Gregory's arrival raised a few eyebrows. People knew who he was, and most wanted to give the six-foot, barrel-chested mobster a wide berth. Even if they didn't know his organized crime ties, his "don't fuck with me" attitude had people running. The staff behind the counter didn't greet him, and he just stood there intimidating everyone until a hesitant hostess finally asked if he needed a table. By that time, he'd seen me and waved her away, pointing to me.

He wore a bright-blue summer-weight blazer in a tight weave, a gray collared shirt, tan khakis, and sockless loafers. He maintained a close-cropped beard and mustache, and his hair remained short and carefully styled. Arresting blue hooded eyes peered at me as he approached, and I silently admired his tan. Guess he'd been sailing. His house did have a dock. Maybe he sunbathed by his crystal-clear backyard pool. Whatever. He looked like a man who lived the good life.

He slithered into the booth opposite me, and something rattled in his pocket, a *schick* of metal against metal. Probably his key fob against a money clip. He leaned back, folding his arms across his chest, mimicking my position.

"Rebecca." He inclined his head.

"Gregory."

"You asked for a face-to-face. Why?"

Before I could answer, Betsy came over. "Coffee?" she asked. "Tea? Soft drinks?"

"Hi, Betsy. Two coffees, please," I answered, jerking my thumb at Gregory. "He's buying."

We waited in silence until Betsy returned, the buzz of the evening crowd and a nearby fly our only company. She set the coffees down, dropped a small bowl with creamer on the table, and scooted away as quickly as possible.

Gregory took a sip of his coffee. Black, naturally.

I added sugar and creamer and stirred them in, taking my time.

Gregory was patient, but he broke first, leaning his elbows on the table. "Ms. Greenblatt, what am I doing here? We could have talked on the phone."

"Do you want me to summon your mother? You, yourself, I mean. Not just Nick."

He sipped again. "Yes, I want to speak with her."

"About what?"

"That's personal."

"Too bad. If I'm summoning, I need to know the reason in advance."

"Why?"

"It has something to do with the power of the summons. I don't exactly understand the way the magic works, but you can't keep it a secret. I'll hear it now or when you ask the question of your mother's shade."

He weaved his head from side to side, considering my statement. "Weren't you taught the metaphysics behind the magic?"

I blew out a frustrated breath. "My training was cut short."

"You need to finish your education."

"No shit, Sherlock. That's one of the reasons I'm talking to you."

He smiled, teeth white against his tanned skin. "Ah. You need something from me. How refreshing."

I ignored his glee. "Tell me why you want to talk to Mimi."

He placed his mug on the table and steepled his fingers. "I want to ask her for advice on finding my true mate."

I should have guessed. Our last, rather violent, interaction, involved his desire for true love, as well.

"Why do you think she'll be able to help you?"

"She found my father. Say what you will about my parents and my upbringing, they loved one another."

"Because your dad overlooked the fact that your mom was an evil psychotic bitch who wiped everyone she didn't like off the face of the Earth. Or, at least, that's how I'm interpreting it, given that you said she taught you everything she knew."

He didn't even flinch. "Merciless, yes. Psychotic? No."

I moved on. "What does Nick want to know?"

"He aches to see his mother again."

Despite myself, my heart hurt for Nick's inner child, a little boy who just wanted to see his mommy again. I understood the feeling. There was only one problem, and I had to mention it. "You know I can't guarantee she'll come, right? And I don't know what shape she'll be in."

He shrugged one meaty shoulder.

"One other thing. While this may not pertain to your mother, righteous people move on, and I can't say specifically where they go. Many people call it Heaven, or you may call it the Elysian Fields. Whatever the name, I may not be able to summon a person from a better existence."

"Can't good people become ghosts? Surely not everyone proceeds to the next stage. Or goes into the light." He flapped a hand. "Whatever it is."

"Summoning a shade from the underworld isn't the same as summoning a ghost. Ghosts choose to linger, and Mimi Adamos is not a ghost, or you would have seen her already. It's not comparable."

Now it was his turn to blow out an irritated breath. "Well, we don't know where she is, that's for sure. Still, we'll have to try." He drained his coffee and offered a questioning palm, a gesture to say it was my turn. "Now, what can I do for you?"

I pushed my unfinished coffee away, a sour taste in my mouth. "As you noted, my schooling is incomplete. I need a teacher, but I don't know how to find one. I'd like you to use your resources to find my old trainer. I can give you a picture and tell you his first name."

"Not his last?"

"I never knew it."

"What's his first?"

"Trace."

"Could it be short for Tracy or something else? Could it actually be his surname?"

Scowling, I answered as best I could. "It's what I called him."

He sat back and counted on his thick fingers. "You have a name, but it could be first, last, or a nickname. You have a photo. You have the last location you saw him." He held up three fingers. "Not much to go on."

"You're the all-powerful man with the contacts. Surely, this isn't too hard for you?"

He didn't rise to the bait. "When did you last see him?"

"Thirteen years ago, when I was fifteen. I've had two years of instruction."

"Hmmm. . . ." He crossed his arms and stared at the ceiling above my head, a mile long stare in his eyes. I waited him out. Dishes clattered in the background, and customers paid and left as we sat together.

Finally, he clapped both hands together. "You are correct to assume I have an extensive network. I'll put the word out. After all, if I find him, I'll have two summoners at my beck and call."

"You're always out for yourself, aren't you?"

He smirked. "Who else is worth worrying about?"

I shifted away from him, and the bench squeaked. "Your brother. Perrick. Other people who work for you. Your victims."

"Victims? My opponents are just as culpable for my actions. They provoke me. They're not innocents."

"Really? What about Oded?"

He shook a finger at me. "I wasn't responsible for that."

"Not directly, but ultimately you were. You were the catalyst."

"You see it that way. I do not. Perrick made his own choices."

I leaned forward, hands flat on the table. "You refused Perrick home soil, so he'd get sick. He sought a way to impress you and made a deal with Valefar to take out your enemies. Oded burned as a result. It *is* your fault, you cruel bastard."

Cold, menacing, he leaned in to me too, so our faces were only a few inches from each other. "Home soil is Perrick's weakness. He can learn to live without it."

"It's not a craving for chocolate, you moron. It's a troll's biological need."

"He can break its hold and should. It will make him more effective. Stronger."

We'd moved so close to one another that a drop of his spittle hit my cheek. I wiped it off with the back of my hand. I sat back, not trying to hide my revulsion.

"You threatened to out Perrick's son as half-troll. What's that have to do with Perrick's need for home soil?"

Gregory straightened his blazer sleeves. "He is my employee and knows where he stands."

"You're an evil creep."

"I'm the evil creep who can find your trainer."

I dropped a few bills on the table for the coffee, changing my mind about him buying, not wanting to owe Gregory anything. I stood, vibrating with rage. "And I'm the summoner who can call your mom. Don't forget it. You aren't doing me a favor. It's an even trade. And, if you so much as hurt one hair on the head of anyone I love, I'll find a way to bring you down. Don't doubt it."

He settled onto the bench, a cool, detached smile on his face. "You can try."

"I'll do more than that. Don't forget—I know your deepest wish. I know your soul's desire. That means I own you, Gregory."

Ignoring the terrified looks of the other customers, I stalked away.

Chapter 11

You never know who you'll see in a fae bar, and I sure as heck didn't expect to see Pinky. I also didn't expect Pinky to be surrounded by elves and dwarves clapping him on the back with hearty "Well met" gestures. Pinky had always been odd man out, so this new behavior made me suspicious that it wasn't Pinky they cared about, it was Oberon.

I, on the other hand, gathered him in for a big hug, his dislike of touch be damned. I needed the contact.

"Pinky! I'm so happy to see you."

He extracted himself from my grasp and sat on a stool, ears pink and cheeks flushed. I shooed the other fae away, and he breathed a sigh of relief.

"Thanks, Becs," he said softly. "Why do they like me all of a sudden? They never did before."

I purposefully ignored him, not wanting to answer him. I tried distracting him by offering his favorite drink. "Honey mead, Pinky?"

Keeping his head down and still speaking in low tones, he said, "That would be nice."

I went behind the bar and poured him a double thimble of honey mead. "Have you seen Joey?" I asked, looking around for her.

He brightened. "Yes, she's in the back. She'll return in a moment." He closed his eyes and sniffed. "You smell like coffee and French fries."

There was that sensitive nose. "I was just in the diner."

He leaned forward and inhaled. "Did you meet with Gregory Adamos?"

I quirked my head in surprise. "How did you know that?"

"You're carrying a touch of his aftershave."

I plopped down a menu I'd been holding. "You know what Gregory Adamos's aftershave smells like?"

He shrugged. "It's unique."

"Probably gets it custom made in China by small, indentured children."

Pinky frowned. "Do you really think so? Children make aftershave?"

I'd forgotten how literal he could be. "No, not really. I meant that it's probably an expensive, imported scent from Europe or something like that."

He sat back. "I'm glad children aren't involved."

"Don't worry about it. Tell me what brings you back." An elf flashed a twenty. "Ah . . . hold that thought. Let me get this guy his drink."

I made the elf his Dainty Dogwood, silver tequila with lime, simple syrup, and soda water, and then had to make his friend a Bellini, of all things. These elves had interesting tastes. I served them and went back to Pinky.

"How's your mom?" I asked.

"Good. She hugged me so hard when I made it back. A little bit like how you hugged me now."

"That's what people do when they miss each other."

He blinked at me. "I didn't know that."

I poured four draft beers and carried them to a table of squat rock trolls. A group of dwarves raised their empty wine glasses, and I brought them two chardonnay bottles and let them have at it, telling them they'd better even up before they left, or I'd sic Joey on them. The moment I said that, my boss emerged from the back.

"You better listen to her," she said, shaking her fingers at the dwarves. "She's being generous by giving you two bottles before you've paid for them."

"You know our money's good, Joey. Don't be poppin' your top like that," said one as he filled his glass to the rim.

I gave them a mock stern look. "Don't get me in trouble, now."

A dwarf with a red kerchief shuddered. "Never, Becs. We know who's watching you."

The reminder of Oberon chased the smile off my face. But it returned when I saw a new body had bellied up to the bar next to Pinky.

"Timothy! Never seen you in here before," I said as I made my way back behind the bar.

"Been here once or twice," Timothy answered. "May I please have a small cognac?"

"Absolutely," I replied. I had to open a bottle because no one ever asked for the finer spirits, and I handed him a snifter of Hennessy. "Do you know Pinky?" I asked, gesturing to the six-foot tall fairy with pink wings.

"Don't believe we've met. It's nice to make your acquaintance," said Timothy, holding out his hand.

Pinky swallowed hard, lifted his hand, touched Timothy's fingertips, then snatched his hand back and wiped it on his pants.

"Pinky just returned from Faerie," I said, to cover for my pink friend's discomfort.

"I wish I could go there," Timothy said, slumping on his stool.

"Why can't you?" Pinky asked.

"I'm only quarter fae. I don't know how to get in."

"You can see Joey's, so you've got enough fae in you, I would think," Pinky remarked, spinning his bar stool in full circles, round and round. "Maybe a relative would invite you? I've seen a human in Faerie before."

Timothy sat up straight. "That's it! Becs, that's what the sweetgrass ring does."

I cocked an eyebrow at him. "Say, wha . . . ?"

He gulped down the rest of his cognac, so excited that he bounced in his seat. "It's an invitation. Like Pinky said. It lets my kid go to Faerie for a night and a day. The clan doesn't come here. She goes there."

I bobbed my head. "That could be. All she can do is try it. I don't believe Granny gifted her something harmful."

Pinky stopped spinning. "A fae gifted something?"

"My great-great-great granny. She gave me a present for each of my children," said Timothy.

Pinky sat on his hands and swung his legs, concern on his face. "Fae gifts are never free."

"He's right," I said over my shoulder as I made a gin and tonic for a tree sprite. "But you knew that."

Timothy nodded. "I'll make sure she brings something suitable to trade." He clapped his hands together. "This is so exciting. She'll actually see Faerie."

"She may be gone a while," Pinky warned, his face glum. "I was gone longer than expected. Time works different there. A night and a day may be a month over here. This is the Slow World, after all."

I wiped rings from the counter. "I don't understand that at all. If a month over here is a day and a night over there, wouldn't we be the Fast World? It's backwards."

Joey stopped carrying a massive tray laden with drinks and snacks long enough to answer. "Don't try to figure it out. Sometimes there's no difference at all, and other times, it's only a few hours. That's why fae commute between here and Faerie for work. It depends on where home is and the capriciousness of Faerie, whether it is fast or slow. You-Know-

Who can make a change on a whim. As can his wife. Point is, Pinky is right. If your daughter goes, she may have what seems like an extended stay."

"There's someone named 'You-Know-Who?'" Pinky queried, his face scrunched up in confusion. "That's a funny name."

I shook my head. "No, Pinky. She's referring to the king of the fae and the queen."

"I know who they are!" Pinky exclaimed. "Oberon and Titania."

An instantaneous "Shhhhhhhh!" filled the room, the various voices, elven, dwarven, sprite, and troll creating a multi-tonal, multilayered, loud and ardent admonition.

Pinky froze and murmured to me. "What's going on?"

Joey ran over, holding her hands up as if to clap them over Pinky's mouth, eyes darting wildly back and forth. "Pinky, don't say their names!"

Pinky hunched over, confused, and upset at being chastised. "Why?"

I tapped the bar top to get his attention. "Saying their names may make them appear, and no one wants that."

He held his arms out wide. "Why?" It was all he could say.

"They bring a lot of power, and the king has already been here once."

"Yeah," said the dwarf with the red kerchief, lifting his glass Pinky's way. "And he mentioned you, son."

"Me?" Pinky pointed to his chest.

"He might have been a teensy bit upset that no one helped you get back home to your ma," the dwarf continued. "And he finds Becs 'interesting,' which I don't mind saying is a scary prospect. A scary prospect, indeed."

My six-foot-tall pink friend sat there, still, and slack-jawed.

"You okay?" Timothy asked.

He shook his head. "I didn't know Ober . . . I mean, the king, knew I existed."

"Well, he does," I said.

Pinky drank the rest of his honey mead and then jerked his head toward the dwarf. "What did Rumbleshots mean about him finding you 'interesting'?"

Joey plunked down a banana in front of the fairy. "Eat. You'll feel better." Pinky didn't blink, just picked up the banana and peeled it.

I hadn't wanted to share this with him. "It's probably no big deal. The big guy showed up in the bar and mentioned that he found me interesting. I think I've met him before. Twice, actually. He told me to call him Liam."

Timothy's mouth fell open. "He's following you?"

I waffled my hand back and forth. "*Follow* is a strong word."

Joey stepped behind the bar and grunted. "*Keeping tabs on* may be more appropriate, but it amounts to the same thing."

Timothy gulped. "The fae king wants something from you, Becs."

"Or he wants to stop you from doing something," said Joey.

I poured myself a shot of vodka and took it in one go, thunking down the glass. "But what? What could it be? Does he want me to do something and is going to request it? Or does he want me not to do something but hasn't told me what that is? Why me?"

Rumbleshots clambered up on a stool next to Pinky. "You helped Pinky. That may have been enough."

Timothy turned green and held his hands to his mouth. "And you summoned Granny from Faerie. Didn't you say you'd never even considered doing that before I asked you?"

"You're human and can see a fae bar," added Joey.

A selkie lifted a glass and chimed in. "You make a decent Salty Dog."

An unfortunately familiar elegant, tall elf materialized out of the shadows near Joey's melted magical sundial and joined us. "All that makes ye interesting lass, that's fer sure."

Everyone in the bar stopped what they were doing, some mid-drink, others mid-chew. Everyone looked at their feet, the table, or their hands, not at the fae king.

"Why are you here?" I stammered.

"Someone said my name."

"That's not enough, with respect. You came to see me. Why?"

"I came to check on Pinky," Oberon said, turning to the fairy whose eyes widened in shock. The fae ruler clapped a hand on Pinky's shoulder, and my friend flinched.

"Ah, sorry, son. Didn't mean to touch ye. Makin' certain ye know how to return to Faerie this time, lad. Your ma left you with instructions?"

Pinky nodded, a quick up-and-down motion of his head, his eyes trained on the thimble of mead.

"That's good. Becs, in case he gets lost again, here's a couple coins in payment to make sure he gets home." He pushed three gold coins to me. I knew better than to touch them.

"Nnnooo. I can't accept that. I'd help him no matter what. No payment needed."

"They're not a payment. They're to pay his way if he needs help again, like last time. Or, if needs must."

"If needs must?"

"A sayin' from another time. You'd say, 'in case of emergency.'"

"I can't accept them."

His face darkened, and the lights in the bar dimmed. "Ye can't refuse them."

"We'll keep them here, in the bar, my lord," said Joey, with a bow. "For emergencies."

He smiled, and the lights flared. "Excellent. I'll take my leave, then. I see the crystals are workin'. That's good. Nice job, Evans."

Evans, who'd shrunk into a corner, squeaked out, "As you requested, my liege."

"Yes," said the fae king as he strode to the door. "As I requested." He did a quarter turn to face us. "I always get what I want. Or what's the use in bein' king?"

With a whistle and a puff of wind, Oberon vanished.

The king had appeared to check on Pinky and provide coins if he ever needed help getting back? Absurd. Something else was up.

Trying to read that enigmatic jerk gave me a headache, but there was one thing I knew for sure—I was playing Go Fish while he played poker. Whatever the outcome of his game, I was certain I wasn't holding the winning hand.

Chapter 12

I'd read up on Marianna "Mimi" Adamos, the former queen mobster of Smokey Point, Ohio and environs.

She built her empire by intimidation, guts, and sheer determination. A woman with an exacting mind, little patience, and no motherly instincts, she'd had two sons and trained them to follow in her footsteps. Gregory, the oldest, learned at his mother's knee and apparently had taken every lesson to heart.

One Mimi story, which I'd put down to urban myth except it was reported in the papers back then, claimed that Mimi personally drove over a groundskeeper who had accidentally killed her favorite rose bush. Literally hit him with a car and kept going. The man died. Although originally out for vengeance, his widow recanted her police report three weeks after the incident. The reporter who'd written the original article found the man's wife vacationing in Italy.

Another story said she'd ordered the extermination—this word typed in quotes—of an entire family of newly immigrated Greeks because their family, the Cirillos, had once been rivals of the Adamos clan decades ago, in Greece. While the new immigrants didn't have a penny to their names, that didn't matter. The mother and father were found shot in the head, and the grandfather was poisoned. The three children, two teens and an adolescent, received letters telling them to go back to Greece, which they did, but all died under mysterious circumstances months later. One drowned, a second fell from the top of a tree, and the third got hit by a truck.

So ended the Cirillos.

While commercial real estate and extortion comprised Mimi's daily activities, she eventually discovered gambling, most importantly, racing. Horses, motorcycles, stock car, you name it. She didn't care who or what raced, just that she owned the tracks and charged exorbitant fees for their use, plus grifted a bit of the winnings off the top. If you wanted to race a Hot Wheels diecast toy car around a wooden race track you built in your backyard, you'd have to deal with Madame Mimi. If you didn't, she'd send her literal trolls to demolish you. Oh, and I read that she had a nice import/export business in Greek and Roman antiquities. Totally illegal, of course, but many collectors didn't care.

A crime household for generations, the Adamos family's reputation grew under Gregory's administrations. He'd inherited his mother's dispassionate cruelty.

I wanted to summon her like I wanted a hole in my head.

Already rattled by Oberon's surprise appearance, I almost refused Gregory when he texted that morning after my last shift, asking if we could summon her that night. He informed me that he'd started the search for Trace, so I was obligated to follow through on my end of the deal.

I told him to meet me at dusk.

I'd slept late, which meant I didn't have a lot of time to prepare. I fed and watered the birds, shoved food down my own gullet, took a quick run, and made a list of things to purchase. I stopped at several stores, a cemetery, and at a small medical clinic where a nurse I knew owed me a favor. By the time I arrived at my office, I had several bags to unload and a small vial in a cooler.

I'd opted for comfortable clothing, knowing I had to prep the space. Blue slip-on, high-tread shoes, a pink tank, and navy leggings did the trick. I threw a hooded zipped sweatshirt around my waist in case it got cold later and got to work. I unrolled the door and grabbed a broom, since it was never a good idea to summon in a dusty or dirty location. It simply wasn't good manners, and even though I didn't need a protective circle, if I was going to use one, I didn't want some random strand of hair to break it. I swept widdershins, counterclockwise, and, after that was done, I wet-mopped the whole place the same way.

When the floor was dry, I drew a large circle with white chalk. Then, I used a Hula-Hoop I'd shlepped from home to draw four overlapping circles within the bigger one. I didn't know if there was enough belief in the world to power Hades, but I'd give it my best shot. Relying on the idea that the intention is what mattered, I'd made up a symbol and offerings to represent the Greek underworld.

Each circle represented a level because I didn't know where Mimi resided, if she was there at all. The first circle represented the Asphodel Meadows, where the myths said most people went upon dying. I drew this circle in green.

The second circle, I created in sky blue, representing the Elysian Fields, the Isle of the Blessed, where only the most chosen heroes spent their afterlife. The third, sketched in gray, represented the Fields of Mourning, an area reserved for those pining for love.

Finally, I used black for the fourth level of Tartarus, the deepest plane which housed evil perpetrators. I'd bet money that was where she was, but maybe the measuring stick used to assess evildoers judged people much worse than she was, and she seemed tame in comparison.

Next came the offerings to the dead. Sweet strawberries for the Asphodel Meadows. A nice merlot for the Elysian Fields. Chocolates in a red heart-shaped box for the Fields of Mourning.

Last of all, a small vial of my blood for Tartarus. Life for those who had none.

In the center, I added a bouquet of white lilies, for the Lord of the Dead, and narcissus, an offering to Persephone. The narcissus grew wild in the cemetery, but the lilies I got from a flower shop. It occurred to me that whoever planted the narcissus might have been aware of Greek myths and had been currying a little favor of his or her own.

Gregory and Nick arrived in a black Mercedes sedan with a tan interior. The car cost more than your average college education. At least, I believed so. I never went to college.

Perrick drove. He stayed in the car wearing sunglasses, despite the fading light, and didn't look at me. The brothers stepped out and entered the storage space.

I didn't want to engage in any small talk, so I started in with business. "Let's get this contract signed."

I motioned for them to follow me to my desk, and they waited while I withdrew a blank contract, filled in their names, my name, the subject being summoned, and the reason for the summoning. I signed it with a flourish and handed the pen to Gregory, who signed next to his name, and then Nick signed next to his.

I extracted a needle from a pin cushion I kept for such occasions, wiped my second finger with alcohol, and leaked a drop onto the contract. Gregory and Nick followed suit. I offered bandages, which they accepted.

We did all of this without a word between us.

I pointed to the other side of the room, and they obeyed my directions. They both stood, neither taking the chair. I closed the door, and the battery-operated lights brightened.

"You two ready?" I asked.

Gregory adopted a nonchalant air and nodded, eyes aloof, face impassive. Nick pumped his fist. "Yes," he said. "Is it okay that I'm nervous?"

"Of course, it is. You've been down this road once before, and it didn't end well. This time, stay away from the divider."

Nick sobered up at my reminder.

"Remember, ask only what you've come to ask. Mimi may have very little time."

I kept my protective cuff on this time. Staring at the symbols and offerings, I said, "Marianna Adamos, we call your shade to the land of the living so you can speak to your sons. As a bearer of the Kiss, I summon you. We ask Hades to let you visit and show your true self. We submit gifts in exchange."

A ring of cold blue flame manifested and grew outward from its center. Pitch black in the middle, it spread in a wide radius, several feet across. I backed away until my back hit the wall, apprehensive about touching the flame's edge. The blackness was the black of a raven's wing, black with swirling purples and blues, slick and wet. It hurt to look at it.

Mimi Adamos stepped through, and Nick gasped. Gregory touched his hand to his heart.

Their mother wore ragged, torn clothing. Her skin, pale in life, was now ebony, a color not seen on a human ever in creation, but the darkness couldn't hide the bruises that speckled her whole body. A footprint on one half of her face shone in bright white. A chain girdled her skeletal waist, and her emaciated wrists clanked with metal cuffs. A red rose hedge, three inches thick and wide, replete with thorns, wove through the holes in the chain belt so that no matter where she placed her arms, she couldn't help but be pricked, unless she held them away from her body. Her wrists were the only place protected, and that was because of the cuffs. Tiny specks of red blood dripped onto the floor from her hands and forearms, glistening in the light.

Her eyes shimmered with unshed tears and a flaming hot rage.

"Gregory, ask your question," I said.

He took a tentative step closer to the divide, never taking his eyes off his mom.

"Mom, what happened to you?"

I clapped my hands to my face. He'd asked the wrong question. I understood, but it wasn't what he was supposed to do. I gestured to him to hurry up and ask the correct question, but he didn't. He just stared.

Mimi turned to face her sons, raised her right arm, exposing a silver filament that tied the cuffs to the metal belt. "Every death is a black mark against you," she said.

"I . . . I don't understand," Nick stammered.

Soot drifted from her arms onto the floor. "Every harm is a black mark. Look at all I carry." She spun in a slow circle to display her figure, dark as pitch, as if a black hole had fallen from the sky and landed on her body. More soot wafted from her hands. Even her fingernails gleamed like obsidian.

"Hurry, Gregory. Do it now. Ask your real question. You can't do anything for her," I said.

Gregory shook himself. "Mom, how do I find my soul mate? My true love?"

Mimi glanced over her shoulder, and her eyes widened in fear. "It's not a game. You can't treat it that way," she said, tugging at the metal girdle.

A scaly arm reached through the ring of blue fire and grabbed her around the neck. She cried out, and her hands flew to her throat, but the reptilian appendage yanked her backward into the hole. The baying of hounds and the sound of a hunting trumpet echoed through the opening from which she'd emerged. A churning, eddying wind sucked the gifts off the floor and through the ring, which caved in on itself and vanished.

Nick wept, sobbing into his hands. He collapsed and folded himself in a fetal position on the floor, something he'd done in my office once before, a painful memory and reminder that summoning could bring answers but also harm. Gregory sat in the one chair, glowering into the distance.

I took a seat in my own chair, worrying a cuticle and thinking about what we had witnessed.

No doubt Mimi resided in Tartarus, and it appeared the saying "a black mark against you" had literal meaning in Hades. The god of the Greek underworld took things seriously. I wondered if Gregory would heed his mother's warning.

I couldn't predict what Gregory would do, save for one thing.

He'd blame me for not getting the answer he'd bargained for.

Chapter 13

"You did something wrong," Gregory said, pacing close to me, getting in my face. His hands gripped his hips, and ire emanated from his body in palpable waves. I placed a hand on his chest and shoved him back.

"Don't invade my personal space or criticize me because you're disgruntled. Your mother suffers in Tartarus, and she warned you about what would happen if you continue down your present path. She cautioned you that love is not a game, and you can't treat it as such."

"That's not what she meant!" Gregory growled. "And I don't believe in Hades."

I felt like I'd been slapped. How could he ignore his own eyes? "You saw her! You heard her. How can you not believe?"

"I don't worship those gods. They mean nothing to me."

"You're putting your head in the sand. Wherever she resides, her appearance is a warning. Stop being a massive douchebag, Gregory. Clean up your act or bad things will happen. You could wind up just like your mother."

"Maybe that wasn't really her," he said with a stubborn set to his jaw.

Nick, his face wet with tears, reached for his brother's hand. "It was. Becs didn't fail. Mother did, and we witnessed the results."

Gregory ripped his hand away and cast us both furious glances. "Bull. Shit." He stalked out to the car, and Nick followed, still weeping. Gregory held the back door for Nick, shoved him inside, and barked at him to buckle. He took the passenger seat, Perrick revved the engine hard, and they peeled out on smoking, squealing tires.

"Sure, leave me with the mess," I shouted after them, but they were long gone. I rolled the doors back down for privacy and grabbed my mop. I squirted some cleanser and water on the floor and got ready to clean up.

A sizzle drew my attention back to the circle which sprung to life like a dormant fire exposed to new oxygen. It turned red, then orange, and then flames burst forth, jetting three feet in the air. It burned so hot that I feared it would scorch the floor. The blaze expanded, thickening into a six-inch wall of flame, and I scooted back, terrified of what this might mean.

A familiar demon surfaced in a flurry of gold motes. First his head, a human visage with spikes on his head and face. His body next, a lion's frame with griffin wings. His long lion tail, complete with a tuft of hair on the end, emerged last.

Except he didn't look like himself. He appeared thinner than normal, as if he'd been sick, which was impossible. I waited for him to fully materialize, but he remained semi-transparent.

"Rebecca Naomi Greenblatt," Valefar said.

"Duke of Hell," I responded.

His human lips twisted. "I cannot claim that title."

I gasped. "You're no longer a duke?"

"It shall be remedied shortly."

"Are you saying that you got demoted?" I asked. A smile threatened, but I held it back. What darling news. A weakened Valefar meant a less terrifying Valefar.

I shelved that thought. He still had power or he wouldn't be here.

"I didn't summon you," I said.

He tapped his claws on the cement floor. "True, but you reached into Hades. We're—how should I say it—connected."

Interesting.

"Is every underworld connected?"

He batted his eyes. "If you want me to explain, it will cost you."

"Seems like something already cost you."

He roared at me, a huge, belching roar filled with fury. It flattened me against the wall, shoving me so hard I almost lost my footing. Smoke rose from his body, and his torso flickered with flame. The scent of brimstone filled the room.

"DO NOT MOCK ME, GIRL!" My bobbleheads tipped over, my chair slid back a foot, and the papers on my desk blew to the floor. My eyes watered, and I blinked to get the ash out. I breathed in smoke and coughed like an asthmatic. It took several seconds to recover. Valefar licked his wings like a cat and waited.

I finally caught my breath. "Yeah, got it. No mocking," I said, my tone bitter. "You're still the big, bad demon."

He flicked something off a claw. "I most definitely am."

"Okay, fine. You've proven your point. What are you doing here?"

"I simply desired the pleasure of your company. Is it wrong to wish for time with your best friend?"

My jaw dropped. "I'm not your best friend. I'm not even an acquaintance."

"Oh, you will be," Valefar said with a devious smile.

"Yeeeah . . . no. I'm never gonna be your friend."

He tilted his head to examine me. "I think otherwise. Want to bet?"

"No need to bet, you monstrous creepazoid. I hate you, and you shouldn't be here."

Valefar drew up, chuckling. "Why, that's a *new* insult. Quite pithy. I'm wounded. After all we've been through, I can't believe you don't trust me." He brought one clawed paw to his heart.

Oh, I trusted him. I trusted him to do whatever benefitted him, and from the looks of it, he'd fallen in the pecking order and his power had gone with it. Whatever he wanted, it had to do with regaining what he'd lost.

I licked my lips. "If I'm piecing this together right, you snuck in on a technicality because I summoned from an adjacent underworld. That can't be easy, but you've risked it. Why?"

He peered at me, his body coiled, intent. "Have you seen Oberon?"

"Don't say his name!"

He sat back, a crafty smile on his face. "So, you have."

"What's it to you?"

He shrugged with one furred shoulder. "Professional curiosity." He studied me again. "What did he want?"

Now it was my turn to study him. "I'll tell you if you explain to me about underworlds being connected."

He settled down on his belly, head up. "Deal. And, as a sign of *trust*," he said, emphasizing the last word, "I'll go first. You've already guessed it, anyway."

He rolled his shoulders and folded his wings, taking on a professorial demeanor. "All underworlds are connected—Hell, Hades, the Duat, Diyu, Abbadon, Niflheim, you name it. They touch, overlap, converge. While we tend to stay in our own spaces, we can travel from realm to realm if desired."

"Is it difficult?"

"Not if you know where to find the doorways."

"A hellmouth?"

"That's one type of doorway."

"What's another?"

He grinned wide, showing his incisors. "Well," he said, with a coy incline of his head. "The easiest way is to die."

I frowned. That tracked, unfortunately.

"When I summon you, do you come through a door?"

He shook a paw at me. "Ah, ah, ah. That's beyond our agreement." He paused and held up a paw. "I could tell you more, for a price. Maybe a tidbit on your sister or, better yet, your young niece?"

I kept my temper, but barely. "No chance. No way. No how. And you can't touch children. I know the rules."

He rolled his eyes with a yawn. "It was worth a try. Now, I've told you what you wanted to know. Tell me what Oberon wanted from you."

I shrugged and gave him a thin smile. "Nothing."

He unfurled his wings. "What did he say to you?"

"That he found me 'interesting.'"

Valefar considered that a moment. "Ah. I see."

"What does that mean? Do you know?"

He ignored my question. "Tell me more. You owe me."

I shrugged again. "He thanked me for doing something I'd have done anyway."

"He admitted a burden?"

"Not really. He wanted to make sure one of his subjects was taken care of."

Valefar sat back and crossed his arms, a funny look for a lion. "He asked you to take care of this fae?"

I wagged my hand in a see-saw motion. "Sort of."

"Did he give you anything?"

"Fae coins, which are useless here. And that's all I'm telling you. We're even."

"Yes, I believe we are." He tapped his claws again. "Tell me, how's the search for your trainer going?"

I jolted upright. "How did you know I'm searching for my trainer?"

"Tsk, tsk, Rebecca. I keep tabs on you. People whisper to me in the dark."

"What kind of people? Who?" I demanded, taut as a bowstring. Who was spying on me?

"You can't really believe I'm going to answer that."

"This is more than annoying. This is invasive, and you don't have the right. I don't owe you anything anymore!" I got right up to the white circle, which I'd noticed he hadn't stepped out of. I made sure my toe didn't touch it. I wanted this soul-sucking, conniving bastard contained.

My voice seethed with malice. "Stay away from me. Stay away from mine. And when I find out who is eavesdropping on me and reporting to you, I'm going to make sure they stop and stay stopped."

He chuckled. "Oh, I like the sound of that. Go ahead. Find out and kill them. Destroy them, Becs. Do it." He bent and stretched his neck right through the flames, so we were almost nose to nose, his fetid breath filling my nostrils. "I'd like to see you become a murderer."

That drew me up short. I scurried to the farthest corner of the room, near my steamer trunk, and took three deep breaths, my eyes closed. When I got myself under control, I opened my eyes. "Don't you have somewhere to be?"

He jutted his wings out to touch the barriers of the circle. "I have all night."

"Well, I don't." I hurried to my desk and withdrew a plastic container, intent on trying something I hadn't done before. I shook out a handful of dried sage, rue, dill, lavender, and rosemary and threw it at the demon. "Valefar, former duke of Hell, begone with you. As a bearer of the Kiss, I send you back to Hell where you belong."

He shivered as my command took hold. He held up a paw and said, "I find you interesting too, Rebecca. Very, very interesting."

His already diminished form dwindled away. The scent of brimstone lingered.

A disgusting muddle of chalk, Mimi's blood, soot, Valefar's ash, cleanser, water, and a few smashed strawberries, remained. I sat in my chair, thinking about the demon's visit. Why ask about Oberon? What did that information mean to him? The questions jumbled in my head in a chaotic mix of alarm, foreboding, and apprehension.

Confused and worried, I heaved myself out of my chair and opened the storage facility door. I splashed clean water on the floor and mopped the slop out onto the pavement. Anyone who saw it would think someone perished horribly, and I prayed I wouldn't be arrested. I'd never seen anyone in the adjoining units, but you never knew. I looked up at the sky.

"My life is in upheaval, and I'm terrified I'm going to mess up and put my family back in danger, or hurt Pinky, or do something dumb and ruin Joey's bar, or get myself killed. Any guidance would be appreciated."

I had no idea if anyone heard me, but it didn't hurt to try.

Chapter 14

I don't think well at one in the morning. I usually managed to muddle through at the bar but pulling drafts and mixing martinis doesn't take the same concentration as summoning. Summoning drained me like nothing else.

Which is why I didn't hear the car stop outside my unit.

But I did recognize the voice.

"Becs?"

I stopped mopping and peered into the dark. "Asher?"

The sexiest man I'd ever seen stepped into the light, moths flitting around him. He wore faded jeans, black sneakers, and a gray T-shirt. His fine jawline was roughened by the beginnings of a beard. He'd cut his hair, so it was clipped close on the sides with a hint of waviness on top. My first thought was how I would miss running my hand through his curls. His dark eyes held a mixture of wariness and hope.

My breath caught in my throat, and I dropped the mop. It clattered as it hit the floor, and I kicked it out of the way.

"Is it really you?" I asked. Then, more pointedly, I added, "Where have you been?"

He walked toward me, determined, like a lion stalking prey, but I wasn't scared. On the contrary, it thrilled me and I heaved a huge breath, trying to remember I was mad at him, an impossibility with the heat of him this close.

Close enough for me to touch, his eyes fixed on mine, holding my gaze. I couldn't move or ask any of the myriad of questions that rattled through my brain. *Why'd he leave? Where'd he go? Would he stay?*

"You look great," he said, his voice low and insistent. The simple compliment held the promise of other things, of things he wanted to say, things he yearned to tell me but didn't.

I stopped short of reaching for him. "You, too," I said. Finally, I shook myself and asked, "What are you doing here?"

He didn't answer, just closed the space between us, brought his hand to my hair, and brushed it with his fingers. I closed my eyes and swayed against him, and he brought his arms around me and held me close. His heartbeat galloped against my cheek and was echoed by my own. Warm and solid, he enveloped me in a bubble that was somehow both safe and brimming with ardor, and I wanted to stay there forever. He'd always been clean shaven, and I'd liked it, but now that I was up close, I thought that the beginning of the beard looked good on him. I wanted to trace his jaw with my fingertips and rub my cheek against his chin stubble like a cat in heat.

But I didn't. With a reluctant sigh, I drew away and looked up at him. "Where have you been?"

"Away." He released me, and I instantly pined for his embrace. It was a physical pain, like a phantom limb, and I had to steel myself against it. He rubbed his face with both hands, avoiding my gaze.

It pissed me off. "Away? You leave without warning, come back uninvited, and all you can say is 'away'? Not good enough."

"I'm sorry. I want to tell you, but I can't."

"Why?"

Asher curled his hands into fists at his sides. "It's sort of family stuff."

"Family stuff? I thought both your parents were dead."

"They are. It's more of an extended family." He walked past me, examined my desk for a second, and then turned to face me. He gestured to the half-mopped floor.

"Who did you summon tonight?" he asked.

"None of your business. If you can't be honest with me, I don't have to be forthright with you."

"I've never lied to you."

My voice rose, my anger spilling over. "Not directly, but lies of omission are still lies. What extended family? Why did you have to go? Why can't you tell me what is going on?"

"Because I can't, okay? Because there are *rules*." The vein in his temple pulsed, and he brought his hand up to massage it.

I snorted. "Rules, schmules. You could have at least said goodbye and told me when you'd come back."

Asher hung his head, chagrined. "I should have done that, but I was a coward. I'm sorry I hurt you."

I threw my hands in the air and turned toward the door, keeping my back to him. "Hurt is an understatement."

He crossed the room in a flash, wrapped his arms around me, and nuzzled my neck. Longing filled me, and despite my frustration and anger, I leaned against him again, letting him explore my neck and ears.

He placed soft butterfly kisses on my cheek, and a deep, pulsing need rushed through my body. His equal desire was obvious, pushing against my back, and I rubbed against him.

With a sharp intake of breath and a small cry, Asher let go of me. I stumbled and had to catch myself on my chair. I whirled on him.

"What game are you playing?"

He pressed his lips together and shook his head. "No game."

"Then what's going on?"

He looked right at me, a penetrating gaze that made him seem like a cop.

"Who did you summon tonight?" he asked.

"Why?"

"I smell brimstone."

I frowned. "I cleaned everything. I even sage-smudged every corner."

"The scent is still in the air."

Crossing my arms, I studied him. "Why do you care?"

"I don't want to see you hurt, and it smells like demon."

"Well, Mr. 'I disappear and then come back and want to run your life,' it was Valefar."

His jaw dropped in disbelief. "How could you summon him again after all we went through?"

I narrowed my eyes, anger coursing through me, replacing the passion of a moment ago. I'd never met anyone who could make me run this hot and cold. "First, I didn't summon him. And, puullease. What's this 'after all, we went through?' There's no *we* after you left in the middle of the night, so don't you dare lecture me."

He rubbed his temple again. That must have been a crasher of a headache. He started to say something, stopped, and then continued. "I'm not lecturing. I'm asking. Politely. Please. Please tell me why you're dealing with Valefar again. He's dangerous."

"I'm well aware of that."

He clenched his jaw and struggled to get his next words out. "You and I did everything possible to unentangle you from that demon."

"Yes, we did. And I repeat, I didn't summon him. I summoned someone else from Hades, and he showed up uninvited—much like you, actually—and asked questions about my life. It seems the two of you have a lot in common."

"I have nothing in common with a demon!"

"Except showing up out of the blue and prying into my life!"

"That's not what I'm doing!"

I shook with rage. "Then what are you doing, exactly? Providing unsolicited, unneeded advice? Are you going to disappear again?"

"I'm trying to protect you." Asher ran his hands through his hair and massaged his neck.

Once, I'd have massaged his neck for him. Now, I thought, he deserved the discomfort.

"Protect me from what, Asher?"

He strode over to me, so we were only a foot apart. "From making a big mistake."

"What mistake would that be?"

"Dealing with Hell, in any form. It's not safe. I'm pleading with you, leave the underworld alone."

"I'm doing my job."

"You could put everyone in danger."

He'd said something like this before, in my dream. "Did you dream walk to me?"

"Maybe? I don't know. I can't remember."

I rolled my eyes. "You can't remember? 'Cause dream walking is old hat to you?"

Asher tapped the tips of his finger together, not quite a clapping motion, but enough to reveal his agitation. "Of course not. Maybe we dreamed of each other? I honestly don't know."

Suddenly, fatigue overwhelmed me. Perplexed that Valefar showed up when I hadn't summoned him and confused by Asher's equally unexpected appearance, I sank into my chair, exhausted. Arguing with Asher was like going in circles. He didn't answer anything directly.

I addressed my sorta ex-boyfriend, reminding myself to guard my heart. "Look, I get that dealing with Valefar is a bad idea and that it could endanger Mickey and Ruthie and everyone I care about, but for the third time, I didn't call him. I never mentioned his name. I summoned Mimi Adamos from Hades, and afterwards, he materialized on his own. If it is any consolation to you, he doesn't look well."

That piqued his interest. "How so?"

I flapped my hand back and forth, searching for the words. "He's pale? Thin? Diminished? He appeared semi-transparent, not his full materialization like before. He intimated that he'd lost power and couldn't use the term 'duke,' anymore. He also said he'd remedy that soon. And before you ask, no, I don't know what that means."

Asher turned and paced the length of the room. "That's unheard of. A demon of his history and strength? A duke falling in the ranks?"

"And . . . how would you know this?"

"I did my own research. Like I said, I'm trying to protect you."

I was too worn out to push. I fluttered an indifferent hand. "Sure. Okay. Whatever. Look, I didn't push for specifics. I was too interested in how he showed up."

"What did he say?"

I leaned back in the chair and closed my eyes. I could fall asleep right there. "He said that all underworlds overlap, that they touch each other, and you could use doorways to get from one to the other if you knew where they were."

"Did he say how to find the doorways?" His voice was suspiciously eager.

I opened one eye. "Why? Want to go there?"

"No, but I'm curious."

I closed my eye again. "He said the easiest way to get in was to die."

Asher snorted. "Not helpful."

"Tell me about it. And it doesn't answer the main question, which is how and why he surfaced in a summoning circle when I didn't call him."

Asher circled behind me and rubbed my shoulders. "It's perplexing."

"It is, and now you know that I didn't invoke him on purpose."

He worked a knot near my right shoulder blade. I groaned in pleasure.

"This information fascinates me," he said.

"Uhm hum. Can you dig a little harder?"

The pressure increased, and it was almost a sexual experience. Of course, any physical contact with Asher was a sexual experience.

"God, that feels great. Thank you."

He chuckled. "I'm sure the Almighty appreciates the gratitude."

I giggled. "I meant you. Thank you."

"You're welcome."

We hung out in silence for a few moments while he worked on my back.

"Asher?"

"Hmm?"

"Are you back to stay?"

Regret colored his words. "No."

I pulled away from his touch. Reluctantly, I whispered, "Then you'd better go."

Asher released the back of the chair. "As you say." He kissed the top of my head in farewell.

I watched him leave, my heart in my throat. I wanted to call him back, to beg him to stay and explain, but I couldn't do that anymore. If he wanted to share himself with me, he could. But I needed all of him, not pieces and parts, not mystery and dishonesty.

"You know where to find me if you change your mind," I called to his back. "I won't wait forever."

His voice carried through the night. "I understand." He slipped away.

The moths gathered around my lights, flying in jerky circles, as I cried into my hands.

Chapter 15

The black-clothed woman walked into So Long Noodles while I ate veggie lo mein and attempted a word scrabble to clear my head. My wee friends had given up helping me with the puzzle and were building a house out of toothpicks on the adjoining table. They scooted farther away when she took the seat opposite me. Kenneth and the Longs, working in the kitchen, popped their heads out to see who had entered.

The woman's black veil and tiered jet lace dress certainly caught the eye. Jet-black hair streaked with gray hung down her back, and her pointy shoe boots rounded out the ensemble. The whole getup screamed Halloween witch costume, but I didn't think she meant the outfit to be ironic.

It took a second, but I recognized her as the woman who'd stared at me across the street from Joey's—the woman whose shop vanished from sight the second I turned away.

She sniffed, threw back her veil, and I got a good look at her pale-blue eyes, like a husky's, striking against the black. The gray hair and jowly, loose skin hanging from her jawline and neck indicated advanced age, but she didn't move like she was old, and those blue eyes were sharp and clear. She shifted in the yellow plastic chair, as if trying to get comfortable on a plushy chaise. I could have told her not to bother. Though a take-away place, the Longs had a few scattered red molded plastic tables with gold chairs for the customers who wanted to eat in and the other hungry patrons who lingered for orders. The hard seating was for dine-and-dash, order and wait, not comfort.

"What do you want?" I asked, my voice brusque and suspicious, because, well, I was totally suspicious of this woman and why she'd sought me out at my home. "Who are you?"

She pointed a finger at me, a yellow talon-like nail leading the way. "The Warlock sent me."

"Which warlock?"

"The Warlock whose shade resides in Hell."

I leaned back in my chair and crossed my arms, though I had to suppress a shiver. "Really? He's dead and reaching out to me from the grave?"

"He doesn't have a proper grave." Her voice held a faint note of disapproval.

"It was kill or be killed, and the fact that he wound up in Hell is not my fault or my problem. As for his body, Gregory Adamos took care of his burial, not me. Who are you anyway?"

"My name is Madame Francesca Pietrov."

"Okay, Madame Francesca. The goth makeover guys really went to town on you, didn't they? The '80's called, and they want their dress and veil back." When she didn't respond, I tried a more direct approach. "We're done talking. Feel free to leave."

She lowered her voice, her piercing eyes studying me like an ant under a microscope. "He left his death curse on you. I see it clinging to your body like a shroud. He's sent me a message to give to you."

Derrick, the self-styled "Warlock with a capital W," had indeed been an actual magic-user who'd hit me with a blight curse right before he died. It disturbed me that this crone could see it.

She stood, unfurling herself inch by inch. She was tall, and by the time she reached her full height, she towered over me. I stood, too. The wee ones hid inside their toothpick house.

Madame Francesca lifted both hands, as if she were cradling my head from two feet away. "The Warlock says to tell you he's looking forward to your visit to Hell and that he'll own you there, Rebecca Naomi Greenblatt. His death blight will bring you to him, and you will be his." She dropped her hands. "That's his message, word for word. I have discharged my duty."

Inwardly, I groaned. When the Warlock had died, he'd thrown a death curse on me using the word "blight." I'd never gotten sick and had forgotten all about it.

I rose. "Ugh. This creepy act isn't working for you. Don't come around here, witch, and try to scare me with warnings from beyond the grave. They won't work. All you're doing is making a fool of yourself."

She jolted at my words, affronted. "I'm not a witch. I'm a *medium*."

"I'm a small. Large will be here later, and Extra Large is coming tonight."

"He warned me about your smart mouth."

I shrugged. "I'm smart, alright, so I know a fraud when I see one."

"How can you be so flippant? I give you portents."

Portents. Omens. While I was playing hard at being glib, what she said frightened me. Acid rose in my throat, and I held my hand to my chest. "What you give me is heartburn."

Mrs. Long walked out from behind the counter holding an ancient Devil Chaser Mask in front of her and peered at Madame Francesca through her red half-moon reading glasses. She'd once hung the mask on my door to repel evil spirits.

My landlady shoved the mask toward the medium, her gold eyeglass chain swinging with her effort. "Get out of our domain," she said, holding the mask in front of her like a shield. "You're not welcome here."

Madame Francesca replaced her veil. She pivoted on her heel and stalked to the door, opening it with enough force that the dainty bell jangled rather than tinging its usual welcoming ding. "I have done what I came to do. I have fulfilled my obligation to the dead. Heed my warning, Ms. Greenblatt, or suffer the consequences." All she needed was lightning, a cape, and scary organ music and she'd be set.

Mrs. Long pushed the mask toward her. "Begone."

The medium dismissed the mask. "That mask deters evil and thus does not bother me." She flicked her eyes at me, hesitated as if to say one more thing but instead held her tongue. She departed, leaving a faint musty odor behind.

"What was that about?" Mr. Long asked, his gentle voice unusually high-pitched. The weirdo medium had unsettled all of us.

"I honestly don't know," I responded, sitting down with a thump, my bravado all gone now that she'd left. "I saw her once before, near Joey's, but this is the first time she's spoken to me."

Mr. Long pressed on. "You knew the person, the warlock, she was referring to. Is that the same man that sent the death magic to you? The magic that eventually morphed into those arrows you have upstairs?"

I put my head in my hands, my elbows on the table. "Yes, it's Derrick, a warlock. And it turns out we knew each other in high school. Can you believe that?"

Mrs. Long peered at me, stretching her neck long, like a swan. "Someone you went to school with turned into a bad magic practitioner?"

I held out my hands in a "what can you do?" gesture. "I know. Who woulda thunk it?"

Mr. Long placed his chin in his hand and leaned on the counter. "Something must have driven him to it."

"His father did something awful—I don't know what—and wound

up in Hell under Valefar. I think Derrick sought out magic as a way of getting him back. That's why he followed me. He sought to use my Kiss to free his father's spirit."

Jimmy piped up. "But that's impossible."

I inclined my head at the little one. "Exactly. That's impossible. The whole thing was crazy."

Rin stroked his beard. "How did Derrick wind up in Hell?"

Trick nudged him with a foot. "Don't you remember? He tried to kill Becs and Asher, but he died."

"Good memory, Trick. Right. He died at Gregory Adamos's estate, and Valefar whisked him off to Hell."

Mrs. Long spoke up, peering at me through her reading glasses. "What about this death blight thingee?"

I rubbed my eyes, tired. "Before his death, he threw a death curse at me. He cast it, using the word, 'blight'."

Mrs. Long pushed past her husband, her eyes wide in alarm. "You've been carrying around a death curse? This blight? This is terrible. You bring disease into my house." Mrs. Long didn't even take a breath, but continued, her voice getting more strident by the syllable. "You can no longer live here. Find another place to stay. Out. Out!"

I stared at her, confused. "Why? I'm not sick. Even if it's a real thing, it doesn't affect you."

Mr. Long tried to intercede, walking over to stroke his wife's arm. "Nothing bad has happened so far."

She shook him off. "It will. When Asher was here, I didn't worry as much. But without him. . . ." She went behind the counter, still carrying the mask, muttering quietly so I couldn't hear her, but I could tell by the tone that it wasn't complimentary. She slipped the mask into a protective case.

I pressed the issue. "Why does Asher matter? What is it about him that made you feel more secure? He's just a guy."

"How do you not see?" she demanded, slamming her palms flat on the counter.

"See what?" I exclaimed, flinging my arms out at my sides, exasperated.

She hit the counter again. "He's an angel!"

My face grew hot. "He's not. He's not even nice. He pretended to be my boyfriend and then left the second we got close. I know you like him, but don't you think you're overdoing it? He's not that great."

Mr. Long pushed his body between me and the counter so I

couldn't see his wife. He put both hands on my shoulders. "Becs. Listen."

I fumed but paid attention because Mr. Long never said anything that wasn't important. "What?"

"Asher is an angel. Literally. He's your guardian angel."

I blinked at him.

Mrs. Long sidled left so I could see her again. "I saw his light immediately but was unsure. He told us the truth when you got so sick with the death magic. We wanted to take you to the hospital, but he wouldn't let us. We demanded to know why."

I rocked in place, swaying with this news. "This can't be."

"Why couldn't it?" Mr. Long gave me a kindly smile with a small bow to offset his arguing with me. "After all you've seen, you doubt the idea of a guardian angel?"

"No. I doubt the idea that I have one."

Mr. Long motioned me back to my little red table where the wee ones stared at us, wringing their little hats in their hands.

"Asher made us promise we wouldn't tell you. He said he'd tell you himself."

All the energy left my body, and I slumped in my chair. "The origami bird wasn't a bird. It was an angel."

Mr. Long shook his head. "I don't know what that means."

I waved the words away. "Doesn't matter. He should have told me directly."

"I'm sure there was a reason why he didn't," Mr. Long said.

"He's a coward."

Mrs. Long gasped. "Don't speak of an angel that way! Especially under our roof when you have a death curse clinging to you. What do you want to do, kill us all?"

I was too tired to do anything but sigh. "I'm going to my apartment. Please don't kick me out."

Mrs. Long put her glasses back on. "We'll return your rent money. We thought you were a nice girl, but first you have death magic, now a death curse. And your angel gone? Too much trouble."

I opened the door to the stairwell and placed a foot on the first step, unable to deal with her assertions and what they implied.

I'd forgotten about Kenneth, who stood stock still in the back of the kitchen, next to the stove, as gobsmacked as I was.

"Becs, wait."

I turned, looking over my shoulder at him.

"You've had a lot of horrible stuff happen to you. What's the use in having a *guardian angel* if he can't stop the bad things?" He drew out the words 'guardian angel' with enough snark to impress even me. He shrugged. "Sorry Ba`ba, Māma, but I'm not buying it."

Rin's little voice floated to me on a soft breath. "But, Kenneth, what if he kept it from being much, much worse?"

Trick offered a lovely follow up. "Yeah, maybe Becs could have died without him."

Jimmy smacked his brother on the shoulder. "Becs isn't going to die. Why did you have to say that?"

But Trick was right, and the thought that Asher had kept me alive slammed into me, making me trip on my way up the stairs.

The question was, could I change my current predicament on my own or would Asher's absence guarantee my death?

I had no way of knowing.

Chapter 16

I ran some errands that afternoon, and when I got back, I climbed my fire escape to my back door, only to discover it wouldn't open. I'd been locked out.

"Oh, for the love of Pete."

I couldn't ask the Longs to let me in, since I was pretty sure they'd been the ones to lock me out in the first place. Not Kenneth or Mr. Long, but Mrs. Long, who'd worked ridiculously fast to get the back lock changed in just a few hours. My groceries sat on the fire escape, and my ice cream was melting.

I needed to get back in without letting Mrs. Long know. If I really couldn't stay here anymore, she at least had to give me time to pack up and find a new place.

There was only one thing to do. I only hoped they wouldn't mind.

I found the jelly rectangles from the Dapper Diner and took three out, placing them on top of my bag. I made a comfy well next to them and called my little friends.

"Jimmy, Trick, and Rin. Can you come here?" It was the most informal summoning, but I wanted to be polite.

Pop! The three wee ones appeared on my backpack. They wore their tiny little sleeping caps, and Rin showed up on his side, snoring. Trick stretched and yawned. "What's the big idea summoning us during our nap?" he demanded.

"I'm so sorry. I hated doing it, but I'm locked out. I know your special talents. Can you assist?"

Trick nudged Jimmy who sat there staring at the jelly without blinking. "Jimmy! Jimmy, you lug nut, Becs needs your help." He poked him again, saying, "Jimmy's the one who's good at locks."

Jimmy tilted his head to look at me, his eyes blurry with sleep. "Where are we?"

"Wake up, you big fairy fart. Becs needs you to unlock her door."

Jimmy blinked and scratched his bottom. "She locked you out for reals? Aw, Becs, you know, she's technically our employer. If she finds out we let you in, she might tell us we can't stay."

"She can't evict me and lock me out with all my stuff inside. I have to get in."

"Hold on. I've got another idea."

Jimmy winked out, and three minutes later, Kenneth wandered around to the back of the building. He called up to me. "I've got a copy of the new key. She had two made."

"Thanks, Kenneth. I'm sorry if this gets you in trouble with your mom."

Kenneth climbed the fire escape and handed me Jimmy, who hopped into my palm. "Legally, she can't lock you out as a means of evicting you. I'll talk to her." He opened the door and handed me the new key. "But, you're right." He swallowed hard. "I don't usually go against them. Respect for your parents and all that. My mom is already upset that I said I didn't believe Asher was an angel."

"I know, and I'm sorry. Thanks again. . . ."

"Ahhhhhh!" Trick and Rin broke out into screams, and I almost dropped Jimmy when I saw the owl, out for an early snack, gliding out of the trees to land on the fire escape platform. The Eastern Screech Owl is small compared to the Great Horned Owl but to my little friends, who were only four inches tall, that was no consolation.

I scooped the two remaining wee ones up in my other hand and shooed the bird with my foot. "Sorry, darling, but you've got to hunt elsewhere." The owl clacked its beak in annoyance, vaulted into the air, snatched a dragonfly mid-flight, and left.

Kenneth, scrunched in the corner next to the door, his mouth open. "Darling?" he asked in disbelief.

"Owls gonna owl. They eat, too, you know."

"That was close!" Rin said, pulling his hat down over his ears. "Kenneth, your mom won't evict us, will she?"

"No. Don't worry. Becs, go inside. I'll explain the regulations to my folks." He jogged down the steps murmuring something about sharp, pointy talons.

I opened the door and placed the wee ones on a couch pillow. Then I went outside for my bags. After putting the groceries away, I opened the three jelly squares and handed them to Rin, Trick, and Jimmy.

"Here you go. As promised."

They dove in head-first like puppies lapping at a water bowl. Total carnage.

Rin sat up first, holding his head. "Sugar rush!" he exclaimed, squinting. The other two followed suit.

"Sugar rush?" I asked.

"Like when you humans get a brain freeze," Rin explained, but it didn't keep him from licking his fingers.

I handed them each a tissue, and they wiped their hands and faces.

"Now," said Trick, sitting down and rubbing his hands together, "tell us what's going on."

"How do you know something's going on?"

"You have worry lines between your eyebrows."

"I might have gotten Kenneth in trouble with his parents."

"That young man is already breaking free a bit. It's the girlfriend."

"That's interesting. Tell me more."

"It's good for him," Trick said with a wave of his tiny hand. "Nothing else to say. Now, tell Uncle Rin, Trick, and Jimmy what's bothering you. You know, in addition to the death blight and the scary medium lady."

I laughed at the thought of them being my uncles, but I told them the whole sordid story, from my sister to Gregory to Valefar. I mentioned Asher but left out the personal details. They listened attentively, not interrupting.

Rin rubbed his belly and burped before speaking. "Let's get this straight. First, your sister thinks you're addicted to magic because she doesn't understand the Kiss and you don't know how to explain it to her?"

"Correct."

Jimmy held up two fingers. "Second, your last two summonings worked, but weird things happened that you didn't expect."

"Again, correct."

"Third," Trick said, holding up three fingers like a toddler proudly showing you his age, "Valefar appeared without you directly summoning him, and that's yet another thing you don't understand."

I wobbled my hand in the air in a "so-so" manner. "I understand it a little bit, but no, I don't know why that happened."

"Most importantly, Mickey says that until you get control of your magic, you and your family will never be safe," said Jimmy, his face solemn. "Which means she won't let you see her or Ruthie."

I bit the inside of my cheek and nodded.

"It all boils down to the same thing."

I waited for him to tell me what that was.

The three of them waited expectantly for me to figure it out.

"I'm not getting it."

Jimmy looked at me as if I was an idiot. "There's one underlying problem to all of those things. You've said it yourself. Your summoning lessons were cut short. You lack instruction."

I stood and paced the room. "I've already explained all of that. Trace left without a forwarding address. Without a phone number. I don't know if Gregory can find him. I've never met another person with the Kiss, and my mom passed away, so I can't ask her how she found Trace in the first place. And no, I'm not summoning her ghost."

Rin giggled. "Hey, you rhymed! Trace, place."

"Seriously?"

He shrugged.

Trick crossed his arms, thinking. "Have you tried summoning Trace?"

I blinked at him. "No. He's human."

"You can't summon humans?" they asked, at the same time.

Huh. That was something to consider. I could try it. If it didn't work, it didn't work. No harm, no foul. I got up and made tea. I ate a cookie. Deciding that wasn't nutritious enough, I scrambled some eggs, as I pondered their question.

The truth was, I didn't know for certain that I *couldn't* summon a human. It had never occurred to me to attempt it. Humans weren't magical, and summoning was a magical process. Like attracted like, so calling a human by magic shouldn't work.

But Trace had magic. He had magic like mine.

Could that work?

I brought my eggs into the living room and spooned some onto a clean coaster. The guys slurped them up, making their bellies stick out like beach balls.

"I'll check with Gregory to see if he's found Trace through normal means, first."

"Goosh ideash," Rin said.

"Excuse me?"

He swallowed a last mouth full of egg. "Good idea."

I tapped my fork against my teeth. "Maybe I'll also seek Joey's advice."

Jimmy nodded. "Smart. Good to be cautious."

Did I know anyone who was an expert in magic?

A memory caught me. Pinky once referred to Oberon's "Rules of Magical Harmony." The fae king had had dozens of lifetimes to study magic.

Well, too bad. I wasn't about to say his name. Even if he knew about my particular flavor of magic, it was unwise to bring more attention to myself, especially if it involved something that could be construed as a request. Besides, even if he would help, I didn't dare risk invoking the wrath of his wife. The thought gave me the heebie-jeebies.

But my friend Pinky might be the next best thing.

I didn't know if he was still on this side of the Faerie portal, but if he was, I knew where he'd be. After all, cork rot waited for no man. Or fairy. Once he saw those apple trees, he'd stay around to make sure they survived.

"Gentlemen, thank you for your advice. I need to see a fruit fairy."

"Nap, Becs," Trick said. "Best to get some sleep first."

"Thanks, Mom."

"Mean it, Becs."

"Okay, I will." I acceded easily because Trick was right. I couldn't go much longer without rest.

Trusting that they'd make their way downstairs, I washed up quickly and changed into a T-shirt and pajama shorts. I read for a while, but as soon as it was dark out, I put my book away and curled up under the coves.

Sleep wouldn't come. Instead, I was plagued my bad memories. One in particular.

I was thirteen, and I'd just gotten my Kiss. I sat at our kitchen table doing homework, my mom at the stove stirring Beef Bourguignon. I smelled the cabernet and hoped she'd remember the tiny onions. The kitchen's yellow curtains swayed with a light breeze coming from the open window, and the clock ticked each minute, but I'd learned to ignore that sound. It was part and parcel of our cozy space. I'd have missed it if we replaced the clock with something else.

Mickey barged in the back door and ran to where we were, sliding onto the bench next to me. Our table had two chairs on one side and a bench on the other. We added a chair on each end when we had guests, but that was rare. I couldn't remember the last time we'd had someone over. I remembered playdates from my elementary school years, but when the Kiss had come in, they'd dried up. I had a few acquaintances at school but no one close.

"I'm staaaarrving," my sister said. She craned her neck to see what I was writing. I elbowed her out of the way.

My mother smiled at us. "Eat a banana. Or grapes."

"I want chips."

"You can want until the cows come home. You're eating growing food."

The front door swung open. "Maya? I'm here for the lesson."

My mom stiffened and then, with a conscious effort, relaxed. "Thanks, Trace. Becs, go with Trace now. To the backyard, please."

I followed Trace, unable to keep up with his long stride but excited enough to run.

"What are we learning today?" I called to his back, hurrying to catch up. My white canvas sneakers soaked up the wet from the grass, but I didn't care. I was learning magic!

"Closing a circle."

In the middle of the small lawn was a circle of stones, evenly spaced. A canister of sea salt lay next to it. The surrounding oak trees grew tall around us. I couldn't even climb the smallest of them.

"Pour the salt in between the stones to connect them together in a circle," Trace instructed. "When you cast a circle, try to get it as round as possible. It isn't necessary for it to be perfect, but get as close as you can. The stones are here to provide you with a template for the proper shape."

"Like connect the dots."

"Exactly."

"I thought we didn't need a circle."

"In the beginning, you'll use one to protect yourself and others." Trace rubbed his silver chin stubble with one hand. With the other, he motioned for me to start. "Get on with it now."

Tongue between my teeth, I held the cannister in both hands and poured the salt in a thin line all the way around, going slowly and concentrating hard. Trace watched with his serious green eyes.

"Make it thicker, Rebecca."

"What if I run out?"

"Don't."

"But what if I do?"

Trace ran his fingers through his salt-and-pepper hair, which stuck up in a cowlick over his forehead.

"Get another cannister of salt. You can't afford a weak spot." His cheekbones stood out more than usual, and I wondered if I should ask him to stay for dinner.

No, Mom wouldn't like that.

We practiced pouring a perfect circle three more times. Once I had a good one, he instructed me on what to do next.

"Now, touch the salt and imagine it glowing bright white all the way around."

I touched the ring with my finger and did as he said. A click reverberated in my head.

"What was that?" I asked, jumping back.

Trace smiled and held out his hand for a fist bump. "That was you closing your first circle. Good job."

I weaved on my feet, and he caught me. "Come on, sweetheart, let's get you inside. You need food and a good night's sleep."

Walking with him, proud as I'd ever been, I cast my eyes backward to look at my circle. The complete one gleamed pure white. One of the imperfect ones glowed a sickly yellow-green, and mushrooms had sprouted up along the edge.

I tugged his sleeve. "Trace, what are those doing there?" I pointed.

He whirled around and rushed over. "What *are* these doing here?" He stomped on the mushrooms with his feet, grinding them into the dirt.

"Becs, get the hose."

I dragged it out from the side of the house and gave it to him. He used it to wash the salt and mushroom bits away.

"Don't come back, you evil buggers," he muttered, shaking a finger at the ground. "She's not yours. Stay away."

"Who are you talking to?" I asked.

Trace let out a small laugh, but he didn't sound amused. "Those are deadly mushrooms called Death Caps. If you see them again, do what I did. Squash them and drown 'em with water. They hate getting their feet wet."

I'd gone to bed that evening in my little shared bedroom, Mickey already fast asleep when I put my head on the pillow. I'd dreamed of the Death Caps that night. One grew larger than the rest, becoming a specter so big, I couldn't see its head or ankles. It loomed over me, and I shouted at it to go away. I pushed at it as hard as I could.

"Go bother someone else!" I yelled, thrashing in my sleep. "I'm not yours! Trace said so."

The next morning, we learned that our neighbor had had to call an ambulance for her elderly father during the night, who'd fallen ill. He'd been living with them for the past year.

Their little boy got sick too, but thankfully, he recovered. The parents tearfully recounted how the grandfather had whispered, "Take me instead." They prayed, family and friends coming over to be with them for *shiva*, the Jewish mourning period. They asked that his memory be a blessing and thanked God that their five-year-old had escaped unscathed. We brought a sandwich platter, and I wandered the house glad for the covered mirrors, afraid to face myself. Standing on their deck, I saw the mushrooms growing in three concentric circles in their backyard. I rushed down the steps, pulled out their hose and doused them, but I heard their mocking laughter. I stomped them with all my might, ruining my first pair of heeled sandals.

I attended the memorial service, wearing a sweater in June. My heart was frozen, and my brain fixed on one cruel truth—a truth I still couldn't deny.

It had been all my fault. I'd sent the Death Caps to them.

I pushed the memory aside and fell asleep, but their laughter still rang in my ears.

Chapter 17

I woke mid-morning, trapped in rolls of bedsheets and blankets. I thrashed my way out of the mess, made a pathetic attempt to straighten the covers, and stumbled to the kitchen. Food, I thought. Coffee.

I set up the coffeemaker and took a shower while it percolated. Once I was suitably lathered, rinsed, and dried, I dressed in bar clothes, black pants, a black T-shirt, and non-skid shoes. I scarfed down a bowl of unsatisfying cinnamon-something squares and a glass of orange juice. Bunching my hair in a loose bun, I left the apartment, coffee thermos in hand, and sneaked downstairs.

"Good morning," Kenneth said as soon as he saw me peeking around the corner. His shirt said, "Why Soy Serious?"

"Good morning. Is your mom around?"

"No," he said, wiping his hands on his apron. "My parents are at the bank. You hungry?"

"I had cereal, but something smells good." I sniffed to get the full effect.

Kenneth reached over his head to get a bamboo steaming basket. "Baozi?" he asked, waving the basket at me. "I've got mushroom, bean curd, and bok choy for you."

"Really?" I clapped my hands together in glee. The stuffed wheat buns were my favorite, but I'd never asked for them because they were a circus to make. Usually containing ground pork and vegetables, sometimes the Longs made vegan ones that were seasoned with soy sauce, sesame oil, sugar, and white ground pepper. Once you had one, you'd never forget it.

"I had a feeling you'd be down today," Kenneth said, as I took a seat at one of the small plastic tables. I swigged the rest of my coffee and bounced my knee in anticipation.

"Really? I'm afraid of your mother, but I need to talk to her to clear the air."

"The guys said you needed a lot of sleep. Something happen you need to talk about? Anything I can do to help?"

"You are helping by making the baozi. That's the best thing anyone could do for me right now."

Something caught Kenneth's eye. "Hey!" he yelled. "Watch the wok."
He flapped a dish towel, as if shooing a fly.

My little friends climbed on top of the counter, slid down a long
strand of Golden Pothos, a plant the Longs had placed on the counter's
edge to liven up the place, and bounced their way over to me. I picked
them up and placed them on the table.

"You're going to fry your tushies off," I said to them, wagging a
finger.

"How are you feeling?" Rin asked

"Better, thanks."

Jimmy eyed me, his face serious. "Truly? You're not fibbing?"

Kenneth placed the steamer of buns in front of me.

"I'm telling the truth, especially now." I caught Kenneth's gaze and
smiled. "Thanks, Kenneth."

"You're welcome," he answered with a smile of his own. "My
pleasure."

Trick rubbed his tummy. "Are those what I think they are?"

"They are," Kenneth said, his voice stern, but his eyes twinkled. "And
they're for Becs."

Tricks crossed his arms and jutted out his chin. "It's rude to not share
when you have plenty."

"I'll share. Kenneth, may I have a plate?"

Kenneth good-naturedly grumbled about ungrateful wee fae but did
as I asked. I extracted one steaming bun and gave it to the guys, who stared
at it with reverence.

We dove in, and despite my worries, I blissed out on the yummy
deliciousness. Kenneth joined us, and we chatted and slurped down our
food with sugary hot oolong tea. My anxiety faded with a full stomach and
good company.

When my phone rang, I answered it with a chirpy, "Hey, Zara!
Haven't heard from you in a while. How are you?"

"Oded's in the hospital again. Infection in his arm." Zara's flat voice
reflected her sadness. She'd given up knowing what to do and was losing
hope that he'd ever be well.

"This is terrible. I'm so sorry." My good mood evaporated, and my
voice mirrored hers. Oded deserved so much better than this. He'd done
nothing wrong.

"More bills. More pain. He's tiring, Becs. I've got to figure out a way
to help him."

"Do what you're doing. Keep the studio running. That's all he wants."

"Yeah, but I'm calling because I was hoping you'd know a good lawyer. I need someone to sue the pants off the Andino Trading Company and make them pay all his medical costs."

Did I know a law firm?

No, but I knew *of* a law firm.

"I'll get back to you. I have an idea."

"Thanks, Becs."

"We're going to fix this, Zara."

"I wish I could believe you, Becs. We'll need a miracle."

No, I thought, *we'll need a mobster*. Perrick hadn't come through on his own, but I could go to his boss. Zara and I disconnected, and I placed my phone in my pocket. I stood, the wee ones and Kenneth looking at me expectantly.

"Thanks for the food and laughs, guys. I've got to place a call."

"What's wrong?" asked Kenneth.

"It's Oded. He's not doing well. It's time I did something."

Upstairs, in privacy, I called Gregory Adamos at his office.

I got Perrick.

"Becs, Gregory is unavailable at the moment," he said.

"Tell him to make the time."

"No can do, and you know it."

"Perrick," I said, holding on to my temper. "Do you recall when you said you'd help Oded in any way possible."

"Yeeessss. . . ."

"This is helping in any way possible. Oded is back in the hospital with an infection, and I need to talk to Gregory."

Perrick's silence spoke volumes. He knew he was the reason for Oded's suffering. At last, he said, "I've got something to give Oded to help, but I'll get Gregory. I'll see you at the bar later?"

"I have a shift."

"I'll stop by."

The green troll put me on hold. Barbra Streisand's "The Way We Were" played in my ear. Neil Diamond's "Play Me" picked up where it left off. "Mandy," by Barry Manilow, followed. I was on Billy Joel's "Piano Man" and tearing my hair out before Gregory picked up.

"Ms. Greenblatt."

"Took you long enough, and your playlist needs an update."

"I'll tell my people." His voice was as dry as sandpaper. "Why are you calling?"

"Have you found Trace?"

An exhale. "I have not."

"How hard have you been looking for him?"

"Believe it or not, Rebecca, I'm a man of my word. I've had my best team on it, but there's no sign of him. It's difficult for someone to become invisible in this day and age. He's either gone completely off the grid and is living in the hills somewhere or he's dead. I'm betting on dead."

I hated to think my trainer had died. I hated it more than I expected. A weight settled in my tummy, and my breath hitched. I mean, I'd known it was a strong possibility, but I'd held onto a thread of hope.

I gripped my phone tighter. "Fine. Stop looking. I have another way you can pay me back."

"Ah, ah, ah. I said I'd look for him, which I have. I didn't promise I'd find him. I've fulfilled my end of our deal."

"No, you haven't, you monkey-brained thug, but have no fear. I know of a way you can, and you might even like it."

"Monkeys are quite intelligent. Compliments will get you nowhere. I'm hanging up."

"No, wait. Seriously, you'll enjoy this."

Gregory spoke through clenched teeth. It made me smile to hear him so aggravated. "You have two minutes."

"I need one. You're on the board of Hart & Wells Litigation, correct?"

"I am. As you know from the letter Walter Hart sent to you regarding the car accident you were involved in."

I scoffed. "Oh, yes. I got that letter. I wrote them back telling them that I'd send my own medical experts to check up on the client, and miraculously, he recovered."

"I'm so pleased to hear it. He suffered significant injuries."

"That man didn't suffer for a moment, and you know it. That was a strong-arm tactic, and it didn't work."

"Your tickets would say otherwise."

"I went to court and fought them and paid the minimum plus court costs. No points. And, by the way, the judge didn't buy the client's allegations at all. Maybe because someone spied the guy playing racquetball not twenty-four hours prior. Not to mention the responding police officer recalled the man stepping out from his car to scream in her face."

Gregory cleared his throat. "Your point?"

"Don't try to bullshit me. I've got a serious proposal here. How would you like to go after the Andino Trading Company, legally, for not paying Oded Levi's medical bills from the flower shop fire?"

"They're not paying?"

"His girlfriend says they've paid some but not all."

"This has merit."

I had him. "Think of it. It's all above board, on the right side of the law and public opinion. It would be a public relations win, and you'd get to harass your rivals."

"This will call us even?"

"Even Steven."

"I'll see what I can do." Gregory hung up.

I called back. Perrick answered again. "He won't speak to you a second time."

"He disconnected our call without saying 'hugs and kisses.'"

"You're really pushing it."

"Gregory likes to be pushed. It's foreplay to him. Put him back on the phone."

"He's going to deprive me of home soil if I keep bothering him."

I sighed. "Perrick, as soon as your son graduates, get the hell out of there. What's the worst that can happen?"

"My son might make the pros. He's a damn good power forward. Tall and athletic. Physical, ya know? Great midrange jump shot. Able to hit a three-pointer consistently."

"So? You're Gregory's prisoner until your son hangs up his shingle or gets hurt?"

"He can make him get hurt, that's the problem."

I closed my eyes and nodded, although Perrick couldn't see me. "Gregory's a bulbous snot rag of a person. You're right. He'll out your son as half-troll if you don't do what he says, and if people don't believe it, he'll allege drug use or make sure he gets hurt so he loses his scholarship and future."

Perrick's voice grew suspiciously formal. "Ms. Greenblatt, Mr. Adamos exited his office. What message do you wish me to convey to him?"

"Tell him to call me as soon as he has a response from Hart & Wells."

"I'll pass the message on. Thank you for calling."

"I'll see you tonight, Perrick."

"Yes. Of course."

Perrick was caught between a crime boss and a hard place. He didn't want to cross Gregory, since his son might pay the price. Luckily, I had no such reservations.

If Gregory didn't do as I asked, I'd find a way to force him.

Belatedly, I realized I hadn't checked on Nick. I wondered how he was doing after the whole Mimi summoning fiasco. I promised myself to ask Perrick that evening.

I mentally made a list. Talk with Perrick. Find Trace. Reassure Mickey. Repay Laurel. Evade Oberon. Block Valefar.

And most of all, stop thinking about Asher.

It was a to-do list from Hell.

Chapter 18

The bar buzzed with a hive of activity. Literally.

"What are these?" I asked Joey, barely refraining from swatting the tiny insects whizzing by my head. "We have enough bugs this time of year. Everywhere I go, annoying little insects." I grabbed a clean apron but didn't put it on, distracted by the bugs.

"They're Humbees," Joey replied. "Small pixies, basically cousins to Laurel and her posse. The whole hive is in here today."

"I thought a group of pixies was called a chorus."

"Those are the big ones." She caught my arm as I waved one away from my face. "Don't kill them."

"They should stop doing fly-bys next to my ear, then."

"Tell them."

I shook my apron at her. "How am I supposed to do that?"

Joey put two fingers in her mouth and blew a shrieking whistle. Everyone in the bar turned toward her, even the Humbees, who flickered in mid-air like centimeter-long hummingbirds.

"Queen Clarissa, could you kindly ask your hive to stop dive-bombing our heads and hands? Have some respect, please."

One of the itty-bitty pixies landed on my shoulder. I held up my palm, and she walked down my arm to my hand. I squinted to see her.

"My apologies," she said with a tiny curtsy.

"Queen Clarissa, I presume?" The gold crown balancing precariously on her head was the giveaway.

"Yes. Please forgive us. We are excited to be back in the Slow World."

"What brings you to this side of the portal?" I asked.

"Pinky!"

"What does Pinky have to do with it?"

Queen Clarissa vibrated with joy. "Flowers. Lots and lots of flowers! He asked if we could come to help the park where he tends the apple trees. He said the flowers were dying, and they were! We came to give a helping wing."

I eyed her. "What's in it for you?"

"Pollen," she said, swooning.

"I don't understand."

"The pollen is divine." She sniffed and lay down in my hand, stretching sensuously.

"It's like cocaine to them," Joey whispered. "They roll in it, sniff it, even eat it. It's bad for them, but occasionally they get permission to come here and indulge."

"Who gives them permission?"

Clarissa shimmied in her tiny green gown. "Ober—"

I clapped my hand over her, keeping it cupped so I wouldn't squash her. I hinged my hand open like a clam shell and peeked inside. "I get it. The fae king. Don't say his name, please. He has a bad habit of showing up." I lifted my hand all the way and eyed her. "Understand?"

"No worries. Mum's the word. We've been here a couple of weeks and will do whatever we need to do to stay." She eyed me up and down, and for some reason I didn't like it. She fluttered her eyelashes at me. "If we're clever, we may be able to bring some of the good stuff home with us."

I tossed her in the air. "Well, have fun." She flew off.

"Joey, do they pay?"

She rolled her eyes. "They wanted to pay in pollen! I refused, naturally, and she managed to convince a dwarf to advance her some local currency."

"You mean dollars."

"I mean dollars. She'll have to repay him when they get back to the hive in Faerie."

"How will she do that?"

"Probably sexual favors." Joey grabbed a menu, then took it over to a table, while I pondered how the size difference worked. I dipped glassware in a cleaning solution, waiting for her to return.

"Okay, I have to ask. I tried not to, but I can't stand it. How does an itty-bitty pixie provide sexual favors to a full-grown male dwarf?"

Joey chortled. "Not one pixie. The whole lot of them. That's why a group of these little ladies is a called a 'harem.' A harem of Humbees."

"Oh, dear God."

"You wanted to know," she said with a grin. "Now, go take the mermaids' order before they start singing. I don't want a riot."

"On it."

The mermaids ordered margaritas on the rocks with extra-salty rims. I squeezed limes like my life depended on it and got out a whole box of kosher salt. They kept themselves busy comparing shell bras and braiding one another's hair.

The night flew by, a mixture of drink making, draft pouring, and payment processing. Plus, the flirting and off-color jokes that were prerequisites to bartending. But it wasn't getting me the advice I needed, and the crowd wasn't slowing down. I kept looking for an opportunity to speak to Joey, but none opened up. Finally, almost at closing, we got a break in the action.

"Joey?"

"Yeah?" Joey wiped her brow with a towel.

"Have you ever heard of anyone summoning a human?"

She stopped wiping down a four-top to answer me. "No. I mean, why would you? Summoners, as far as I know, although admittedly my knowledge is scant at best, are all humans. Humans don't summon other humans. That's what cell phones are for."

She cleaned off the four barstools around the table. "Why are you asking?"

I dumped coffee grounds in the trash and tried to look nonchalant. "Something our three wee friends said. They suggested summoning Trace, if I couldn't locate him by other means. And by other means, I mean Gregory Adamos, who thinks he's dead."

"If Gregory can't find him, then he is dead."

Joey came out from behind the bar, holding a tube of hand lotion. I held out my hand and she squeezed some into my palm and then squirted some into her own. Constant dishwashing dried our skin.

"It's dangerous." She rubbed her hands together, thinking. "Really dangerous."

"Why?"

"It's unnatural. Summoners call to 'Powers,' powers that live in different planes. Humans don't fit in either category. No offense meant to humans, but they aren't demons or fae, or gods. They exist here on Earth, in the mid-realm, the crossroads to the other dimensions. A good internet connection and email seems to work just fine for people."

"Wait," I said, turning to face her. "Say that again. Earth is the crossroads?"

"That's how it was explained to me. Earth exists at the apex of all dimensions. You can't go to one without traveling through Earth. This keeps Hell out of Heaven, for example, but also Hades out of Faerie. It makes sure Zeus doesn't meet Lucifer, as another way of thinking about it."

"But Valefar said different versions of the underworld are connected by doors."

Joey pursed her lips. "That's something I didn't know. It is entirely possible that Lucifer and Hades are two sides of the same coin and thus can communicate if they wanted to. But Lucifer can't march onto Olympus to see Zeus, nor can he slip into Faerie to see the fae king either."

I tapped my finger on the bar counter. "If Hades wanted to talk with Lucifer, he could probably do that on his own. But if Hades wanted to talk to the fae king, or an angel in Heaven, or visit the Hindu Svarga Loka, he needs an intermediary."

Joey pressed a finger to her lip. "I never thought of it that way, but theoretically, yes."

"Do you think Pinky might know more?"

Joey heaved the last tray of dirty dishes onto her shoulder and shot the last few stragglers a pointed look. "He may. He's had formal education in magic theory while I've learned on the job."

"Have you seen him lately?"

"No. He hasn't come in here. I think the last time sort of freaked him out. Everyone was fawning all over him, including an actual faun, I might add."

"I missed a faun?"

"They come and go like the wind. They're hard to catch."

"Damn."

For the next forty-five minutes, I squeezed all the lemons for the next day and then transitioned to oranges and limes. Joey cleaned the taps and wiped the wine bottles.

"Becs?" she asked when we were getting close to closing for the night.

"Yeah?"

"What was your dad's name?"

I held up a finger to tell her to wait a moment, went to the back to retrieve a broom, and returned. "Why?" I asked as I began the nightly floor sweep.

"Just tell me."

"Gideon. My mom's name was Maya. Why do you want to know?"

Joey got to work on the rails as I continued to sweep. "I was just thinking. You want to talk to Trace so you can learn about summoning, but it occurred to me that you've never mentioned finding your dad. Why not summon Gideon?"

"I don't care about him. He left when I was very young and never came back. If he doesn't want me, I don't want him."

Joey continued cleaning the rails. "But Trace left, too."

"Sure, and I don't want to talk to him either, but he has the knowledge I need."

"I don't buy the whole 'I don't want to talk to them' thing."

I swept the detritus from the floor into two big piles. "Well, it's true. I don't want to *talk*. I want to yell at them. Scream at them. Tell them how much they hurt me."

Joey stopped her sanitizing for a moment to study me. "Don't you want to know why they left?"

"No."

"Yes, you do, but you're afraid of the answer."

"What if I am?" I raised my voice. "What if the answer is that I was unlovable? A total fuck-up? Unteachable, unwanted? How would you feel in my shoes? Two men that you depended on left without any explanation."

She took a shuddering breath. "My father left me here in the Slow World with my mother. I'm an embarrassment to him."

I stopped my clean up. "I'm so sorry, Joey. That must have been very hard." I started to sweep the rubbish into a dustpan. "I don't mean to be rude, but many fae have children here. There are tons of half-breeds. Why was your birth such a problem?"

She shrugged. "Gnomes don't usually have half-human children. I've been to Faerie only once."

"What happened when you went?"

"My father's family wanted nothing to do with me. He gave me enough money to start this tavern, and that was the last time I saw him."

"Wow. Again, I'm so sorry."

"It was hard on my mum. She sent me to a special high school for fae-mixed kids. It was the only place I could feel safe. Safe-ish, at least. School wasn't easy though. I got teased a lot about being a lowly half-gnome, not a cool part-elf or a strong half-troll. 'Hairy, short, and round' was the way one part-pixie expressed it."

"That sounds like a pixie. Mean through and through." I was getting mad for my friend.

She shrugged. "My mom loved me, but even with the teasing, it was better to be at school. I think she was ashamed of me, too. I didn't fit in with the other kids on the cul-de-sac."

Joey cleared her throat. "My point is, you're not the only one who's been discarded, but I'll bet there is more to it than you're 'unlovable,' because that doesn't make any sense. Your mom loved you. Pinky loves you, and I. . . ." She scowled. "I like you. In my own way. Doesn't mean much so don't get too excited."

I put down my knife before I slipped and cut a finger out of shock. Joey had turned her back to me so I couldn't see her eyes.

"It means everything. I care for you too."

She whirled around, holding up a finger. "I said 'like,' not 'care for.' Don't read too much into this."

I held up both my hands. "Got it."

"As for 'unteachable,' that's clearly incorrect. I've turned you into a fairly okay bartender."

I kept my face straight with concentrated effort. "I'm glad I'm fairly, sorta, basically, okay."

"Humpf." She wiped her brow on her sleeve. "At least we got that straightened out."

I watched her walk away, a tiny glimmer of something new in my heart.

Chapter 19

I stepped out into the night air with my knapsack thrown over one shoulder and leather jacket draped over my forearm, and walked toward my car in the side lot. The unseasonably muggy weather made me wonder where the earlier chill had come from, and I regretted not bringing flip-flops. I'd prefer driving home with cool feet. My black non-skid bar boots were heavy.

The street lamps created dark silhouettes, sharp demarcations of chiaroscuro where black shadow hit yellow glow, like a Rembrandt painting. Nobody walked the street except a cat that crossed my path and ran toward the alley behind the diner. Moths and larger insects darted about the lightbulbs, every so often hitting the bulbs with an audible *ping*, and I had to wonder if it hurt to do that. Did they get injured? Die? Was it like a bird flying into a glass door? Or did they keep doing it over and over again, like a chicken pecking at the same spot on the ground?

Idle thoughts for an indolent evening. I yawned and dug in my pocket for my key fob.

A millisecond before I reached my car, a thick arm cut me off, and the matching hand slammed, flat-palmed, onto my car door. I gasped but had enough presence of mind to turn and run. I made it back to the street before I heard the man's voice.

"Becs!"

I turned, hyperventilating because of the adrenaline rush. "Dammit, Perrick! When you said you were coming tonight, I thought you meant into the bar during business hours, not afterwards, accosting me in the dark like a mugger!"

The light-green troll wore a trench coat and a brimmed hat, which made him look like a ninja turtle. My brain wanted to say, "kowabunga, dude," but my stuttering heart wasn't ready for humor and told my head to shut the fuck up.

"Move," I ordered.

Perrick shifted out of my way. I unlocked my car and threw my belongings into the back. Then I spun around, rested my back against the car door, and crossed my arms.

"Why are you here?"

Perrick dipped his left hand into the trench coat's side pocket, and although I thought I could trust him, my baser instincts noted that he was right-handed and if he'd had a gun, he'd have used his other hand. Instead of a weapon, he extracted a squeeze bottle, like a mayo or mustard bottle you'd see at the ballpark, cylindrical with a tiny nozzle on the tip. An ivory viscous fluid swirled inside the clear plastic. He handed it to me, and I took it.

"What's this?"

"My mother made it. It should help Oded's skin heal faster. She used dried herbs from Faerie so if he runs out and needs more, it might take a while. Nothing in it grows here."

An ugly, evil thought crept into my brain. "Do you promise this won't hurt him? This isn't going to make anything worse, will it?"

"Of course not."

"How'd your mom get it to you?"

He looked off into the distance, frowning. "My brother drove it out here, along with a bag of home soil. He did me a solid, and now he won't let me forget it. 'You owe me, bruh,' and all that."

Despite myself, I laughed out loud. "Siblings."

He pointed toward the bottle. "You ask them for one small thing— a little understanding and a way to help someone—and they lord it over you for the rest of your life."

I laughed again, but I couldn't keep the sorrow out of it. "Perrick, my man, you're singing my song."

He gave me an equally sad smile. "Let me know how it works. I hope it helps Oded. I have to get back now before Gregory notices I'm missing."

The hulking troll drifted off into the night. Had I had a bonding moment with Perrick? I thought I had. I shook my head in disgust as I got in and started my car.

My standards kept plummeting. Honestly, how much further could they descend?

I drove home taking it easy. Cruising at the speed limit but without traffic, I made it home in less than twenty minutes. I pulled into my spot, gathered my belongings, and climbed the fire escape to my apartment.

A white envelope taped to my back door made me tense. I opened it.

Rebecca:

We cannot evict you under the law, and now that we've had some time to think about it, we've realized that legal action is not warranted. However, we are sorry, but it is unsafe for you to be here in this building. We are not forcing you out, but we are asking you to move. We must protect our family and our other tenants. You have a blight curse clinging to you, and you no longer have a guardian angel to protect you. Disease will come, and we cannot take the chance that it will spread. Evil has a way of doing so.

Your friends, nevertheless,
The Longs

Well, *now* I knew how low I could sink.

Chapter 20

Sleep came slow, and morning came fast.

The weight of Laurel's debt stung all night, keeping me up, the pressure intensifying at an alarming rate. She hadn't asked for anything to even things out, and I had nothing to offer her. I took a deep breath, stretched, and pushed it aside. A shower, coffee, and some cereal later, I was suitably fortified to face what I had to do. I wasn't happy about it but more or less resigned.

I dragged out my one dusty suitcase and stuffed it with clothes—just the necessities. Toiletries got dumped in an old gym bag as well as a pair of running shoes. I grabbed a pillow, sheets, and two blankets and shoved all of it in my car. There was enough room for a box containing fruit, chips, granola bars, and cheese crackers, plus a large thermos of water. My workout bag was already behind my seat. I rolled up two towels and a washcloth and wiggled them in between all the other stuff, using whatever cracks and crevices I could find. When my car couldn't handle anything else, I went back upstairs.

I found a pen and paper and wrote the Longs a note saying I'd stay away for now, but I intended to be back so I requested that they not sell my stuff. I left a month's rent in the envelope to buy some time and asked that Kenneth feed the birds. I put all the bird seed outside under a tarp. After taping the note to my front door, I retrieved the bow and arrows and left via the fire escape, closing it behind me without looking back.

I refused to cry.

I understood the Longs' position but the acid bubbling in my stomach told me I resented, more than accepted it, at this point.

Officially homeless, I drove to check in on Oded.

My Krav Maga teacher sat slumped in a chair in his office. I dropped my bag and rushed to his side.

"Oded, what's wrong?"

"I'm tired. I'm so exhausted all the time because I can't breathe right. My lungs haven't fully recovered. I'm not sure they ever will."

"They will." They had to. "Healing zaps your strength. Don't push yourself. Give yourself time."

He popped to his feet, pushing me aside. "I don't want to take any more time, Rivka! I want to be better now. Now. These people did this to me, and I can't use my arm properly, can't take a deep breath, and my skin itches."

He coughed a deep asthmatic cough. It was terrible. He finished, waited a second to catch his breath, and carried on with his rant. A deserved rant, most definitely. I would listen as long as he needed me to.

He lifted his elbow so I could see the underside of his forearm. "Do you know how maddening it is to have an unrelenting itch? Take your worst mosquito bite and multiply it by a thousand. Then imagine it never stops. Not to mention the pain. The skin hurts with pressure, a breeze, even water."

I reached into my bag and withdrew the squeeze bottle containing Perrick's mom's lotion. I held it out.

"A friend made this for you at my request. It's a special concoction that she swears will accelerate the healing."

He didn't take it.

I shook it at him. "I believe this will help you. Please promise me you'll try it."

"What's in it?"

"Honestly, I don't know. The woman who made it is sort of a hedge witch. I know you don't believe in that kind of stuff, but what do you have to lose?"

"It could make it worse."

"Let's try it on a small patch."

Oded hesitated but eventually gave in with an exasperated exhale. "Fine. Here, try a little on my forearm. It's the worst."

I pressed my lips together as he put on latex gloves and then removed the loose-fitting bandage on the lower part of his forearm, near the wrist. Cherry red with white spots, the burn oozed fluid and looked worse than ever, although I knew, intellectually, that it was much better than it had been. I constrained my instinctive flinch, turned the bottle upside down, and squeezed it on my fingertip. To my surprise, it wasn't a cream at all but a clear gel.

Without a word, Oded pulled a burn dressing from his drawer. I donned my own pair of gloves and opened the clean dressing. He squeezed Perrick's mother's gel on it, and then I placed the new dressing on it for him. He gritted his teeth through the whole process.

We sat in silence for a moment while he sipped a bubbly water and caught his breath. I couldn't imagine the pain of having to do that every day. He suddenly looked up and caught my eye.

"It's cool," he said. "It feels nice, like it's dissipating heat."

"That sounds like a good thing."

"It is." He rotated his wrist in a circle. "It's alleviating the itch, too."

I smiled and said, with a dramatic flourish, "Then my work is done here."

He smiled back, the first smile I'd seen on his face since the fire. "Go on, get out. I'll use this and let you know how it works."

I held my fingers up to my ears like a telephone. "Call me. Or text."

"Are you working out or chatting with an injured old man? Find someone to spar with you already."

"I don't see any old men here," I said. I blew him a kiss and went to the main part of the studio to work up a good sweat. I'd pretend the punching bag was Gregory's face. Or Valefar's. Even Mrs. Long's.

No, I wasn't angry. Not me.

I felt put upon, sulky, and furious, none of which accomplished anything except impoverishing my soul, but I recognized my emotions for what they were. Reactions to feeling overwhelmed and helpless. Point for me for that flash of emotional insight.

Keeping my toiletries and towels at the studio would help, so I rented a locker. At least I'd have access to a shower when the gym was open. Stupid warlock. He was still ruining my life from beyond the grave.

What an asshole.

I'd had a lot of time to consider my next move, and after a while, the urge to punch someone transferred from Mrs. Long to Derrick, the pinhead dead warlock who still haunted me. Thinking about him gave me an idea though.

Not a *good* idea, but *an* idea. I took my second shower of the day, redressed, and went looking for the most mysterious woman I'd ever met.

The best way to find someone who didn't want to be found was to not look for them—to do anything else. Walk aimlessly. Talk to random people. Pet a dog. Buy a bouquet of flowers. When you weren't looking, there they'd be.

If you wanted to find someone who *sorta kinda maybe* wanted to be found, you'd need a different tactic. If you wanted to locate an individual who'd revealed themselves to you twice but only wanted to interact with you on their terms, you had to shake things up a bit.

I favored brute force.

I made my way down the street, passed Joey's, and stopped a few feet from the diner. The medium's storefront? Office? Whatever it was, it hid between the sushi place and the pottery studio, a spot of hazy air begging to be ignored, surrounded by—of all things—colorful rose bushes. I assumed there was some witchcraft associated with it, despite Madame Francesca's protestations that she wasn't a witch herself. A "no-see-me" spell, perhaps? That could be housed in an. . . .

Amulet.

Bingo.

If you concentrated on the fuzzy space where the shop was supposed to be, you'd see something dangling in mid-air. Chances were good no one ever noticed this because the magic made people look away. But, as hard as the magic worked to hide the door, the amulet was visible. An amber oval about an inch in length, it floated there, small and unassuming. But if you didn't know to look for it, you'd miss it. I jumped and yanked it down.

A furious screech emanated from inside, and I knew I'd guessed right. Ignoring the strident curses that followed the screech, I opened the suddenly visible entrance and walked in, as if I owned the place.

This woman owed me answers.

Madame Francesca shook her fist at me. "You could have knocked."

"You made that difficult by hiding the door."

"You knew where to look. Now I must replace the entire amulet. Once removed, the magic dissipates fast." She reached over and snatched it from me. "Well, close the door. We've got mosquitoes." She reached behind me, pulled it shut, and secured the latch.

The narrow shop, decorated in soothing browns and greens, extended far back, maybe fifty feet or more. It ended in a closed door. Soft, comfy chairs arranged in a simple seating pattern sat to my immediate left with a small round table in the middle. A vase of stunning apricot-colored roses rested on the table. A vintage bronze cash register took up half the counter on my right with a transparent display case underneath containing various knickknacks with price tags. The tags lay face down so I couldn't see how much each item cost.

Endless rows of books occupied countertops and the space on top of the cabinets. A tiny red imp statue grinned at me from a high alcove, and something that looked like an Easter Island Moai stared out into space. It looked like it was ignoring the imp.

An amulet like the one I'd snatched from the doorway, but in green, nestled in a black jewelry box. A beaded bracelet in earth tones designed to fit a woman's arm sat on white cotton. The white beads looked suspiciously like bone. A statue of a pregnant woman rested in the corner opposite a phallic carving the same size. A ceremonial knife, a malachite ring, a chunk of rose quartz, and several crystal balls of various sizes filled out the rest of the case.

Except for the middle shelf, which featured an honest-to-God, freakin' tiara. An open circlet of gold filigree with a garnet in the center, it screamed power to me, but I couldn't tell why. It made me wonder why such a piece was in a display case and not in a vault.

I pointed to it. "What is this?"

"A trinket," Madame Francesca replied, motioning me toward the back area to three chairs surrounding a small, circular table. Guess she didn't want to say. To me, it looked like it was something either you hid because of its value or you kept in easy reach for personal reasons. She clearly wasn't going to tell me.

She inclined her head. "Now that you're here, ask me what you've come to ask."

I glanced at the chairs, wooden ones with arms and backs and dark-green cushions on the seats. They looked terribly uncomfortable. I placed my hand on the back of one but didn't sit.

"How did the Warlock contact you?" I asked.

"That's not what you want to know." She sat in her chair, a duplicate of the one I stood behind. She fluffed her skirt, a dark sienna this time, and straightened the sleeves of the matching peasant blouse she wore. The scooped neckline set off a thin silver chain, completely unadorned. She glanced at the case, and once again, I wondered if she wore the tiara. Maybe she liked to play dress-up, with bling and the whole goth thing was an act.

"Tell me," I insisted.

She sighed. "At least sit. Be courteous."

I took my seat but didn't relax, keeping my knapsack on my back.

She sighed again, then pursed her lips. "As I said, I'm a medium, which means I commune with the dead. I don't always have a choice about who I speak with or for what reason. A strong enough spirit can reach out to me. The Warlock did so, gave me a warning for you, and I delivered it." She wiped her hands together. "Job done."

I slapped at an insect on my neck.

She stood and walked to a mantle behind her, then lit some incense.

"It's the roses. This will help." The scent of citronella and peppermint filled the air.

"You look different than the last time I saw you," I said, trying to place what was off about her. I snapped my fingers. "You look younger." Cringing, I rushed to add, "Not to say you appeared old before, but your skin and hair look great. What's your secret?"

She laughed, a self-deprecating giggle more suited to a teenager than a grown woman and dismissed my observation with a flick of her hand. "Good lighting. The fluorescents in the restaurant are murder on the complexion. That, and a little hair dye." She winked at me. I shuddered. Girl talk didn't suit her.

"I understand having powers you can't ignore or control. I'm like that with summoning. The Kiss happened to me. I didn't seek it."

For a moment, she gazed out the window at the roses, thoughtful. "It's tiring when you don't have a choice."

Resuming her seat, she pressed her hands together. "Now. Ask your real question."

It was there, pressing against my skull but still I held back, reluctant to show this strange woman any weakness. But somehow, I also felt a kinship. She, too, had been born with a power she didn't ask for. Her blue eyes waited patiently, but she tapped her foot in exasperation.

She slanted her angular chin at me. "Ms. Greenblatt, I don't have all day."

Taking a deep breath, I finally blurted it out. "Can you reach my trainer, Trace?"

"Your trainer?"

"The teacher who taught me about summoning. I haven't seen him since I was fifteen, and I'm assuming he's dead."

"Why do you assume he is in the life beyond?" She pressed her hands together in front of her chest and bowed her head.

I told her about Gregory's failed efforts.

She narrowed her eyes and nodded, finally allowing her lids to droop to her cheeks. She hummed a low tune and pressed her palms to the table.

She opened her eyes and peered at me like a hawk eyeing a fish. "I will do this for you, but for a small price. Do you have any information on Trace other than this one name?"

"I have a photo."

"Well, why didn't you say so in the first place? Let me see."

I'd taken a photo of the framed picture, so I swiped in my photos app until I found it. "What's this going to cost me?"

"A personal piece of information."

"Like what?" She wanted a deep, dark, secret?

She folded her arms in front of her chest. "I get to ask you a personal question."

"I don't promise to answer it."

"Then I don't promise to try to reach your trainer."

I considered it. "What do you want to know?"

"Besides your sister and your niece, who do you love most in the world?"

I thought about it. Would I tell her this? Would it matter? Anyone who knew me could guess the answer.

"If I tell you this, you'll reach Trace?"

"I'll try to reach Trace. If he's not dead, I won't be able to."

"Try. If you do, I'll tell you the answer. If you don't, I see no reason to pay."

She studied me across the table. "Agreed. Place your hands in mine."

I lay my palms on hers. They were dry, like stale bread. I didn't recoil, but it was far from pleasant. She closed her eyes and concentrated.

"Trace, trainer of Rebecca, your spirit to my spirit. Your life force to mine. Your voice to my throat. Speak to me and through me."

I waited.

She tapped my phone and indicated I should open it to the picture again. I did and then she held my hands tighter.

"Trace, the image in front of me shows me your face. Where do you rest? Rebecca seeks you."

After a long silence, frustration crept into Francesca's voice. "Trainer of summoners, we seek you as friends."

The medium's head rocked back, her mouth opening so her throat lay wide like a gaping fish. A voice spoke through her, a voice I knew as well as my own.

"Rebecca, Trace is the changeling."

Francesca flopped forward, her brow hitting the table while I jumped to my feet.

"Mom?" I barely got out the word before emotion choked my voice.

Madam Francesca moaned and sat up, holding her hand to her head. I ran to the back, found a tiny kitchen, and poured her a glass of water.

"Here." I handed it to her. "That was my *mother's* voice. Is there anything else?"

Francesca gulped the water, and I studied her hands. She'd aged a decade in a few minutes. She wiped her brow and frowned at me. "That's all. Trace isn't dead or I would have found him. Instead, your mom found me. Now, tell me the answer to my question. I've earned it. Who, apart from your sister and your niece, do you love the most?"

"Where is my mother?"

"I don't know. Fulfill our bargain."

"Pinky," I said, though I hated admitting anything so personal to her. "I love Pinky the most."

She smiled with satisfaction.

"That will be all. See yourself out."

I walked out in a daze, hardly able to see where I was going. My mother? Trace was the changeling? The changeling who wasn't a changeling?

But it was the memory of her voice, that sound, that pitch, the intonation. I knew it in my bones and in my heart. I missed it with the deepest part of my soul. Hearing her voice again was a knife to the gut and a balm for my spirit.

I'd gotten to hear it for less than a second before it had been ripped away from me again, leaving me as bereft and empty as the day she died.

Chapter 21

I wandered to my car and sat in the driver's seat, my head spinning. When had my life gotten so weird? When the Kiss came in? When I summoned Valefar? When I took the job at Joey's? When I stole Asher's Wi-Fi? Every life choice I'd made floated through my brain, and I questioned each one.

People passed my car without a care in the world. Or, maybe they had their own share of worries. But had anybody else visited a medium to find their magic trainer and heard their dead mother's voice come out of someone else's body?

I doubted it.

I mean, really, this couldn't be a common experience.

I rummaged in my bag for a pen and paper, pulled out the small journal, and made notes. When in doubt, I always made a list.

1. *Main concern: someone to finish my training.*
2. *Trace was alive, but no one knew where he was.*
3. *Asher was apparently my guardian angel.*
4. *Asher told me some stupid prophecy about a changeling who wasn't a changeling.*
5. *My dead mother told me that Trace was the changeling.*
6. *What did that mean?!!!!*
7. *Where was my mother? Why did she choose now to talk to me? Could I talk to her again?*
8. *Oberon found me interesting. Valefar found me interesting. My landlords did not.*
9. *I was homeless.*
10. *Oded still needed help.*
11. *Oh, yeah, my dead mother. I heard the voice of my dead mother. This bears repeating. Oh, God. Do I tell Mickey?*

The last one was a kicker. I performed some of the deep cleansing breaths I'd learned from Oded, trying to calm down. Once I'd done that for a good three minutes, I had the answer.

No. Nope. Absolutely not. Fuhgeddaboudit. If I wanted to repair my relationship with Mickey, I could not tell her Mom's voice had come out of a stranger's mouth.

That solved that.

Moving on. My experience with Madame Francesca confirmed that Trace was among the living, but Gregory, even with his extensive network, couldn't find him. And if my list told me anything, it was that my continuing number-one problem was that I needed a teacher. If I knew more about my powers and how they worked, maybe I could avoid half the messes I found myself in. Plus, having a second person around to tell Mickey what the Kiss meant could clear my way with her. And Jonah.

I had to find Trace. If I couldn't go to my trainer, I'd find a way to make my trainer come to me.

Time to prep.

Intention mattered in summoning, so the elements had to reflect my inner thoughts. Unfortunately, anger colored my feelings about Trace— fury that he left. Anger that I couldn't find him and had to resort to summoning. Frustration that his abandonment left me and my loved ones vulnerable. I pictured him in a sunny field somewhere, educating a new summoner, pleased he'd dodged a bullet by escaping me and my meager talents.

My imagination played out the scene in my head.

Opening setting: Sunny field in a far locale. Fiji perhaps.

Trace, sitting in a full lotus, face unlined and carefree, turns to an adolescent, fresh-faced girl with long black hair and says, "Ah, Rabbit. I'm so glad I'm here to train you. At least you have skills."

Rabbit: "Doesn't every summoner have the same skills?"

Trace: (Laughs heartily) "Oh, no. You should have seen this one girl I tried to train. Useless! I left because she was so awful. She couldn't control her dreams and killed the old man next door."

I jolted out of my reverie and shook myself. I couldn't—wouldn't— accept that guilt anymore. The Death Caps had escaped my mental grasp, true, but I'd been a child. It hadn't been my fault.

Well, not totally my fault, but some of it was.

But maybe I could use it.

I ran around gathering a few things and drove to my office to set up.

I cleaned my summoning space again, sweeping and scrubbing until it gleamed. I left the door open so fresh air could blow through, and when I was satisfied that it was as pristine as I could make it, I grabbed my chalk.

Working off a drawing in my *Celtic Fairy Tales* book, I sketched five interlocking circles. The Five Celtic Knot symbol represented balance, something I sorely needed. Some folks interpreted it as the harmony of seasons or the balance of elements—earth, water, air, and fire, and the central ring symbolized those concepts brought together.

That was another interpretation, and the one I was relying on. Those circles represented Heaven, Time, Spirituality, and the Universe, with a central Spirit in the middle. Call that Spirit God or another name, the underlying theme seemed to work here.

Or maybe it didn't? I was playing by the seat of my pants.

I placed Trace's photo in the center of one circle. To represent my childhood, I placed my stuffed lamb in the second, a paper bag of mushrooms from the local organic farm in the third, and a blank summoning contract in the fourth. Hopefully, these elements connected to Trace through reminders of my youth and the magic of summoning, including the Death Caps.

I stood in the center holding my bow and arrows. I debated the weapon but decided to hold onto them in case something unexpected happened.

I pricked my own finger, threw droplets of blood in each cardinal direction, took a deep breath and intoned, "Trace, my former trainer, I summon you."

Nothing.

I tried again. "Trace, my former trainer, who is neither dead nor findable through other means, I summon you to my side to fulfill the contract you made with my mother to train me in the summoning arts."

Crickets.

Rolling my neck to relieve the tension in my muscles, I removed my bracelet and stuffed it in my pocket.

"Trace, I summon you! By my power as a summoner, I call like to like. Thrice said, thrice done."

A wave of nausea hit me like a tidal wave, and I dropped to the ground holding my stomach, the bow and arrows pressing into my back. Pressure built inside the room as hard and fast as a summer thunderstorm, and my head pounded with it, the compression muffling external sound. Nevertheless, I yelled, "Trace, dammit, what's wrong with you! Why won't you answer me?"

A torrent of artic air blew up out of the center of the circle, throwing me out of the way. The squall roared as it rocketed through the room, and the pressure popped like a balloon. A turquoise lake burbled up with the crackle of breaking ice, and white, frosty air spiraled up from its center, stretching to the ceiling. I scooted back, chilled to the bone. My hands were so cold, I couldn't have nocked an arrow if I wanted to.

Long blond hair, a kick-ass figure, and the meanest, angriest pair of eyes stared out at me from the filmy, white tendrils dancing in the center of my Celtic Knot.

"Laurel?" I scrambled to my feet.

"Yes, it's me, you ignorant, stupid fool!"

"What are you doing here?" I floundered for my words, my hands waving helplessly.

"You tried to summon a man!"

I held out my hands in protest. "Don't get mad at me. I'm trying to learn the rules here. That's why I'm summoning my trainer in the first place."

Laurel crossed her arms. I couldn't see her feet through the swirling white fog floating around her legs.

"Summoning humans goes against Oberon's Rules of Magical Harmony, you mortal idiot."

"How was I supposed to know that?"

She huffed out an exasperated breath. "You have Pinky. Did you ask him before you tried this crap?"

"Uh. No."

"Well, you done fucked up. Again."

"I'm pretty sick of being accused of messing up when no one's actually helping me learn anything."

"Well, boo hoo on you, princess. Ignorance is not an excuse."

"Why are you here, Laurel? Why did you appear when I summoned Trace? You, of all people?"

She gave me a look usually reserved for small, temper-tantrum-throwing children. "Summoning a human violates the laws of magic."

"Yeah, so you said. That doesn't explain your appearance. Why did you get this job? Why are you the messenger?"

She sniffed, looked up at and away, not meeting my eyes, and I detected a small blush to her cheeks.

"Lauuuurreelll?"

"If you recall, I made a small, off-the-cuff crack about the fae king's sexual ability."

I thought about it.

"Ah, you mean in Gregory's bar, The Three Arrows when you said, 'from what I've heard, calling him the Big O was hardly true?'"

"I didn't *mean* it." She pursed her lips. "But . . . his wife didn't like the joke."

I raised my eyebrows. "So delivering a message to me is a punishment?"

"I was told to deliver the findings of your trial."

"My trial?"

She sighed a beleaguered, heaving breath. "You violated the rules, and judgement was rendered."

My eyes narrowed, and my chest tightened. "What does that mean? Who rendered a judgment? From what court? I wasn't there to defend myself."

"You don't get to be there, moron. No human attends the Fae Court. Titania herself made the decree."

"Titania! What decree?"

"You are barred from interacting with the fae."

"I work at a fae bar."

"Not anymore."

"Titania can't tell Joey who can and can't work at her bar."

Laurel coughed "bullshit" into her fist.

"Seriously? She can make these rules for the Slow World?"

Laurel laughed, but it was wry and strained. "She's freakin' Titania, Becs. She can do whatever she wants to any of her subjects at any time."

"I'm not one of her subjects."

"Not sure she cares."

I focused on the ban from all things fae. "My best friends are fae. The wee ones, Joey, Pinky, Timothy. . . ."

"They're not your friends now."

"For how long?"

"Permanently."

"How did a trial happen in the mere seconds it took for me to issue the summons and for you to appear?"

Laurel examined her cuticles. "Time works differently in the Slow World. You know that."

"Yeeeaah, but this feels faster than fae fast. This feels like she had a summary judgment waiting to go in case I tried to summon a human. Why didn't she tell me it was against the rules of magic instead? What's her game?"

She shrugged and gave me a pitying look. "No one knows her game, Becs. She's the queen of Faerie. She's as old as time. You can't outthink her, outplay her, or outmaneuver her. Maybe she had this planned. Maybe not. It's immaterial."

"It's material to me!"

Laurel drew out a powder compact and checked her lipstick, which was flawless. "Whatever. Believe what you want. It makes no difference."

"Laurel, there has to be a way to get out of this. It isn't fair."

"Life isn't fair. Magic, especially, isn't fair. Cinderella got to go to the ball but had to get back by midnight. Rapunzel lived alone in a tower. Rumpelstiltskin was really the milliner's daughter's boyfriend and the father of the child in question. It wasn't about turning straw into gold. It was a custody battle."

That one stopped me in my tracks. "Really?"

Laurel sniffed and began braiding her hair. "My point is, when the fae are involved, magic is involved. And when magic is at the heart of the matter, there the fae lie. You can't have one without the other."

"What about you? She's enslaved you?"

She kept on braiding. "Enslaved, no. Indentured servitude for a really, really long time? Yes." Her face mottled, and it was the first and only time I'd seen her not looking haughty and perfect.

"Can you get out of it?"

She stopped braiding and, instead, finger-combed her hair with unnecessary roughness. It had to hurt, but she didn't seem to notice. "Not that I know of."

My debt to her creaked between my shoulder blades. I wondered if I could help her and repay my obligation. I hated owing the pixie. It chafed under my skin, and the longer it lingered, the more it burrowed in.

"So, what do I do?" I asked, returning to my personal situation. "I'm wrongly sentenced."

She gave me a baleful stare. "Get used to it." She grimaced and held up a hand. "Coming!"

"Who are you talking to?"

"Who do you think? Gotta go. Other messages to deliver, a game of four-dimensional chess to lose. You know how it is."

No, I didn't know how it was, and didn't freaking care.

Chapter 22

Laurel faded away and the water portal closed, leaving me sitting on the freezing floor, tears streaming down my face. I was alone and the emptiness echoed through my heart. How was this possible? Could the fae queen really make my friends turn on me?

There was only one way to know.

I closed the rolling doors, not even bothering to clean up, and drove to Joey's. I parked where I usually did and ran to the bar.

Or tried to.

I couldn't see the door.

I knew where it should be. I knew it like the back of my hand. Going to Joey's was second nature.

But . . . the door wasn't there. A narrow alley, completely empty except for a couple of rats, was all I could see.

I'd been kicked out. Banned. Blackballed. Treated like a regular, vanilla human, the door glamoured from my sight.

"Hey!" I yelled into the night at the space where the entrance should be. "I know you're in there! This is ridiculous and unfair. How can I be held responsible for rules I didn't know existed? Let me in!"

"You okay, lady?" asked a black man carrying a brown paper bag, which he gripped like his life depended on it. He had a guitar slung over his shoulders. "I've screamed into the void a few times myself. It doesn't work."

"There's a door here. I know you can't see it, but it's there. I have to get inside."

He nodded. "Like Narnia, right? Listen, I'm not much to look at, but you can trust me. There's a shelter I can get you to if you need a place to sleep tonight and maybe a meal? You look like you could eat. Tell them Jack sent you."

"Thank you, Jack, but no. I'm fine. I have a place to sleep. . . ."

I didn't have an apartment. I didn't have a job. My landlords and friends had turned on me.

He gave me a sympathetic look, his deep-brown eyes warm and kind. "I get it. No one wants anyone else butting into their business. But when you're knocking on doors that aren't there and talking to imaginary people, you may need a little help."

"There's a door here, really, and the people inside are real."

He took a swig from the bottle in the paper bag. "I get you. 'Salright. It's still warm out so you'll be fine if you hide well enough. Don't sleep in that alley though."

"Why not?"

He leaned in, and I smelled the whiskey on his breath. "The rats, man. That's their place." He shuddered. "And the mushrooms. They shouldn't be growing there, but they do. It's hinky."

Mushrooms?

"Thanks for the warning," I replied. "Hey, don't I know you?"

"Maybe. Play a little here and there."

"I saw you busking in front of the library." I'd been heading to the library to look for more information about my summoning powers, and he'd been singing in the open space in the square. "You warned me about a power taking control of UnderTown."

He studied me, and I realized that his eyes were clear despite the whiskey. "It's better down there now," he said. "Seems someone took care of the bad juju. People that live down there are grateful."

"That's . . . that's . . . good," I responded after a beat. "People have a right to be safe."

"Damn straight, which is why I'm warning you 'bout that alley."

Before I could respond, he left, faster than was realistic for a drunk, so late at night, but I couldn't call after him. He was already gone. I set that mystery aside for another day.

Despite his warning, curiosity got the better of me. Besides, I was feeling ornery. I stepped into the alley, no more than a few feet, but that's all it took. A rodent phalanx assembled at the opposite end, and visions of the *Nutcracker's* rat king danced in my head.

But that wasn't what scared me the most.

What terrified me were the Death Caps lining the sides of the alley, growing at the junction between the brick and the asphalt and hanging down at the cornices between the walls and the neighboring buildings' roofs. They formed a menacing brigade outlining the edges of the alley, a narrow, long rectangle of terrifying killers who'd rip apart the minds of anyone attempting to shelter within.

This was the fae version of a "Stay Out, Guard Dog on Duty" sign.

"Fine," I said, not trying to hide my voice's bitter tone. "Message received."

"Becs."

I turned and stopped dead in my tracks. "Joey?"

The half-gnome glanced furtively to each side. "Here," she said, shoving her hand out to clasp mine. "Take this. I'm sorry we can't let you in, Becs, but the fae queen's orders bind us all. I'm risking her wrath by talking to you now. Only one can countermand her, and well, I'm not facing him."

She closed my hands around a small, brushed chocolate-brown velvet bag and shoved me away. "Please go before the Death Caps get creative." She gave me one last sad smile and twisted her hand in the open air, revealing a sliver of light and the sound of happy, drinking customers. "Gotta go. Can't get good help anymore." She slipped inside, and the door clicked closed, leaving me alone in Death Cap Alley, with only the rats, a faint streetlamp, and fluttering insects for company.

The bag lay heavy in my hand. I opened it and poured the contents into my palm. The three gold fae coins from Oberon tumbled out, plus a wad of twenties wrapped tightly in a strip of white paper. I didn't count them because the urge to run and hide settled on me like a shroud, tickling the back of my neck. My feet itched with the sudden need to move. I glanced behind me and saw a pack of Death Caps gathered in the middle of the alley, gliding toward me in a slow but inexorable march on oozing, muscular feet, like slugs with stems. I heard their whispers as they advanced.

Hungry. Ours. The fae queen promised if you came near.

"Not yours, you homicidal fungi. Not now, not ever." The front line hit the pavement squares where I was standing, and I stomped on them hard. Their shrill, thin cries were music to my ears, but I didn't hang around long enough to attack any others. They'd be out for blood like sharks circling chum, and their psychological assaults could cripple even the strongest minds. I'd been responsible for the death of one human already, and I didn't want anything like that to happen again.

I bolted, trying to get out of their reach as fast as possible. I tripped in my rush and fell to the ground, the bag tumbling out of reach. I scrambled to my feet, walk-crawling to retrieve it when a brown-booted foot blocked my path.

"Rebecca, what's going on? Why aren't you in the bar?"

"Evans, you're going to need to move. I need that bag." I hopped-stepped around him and bent to retrieve it. He tapped me on the back.

"Fill me in on what's happening. I know something has, but I've been on an errand for the fae king, and I don't know what."

I rose to look over his shoulder and saw the shadow of a specter, the giant Death Cap who haunted my nightmares, creeping up the brick wall next to the parking area. He'd report whatever he witnessed to Titania. Evans couldn't be seen with me.

I screamed at him and pushed him away.

"I know I can't be near any fae, you cruel elf! How could you be so callous? No need to rub my nose in it. If Titania says I have to stay away, then I will but there's no need to mock me!"

Evan gasped and tweaked his eyes to the side, seeing the specter pressing forward. He backed away, realization dawning. "Don't come back here again, Becs. It isn't good for your health."

He cast one last glance at the Death Cap shadow and hurried off. I rushed to my car and kicked the engine to life, peeling out onto the street. I looked in the rearview mirror and saw the Death Cap retreat to the alley. I hoped I'd covered for Evans.

I drove to my office, skidding to a stop and exiting the vehicle while the engine pinged. I rolled up the doors, closed them behind me, and sat in my rolling chair, breathing hard.

It took a few minutes for me to feel safe.

I poured the bag's contents on the hard desk surface. Three gold fae coins and a roll of bills held together by a rubber band and a circle of paper.

I unrolled the bills and realized the paper encircling them had writing on it.

Becs,

The money is your pay from your last few shifts plus some extra a few of our regular customers threw in as tips they'd forgotten to give you earlier.

I was grateful for the pay and tips, both positioned as earnings, not gifts, therefore not incurring debts. That was thoughtful of them. Tears gathered in the corners of my eyes, and I swiped them away with the back of my hand.

I opened my bottom drawer and extracted a granola bar and a bottle of water. The guitar man on the street was right about one thing—I needed to eat. But without So Long Noodles, my apartment kitchen, or bar food, I'd be eating out or choking down chalky protein bars. I'd get sick if I wasn't careful, and my funds, even with the money Joey gave me, would dwindle fast.

I needed a plan, but first, I needed sleep.

I gathered most of my belongings from my car and curled up in my comfy chair, making a nest with a pillow and a blanket. Ten minutes in, I vowed to replace the chair with a recliner the next chance I could.

The dream came on quiet, pitter-patter feet. Asher kissing me on my neck, my eyes closed, his heat against my skin, and the soothing coolness of the sheets in my bedroom. I sighed, letting his smooth touch calm my spirit.

He kissed me again, on my mouth, more insistent, and I pulled him closer. His hands, more desperate now, running up and down my sides, caressing my breasts. He brought his head to my nipple and sucked, and even through the fabric of my shirt and bra, sensation ran like an electric wire from my breast down my body and in between my legs. I moaned in pleasure, and he pulled away, bringing his hands to cup my face. Quiet, tiny nibbles on my bottom lip had me panting with need.

"Look at me."

I did as he asked. Wouldn't I always?

His beautiful brown eyes peered into mine, as if he could see through to my soul. "You are a beautiful person, Rebecca. I wish I could give you more."

"You're giving me everything. Don't stop."

"Please forgive me," he whispered and touched his thumb to my lips. I flicked my tongue out and sucked, and now it was his turn to groan. I wiggled out from under him, pushed him down, and with an audible sigh of surrender, he let me love him. I took my time, smelling his skin, kissing my way down to where I wanted to be, licking him, and tasting. I settled on top of him, intertwining my hands with his. After my release and then his, my life finally made sense. I'd come home.

We lay entangled in my blankets, our limbs intertwined. An owl's hoot and a dove's coo were the only sounds coming from out the window. A cool breeze ruffled my curtains and lifted Asher's hair like a mother caressing her child's forehead. I traced my fingers down his arm, admiring his unblemished skin. Not a freckle. Not a birthmark. Just a gorgeous expanse of touchable flawless perfection. I snuggled against him, burying my nose in his neck, trying to memorize the moment, then fell into a dreamless sleep.

It wasn't a dream, but a cherished memory. It had been my last undisturbed night of sleep. He'd left me with nothing but his head's indentation on the pillow and a crushed origami bird.

Or an angel, if the Longs were to be believed.

Chapter 23

My mind roiled with a burning need for answers.

Here I was, locked out of my apartment, my place of work, without friends, trainer, or boyfriend, and when I thought about it, really pondered it, who was at the center of it all?

Asher.

The sexiest man on the planet, and maybe off the planet, could answer all my questions if he wanted to.

Where was he?

God only knew, and that might be literal.

Maybe hitting something would help. I straightened the storage unit and went to the Krav Maga studio, my mood as black as my sneakers.

My grumpy disposition lightened when Oded greeted me with a smile.

"Rivka! That medicine you gave me is miraculous. It takes the itch and burn away. I may also be healing faster, and I'm more comfortable. I'm so grateful to you and your friend."

I air-hugged him, still uneasy about touching his injured body, but gave him a real kiss on his good cheek. "I'm so glad, Oded. This is the first good news I've had in a couple of days."

"What's wrong?" I glimpsed the old Oded, the one before the fire, as he examined me from head to toe, concern in his eyes.

I shrugged. "Just about everything."

"You want to talk about it?"

"Not yet." I did, but I didn't know what to say. He'd already been hurt because of me.

"A good sweat, then a hot shower. You look like you've been to hell and back."

"Thank heavens, that hasn't happened yet."

"It's an expression, Rivka. A figure of speech."

"I *know*," I said with a snarky eye roll. "I was kidding." I brushed passed my instructor and scampered to the changing room. *Whew.* I had to stop taking things so literally.

When I emerged dressed and ready, students lined the room, all eyes on the middle of the big training mat. A six-foot-something hairy guy in tight shorts and a muscle tank stood facing Oded. His biceps flexed and relaxed and flexed again as he shifted from foot to foot, like a posturing gorilla from a nature documentary. Oded stood calm and still, his arms loose at his sides, his bandages on full display.

The man's aggressive posture seemed odd for this studio. Students were usually more respectful.

Suddenly, out of nowhere, Gorilla Guy backed up a few feet and snapped a sidekick at Oded, who nodded politely and stepped back to allow him some room. Another sidekick, and once again Oded moved out of the way. "That's impressive," Oded said. "You've studied."

"I have," Gorilla Guy grunted. "But I wanted to learn what you're doing here. That's why I paid for six months' membership up front. I heard that Israeli Krav Maga teachers are bad asses, but I'm looking at a total candy ass."

"As I explained to you, we aren't a traditional dojo," Oded explained, his voice never rising. "We're a Krav Maga studio. An academy. A teaching facility that focuses on mindfulness and defense. I refunded your money because I think you're looking for something we don't offer."

"This place is a joke," the hirsute man said, gesturing to Oded's burns. "Who trusts an injured man to teach them anyway? Couldn't defend yourself in a fight? Is that how you got hurt?"

"It's hard to defend yourself against fire."

"Likely story." The large man backed up as if he was going to leave but then stopped and with a sick grin threw a roundhouse kick followed by a flashy spinning kick I'd only seen done in pro wrestling or a Muay Thai competition. He aimed for Oded's head.

The kick would have been devastating if it landed, but Oded wasn't ten feet near that guy's foot, having already stepped out of the way. I didn't know what this man's deal was, but rarely would someone throw a fancy kick like that in a real-world fight. They wouldn't have time. Real-world fights were surprising, fast, vicious, and exhausting. For your average person, the goal was to avoid one altogether or, if impossible, to create enough space to run away or to distract and disable your opponent so you could flee. Unless you were in a movie or were an extremely well-trained fighter, that was about it.

So, I laughed.

I couldn't help it, but Oded threw me an exasperated look when Gorilla Guy's attention slipped past Oded and landed on me.

Oops.

"You think that's funny?" he grunted.

I sobered right up. "No. I don't. Sorry, I didn't mean to laugh at you. I laughed at Oded's face when he scrambled out of the way. You're super quick and flexible. That was a high kick."

I tried for genuine, I really did.

"Let's get you the names of some other gyms, shall we?" Oded said, calling the man's attention back to him, but Gorilla Guy wouldn't budge.

"Do you really think you could defend yourself against me?" asked the man.

Oded called out. "Zara, please call the police." I supposed she did as he asked, but I didn't look. I had eyes for Gorilla Guy only.

I knew I shouldn't have egged him on, but this man was everything wrong with the world.

"It depends," I said with a nonchalant shrug.

"On what?" he asked, bouncing on his toes.

"No fighting!" Oded commanded, but his voice sounded far away.

"If your eenie weenie is big enough to kick."

That did it. Gorilla Guy lost his shit and came at me, hands outstretched to grasp my neck. Before he got a good hold, I placed my left hand on his right wrist, brought my other one up inside his arms as if to touch my forehead and twisted to my right, using the hinging motion of my shoulder and my body weight to break his hold.

Which I did, but it didn't matter because the man stumbled backward as his knee crumpled inward. He fell to the ground, howling. Oded stood over him.

"The police are on the way," he said, as the man regained his feet. He balanced on his good leg, and I thought for sure he'd yield.

But, no.

He snapped a fist at Oded's throat and Oded floated to the side, grabbed him by the right shoulder with both hands, and took advantage of the man's forward momentum to yank his torso downward . . . and simultaneously strike him with an obliterating knee to the ribs. The fact that the man was breathing and not dead told me Oded had held back, but I knew the guy's ribs had to be broken.

The whole thing took less than sixty seconds. The man lay on the floor, beaten and in agony.

Zara arrived with the cops, and then it was explanations and statements and promises to provide more information if needed. Oded downloaded the security camera's footage for them, and when they viewed it, they just shook their heads.

"Got what was coming to him," muttered one of them, as the ambulance loaded the man on a stretcher. He was met by murmurs of agreement.

"Hey, Oded," asked a lieutenant who'd shown up specifically because he'd heard who'd originated the call. "When are you doing another training for the Bureau of Community Policing?"

"Monday evening at seven p.m.," Oded replied.

"I'll be there."

The cops finished getting their info, spoke quietly to Oded, and departed.

"Everyone else, get back to what you were doing," my mentor said, his face a mask of calm. "Party's over."

The room was soon filled with the thwack of people hitting punching bags, instructors barking directions, and a woman counting down seconds as she led a series of planks, but the normal sounds couldn't quite cover the excited buzz as students discussed how Oded had taken the guy down.

"Rivka!"

I reacted to the sharpness of Oded's tone. "Uh? Yes?"

"You should not have challenged that man. I was trying to deescalate the violence, not ratchet it up."

Good thing my momma taught me the value of silence.

"Your lack of control could have gotten you hurt. As it is, I now must deal with the fallout from this fiasco. Whether he deserved it or not, I had to injure a man to protect you. You should not have forced his, and consequently, my hand."

"I'm sorry."

"You should be."

"Are you kicking me out of the studio?" I asked, hating the sulky tone to my voice, but I'd been barred from everywhere else. Why not here, too?

Not for the first time, Oded surprised me.

"Absolutely not. You need to train more, not less. Learn discipline. Remember why you're here. I blame myself. Your lack of steady training is what led to this."

Lack of training. The story of my life.

"You couldn't train me while you were in the hospital."

"True, but now that I'm feeling better, we will be rigorous in your lessons."

Tears threatened, but I refused to let them fall. "Thanks for letting me stay."

Oded exhaled, reached up with his injured arm and caressed my face. "My friend, I'll never abandon you. Teachers don't push their students away when they make mistakes. They bring them closer."

"Then why did my other teacher leave me?" The question popped out before I could hold it back. And once it was out there, I couldn't suck the words back in.

Oded quirked his head at me. "Which teacher?"

"Not anyone you knew. I haven't seen him since I was a teenager, and he left without saying goodbye."

"What was he teaching you?"

Ugh. I'd opened this can of worms and now I had to close it. "Sort of . . . a type of art."

"I didn't know you were an artist. This instructor left while you were a child?"

"Yes, and no. I'm not an artist, but I wanted to be, and my mother hired this person to teach me. I thought we had a special bond, but he left too."

"Too?"

Holy Moley! My mouth was running off without my brain to guide it. I had to finish it now. "Like my father. He left when I was little."

"Ah." Oded fell silent, studying me, and I wilted under his gaze.

"Stop looking at me."

"I don't mean to embarrass you, but I think I've learned something about you that I didn't know before, something that explains a lot. You hit first because you're afraid. You strike without thinking because you want to push people away before they can leave you."

"I do not." Yeah, I did.

Oded grasped both of my hands. "Rivka, look at me."

I winced, remembering how Asher had said that same thing to me on our last night together.

"Rivka, I'm serious. Look at me."

With a huff, I brought my eyes to his.

"Sometimes people leave, or change, not because of you, but because of *them*. Everyone has secrets. Their own stories. You don't know what those were. And while I think a father leaving his family is awful, and I can't imagine doing it myself, I won't judge him without knowing more."

"I'll never know more."

"Then, you'll have to live with the unknown. It's uncomfortable, but it's not debilitating."

"Says you."

He laughed. "Yes, says me."

"I want to know *why*. Not knowing hurts."

"And I didn't want to get hurt in a fire I didn't cause. I don't like being in pain either, but it's a part of life. Accidents happen. People change, face unreasonable choices, and sometimes, they leave."

"What about rotten boyfriends who ghost you?"

"That's what margaritas are for, or so I hear. Zara's the expert. She tells me stories."

Now it was my turn to chuckle. "Maybe I should call her."

We shifted off the mat to avoid interfering with a women's self-defense class gathering for their first lesson. Women of every ethnicity and size assembled because they refused to be victims. Maybe some had already been victimized or had friends or sisters who had been. It wasn't about looking backward for them. They were looking forward.

And I could do the same. Rebuild my life. Move to a new apartment, get a fresh job, especially now that I had bartending experience. I couldn't use Joey as a reference, but I could offer to work a night for free and prove myself. As for summoning, I could operate a business based on the small rituals I knew how to do well. Continue to take on simple jobs, and with a new bartending gig, I'd have somewhere Mickey could visit. I could get her and Ruthie back. I'd spend more time working with Oded and Zara. Open myself up to a more disciplined, stable way of living. I eyed the guys working out around me, teaching and practicing. Maybe I'd ask one out on a date? Forget about my missing father, my lost summoning trainer, and Titania.

As my sister said, put them in my rearview mirror.

"Join the class, Rivka," Oded said, patting me on the shoulder. "Dig back in. Practice the basics. Though . . .," he said with a wink, "that was a nice move you did earlier. Well done."

I snorted a half-laugh, half-choke. "Are you kidding me? You took that man down like he was an elementary school bully. You're a superhero."

He shook his head. "No, I'm experienced. What I did was control my temper so I could think clearly."

"I shouldn't have goaded him."

"Nope, you shouldn't have. But learning how to slow down and think in an emergency is a matter of physical practice and mental preparation. You just had an apt lesson." He hugged me. "Go join the woman's class and work off some of that adrenaline."

I hugged him back and then jogged over and joined the class. One of the teachers used me to demonstrate some techniques. My negativity floated away while I worked with the new women.

Afterward, I took a shower with a new lease on life, ready to focus on the positive and move forward in a healthy way.

I wondered how long it would last.

Chapter 24

Clean and calm, I returned to my storage unit office, the only home I had at the moment. Sunlight beat down on the endless rows of concrete and metal, making it unreasonably and unseasonably hot. Storage facilities weren't known for cooling foliage, and the heat coalesced into mirage-producing waves that shimmered several inches off the ground. I left the door open to allow air in and reminded myself, again, to get a fan.

As a small indulgence, I'd stopped and used some of Joey's money to buy a salad and fresh fruit. Healthy eating for a healthy mind, right? I suppressed my craving for fries and ice cream, although chocolate chunk with brownies sounded divine. My body hadn't caught up with the new positivity program. All it knew was that I'd worked out hard and craved greasy, fattening calories. I told my body to shut up.

My phone rang, and its quiet tone reminded me that I'd better check my online bank to make sure my bills were paid on time. Unfortunately, the utility companies didn't care that my life was in an existential crisis. If I didn't pay by the fifteenth, they'd cut me off. Everyone was so mercenary. I paused stuffing my mouth with lettuce and tomatoes and wiped my hands with a wet nap.

My phone rang again, and I answered.

"Hello, Gregory."

"Rebecca."

"You called?"

"Obviously."

"Gregory, why are you calling? Do you have news?"

"Say 'thank you.'"

"Thank you."

"Say, 'thank you very much.'"

I couldn't stand his smug tone. I gritted my teeth and said, "Thank you, Gregory, O Wise One for blessing me with your melodious vocal tones. Does that suffice?"

"Now, see, that's just rude."

My Krav Maga-imposed Zen cracked into a multitude of hairline fractures.

"I'm losing my patience. Either you have good news to tell me or you're calling to gloat about something. I can never tell."

"You're no fun anymore. I called to tell you that Hart & Wells Litigation sent a letter to the Andinos informing them that they were liable for the medical bills incurred by Oded Levi and the firefighters who responded to the fire. The firm's been officially retained by local government and is providing services pro bono on behalf of the victims and our city's residents who rely on its corporate citizens to behave honorably."

I barely kept from gagging. Instead, I said, "Wow. That's quite a mouthful."

"Do you like? I practiced in the mirror."

"It sounds good, I admit."

"Grudging, faint praise but I'll take it."

"I hope it helps, that's all."

"It should. The Andinos don't want to be on the city's bad side any more than I do. It would be bad business, not to mention short-sighted on their part not to be magnanimous in this instance. I'm wondering if Phillipe is losing a step."

"He's the head of the family?"

"Yes." Gregory couldn't keep the glee out of his voice. "I've been waiting for the old man to slip up. Thanks for presenting me with this opportunity."

"It's all a game to you, isn't it? Who wins? Who loses?"

"Power. Money. What else is there?"

I reminded him. "Love."

Silence.

"Gregory?"

He sighed. "Yes, Rebecca. Love. But I don't have that, so I'll take what I can."

"Maybe taking isn't the right approach. Maybe that's the problem?"

His voice hardened. "Thanks for the therapy session. I'll let you know what happens."

He hung up, and I placed the phone on the desk.

Part of me pitied Gregory Adamos. He'd survived a rough childhood at the hands of an emotionally abusive mother and a neglectful father, and the thing he wanted most in the world was true love.

The other part of me remembered that he killed people, leveraged their weaknesses to take advantage of them, and told me flat out that he hired warlocks to do some of his dirty work.

Yeah, my sympathy only went so far.

His wish for true love resonated, though, and with Asher dominating my thoughts, I shared his yearning. No matter how far I pushed Asher away mentally, all I could think about was the last time I'd been with him. The feeling of his lips and hands on me. His skin and scent. His sighs and moans. The way he felt inside me.

Also, my deep disappointment when he'd disappeared and my frustration when he'd shown up out of the blue issuing dire warnings.

I gnawed a carrot and reviewed my conversation with Gregory. I'd advised him that taking was the problem. But when it came to Asher, was I the one taking? Did Asher need me to give him something?

"Asher?" I called into the steamy air, standing at the door's opening. "Asher? If you can hear me, I'd like to talk to you. I've learned a few things, and I think it's time we spoke plainly, no riddles."

A hawk's screech echoed through the air, and sweat beaded on my forehead. My feet baked right through my shoes, and I held my hand to my brow to search the area, my eyes blinded by the glare. Nothing. No Asher. I swatted at the ever-present bugs and smashed one on the back of my neck, coming away with a splash of blood.

Ew. It must have been mid-bite. I'd have a welt soon. I wondered if I had any antihistamine cream. It stank not being at home with a bathroom cabinet full of supplies. I couldn't even clip the hangnail on my thumb without a trip to the pharmacy.

Discouraged, I sat in my chair, pensive and alone, until an embryo of an idea perched on the edge of my consciousness, thin and indistinct. Staying still, trying not to think about anything at all, I let it take form.

If I could summon a demon, why couldn't I summon an angel?

Weren't demons and angels equal opposites? If I could summon Valefar, could I summon Asher?

A tiny voice told me that this wasn't a great idea. I argued with it. Sure, it wasn't a fantastic idea, but was it a terrible idea? Mildly awful? Middling?

There was only one way to find out. I pulled books from my little library and went to work.

Drawing the *Ten Sefirot* of the Kabbalah in chalk was no easy task. Comprised of ten circles representing the principles of unity, harmony, and benevolence on one side, and the necessity for justice on the other, the symbol represented the creative forces that shaped our world. The side symbols were balanced in the middle by God's Presence in the World, *Shekhinah*, and Beauty, *Tif'eret*.

I drew it in white, and then when that piece shrunk to a nub, I used pink. I didn't think it mattered. It took two hours to write the Hebrew letters correctly. I wanted them to be tidy, with clean lines and little flourishes. A search outside found four pigeon feathers, and I placed them at the four corners of the symbols. Pigeons and doves were pretty much the same thing. White or gray, big or little, ring-necked, white-winged, or mourning, they were all *Columbidae*. I wouldn't find pure white ones where I lived so these would have to do. I didn't think Asher would stand on protocol.

I lit a candle for fire and added a bowl of spring water, a clod of dirt for earth, and a small Japanese hand fan for air. I changed my clothes, donning a light summer dress in a deep garnet. It was the only dress I owned.

I let the doors stay open as dusk fell and stood at the edge of the symbol in bare feet. Closing my eyes, I whispered the Hebrew words I'd inscribed on the floor as well as their English meanings. "God's Crown, Wisdom, Understanding, Mercy, Justice, Beauty, Eternity, Glory, Foundation, God's Presence."

An anticipatory stillness settled in the room, and I didn't know how to interpret it, so I plunged ahead.

"Asher, guardian angel, please come to me. I summon you as a bearer of the Kiss and as your charge."

A rumble of thunder echoed in the distance. *A warning?* I waited.

Nothing else.

I continued.

"Asher, guardian angel, I summon you. I know we've been at odds, but maybe if we talk, we can figure out what is going on."

Definitely a rumble, and a crackle of lightning overhead. The air grew thick, and a heaviness fell over my limbs so intense, that I sank to the floor. Drowsiness hit me, urging me to lie down and doze, to forget this nonsense, and rest.

A whisper of sound. "Drift away. Sleep."

I shook myself. "No! Come on! Asher, please come to me."

A beat of wings, the flap of something big, so much bigger than any bird, reverberated through the air, then that presence tore away.

The whisper again, "Turn your face from this path."

"Turn my face? I want to talk, that's all. What happened to 'Do not hide your face from me when I am in distress. Turn your ear to me; when I call, answer me quickly.'"

Wham! A flash of lightning crashed right outside my office, striking the ground with such force that I jolted backward, tumbling ass over teakettle, and landed on my butt across the room. Another strike, another explosion of light, and now I was so flash-blind, I couldn't see anything at all. Acrid smoke filled the air along with the crackle of fizzling embers as they hit the asphalt.

I lay there, panting, aching, and unable to see.

What would it take to get a straight answer? Heaven, Hell, and Faerie were keeping secrets, guarding their dominions, afraid of me for some unknown reason or reasons. I had to believe the whole "child of a changeling who wasn't a changeling will destroy balance" thing was at its root, but I was no closer to understanding what this meant, why it concerned me, or how Trace, Titania, and Asher fit in. In fact, every step I took made things worse.

I trembled on the hard floor, the thunder's boom echoing in my ears. I shivered despite the heat but pulled myself to my feet and stumbled around, feeling my way until I got to my desk.

My phone lay just where I left it, and miraculously, it felt intact.

Hoping she wouldn't hang up on me, I asked the phone's voice activated assistant to dial the only person I wanted at that moment.

"Call Mickey."

Chapter 25

Mickey's car drove into the parking lot and slammed to a stop. "Becs? Becs? Where are you?"

"Here," I replied. "In here."

She ran into my office. "What do you mean you're blind?"

I sat in my chair but turned to face her. "I can't see."

"It's dark in here. I can hardly see anything either."

"I think some of the lights blew out. I have a flashlight somewhere." I got up and felt my way to the desk and rummaged in the lowest drawer for the heavy mag light I kept there. My fingers shook so hard, it took me three times to flick it on.

Mickey gasped. "What is this place? What happened here? What are you up to?" Anger laced her tone, but I couldn't blame her. I'd woken my Jewish mother sister up in the middle of the night, given her an address she didn't recognize, and told her I was blind. It was a natural response.

"Please sit," I said. "Please?"

"Let me see you first." Her hands touched my cheeks, soft and loving, and I almost burst into tears.

"You can't see me at all?"

"No. All I see is an afterimage of a bright light. Like a camera flash that won't go away."

"My God, Becs. You'd better start at the beginning."

"Sit," I said again. I plopped to the floor.

"First, let me see if I can get these lights working. Ah, there we go. This place is a disaster. Why do you have the *Ten Sefirot* sketched on the floor?"

"I'll explain."

"You talk. I'll clean up."

"You don't have to."

"Keeping my hands busy means I won't be tempted to strangle you."

I hung my head. "Yeah. Got it." I waited a beat. "Mickey, thank you for coming."

The scrape of metal told me she'd moved something back into place. "You're my sister."

"I know, but the way we left things last time. . . ."

"I'm mad at you, more than ever, but that doesn't mean I won't be by your side in an emergency, you idiot. Sisters don't abandon one another."

I swallowed hard. "I love you."

She sighed, and the sound of paper told me she'd righted my trash can. "I love you, too. Now spill."

I rubbed my eyes but there was no change. I refused to believe this was permanent and pushed the panic away.

"This is my summoning office. It's here because no one else is. It's safer to avoid people. Also, the company I rent from doesn't ask any questions and lets me modify it the way I want. I know you have doubts that I summon real entities of power, but I do, and I need you to accept that."

"Go on."

The skitter of chalk rolling on the floor joined the slam of my chair being righted. The place must have been a wreck.

"I've summoned demons."

She scoffed. "Real, actual demons like with horns and red tails?"

"More like horns and griffin wings."

My sister let out an unladylike grunt. "Fine, let's say I accept this on face value, since obviously something terrible happened here. You're saying you summoned a 'demon,' and it went crazy and made a mess of this place, leaving you blind?"

"Oh, no. Demons don't do that."

My sister shuffled papers and from the rattling sound, collected fallen bobbleheads.

"Demons don't cause havoc?" she asked, her voice strained and high-pitched. She was keeping it together though. Better than I expected.

"Oh, demons do cause havoc. They're experts at it, but they're more subtle."

"What did this?"

"An angel."

The bobbleheads hit the floor with a loud clatter and the clink-clink of rolling plastic.

"You summoned an *angel*? Like Gabriel, Michael, Raphael?"

"No! Not an archangel. My guardian angel. Asher."

My sister's voice was closer. She'd given up and sat in the chair. I positioned my body to face her.

She blew out a short breath. "Let me get this straight. Your ex-boyfriend is your guardian angel, and you tried to summon him?"

"Yes."

Her breath came fast, and I thought she might be close to hyperventilating, but only close. Not actually panicking. I silently prayed she'd hang on.

"Did this ritual involve the *Ten Sefirot* from Kabbalah?"

"It did. I'm assuming the symbols are still visible on the floor?"

"Oh. Yes. They are."

I barreled on before she could think about it too hard. "Well, it didn't work. I think Asher came, but a larger force intervened. It tried to make me fall asleep so I wouldn't continue the ritual, but when I kept going, it blasted me with lightning."

She couldn't keep the incredulity from her voice. "Are you telling me that a heavenly heavy hitter gently discouraged you from continuing a ritual, you disobeyed and got fried by lightning?" She'd lost her sense of alarm and gained a sense of wonder.

When she put it that way, it sounded bad. "I guess that's one way to put it."

"You deserved it."

"What?"

She clapped her hands together. "You interfered with forces of the natural world, the energies of creation! You're lucky you weren't turned into a pillar of salt or swallowed by a whale."

"Whales don't live around here."

"Don't be a smarty pants." She sounded just like our mother. "Did it ever occur to you that maybe Asher—if he's truly your guardian angel, which I find suspicious, but okay, let's accept that for a moment—shouldn't have had a physical relationship with you?"

"No." It hadn't. "I didn't know what he was at the time."

"But he did. His responsibility."

"I'm not sure it works that way."

"I'm making an educated guess. Do you think messengers and protectors from Above are allowed to use humans willy-nilly as their playthings? The physical world is bound by laws. If you drop an apple, it falls. The Earth rotates around the sun. Living things move, reproduce, eat, and die. And, the one I think you need to remember is, every action has an equal and opposite reaction."

"Who made you science girl?"

"Shut up. I got A's in physics, chemistry, and biology, but that's not the point. If the physical world has laws, surely the metaphysical one does too."

I repositioned on the floor to be more comfortable. "And magical ones apparently, although I can't get anyone to give me a copy of the Laws of Magical Harmony."

"I'm going to pretend you didn't say that."

"Why?"

"Things are too bizarre for me right now. That sounds like something out of Tolkien."

I stretched out on the floor and rubbed my eyes again. Still nothing. Just a bright, bluish-white afterimage. "Not too far off, but that's fair. I'm thrilled you've gone with me this far."

The slap of Mickey's hands on her knees made me sit up. "Look," I said, "I know this is a lot, but why don't we forget the whys right now and deal with the fact that I can't see."

"Come home with me," she said, sounding as weary as I was. "I have a doctor we can call in the morning." She took my hand and pulled me up. Then she wrapped me in her strong arms, holding me close.

"We'll figure this out, Becs," she murmured in my ear. "I've got you."

The deluge of tears I'd been holding back ruptured, and I cried all over my sister's shoulder—huge, wracking sobs I didn't know I had in me. And Mickey held me through the whole episode, patting me on the back, whispering how much she loved me.

"I'm sorry I've disappointed you, Micks."

"Don't say that. I don't entirely understand your world, but looking around at this, I've realized that I've judged you unfairly. This is more powerful and complicated than I believed. Here. . . ." She left me for a moment and came back, wrapping my hand around my bag's strap. "You'll need this. Why do you have all this stuff here? A blanket? Pillow?"

"Landlords kicked me out."

"You're homeless?"

"Sorta. I've got this place."

"We'll call your work in the morning and explain why you can't come in."

"Don't worry about it. They're not looking for me, either."

"You're jobless too?"

"And blind."

Mickey squeezed my hand. "You're in it deep, aren't you?"

I shrugged and wiped my cheek. "I called you, didn't I?"

She sighed again, a deep long sigh that spoke of sadness and too much lost time. "Yes. Come on, let's go home."

"Jonah's gonna be mad."

She took my hand, leading me outside. She helped me close the rolling doors and got me to her car. Then she buckled me in like a little kid. "Becs, he's not gonna be mad. He's going to be incandescent."

"Can we make one stop?"

She yawned and spoke to me as if I was crazy. "Seriously? It's o'dark thirty, Becs. I'm exhausted, and Ruthie wakes up at six a.m. on the dot."

"It's important."

"Where are we going?"

"Winter Medical Park."

She started the car and eased out onto the road. I could tell by the potholes. "Sure. Why not? This night couldn't get any weirder."

She might soon think otherwise.

Mickey cruised down the main road, and I had her park near the apple grove. She walked me across the street and said, "Now what? Why are we here?"

"Pinky?" I called.

A quiet whistle answered. Pinky must have emerged from the trees because Mickey startled. "Who is this?" she asked.

To Mickey, Pinky would look like a tall, lanky skater kid.

"Remember the boy I told you about? The one I helped get home?"

"Yeah, what's he doing here?"

This was harder to answer. "Visiting."

"By sleeping in the park? He could get hurt!"

"I'm okay," Pinky said, from a few feet away. "Becs, why are you here? Why do you smell like chalk and angel dust?"

"You can smell angel dust? You don't mean the drug, do you? I don't do that stuff."

He ignored me. "Who is this with you? Oh, it must be your sister. She smells of baby."

"Is this kid part bloodhound?" Mickey asked.

"No," Pinky replied. "Why would you think I'm part dog? Our ears aren't alike at all."

I loved this six-foot-tall fairy. "It's an expression, Pinky. She meant that you have a keen sense of smell." I patted Mickey's hand on my elbow. "Micks, can you go wait in the car? I promise I'll only be another minute."

"Oh, sure," she grumbled. "I'm just the chauffeur."

"Thanks. I owe you."

"Big, girlfriend. You owe me big," she griped, but went back to the car, leaving me with Pinky.

"Why did she call you 'girlfriend?' You're her sister, not her friend."

I weaved on my feet, a combination of fatigue and being blind with nothing to hold on to. "Pinky? Can you walk me over to a tree, so I have something to lean on?"

His gentle hand touched my shoulder, and he led me to a bench. "How about you sit?" he said.

"Even better. You sit too, please."

His weight settled next to me.

"To answer your question, Mickey and I are sisters, but we are also friends."

"And girls."

Touché. "Yes, and girls."

"Sister. Girl. Friends. That makes sense, but why don't people say what they mean?"

"I'm with you."

"I know you're with me. We are sharing a bench."

I shook my head. "I mean that I understand why you're confused."

Pinky sniffed. He sniffed again, a deep inhale. "I smell ozone."

"Yeeeahhh. I did something stupid."

"Something involving angels?"

"Uh huh. But that's not the point. I came to see you. To tell you that I'm sorry."

"For what?"

I floundered a moment, searching for words. "For not talking to you about the Laws of Magical Harmony before I tried summoning a human."

"Who did you try to summon?"

"Trace, my former trainer."

"He is a summoner, too?"

"Yes."

"Well, you couldn't summon him, anyway. Summoners can't be summoned."

My mouth dropped open, and I snapped it shut. "I didn't know that. How do you know that?"

I felt him shrug. "My mom told me."

"How would she know that?"

"My mother knows everything."

"I'd like to meet her one day."

"She'd never come here. She hates the Slow World." He hummed a few notes of a song I didn't know. "Why are you blind?"

"Same reason you smell ozone and angel dust."

"Angel flash. After meeting Asher, I asked my mom about angels. She didn't know a lot, but she told me about angel dust and that the lightning they produce is called angel flash. I don't think they do it on purpose. It's part of who they are. We don't have angels in Faerie though, so I'm not sure."

"Angels from Heaven can't come into Faerie, and the fae can't go to Heaven. The realms can't touch."

My fairy friend chirped like a sparrow. "I did not know that."

"Yeah. Earth is the crossroads." I switched topics. "How are the Humbees doing? Are they helping you?"

Confusion laced his tone. "They were, but they bugged out."

I laughed. "Pinky! You made a joke!"

"I did?"

"Bugged out? For Humbees, who are like bugs?"

"Oh. Oh. Right. I see what you're saying. Ha, ha. That's funny."

He had no idea he'd made a pun. Typical Pinky. Such an innocent.

The idea of ruining that innocence made me squirm. "Pinky, I shouldn't be talking to you. I've been shunned, and you could get in trouble."

"Joey warned me, but I don't understand why."

"Titania banned me from all of Faerie for trying to summon Trace. She sent Laurel to tell me that it violated the Laws to summon a human."

"It didn't work because he's a summoner. And, yes, it violates the Laws of Magical Harmony to summon a human, but it doesn't break Faerie laws. Nothing bad happens. It simply fails."

"I don't understand. What's the difference?"

"The Laws of Magical Harmony are laws about how magic works. The Laws of Faerie are rules of the land."

"So, like the Laws of Newtonian physics versus the laws of the United States?"

"Uh huh." He sounded proud of me that I'd grasped it. "If you drop a rock, it will fall. No matter how hard you wish for that rock to stay in the air, it won't. It just doesn't work. That's what summoning a summoner is like. It just doesn't work. But no one is going to arrest you for it."

This was mind-blowing. "Then why is Titania so upset?"

Pinky tapped the bench, making it vibrate. "I don't know. There's no logical reason."

I thought about what Laurel had said. She'd explicitly said that summoning humans violated the Laws of Magical Harmony. She hadn't said anything untrue. According to Pinky, it did, but that just meant it would fail, not hurt anyone. There was no cause for a trial and judgment. Laurel also knew the person I'd summoned was a summoner himself, but she carefully avoided that topic.

Tricksy fae. Laurel hadn't lied, but she hadn't told me the whole truth. Titania was mad at me, alright, but not for summoning a human, and I'd been right about it feeling staged. She'd been looking for an excuse.

What had infuriated her so much that she'd had all of Faerie shun me?

"Pinky, have you ever heard the phrase 'the child of a changeling who isn't a changeling can upset the balance'?"

He drummed his fingers on the bench. "Once. I believe that the first part refers to a child who visited Faerie but came back to the Slow World. Someone taken to Faerie but released, not replaced with a fae child. I never understood why anyone would send their child to the Slow World to be raised as a human, anyway."

"I've read that the fae only steal beautiful children."

"Who decides what is beautiful?" Pinky asked, genuinely curious.

Such a poignant question. "I don't know," I finally responded.

"Me neither. I think you're beautiful, and no one stole you." A butterfly kiss landed on my cheek, there and gone. "I'll go home soon. Maybe I can ask my mom."

My sister's car horn blared in the quiet night.

"Gotta go, Pinky. Help me across the street?"

He did, but before he could leave, I whispered, "I think you're beautiful, too." His wings pulsed faster for a beat or two, and then he was gone.

Mickey drove us home in silence. "We need to talk more, but I'm too exhausted now to try. Besides, first and foremost, we need to get you to a doctor. I called Jonah, who was worried sick, by the way. He's made up the couch."

"That's nice of him."

"Did you at least learn something helpful from that conversation?"

"Yeah, I think I did," I said, wishing I could look out the window. "Humbees are insects, and fairies lie."

Chapter 26

Waking up to find out I was able to see had its downfalls. First, while relieved that the angel flash had faded, sight allowed me to see my reflection in the mirror, and it wasn't pretty. Angel flash sure did a number on your hair.

Second, it meant I observed Jonah making breakfast with a chef's knife in his hand. He brandished it like a sword he'd happily use to run me through. He whirled, pointing the knife's tip in my direction.

"You call my wife in the middle of the night and make her drive out to God-knows-where to rescue you, keep her out for an extra stop to talk to a homeless kid, and wake up this morning all fine and dandy?"

"I was blinded by lightning. . . ."

"Bullshit. You're weaseling your way back into your sister's life on false pretenses."

I barreled on. "Luckily, the flash blindness was temporary."

"I've told you a million times that I don't want your special powers, or the troubles they bring, anywhere near my family."

"They're my family too."

"You don't respect them like family. You don't treat them like family."

"What do you mean?"

"You *protect* your family. You don't drag them into danger."

I'd heard all of this before, and Jonah wasn't wrong. I didn't think they were in any danger this time, though. My current predicament was all mine.

Jonah chopped an onion like a pro and continued his tirade. "What do you want? Money? Mickey informs me you're out of a paying job again. Well, we don't have any to spare."

"I'm not asking for money."

He slammed the knife down hard enough to make the onion pieces jump. "What do you want, then?"

"Now that my eyes work, a ride to my Krav Maga studio would be good."

Jonah scraped the onions into a bowl, washed the knife, dried it, and carefully stored it in a knife block. When done, he grabbed a ballcap from a nearby closet. "Get in the car and tell me the address," he said, opening the door and motioning for me to exit. "Mickey's resting upstairs with Ruthie. I'll tell them you said goodbye."

"I need my bag. One moment." I walked into the living room and sent Mickey a quick text thanking her for everything and letting her know the flash blindness had receded. I told her Jonah was kind enough to drive me to the studio and I didn't want to wake her.

I hadn't told Mickey about Mom's message or answered her questions about Pinky. My stomach tightened at the thought of addressing those issues. Better to leave with Jonah. Besides, as much as I hated Jonah for giving me crap, I'd never blamed him for putting his wife and child first.

"Can I take a banana?" I asked Jonah as I returned to the kitchen.

He jerked his chin at the fruit bowl. "Help yourself. Take an apple, too. Anything. Just get a move on."

I grabbed the fruit and followed him to his truck.

We rode to the studio in silence, and when we arrived, Jonah gave me a terse nod with a begrudging, "Be safe."

"Thank you." He drove off with a rumble of his truck engine and nary a backward look.

It was too early for the studio to be open, so I sat on a bench outside and watched the clouds skim by, considering my position in the universe. To say I was on the losing end was an understatement. The temporary but terrifying loss of vision had nailed that coffin lid down hard.

Yet, summoning was my only power. It was what I did. I'd been marked with the Kiss for a reason. I had to believe that. There had to be more to me than a fluke of fate.

"Look who's bright-eyed and bushy-tailed this morning." Oded smiled at me as he came up the walk.

"I hoped to catch you early. I need your help again."

"Rivka, you always have me. Look at my face and my arm. Your wonder cream heals faster than anything I've tried before. I can't swear to it, but I think I'm breathing better too."

That's when I noticed he'd removed his bandages. His pink skin lay smooth and supple—no scars or angry red welts. Nothing sloughing or peeling.

"You look like you were in the sun too long, not as if you were burned," I commented, placing my hand on his chin to turn his face this way and that and then examining his forearm. "Amazing."

"I owe you."

I choked back a grunt of disbelief. "No. You owe me nothing. Don't say that."

He unlocked the door, and I followed him in. He locked it behind me and studied me for a moment. "How can I help you this morning?"

"Do you remember when you took me on that vision quest?"

"The guided meditation?"

"Whatever you call it."

"I guide. You meditate. You see what you need to see."

I paced farther into the studio and turned to face him. "Can you do that again for me? I think I'm approaching a problem the wrong way."

Oded raised his eyebrows. "You'll open up? Dig in? Let your mind see whatever it wants to, no matter how painful?"

I exhaled a long breath but firmed my resolve. "Yes."

"Well then, I require coffee. Dark roast?"

He brought me into their tiny little break room, popped in a coffee pod, and leaned back against the counter. "Tell me why you are asking this now."

"I'm trying to solve a problem."

"Yeeeeesss . . . ?" He grabbed his mug and added cream. No sugar.

I motioned him out of the way and nabbed a pod to brew my own cup. "I've been attempting to talk to a number of people who don't want to talk to me."

"And why is that?"

I hit the button, and the machine gurgled as it got going. "I don't know. But you said something the other day that made me think differently."

He sipped. "What was that?"

"You said that sometimes people have secrets that force them to make hard choices. I recently also told someone that maybe the reason they weren't finding what they were looking for was because they were taking, not giving."

"I'm not following exactly, but generally I like where you're going."

The bitter coffee needed more than cream and sugar. It needed to be thrown out. "Jeez, how do you drink this stuff?"

He chuckled. "Have you ever had Lebanese coffee?"

"No."

"I grew up on it. Sweetened only with cardamom. Drink that, and then this will seem tame. Now, don't go off topic."

Sipping slowly, I considered my next words. "I thought my

problems were all about me. But what if I'm wrong? I mean, they are about me, but what if they are equally about other people? What if instead of stewing on how people abandoned me, I examined why they left and try to figure out what I can do to improve that situation? Instead of asking them to give to me, see what I can do to give to them? Maybe they'll return and confide in me."

Oded set his mug in the sink, leaned over, placed his palms against both my cheeks, and kissed me on the forehead. "Finish that coffee. It's time to get to work."

We sat in the quiet of the empty studio. I'd closed my eyes and, for once, didn't peek to see what he was doing.

His soft voice floated to my ears. "Breathe in and out, comfortably. No counting. Just relax."

I released a huge breath, letting go of my confusion, anger, and frustration.

"Let your inhalations bring clean air into your lungs, and as you breathe out, release the tension. The air will clean your mind and spirit. The exhalation will rid your body of things it doesn't need to carry."

My body grew heavy, and instead of sitting up straight, my spine curved forward, as if my head weighed too much to keep it erect.

"Lay down, Rivka. Your body knows what it needs. Meditation doesn't judge you. It doesn't think anything is wrong with you in the first place. It just lets you see what is."

Sinking deeper within myself, I saw a staircase. I'd seen it before in a prior vision. It wound down in a spiral.

"I see the same staircase I saw before."

"Do you want to go down it?"

"Yes."

"Then go."

The staircase wound downward, seemingly forever, but a light appeared just as I was about to stop. Dim at first but then brighter as I progressed, it glowed yellow with pink and orange at the edges, like a sunset over water. I described it to Oded.

"Step into the light, Rivka."

My foot touched the spongy, moss-covered ground. A trickle of water flowed somewhere to my left, but I was unable to see the source. A flute played in the distance, answered by violin, not a duet but a conversation. The cool moss carpet soothed my feet, and when I looked down, I saw my bare toes polished in baby pink. I checked my hands, and my nails were the same color. My workout clothes had disappeared, replaced by a flowing mulberry A-line V-neck chiffon dress with a ruffle hem. I'd never worn anything like it. The dress trailed behind me, and I vaguely worried that the dampness would ruin the delicate fabric.

A pink, iridescent flash in the distance made me lift the dress and run. The iridescence reminded me so much of Pinky's wings. "Pinky?" I shouted. "Pinky? Is that you?"

If not Pinky, another fairy, I thought, but no matter which way I turned, I saw nothing but trees—trees lined up to the right and to the left, creating a path forward with no other way to turn. The glowing light intensified, and I squinted to see farther. Leaving the dress to droop as it may, I kept to the moss-covered trail. A tendril of fear wiggled through me, but I pushed it away with a mental shove. I needed to see what lay ahead.

I came upon a gray stone bridge, big blocks piled on even larger ones to make the superstructure. It had wooden abutments at the entrance in front of me. The bridge's stone floor, the deck, differed from the sides, made of tiny, interlaced river rocks that created a pebbled mesh, with no evidence of mortar of any kind.

A gigantic boulder blocked my path. I approached to see if I could walk around it. But as I did, the boulder shifted, issuing a painful, grating noise like rusted gears scraping against one another. I jumped back and watched the rock unfurl itself until a stone troll stood in front of me.

The troll's rough voice chafed my ears.

"Why do you come this way, human girl?"

"I don't know."

My answer amused it.

"You don't know, and yet, here you are. No one comes here without a reason, especially not a human."

"Where am I? Where is here?"

If a rock had eyebrows, his would have flown to the top of his head.

"You do not know even that?"

"I can guess," I answered, less afraid now. "I'm in Faerie."

The troll let out a satisfied rumble. "Correct. Now, why are you here?"

"I'm looking for answers."

He belly-laughed, his rock belly jiggling up and down like Santa's. "Everyone's looking for answers. What matters is the question." He beckoned. "Come closer."

I took two steps, then a third. I craned my neck to look him in the eye.

"Hum. You're here, but you're not. A quest of spirit but not of body. That's interesting."

"Why?"

He leaned down so his giant rock head was even with mine. "You don't know why you're here, and that's a question for you. The question for me is: Why did Faerie let you in?"

I wrinkled my nose. "Because I'm a nice person?"

He belly-laughed again, and I stumbled backward at the force of it.

"Not nearly enough a reason, but I like your spunk."

My shoulders drooped. "I'm not sure I'm a nice enough person though. I may be wrong about that. I try hard, but I'm selfish and confused."

The stone troll shrugged, a heaving motion that made the trees bend. "Why should you be different from anyone else? All we can do is try." The troll grew serious. "Is that why you're here?"

I decided to go for broke. "On Earth, I'm a summoner. I used to work in a fae bar but now I can't. I'm trying to find information about someone I knew a long time ago, and . . ."—I waved my hands around—"somehow I arrived here."

The stone troll's face grew serious, and he whipped out an axe from thin air. Made of rock with a sharp edge and an axe head the length of my entire body, the weapon slammed into the ground in front of me. "I'm sorry, tiny human, but I know who you are now, and you can't be here, by order of the queen herself."

"I didn't mean to come! It's not my fault."

"I understand, but my duty is clear."

"But I have to cross!" I darted to one side, and while he was enormous, his bulk made him slow. I sprinted over the bridge, ignoring the rushing water below me, and skidded to a stop at what I saw.

Looking off into the distance and apparently not noticing me running toward him, Trace tended a campfire. He was thinner than I remembered but had the same silver hair and beard, and he hummed to himself as he poked the logs and stirred the glowing embers.

"That's enough for you!" The stone troll scooped me up and threw me like a javelin.

I jolted awake in the studio, Oded sitting placidly in front of me.

"See anything interesting?" he asked.

"I saw the most important thing," I said, panting. "I finally know where my trainer is."

Chapter 27

I used a mobile app to call a car. My spiritual jaunt made me realize that whatever action I decided to take, I'd need to do it in private. Which meant I had to take care of first things first.

I directed the driver to So Long Noodles, nervous about how I would be received or if I'd even be allowed on the premises. I walked in the front door of the restaurant, the little bell tinging its welcome, and almost fainted with relief when Kenneth greeted me.

"Becs! You're back. I've missed you."

His T-shirt said, "I hate Chinese food, said no one ever." Truth.

"I'm happy to see you. Are your parents around?"

"Upstairs in our apartment. They'll be down in about an hour. I think they'd let you back in. My mom said maybe she'd been hasty."

"Ya think?" Kenneth's face fell at my snarky tone. I didn't want to hurt his feelings, but his mom *had* overreacted, and I longed to come home.

"I want to talk to them but not now, so it's good they're not here. I hoped I could talk to. . . ."

"Becs!" Three tiny voices piped up all at once. The next thing I knew, I had a wee one on each shoulder and a third on top of my head. Jimmy, the one on top of my head, must have been lying on his tummy because I rolled my eyes upward and saw his little face staring down at my nose.

"Are you home for good?" he asked, with a wide smile.

I rolled my eyes to the right, and Trick angled himself to look at me better. He crossed his arms and tapped a foot on my clavicle. "Not sick, are ya?"

"No, not sick. For goodness' sake." The death-curse blight thing was ridiculous. "I'm fine but not home for good. I'll need to get permission from Mr. and Mrs. Long or get out of my lease."

"Noooooooo!" Rin cried out from my left shoulder. "We'll talk to them. If yer not sick by now, then you probably aren't ever gonna be." He slipped and tumbled off my shoulder, arms pinwheeling. I caught him and placed him on the table. His two brothers joined him, scampering down my body to leap to the plastic tabletop. I sat to keep them company.

"You hungry?" asked Kenneth, already chopping vegetables.

"You know it. Even if I'd eaten a gourmet meal an hour ago, I'd want your food." He blushed, and it was so cute. "How's Petal?"

He got this dreamy look on his face and spoke softly, as if acknowledging something positive out loud would ruin it. "She's good. She had dinner with us last week."

"Wow. That's special."

"She's special," said Kenneth, giving me a shy smile. "And the pantry help think she's great."

"We do!" Trick said. "There's something about her, if you know what I mean." He nudged my hand with his elbow. I did know what he meant. Petal, to my now educated eye, had a little elven fae to her.

"Glowing skin? Delicate features?" I asked.

Jimmy nodded. "Exactly.

"Yeah, she's pretty great," said Kenneth. "Ack. The phone. Let me get this order." He answered the phone with a cheery, "So Long Noodles. How can I help you? What? No, we don't sell tacos, but if you want mu shu pork, we're the place to call." An extensive discussion of the dish's ingredients ensued.

I took the opportunity to whisper to my tiny friends. "She's not glamouring him, is she? Is he in any danger?" I'd rip her limb from limb if so, elven features be damned.

"We don't think so." Jimmy scratched his chin as he spoke, thinking it through. "Don't think she's got enough fae to do that. Think it's too diluted."

"Okay, let me know if you smell anything fishy."

I motioned for them to gather close.

"Gentlemen, I'm being spied on."

Rin tugged at his ear. "Who's spying on you?"

"And why?" asked Trick.

"The 'why' I don't know, but I figured out the 'who'."

Jimmy slipped his hands into his tiny pants pockets and eyed me. "Okay, so who is it?"

"Queen Clarissa and the Humbees."

Kenneth slid my egg foo young in front of me. "Queen Clarissa and the Humbees sounds like a rock band."

The food's smell made my mouth water, but I hesitated before digging in. I'd learned the hard way how hot it could be. I'd gotten a literal mouthful of hurt in the past by eating it too fast.

"More like a filk group, if you ask me, but they're not either of those things."

Trick sneered, an unattractive face I'd never seen on him before. "They're tiny little flying pixies, and they're an annoyin' lot, they are."

Kenneth's eyes grew wide. "Smaller than you?"

Jimmy's face mirrored his brother's. "Teeny tiny."

"Insect-sized, in fact," I added.

Rin flopped on the table. "They've been used as spies before. There's only one thing they demand as payment. One thing they crave."

"Pollen?" I guessed.

Trick pointed at me. "Got it in one. Do you know who they're reporting to? Who they be workin' for?"

"Somehow—and I know you won't believe me—but somehow their information is getting to a demon. . . ."

I drifted off as light dawned.

"What's their most favorite pollen?" I asked, already knowing the answer.

Rin put his hands behind his head and studied the ceiling. "They love it all, especially Slow World pollen. It's supposed to be tastier. But if I had to guess one type above all others, I'd have to say rose pollen. It makes 'em crazy though."

Jimmy sat crisscross applesauce and rested his chin in his hands. "The fae king's abolished roses in Faerie because of it. The Humbees forget to eat, stay up all night, and ignore their families. It's bad for them."

"Not to mention," Rin said with a waggle of his eyebrows, "roses cause great problems in Faerie all around. Faerie has a bad history with 'em."

I thought of *Snow White and Rose Red, The Rose Elf, Beauty and the Beast,* and all the other tales, and realized the truth of what he said.

Though once again, I thought I knew the answer, I needed to confirm. "What do they eat for food?"

"Blood, of course," answered Trick. "They're pixies."

I recalled the insect bite I got on the back of my neck the other night, the one where I'd slapped it and come away with a splotch of blood. I recalled the insects surrounding the street lamps the night I'd been banned from Joey's, but mostly, I remembered the roses in the front of Madame Francesca's store and the insects inside.

Gregory believed Perrick was addicted to home soil without understanding that the troll needed it to live. My sister accused me of being addicted to summoning. Well, they'd never seen Humbees. As angry as I was with them, I was furious with their supplier.

"Thanks for the info, gentlemen. Kenneth, may I borrow your car? I will bring it right back. Promise."

Kenneth looked me up and down. "Where's yours?"

"At my office."

"What are you going to do with it?"

"I've got a medium to shrink down to size."

He waffled for a moment but eventually assented. "Be careful with my car. She's my baby." He threw me the keys and motioned for me to follow him to the parking lot. He owned the cutest Kia Soul in what he informed me was "Mars Orange." I promised I'd bring her back safe and sound.

I stopped at a garden store, made a quick purchase, and drove toward Joey's, parking in my normal spot. I still couldn't see Joey's door, but now that I knew where Francesca's shop was, I headed straight for it. Of the six bushes in the front, two of them were bare, but the other four boasted huge, stunning blooms.

Diving right in, I pulled out my new fifteen-inch lopper and pruned away. Clip, clip, snip, snip, those roses hit the ground. I hated doing this to such beautiful bushes, but then I looked around and realized these roses weren't natural. Hundreds of bumblebees lay dead in the mulch around them and had spilled over to the sidewalk. Growling, I cut with fervor, regretting not getting an herbicide and killing the Humbees outright.

By the time I was on the second bush, Francesca's door burst open, and I noticed she was wearing the garnet tiara. "What are you doing?" she screeched. "You're killing them!"

"You mean the roses, the bees, or the Humbees?" I replied, waving my clippers in the air. A woman on the sidewalk hurried around me.

Madame Francesca balked at my question but then regained her ire and stalked toward me. "Vandalism. Destruction of property. I'm calling the police."

Her unwrinkled skin and shiny brown hair gave her away. "Why don't you show them your driver's license and convince them you're the same person? You've sucked so much life force out of these plants and into that garnet, you look like your own granddaughter."

"My abilities age me. It's not fair."

"It isn't." I meant what I said. It was a terrible side effect. "Let me guess what happened. The Warlock reached out to you and asked you to deliver a message to me."

She gave me a curt nod.

"But then he told you that if the Humbees reported back to you about what I was doing and you reported it to him, he'd teach you the spell to store life force in the garnet which you could use to offset the life force you lose talking to the dead."

Another nod, this time with a frown.

"Which all seemed like an even trade. You pass on a little information and in return, you get what you most desire."

She blushed, a pink flush that colored her cheeks and ears. "Well, when you put it that way. . . ."

"Where did you get the roses?"

"A witch. The same one who powered the amulet that hides the store."

It made sense, but I could see she hadn't thought it through.

"What's your plan when the roses die? Ask the witch for more?"

"Yes. Why not?"

"Because she's obviously Valefar's tool. She won't give them to you without a further bargain. He's planning on claiming your soul."

"I owe him nothing. It was a simple exchange. I got the roses from the witch. The roses attract and feed the Humbees. The Humbees spy on you, report to me, and I pass it to the Warlock. In return, I get the life force from the pretty magical plants to store in the garnet and use as needed."

"I admire your gumption. You push rose pollen on the Humbees, and you get youth to offset the aging of your magic. I can see where you thought this was a good deal." I snipped another blossom.

"Stop it!" She reached for my arm, frantic now. "Using your gift doesn't age you prematurely. You don't understand what it's like."

I pulled the clippers out of reach. "I'm sorry. I truly am. But you're forgetting something important."

"What's that?" She was panting, desperate for me to step away. "Come in for tea and let's talk about this."

"Absolutely not, but I will do you the favor of clipping these bushes. What you've forgotten is that none of this is natural. The Humbees shouldn't be here and certainly shouldn't have access to what is essentially a lethal drug to them. The roses themselves are poisonous— just look at the bees. And oh! Look. Butterflies. Your roses killed *butterflies.*"

"So what? It's just a few."

"It means the roses will eventually kill the Humbees, and possibly you as well, frankly speaking. And then who will own your soul, Francesca? Think about it. You've put your soul at risk messing with a demon and his servant warlock."

Her hand flew to her throat. "No, he doesn't get it. We made a deal."

"Did you have an end date on this agreement? Did he specify exactly how much information you'd have to give him to satisfy the deal?"

"N . . . n . . . no."

"You made an open-ended bargain with a demon's minion, which is the same as making a deal with the demon himself. My entire job is to keep people from making bad deals, and still, even with all my experience, I've failed at it in the past. I know Valefar's tricks. And he nailed you with this one."

"It's not true."

"It is true. Magic, as I was recently reminded, does not play fair, and roses in particular have a bad reputation."

"What do I do?" She sagged to her stoop while I cut off the rest of the roses, taking care to kick them into the mulch where they wouldn't be stepped on by innocent bystanders.

"Next time the Warlock comes calling, tell him this is the end of the deal. He'll relay that to Valefar, who will try to rope you into more time."

"How will this help?"

"Tell him you'll give him one last juicy piece of information about me, something I told you in confidence. But he has to release any hold on your soul."

She took off the tiara and immediately developed circles under her eyes. "What's the information?"

"Tell him that I know where my trainer is. That's something he'd want to know."

She bit her lip.

I cut the last rose.

"Why would you help me like this?" she asked.

"Because that demon's been a thorn in my side for too long."

Chapter 28

Francesca crept back into her shop, dejected but resigned. I carefully gathered several rose petals, storing them in a sandwich-sized resealable bag. Hopping back into the car, I crossed my fingers and drove to my next destination.

The library's square bustled with activity. A soft pretzel vendor. A late-season ice cream truck. A busker with an open guitar. No Jack, though. The man I'd last seen warning me away from the alley wasn't there.

Normal humans crisscrossed the walk, heads down and earbuds in.

I approached the entrance. "Uh, hi Dolphin. Hi Ram. Just me, hoping to get inside."

The statues rotated their heads ever so slightly to look at me. Since it was the first time they'd ever done this, I stood stock still and studied them, making sure I wasn't crazy. A man jogged down the steps, passing me, but he didn't notice. A woman with a child in a pram patted the ram on the side but also didn't notice their change in position.

But I certainly did.

"Ooookay, I just need information," I whispered. "You're sentinels, right? I don't think you're fae. Dolphins and rams aren't traditional fae creatures. You're not fae, are you?"

The ram snorted and pawed the marble foundation on which he rested. I took that as a "most certainly not." The dolphin tossed its head and burbled a laugh.

Thank goodness. I wasn't hallucinating.

"Okay, not fae. Coolio. But guardians of the library, of knowledge, perhaps?"

The dolphin flicked its tail.

"May I pass?"

The statues turned their heads and resumed their normal frozen positions. I took that as a yes, thanked them, and carried on.

The library appeared as it normally did. Two women rushed back and forth, helping people at the information desk. A "Mommy and Me" class with toddlers raised a ruckus in the children's section. Several folks typed away on computers, and a steady hum of activity simmered at the checkout counter. Light streamed through the stained-glass archway.

I took the elevator to the third floor, not sure what I would find. Would the fourth-floor pocket dimension open for me?

I greeted the old books as always, reassuring them they mattered. I took a little extra time, staving off possible disappointment. Then I rounded the corner, eyes closed. When I finally screwed up the courage, I peeked.

No staircase. No access to the fourth floor. Just a little school-sized wooden-and-metal desk with an attached swivel chair and narrow bookshelf under the desktop. It was nothing but a discarded piece of furniture thrown into an open, empty corner, forgotten, and abandoned.

This stung more than the apartment or Joey's.

Libraries were a refuge—a place I'd gone my whole life to read and learn. To escape the realities of growing up weird in a single-parent household. My knees buckled, and I folded into the desk chair, swinging my legs inside with the body memory of a third grader. I slipped my hands into the metal bookshelf for balance and leaned back, staring at the ceiling, willing it to open.

The ceiling stayed stubbornly closed, a vast white expanse of nothingness. Not even a water stain. I squeezed the underside of the bookshelf in frustration.

Something tickled my fingers.

I reached farther into the metal bookshelf opening and touched something smooth and cool. I placed my hand on the top, slid it out, and placed my find on the desk.

"Marks, Seals, Symbols, and Madness, Vol. 1."

Slim, with the same opalescent cover as the second volume, it too contained pages of scrawled, spidery handwriting. My head buzzed with excitement, and I opened the cover with trembling fingers, flipping to the K's.

Kiss, Summoner's Mark: calls forth powers from different planes; one who possesses the ability to bridge the worlds. Typically familial.

Huh?

I read it again.

I understood the first part but the second left me speechless, and the third made no sense.

So many questions. Who wrote this in the first place? Could they be trusted? Could this book be a total waste of time? And who would I ask? The implications swirled in my brain, amorphous trains of thought that petered out into nothing, although I knew I'd have to come up with an action plan eventually.

The only person who could have left me this book was Timothy, but since he couldn't interact with me, he must have left it here, assuming I'd come back to the library at some point. I concentrated on the space between my shoulder blades where fae favors and imbalances rested and sure enough, Timothy's favor to me was gone. The only thing left was my favor to Laurel, which, if I focused on it, gave me indigestion.

Out of sheer curiosity, I read the entry prior to "Kiss."

Kilt: marker of the Scottish Highlands. Pleated skirt worn by Gaelic men. See Unicorns; Kelpies, Nessie, Ghillie Dhu, Selkies, and Blue Men.

I flipped to the C's.

Changeling: Child, human taken, switched. Note: return nevermore or ruin evermore.

I shut the book with an outcry of frustration. "Geez. A little too Edgar Allan Poe if you ask me, and about as elucidating as bad haiku."

A meow caught my ear. "Stacks?"

The orange feline wandered out from somewhere and rubbed against my legs. I lifted him onto my lap and petted him in long strokes and then scratched under his chin. He accepted the attention as his due.

"Are you getting fed, boy?" I asked, rubbing his ears. "The fourth floor still exists, right? It's just me who can't get in."

The cat licked my thumb and nudged my hand, then jumped down and wandered away.

At least someone still liked me.

I tucked the book in my bag and wandered out, patting the ram and dolphin as I made my way down the steps. "Thanks, guys. Appreciate it." The dolphin shimmied against my palm and the ram rubbed against me, as if he wanted me to scratch his flank. I did so, thanked them again, and continued walking.

The music of "Mr. Tambourine Man" floated to me, and I followed the voice to the far side of the plaza. Jack stood there with his guitar, his open case at his feet. I threw a ten in, and he acknowledged me with a nod, switching with a wink to Tom Chapin's "Library Song."

I had allies, I thought. Full-on enemies, too. Friends that couldn't help me.

And adversaries that would.

I picked up my phone and called Gregory Adamos. Perrick answered.

"Gregory Adamos's office."

"Perrick, it's Becs."

"It's lovely to hear from you, Ms. Greenblatt. Mr. Adamos isn't available right now."

"Perrick, do we have to do this every time?"

"Ms. Greenblatt, I'll be happy to take a message. Mr. Adamos is in a meeting and can't be disturbed."

"Disturb him, Perrick. I don't give a rat's hairy ass who he's with."

"Once he is out of the meeting with the Andino Trading Company representative, I'm sure he'll return your call."

Ah.

"Gregory Adamos is having a one-on-one meeting in his office with Phillipe Andino? The old man came to Gregory's turf?"

Perrick whispered into the phone in an urgent rush of words. "No, Becs. His granddaughter, Anastasia Andino is here." Then, "I'll be happy to tell him you called. Have a nice day."

He disconnected, leaving me standing in the middle of the plaza, jaw agape. Anastasia Andino was in Gregory's office? Perrick had pronounced her name as "Anna-Sta-Zia," not "Anna-stasha." Interesting. Pretty.

But boy, did I have a bad feeling about this.

I got in the Kia but didn't start the car. Instead, I pulled out my phone and jumped on Google. The Andino family real estate holdings included malls, theme parks, and multi-cinema complexes. Entertainment was their bag. According to a business insider who spoke on condition of anonymity, business was inconsistent, and they'd recently diversified into corporate hotel offices and flexible workspace, divesting failing investments like a line of movie-themed miniature golf courses that once ran coast to coast. Front men and women, people in ten-thousand-dollar suits, Louboutin's, and diamond-encrusted wristwatches spoke for the family. An older man in a wheelchair, Phillipe, smiled from the church steps at his great-grandson's christening and cracked open a bottle of champagne on the bow of a ship.

There was almost nothing about Anastasia. One photo showed a smiling girl in a lavender party dress in front of a stunning blue ocean. The caption said the hotel was in Santorini and that it was her sixth birthday. The only other picture was a standard class photo when she graduated from Vassar.

I was reminded of my original search for Gregory and how I couldn't find him either. This woman was a phantom.

In my childhood, the word "phantom" was associated with toll booths. Dealing with them always had a cost.

Chapter 29

I dropped off Kenneth's car and used my phone to call for a ride to my office.

"What the hell happened here, lady?" asked the nice Pakistani driver, looking at the fragmented concrete driveway. "I can't drive any farther, it is so broken. This looks like an earthquake I lived through in Peshawar."

"No earthquake here. A lightning strike though."

"I didn't know we had a storm."

I opened my app to tip him and got out. "September's a wacky month around here."

"Be careful," he called to me. "If there is structural damage, the ceiling and walls could still fall."

"I'll remember that."

He waved and drove off to pick up his next fare and left me stranded in the wreckage of my office and the surrounding driveway.

I'd borrowed supplies from Kenneth, so I was able to replace lightbulbs, batteries, and clean up my space. I dust-busted my chair and swept and washed the floors. My sister had gathered my bobbleheads and books, but they required some care as well. I cleaned them off and put them back in the right order. It took hours to get the place set right. I collapsed in my chair, extracted the pen and journal from my knapsack, and reviewed my notes.

Some things on my original list had improved. For example, I knew where Trace resided. In Faerie. I just didn't know why.

I'd decided not to tell Mickey about our dead mother's voice coming out of another woman's body. Solid plan.

Thanks to that uber-upsetting message, I knew Trace was the changeling mentioned in the wacko prophecy of a changeling who wasn't a changeling. I surmised it had something to do with the fact that he was in Faerie and, as far as I knew, had never been replaced here in the Slow World, but that was a wild-ass guess.

Summoning Asher was right out, although the traumatic experience of trying to do so, plus some of his comments in the Dreamscape, made me think someone bigger on the food chain was keeping him away rather than him not wanting to see me. This made me feel marginally better.

Titania's edict banned me from the bar and impeded my friends, but some had found ways to communicate with me. Joey had given me money. Timothy had left me the book. Pinky had spoken to me outright, but I didn't believe anyone would hold him responsible for breaking the queen's decree. Pinky was Pinky.

I'd figured out who was spying on me and had rid myself of that problem, hopefully helping the Humbees in the long run. I was sure they didn't think so at the moment, but for their long-term health, getting rid of the demon's influence and the rose pollen was better for them. Valefar had used the medium and the itty-bitty fae to snoop on my activities and whereabouts and had added drug pusher to his list of crimes in doing so. I hoped Faerie had addiction recovery services.

Gregory was still a self-centered mobster, but our needs aligned for the moment. Though I worried about the new player, Anastasia Andino.

Kenneth and the wee ones intimated that the Longs might let me back into my apartment.

All in all, appreciably better, though not great. I still had no access to Trace, thus no training, so my major problem remained. The blight curse hadn't hit yet, and hopefully never would, but I hadn't tried to remove it. I wasn't sure I could.

I was also running out of money and hated sleeping in my office.

Something had to break soon, but I didn't know what button to push or door to kick down, what questions to ask or who might know the answers. I sat and watched the sun fall beneath the horizon.

When the oranges and yellows of sunset turned to dark pinks and purples, a shadow descended from above, at the corner of my vision. A second later, Asher stood in the open doorway. I didn't move.

"Hi," he said.

"Aren't you breaking some rules by being here?" I asked.

"A lot of them."

"Someone worked hard to keep you from me."

He waggled his hand. "It wasn't so much keeping me from you as discouraging you from summoning me, or anyone else in my position. It's considered. . . ."

He fumbled for words. I assisted.

"Rude?" I supplied.

"Impudent. Insolent. Presumptuous."

"I was going for cheeky and audacious."

He scuffed his shoe on the broken concrete and grimaced. "Not so much. Don't do that again."

"Message received."

"May I come in?" he asked.

"Sure. I don't have another chair for you, though."

He gave me a one-shouldered shrug. "No biggee."

I threw him my blanket. "You can fold this up and sit on it, if you want."

"Thanks." He grinned, a sudden ray of light in his otherwise gloomy demeanor. He tossed it back. "I brought my own." With a small wave of his hand, he conjured a white, fluffy cloud which skimmed the ground. He took a seat like a virtuoso piano player.

"That's handy."

He laughed. "It's a perk."

"Did you create that cloud out of nothing?"

"More like I politely asked if the moisture in the air would mind helping me out."

I stared out the door at the driveway. "Do you think you could ask, politely, if the concrete would mind fixing itself?"

"Concrete doesn't work that way, but because the damage was done by Heaven, I can reverse it."

I turned to look at him, confused. "Why does moisture work one way but the concrete works another?"

"Concrete doesn't have a spirit. It's a composite."

Like that cleared it up. I shifted to stare back out the door and sat up with   a   jolt. A smooth, unblemished driveway lay before me.

"That was fast."

Again, with the one-shouldered shrug. "It's the least I can do."

The sun disappeared and the crickets chirped, recognizing the early evening. My stomach growled, and I considered what I had to eat.

"Can you razza-ma-tazz us up some dinner?" I asked.

"No, but I could order take-out."

"Pizza?"

He pulled out a perfectly normal phone. "Mushrooms and black olives?"

"My favorite. Ask them for extra napkins and a cola." As an afterthought I added, "Please."

He placed the order, and we waited in comfortable silence until it was time for him to go get it. He left but not before he eyed me.

"You'll wait right here?"

"I have nowhere else to go."

And wait I did. I sat there, letting my mind wander. I watched a raven stalk across the driveway and admired his self-confidence. I listened to the rush of the wind. I hooked my leg over one of my chair's arms and swung it back and forth while reviewing all that had happened.

By the time Asher arrived back with the pizza, I was thoroughly befuddled. He doled out a slice on a thin paper plate and handed me napkins and my drink.

"Thanks. Smells delicious."

"You had good topping choices."

"Yup. I know my pizza." I swallowed a big bite. "What do I do now, Asher?"

"You rebuild. Find new employment. I'll ask the Longs to let you back into the apartment. Walk away from everything fae and summoning."

"But why?"

He didn't answer, and I didn't push. We munched the greasy goodness, finishing our first slices before I asked again.

"Why, Asher? Why am I expected to walk away from everything and everyone I know?"

He swallowed and wiped his mouth with one of the provided napkins. It was so thin he had to do it again, this time with a whole wad. He placed the dirty ones aside. "It's safer."

"Safer for whom? Safer for what? I was born with this Kiss." I tore off the leather cuff which covered my mark. "I have to believe it was for a reason. What don't I know?"

Asher set his pizza aside and stood, brushing crumbs off his blue jeans, before kneeling in front of me. He took my hands in his. "Becs, do you know why I was sent to Earth?"

"No."

"To watch out for you. To help you navigate your unique position. You're associated with the fae, but not fae. Summoning from Hell, but not destined for there. You walk a fine line and I—we—worried you'd fall over it, one way or the other."

"What does Faerie have to do with anything?"

Asher dropped my hands but kept his eyes on my face. "Summoners can cross dimensions."

"Yeah, the book said so."

His brown eyes furrowed. "What book?"

I got up, nudging Asher out of the way with my knee, and found my bag on my desk. I plucked the book from its depths and held it out to him. He took it from my hands with a mixture of respect and trepidation, the way one would hold a poisonous snake. He opened the cover and flipped through the slim volume. He repeated the process, turning page after page until he got to the end.

"They're blank."

"What do you mean, 'they're blank'?"

"The pages. There's nothing on them."

"You can't see the writing?"

He handed me the book and then rubbed his forehead, pacing a few steps before returning to my side. "I believe they exist, and that you can read them, but they're invisible to me."

"That's very strange. I promise you, the writing's right here. You can't see anything?"

"No. It's not part of Heaven. It belongs to another realm, which means I'm not supposed to see it."

Argh. This type of metaphysical bull was driving me crazy. "Why is that?" I asked. "Like, who made these rules?"

"Heaven, for one. But think of it however you like. The Universe. The fae king and queen. Buddha. Zeus. Amun-Ra. Take your pick. The realms cannot cross."

"I thought that Earth was the crossroads."

He sat in my chair and placed his head in his hands. His muscles bunched under his white T-shirt, and I admired how his shirt stretched to cover them. Asher was one great-looking angel. His hair tickled the shirt's collar, and, as always, I longed to run my fingers through it.

I bit my lip. *What a bad idea. Not the time. Focus, Becs. Focus.*

He interrupted my musings. "This is the point exactly, Becs. Earth is the crossroads. The bridge. We, meaning Heaven, Hell, and all the other realms, must not touch one another. Earth exists in between all of them. This is what allows balance, harmony, and free will. If the realms touched, the battles between them could destroy everything."

Asher's eyes caressed my face, even though we were feet apart. Warmth suffused my soul as if he'd wrapped his arms around me and we'd sailed close to the sun. His spirit touched mine, and it begged me to believe him.

"Okay, fine, I get this part, Asher. But what's this have to do with me?"

"You're a summoner born." He rubbed his hands together and

popped to his feet as if he couldn't stay still. "What I'm trying to say is that your abilities could cause the realms to touch. If that happens, Hell could get a hall pass into Faerie."

I rubbed my temples. "You're underestimating Faerie and the fae monarchs. They aren't pushovers."

"True, but the fae king's been keeping an eye on you, too, and the fae queen's decree has stifled your access, right?"

I perched on the edge of my desk and pointed at the opalescent-covered volume. "This book says a summoner can cross realms."

"Exactly my point."

"But it doesn't say anything about a summoner bringing two realms together. Nothing about making two realms touch."

Asher held me by the shoulders. He pulled me in close, and his heart beat against my cheek. I breathed him in and wrapped my arms around his waist, interlocking my fingers at the small of his back. I nuzzled his chest, and he let out a sigh, dropping his lips to the top of my head, murmuring soft, unintelligible words that nevertheless calmed my soul. I could have stayed that way forever.

He pulled back and placed a finger under my chin, lifting my head until we stared into each other's eyes. "Hell's been trying to access Faerie since the dawn of time, Becs, and they intend to use you to achieve it. Summoners can make the edges of worlds align." He flinched, swallowed. "Or kiss, if you will."

I jerked out of his arms. This was too much. "Are you freaking kidding me? Is that why the Kiss is called a kiss? Who invented this absolute craptastic garbage anyway? And, who put me in this position? Why me? I'm done with it. Done! You say I have free will?"

Asher studied me with a beady eye. "Yes."

I put one hand on my hip and snapped the other in a circle. "I free will everyone out of my life except the ones I choose to be in it. Get my apartment back for me and then free will your bad self along. And while you're at it, tell the Longs to tell the wee ones to communicate to the fae queen that I'm over her high and mighty self. I'm talking to who I want."

Asher raised an eyebrow. "You really want me to put the wee ones in that position?"

Propelling myself off the desk, I pushed past him, and stomped around the small space while he waited out my temper tantrum.

I threw my hands in the air. "Fine! No. Forget that part. Just tell her I'll never summon from Faerie again, but I do want my job back."

Asher crossed his arms. "I'm unable to talk to Titania directly—as you well know—so the job thing is on you. But not summoning from Faerie? Great. Wonderful. Don't summon from Hell either, and I'll leave you alone."

I didn't want him to leave me alone, not really, but I'd pretty much had it with the magical metaphysics, rules of harmony, and realm talk. I whirled on him. "All these powers had eons to figure this stuff out, and one scruffy summoner could be the death of it all? Failure on their parts—that's what this is. Utter lack of leadership. Poor management. A poverty of vision and communication."

Asher rolled his shoulders as if shifting a heavy weight. "Direct communication is forbidden, which is the whole point. You're not wrong, but you forgot the big wild card."

"What's that?"

"The human race."

"Oh, boo hoo. That's your excuse?"

My guardian angel sighed, a resigned sound that spoke of frustration and helplessness. "It is what it is, Becs. I'm low level here. Don't ask me for a better explanation."

I growled. "I've been steamrolled. Used my entire life. Every power in the universe has kept secrets from me, separated me from Trace, denied me the full use of my abilities, and spied on me, as if I was a covert agent in a foreign country. You came here to watch over me. The big O kept an eye on me. Valefar bugged me—literally! It's time for me to take control."

"Becs? What are you going to do?"

"I don't know yet, but I'm certain you won't like it."

"For Heaven's sake, Becs! Don't you see what is at stake?"

"No, Asher. I don't because no one will tell me! If it's so important, just spell it out!"

"Lucifer wants into Faerie so he can harness fae power and use it to cross into Earth and storm Heaven."

I stared at him, speechless, for what seemed like a decade.

Asher walked toward me, cautious, like he would approach a skittish colt, and took both of my hands in his. He leaned in, his eyes on mine, and I held still, letting him come to me. He kissed me on my lips, lightly at first, a soft touch, but pent-up passion exploded like a comet across the night sky.

We were all over each other, a scramble of T-shirts, buttons, shoes, and socks. My panties went one way and his briefs another. He lifted me in the air, something I'd seen in the movies but assumed never happened in real life, and carried me to my comfy chair. He sat, settling me on his lap. I nipped his lower lip. He growled in response, placed his large hand on the back of my neck and held me in place, his tongue wrestling with mine, his mouth demanding more. I rocked and ground myself into him as his other hand caressed my breast, my nipples, and, as our rhythm staggered, he used both hands to hold down my hips until all we saw were stars.

Afterward, we held each other, reveling in being together. Neither one of us wanted to move, and I wished we'd been able to go home, to my bed, and stay together for days without leaving. I ran my hand down his chest and listened to his breath catch. He sighed into my neck, captured my chin, and brought his lips to mine in a sweet kiss.

He released me but held his forehead to mine.

"I love you, Becs. Promise me something."

"What?"

"Don't do anything stupid."

Chapter 30

Asher left on an updraft of wings and wind, and I stared longingly into the sky for several minutes after he'd gone, wishing he'd come back.

Besides mind-blowing sex, he'd also blown my mind by saying he loved me, although I hadn't said the words back. I didn't get a chance to ask if that was allowed by Heaven's executive board. My guess was a hearty, "no," but since I hadn't seen an angel's rulebook in my trips to the library, I didn't know. I didn't want to know, honestly. If it wasn't allowed, then we could be in for a biblical smiting. They'd been a lot of that in biblical times. Frogs, floods, fire, and—oh, dear—slaying of the firstborn.

The last one was a little too close to home.

Deciding ongoing ignorance was bliss at this point and probably not making the best choices, given how high I was on post-coital endorphins, I made the executive decision that I wasn't going to ask and would keep the ride going as long as possible. If it was the spiritual equivalent of sticking my fingers in my ears and singing, "na na na, I can't hear you," then so be it.

I'd forgotten to remind him to ask Mrs. Long about letting me back in the apartment. I crossed my fingers, hoping angels had perfect memories and excellent follow-through.

I ate a slice of cold pizza and mulled over what I'd learned. Hell wanted to cross into Faerie, harness the power there, slink past everyone via Earth, and combine the forces of both realms to wage war on Heaven.

If that was all Hell had come up with over thousands upon thousands of years, then they hadn't gotten far. I'd meant what I'd said to Asher, too. The plan gravely underestimated Oberon and Titania. It was as if Hell didn't know what the hell it was doing. Greed. Avarice. Envy. Pride. Even Lust. The concept ticked off the deadly sin boxes like a checklist.

I still didn't understand how I was this scheme's lynchpin. In fact, it sounded ludicrous.

What didn't sound ludicrous—and what I knew for certain—was

that Trace was in Faerie. Trapped there? Enjoying an extended vacation? Gone fishing and hadn't come back? I couldn't know without talking to him. I needed to understand why he'd left, if he wanted to come home, and why the "daughter of the changeling that wasn't" referred to me.

Despite Asher's admonishment, I was going to do something totally, truly stupid.

Joey said there was only one being that could override Titania. This same person had been watching me and found me "interestin'."

Besides, summoning him was easy. All I had to do was say his name.

But before I did this monumentally dumb thing, I needed sleep and a shower. I snuggled into my chair and, despite my mind's whirling dervish thought pattern, fell asleep.

The Nightmarescape, the dark side of the Dreamscape, had been my personal bad dream playland since I was a teenager and had received the Kiss. It was where the Death Caps had reached me to kill the old man next door. It was where I'd battled numerous terrifying creatures and won the loyalty of the bow and arrows but had also suffered a debilitating sleep paralysis upon waking.

Always watching and waiting for an opportunity, the Nightmarescape took my fatigue as an opening and slithered in under the light of the fading moon, past my mental safeguards, and into my innermost thoughts.

The Death Caps towered over me, stories high, like a Chicago skyscraper, and they'd grown arms which dangled at their sides, all knobby elbows, and bony wrists. Their domed heads and tiny, glowing, stalk-tentacle eyes glared down at me, darting this way and that. They chattered amongst themselves in a language I didn't understand, encircling me, hemming me in. I was surrounded by Faerie psychological serial killers, and they wanted to toy with me, in the same way a cat played with a mouse before ripping its soft underbelly. Profound, unmistakable waves of hate smashed into me like a tsunami hitting the shore, and I was unambiguously, totally, out of my depth.

My usual smart mouth dried up. I had nothing. These creatures had haunted me off and on since childhood. And if you thought a thousand-foot-high talking mushroom wasn't scary, then you've never seen one. Because it wasn't just a *little* frightening.

It was pants-wetting terrifying.

I wished for my magical bow and arrows, but I'd left them propped in the corner of my office between the filing cabinet and desk, out of sight. I couldn't touch them from where my body was lying.

My breath came in rapid pants, and I fought for control. What would Oded say? "Learning how to not panic in a situation was a matter of physical practice and mental preparation."

Ha! I'd like to see him prepare for this.

I studied their front line and realized they had their skinny guys up front. In fact, they were all skinny guys. They needed to find some bulky recruits. But slender, top-heavy opponents I could work with.

In this scenario, running for it was an excellent option.

I took off fast, swerving to the left, and as their stem bodies shifted to block me, I juked right and fled right past them, as if running between their legs. Mushrooms weren't swift. They screamed at me in a high-pitched whine that hurt like an ice cream headache.

Running until I couldn't see them anymore, I stopped to catch my breath. I bent over, hands on my knees, and something bumped the back of my head. The quiver. The bow and arrows had made it. I noted the newly materialized cross-body strap.

"Thanks for showing up."

The quiver shivered in delight at being on my back in the pitch-black Nightmarescape while our physical manifestations remained motionless in the real world. It practically hummed in happiness.

I chided it. "We're not engaging in fungus fight club."

It burbled as if to say, "We'll see."

A spotlight appeared above me, harsh light illuminating me in a tight circle. I crouched, drawing an arrow. The blinding light meant everyone could see me, but I couldn't see anyone. I closed my eyes, recalling my flare blindness and how I'd listened for my sister's movements. A stagger step to my right had me rotating to keep my arrow pointing in the correct direction. The walk sounded like a one-footed man was dragging a heavy duffel. Step/thunk, swish/drag. Step/thunk, swish/drag.

I smelled brimstone.

"Interesting finding you here, Rebecca Naomi Greenblatt."

I knew that voice.

"Derrick. Are you being a good little warlock for your demon master?"

"We have our moments."

A rush of fire created a perfect circle around me, and the spotlight dimmed as the fire's glow turned everything around me orange-red. The Warlock stepped into the light. I let the eager arrow fly. He dodged it, but it cost him. He stumbled and landed on his side with a cry of pain.

Derrick looked worse for wear. He wore Tour-de-Hell chic, a black stretchy T-shirt with black lycra bike shorts. His normal right foot was offset by a twisted, broken left that ended in a second knee and lower leg, complete with calf, shin, and foot. It looked like he'd had an extra half leg pegged to his original foot. The superfluous appendage dragged across the ground, creating a repulsive homunculus that made me bring my hand to my mouth in horror.

"Oh, this?" the Warlock said, waving off his malformed bottom half. "I made the mistake of boasting to another of Valefar's souls that I was using our connection—yours and mine—to gain a leg up in Hell. Valefar gave me this as a reward."

"Teach you to speak figuratively."

"It's temporary."

I seriously doubted that. "How's your father?"

"Withered to almost nothing." Derrick said this off-handedly, like it didn't matter.

"Why are you here in my Nightmarescape? And how did you get in?"

Thunk/swish, thunk/swish. He moved closer. His skin had melted in a rivulet from his right eye to his chin, as if a steaming hot tear had created a tunnel in his face. His eyes held the same unhinged fervor as before. His iron-bound wrists shimmered bloody red, drops of glistening, pink-tinted fluid plopping to the ground. He gestured, flinging the liquid in a wide arc. I ducked the revolting spray.

"We have a connection, you and I, Rebecca. It's a tiny thread but one I hold dear. I tugged it in order to have a word with you."

The blood droplets hit the ground and sizzled. I swallowed and stepped back. "What do you want?"

"Out," he said, a high flush growing from his neck to his forehead. "I want back to the surface. I want to live again."

"I can't do that."

"You can."

I shook my head. "No, I can't. I don't know how. Even if I did, why would I save you?"

"I'll remove the death curse."

"While that would be nice, I don't have the means to release you. You're dead and in Hell because of your own actions."

The Warlock paced in his jarring manner, and I couldn't help cringing.

"I see your reaction. I look awful. I'm disfigured and disgusting. But this is. . . ." He rushed toward me, stopping at the spotlight's barrier.

"This is *nothing* compared to what I've endured since I've been down here." He pressed against the spotlight "wall," leaning against it like a mime, willing himself through, desperate to reach me.

There was nothing I could do. "It's Hell. You're dead. There's no place for you on the surface."

"Tell Gregory Adamos I'll help get his mother out of Hades, and I'll stick to my promise to remove the death blight. There's got to be something you can do. Summon me each evening so I can serve you."

"That's a hard pass."

A giant, fiery hand surged down from overhead, plucked Derrick up, and cackled an eerie laugh. "Tut, tut, Derrick. Don't talk to the help."

The fire went out, leaving smoldering embers in its wake.

I inhaled one shaky breath.

Then plummeted through a hole under my feet. I plunged into a deep-green inky haze and despite all my efforts at control, I screamed my throat raw, tumbling end over end like a rock over a cliff. I barely held onto the bow and considered dropping it to cover my head. The second the thought entered my head, it vanished from my hands and returned to my back. I landed, hard, on a moss-covered surface, springy enough for walking but not nearly soft enough to cushion a swift, long descent. I hit the ground with an *oomph*. A loud *pop* reverberated through the air, and I couldn't breathe or move. Trying to fill my lungs, I gaped like a fish, mouth opening and closing until finally something released, and I inhaled, the air rushing into my oxygen-starved body.

Moving brought racking pain. I'd dislocated both my knees. I lay on the moss, staring at an unfamiliar night sky, disabled, bruised, and bleeding. Humbees swarmed me, darting in and out, taking tiny sips of my blood from the open cuts, using sharp claws to make new ones. They feasted like hungry ticks on a deer's back. A larger Humbee, about the size of half my thumb, hovered in front of my eyes.

I managed to gasp, "Queen Clarissa."

The queen buzzed in front of me. "You ruined our arrangement."

"Please stop eating me. The rose pollen isn't good for you. I meant well."

"You cut us off all at once." Her wings whirred faster.

I hadn't considered the effects on the Humbees of going cold turkey. I shook my head to shoo her tiny subjects, but they kept at it, covering my entire face except my nose, mouth, and eyes, and I struggled to stifle my panic.

"I'm sorry about that. Is there an easier way to wean you off it?"

"Too late. I've already lost three of my hive. The hunger drove them mad. They threw themselves at the gate until they died."

Weakness coiled through my limbs. "I can't help you if I'm dead."

"Your punishment is pain. Wallow in it, suffer through it. Feel the need for oxygen and blood sing through your body until you're so desperate you'd do anything, promise anything, buy anything, or sell anything to get it."

"Withdrawal."

"Agony. Don't underestimate the power of the hive mind."

"Please, please don't." My feeble protestations failed to move her. Humbees blocked my nose, closed my mouth, and sat on my eyelids. The air in my lungs squeezed out, all used up, until the drone of their wings faded, and my vision tunneled to a tiny black dot with scattered red bursts. My heartbeat throbbed in my ears, louder and louder still, while my muscles cramped and my stomach revolted, nausea gripping my midsection. My whole body burned from the inside out.

Suddenly, I rolled on my side and the Humbees vanished. A hand rubbed my back in circles, and a musical voice urged me to breathe. The hand moved from my back to my destroyed knees. Something sticky and cool dripped on them, and the warm hands rubbed whatever it was into my joints. The pain flared but then receded, and I found I could both breathe and move. I opened my eyes to a mosaic of swirling green and black. I couldn't see my savior.

"Good. You're improving. Now, you'd best leave before the fae queen finds you here. I'll leave this bottle for you."

"I didn't mean to come."

"You're here, nevertheless. Traveled in spirit, true, but she won't care. A trespass is a trespass in her mind. Inflexible, that one is. But she and her husband have kept us safe. As safe as they could. Times are changing though. You being here proves it."

"Thank you for helping me."

"Tsk. You know better than to thank a fae."

I nodded and tried to sit up but collapsed, wracked by hacking coughs.

"Guess you need a little more time. I'll sit here with you and keep the Humbees away. But recover quickly, my child, or we'll both be in trouble."

"I don't know how to return." I patted the ground around me, and the bow and arrows came immediately to my hand.

"You're a summoner born, Becs. It's in you, even in your dreams."

"I'll try."

"Good. I'll be leaving then."

"Wait. You did me a favor, but I don't feel an imbalance," I said to the air as I felt her warm presence depart.

"Because there isn't any. You did right by my Pinky, Becs, when no one else would, and returned him to me. A mother's gratitude knows no bounds."

Tears pricked my eyes as I realized who my savior was.

"I didn't do anything special, just what was right. Pinky wanted so badly to return to you."

"And you, and only you, made sure he did." Pinky's mother squeezed my hand once. "Now, grab that medicine bottle near your right hand and skim the edges home."

Chapter 31

Skim the edges? Sitting up made me wretch, and I was supposed to skim a metaphysical barrier between worlds? These words made no sense to me.

I screwed up my courage and shifted to my newly healed knees, surprised when they didn't twinge at all. Neither did my back or shoulders. I grabbed the bottle of healing ointment and held it tight, not wanting to lose this priceless potion.

Creaky, exhausted but not dead, I got my feet under me and rose, one wooden limb at a time. The quiver lay firm on my back, a constant, reassuring pressure. "Can you hold this?" I asked it, and the medicine bottle disappeared from my hand, settling into the quiver. I guess it had pockets, or a purse. A bag of holding? I didn't inquire but simply said, "Thank you."

How would I find an imaginary border between worlds? If Pinky's mom was right, my talents allowed me to feel this naturally, the way a violinist heard perfect pitch or a painter differentiated butter yellow from summer daffodil. Without Trace to teach me, I had no idea where to begin. Without an instructor, I was all innate talent and no disciplined craft.

An arrow nudged me. "I know, I know. We need to hurry."

Hurry. Movement without thinking first always got me in trouble, as Oded had reprimanded me, and yet, that's what I needed to do now.

That thought brought another one. I did have a teacher. Not Trace, but Oded. Oded didn't want me to act rashly, but he did want me to trust myself and use my inner vision to find my way. I closed my eyes and thought about the staircase.

The staircase materialized in my mind, but this time, instead of leading me down, it wove sideways, like a catwalk above a theater. It twisted, curved, descended, and elevated, but with each step, I moved laterally. I held onto the wooden handrail, taking cautious steps.

I halted when the catwalk rotated so far to the right that I'd be sideways, parallel to the whatever counted as ground in this place. I envisioned myself flying off the walkway, like a plush teddy bear stuffed into a human-sized rollercoaster seat. This wasn't skimming edges. This was fighting a riptide blinded by ocean spray. My throat closed at the thought of flipping over the metal bannister into the fathomless bottom.

Metal? It had been wood. The catwalk was changing along with the realm. Faerie wouldn't tolerate cold iron, but it would be fine in the Slow World. I bit my lip and shuffled along, taking a leap of faith but still gripping the railing for all I was worth. It was as if I walked in the blackness of a moonless night with only my feet and hands to guide me, my brain screaming as I rotated slowly upside down, telling me this was impossible. I blinked and bits of sandy particles found my eyes, but I didn't dare release the banister to rub them. Instead, I batted my eyelashes furiously to clear them while they watered from the irritation. Tears ran down my face in warm salty lines, and I let them drip freely.

I stopped, suddenly wanting to laugh in hysteria.

The tears still ran *down* my face. The standard laws of gravity didn't apply in this place. I walked horizontally with as much ease as I walked vertically. My hair didn't even sway. Gaining confidence, I sped up, holding my breath as I turned upside down and back again. The catwalk existed in space, like the planet Earth or the moon or Saturn. There was no north or south. No east or west. No up and down. Those concepts were human ideas designed to put order to a disorderly universe. Here, in the void, it was the walk alone.

I moved faster, smiling as I surfed the walk's wave with increasing ease.

The more I relaxed, the more I saw, my blindness giving way to vision. The surrounding emptiness cleared, and shapes, then scenery, then an entire panorama emerged. Behind me lay a glowing green light, and if I squinted, treetops oscillated in gentle, swooping motions, obeying a wind I couldn't feel. Something glittered within the trees, accompanied by a tinkling of laughter. Beyond the trees lay mountains and a sparkling, blue sea. The tranquil sea cracked wide open when a behemoth broke the surface, opened its mouth, and swallowed a mouthful of sparkly wings. I'd heard of these giants but had never seen one as gargantuan sea creatures didn't typically visit Slow World bars for ale. A shock of electricity shot out of the trees, striking the Goliathan, which roared before sinking beneath the surface.

I quickened my steps.

Concrete and brick buildings rose in front of me with smoking chimneys, the clatter of train wheels, the toot of a tugboat, and the odor of gasoline. Trees popped into view with macaws screaming from their branches. A small patch of ice floated by, bringing with it freezing air and a huddle of penguins. A curious giraffe stared at me with big eyes and long lashes, and a helicopter buzzed over my head. A baby's cries overcame the macaws followed by the murmurings of its mother. A gorgeous oil painting morphed into a human-sized sculpture which itself turned into a flickering movie showcasing an orchestra playing "The Planets" by Gustav Holst.

Despite my increasing confidence, the sheer magnitude of it all dizzied me, and I closed my eyes, letting the pull of the walkway's wave drag me along.

The sounds faded away, and the walkway spit me out into a brightly lit corridor that could have belonged to any office building. The nondescript hallway took me to a parking lot which ended at a double door with an automated handicap button. "Welcome to the Supercenter," a sign said. "For all your shopping needs."

I walked into a high-ceilinged, fluorescent warehouse filled with giant-sized boxes of granola bars, cellophane-packaged jugs of laundry detergent, twenty-four packs of toilet paper, massive quantities of paper plates, kitty litter, and dog food, and a back counter that showcased rotisserie chickens.

A bright, fresh-faced teenager greeted me. "Welcome to the Supercenter! First time here?"

Uhm. . . . "Yes?" I answered.

"Great!" she chirped. "Let's get you set up with your membership."

"I need a membership?"

"Oh, yes. There's a cost to everything, you know. You can't pass through without buying something. Nobody leaves a warehouse store without buying at least one item. Usually more than they need."

She guided me to a desk where an elderly man with a gray beard and a red vest waited.

"Hello," he said. "Can I please see your pass?"

I patted my pockets. "I don't have a pass."

"Yes, you do," the man said, with a patient air of someone who'd done this before. "Show me your wrist."

Oh! I removed my cuff. The Kiss pulsated warm against my skin. It had never done that before.

"Scan here." He motioned to a card reader on the counter. I placed my wrist on the reader, and it beeped a cheerful tone.

"Excellent. Very good. You're all set, Rebecca."

"How do you know my name?"

He pointed to the computer screen connected to the reader. "It's all here. Get a cart and pick an item." He pointed with his other hand toward giant shopping carts nested into one another thirty carts deep. Extracting one involved a lot of shaking and jiggling. The man and teenager watched impassively.

I rolled my cart through the aisles. *Wow.* Twelve dollars and twelve cents for a thirty-five pack of cola. Thirty packs of trail mix for $8.27? What a deal.

I didn't need any of these things though. I wound my way through the wide aisles, searching for something useful.

Leaving the cookie area, I rounded the corner to find empty shelves except for a few, irregularly stocked cartons, bottles, and canisters. I wandered down the aisle, reading the labels.

Hen's Teeth, Silver Lining, Thick Skin, Hedged Bets, King's Ransom, and *Golden Ratio.*

These intrigued me. Especially one: *Free Rein.* I stood on my tiptoes to reach the bottle, no bigger than a saltshaker. My fingertips touched the edge of the amber glass, and it wobbled. I feared it would fall, so I placed my foot on the lower shelf and hopped up to get it. I tucked it into my palm, stepped off the shelf, and placed it in my cart, following the overhead signs to checkout. I pushed the cart into the narrow space next to the register, removed my one item, and placed it on the belt.

"I'll take this."

The cashier studied me. "How will you pay?"

"I don't know. I don't have any money." This had worried me, but I figured there had to be a way to do commerce.

The cashier flipped through her laminated price list. "You can trade."

"I have nothing to trade."

"Yes, you do." She motioned to my back.

Alarmed, I grasped my quiver's strap. "These are not for trade."

"I didn't mean the bow and arrows. If I wanted those, I'd ask them directly."

Oh, right. "What did you mean?"

"The 'Just What the Doctor Ordered.'"

"The healing ointment?"

She nodded.

I hated to relinquish such a generous gift. It could help a lot of people, including me, in case of injury. I'd called it priceless earlier, but I'd been mistaken. It had a price, and that price was removing the deep itchy ache between my shoulder blades. With deep regret, I handed it over. The cashier smiled, passed the bottle of Free Rein over the scanner, which blipped a jaunty *bing*. The cashier said, "Have a nice day."

I took my purchase, put away my cart, and exited. As I passed through the automatic sliding doors, a woosh of wind from above my head forced me to close my eyes and. . . .

I woke with a start, back in my office chair. The quiver and Free Rein sat next to me on the floor. My body rebelled at its recent travels, and I heaved. I made it outside to the grassy field just in time. I rummaged in my car for supplies, rinsed with mouthwash, and ran my last wet nap over my face. I checked the horizon. The sun hadn't risen yet.

Time to get to work.

The storage facility sat next to the highway, and some nice city planners had created grassy areas around the high-traffic area to help absorb sound. Late-season wildflowers grew in the bit of the field next to my office, among the weeds and tall, reedy grass. When the Warlock had killed the birds at my apartment, I'd brought the bodies here and let nature take its course.

I snipped some of the field's wildflowers, brought them into the office, and placed them along the circumference of a circle I drew in green chalk. It was still a binding circle, but I wanted to make it friendly. I added a shot glass of tequila, a chocolate bar, and the Free Rein.

"Laurel, pixie of Faerie, I seek your audience. Not a summons. An invitation to balance the favors between us."

A blue, icy circle swirled on the floor, wispy vapor winding lazily up toward the ceiling. This time, pink ribbons of warm air joined in, like a soft summer breeze, and the scent of orchids filled the air.

Laurel opened a door I could not see, walked through, and closed it behind her. Her suspicious gaze and tapping foot matched the snarl on her otherwise beautiful face.

"I don't like being summoned," she said.

"I didn't summon you. I invited you as a guest."

She crossed her arms. "I have to get back to Titania, and I'm breaking the rules by being here." She crinkled her nose. "You said you wanted to rebalance the scales between us?"

"I do. Look down."

The Free Rein amber glass bottle lay at her feet. She picked it up and read the label. Her mouth dropped open.

"Is this what I think it is?"

"I can't promise how well it will work, but it cost a lot, so it had better do what it says."

Her voice shook, unusual for this supremely confident pixie. "This will free me from my bond with the queen."

I shrugged. "That's what I'd hoped. I figured 'free rein' and 'free reign' was a trivial matter of interpretation."

She lifted her eyes from the bottle to look at me. "Titania's going to hate you."

"She can't hate me any more than she does already, and she shouldn't object to me correcting an imbalance."

The pink whorls twinkled. "She won't. Imbalance is bad for everyone. You're right." She laughed. "I think you're getting the hang of this. Consider us even."

The imbalance's sting between my shoulder blades evaporated along with Laurel's form as she stepped through the invisible door and disappeared. Rolling my shoulders, I exhilarated in the freedom of movement. I hadn't realized how much that favor had weighed.

I stood straighter and scarfed down a protein bar. It was time to get my apartment back.

Chapter 32

Remembering the adage that it was better to ask for forgiveness than permission, I simply moved back in. The Longs hadn't changed the locks again, so I entered my apartment as if nothing had happened.

The empty bird feeders needed filling, although Kenneth must have filled them every so often because sunflower seed shells lay strewn on the fire escape platform. Leaves and petals covered my small table, and I brushed them off, letting the detritus fall to the ground below.

I dumped my stinky clothes in the tiny stackable washer and dryer unit in my hall closet and showered in my own shower again, luxuriating in my lavender body wash and tea tree shampoo and conditioner. I'd grabbed travel versions of things when I'd left the house, and it was nice to have my favorite products again.

After dressing, I dusted and vacuumed the apartment. Finally, I ordered takeout from the Halal Arabic restaurant in the shopping strip next door, requesting that they bring it to the back. After tipping the delivery guy cash for walking over, I scarfed down spicy cauliflower with tahini dressing and falafel salad like I'd never seen food before and tucked the remaining pita away for later.

Clean and fortified, I curled up in my bed to take a nap. Navigating the Dreamscape and skimming the edges between realms had exhausted me. I prayed I'd be able to rest.

But it wasn't that easy. My mind, weary as it was, ruminated on Trace being in Faerie. What was he doing there, and why? I couldn't get off the mental Tilt-A-Whirl, the questions careening through my brain, reexamining everything I knew about my trainer.

Eventually, sheer exhaustion took me. I dropped back into the Dreamscape, but instead of seeing scary nightmare creatures, I floated to a verdant grass lawn in the back of a white, clapboard house with a large back patio. A lush patch of woods lay off to my left, sun-dappled leaves of several oak trees undulated overhead, and a light breeze cooled my skin. It was a warm, lazy summer day that makes you think autumn is never going to come and popsicles are forever.

Childish giggles to my right made me turn that way. I shifted so I could see the kids better while still hiding in the shade of the trees. Two children, a boy and a girl about age five, played tag on the grass. The boy tapped the girl on the shoulder, and she tumbled to the lawn, laughing hard.

I recognized the girl as a young tree nymph, a Meliae, and I scooted farther away from the beech trees to avoid being in their reach. The sapling tree nymph wore a one-shouldered, flowy silver dress, so airy that it floated in the breeze at the asymmetrical hem with the slightest of movements. She pranced and frolicked like a baby ballerina just getting used to toe shoes.

The boy was human, with a little kid's energy, jumping up and down at the nymph's giggles then falling next to her so they could roll in the grass. He tickled her neck, and she squealed, peals of laughter that echoed through the wood. The boy got up and teased, "Chase me, Tuli! Bet you can't catch me." They ran in circles until they tired themselves out, collapsing into a puddle like puppies.

One of the beech trees lowered its branches to brush their heads and, regaining energy as only children can, they popped up, leaping for the leaves, never reaching them because the beech tree cleverly bounced the branches a little too high.

The children tried again, chortling so hard, tears leaked out of their eyes, but the tree snatched the leaves back. The kids ran into the woods and hugged the tree, begging it to show them its leaves, pleading for more play time. Long branches wrapped their torsos, hugging them back . . .

. . . then sucked them into the trunk. Boy and girl disappeared. I froze, not sure what to do. I snapped my head toward a woman who opened the house's back door. She wiped her hands on an apron and yelled, "Son! Son? Where are you?"

A man joined her, using his hand to block the sun from his eyes. "He's disappeared again, hasn't he?"

The woman clasped her hands together, rubbing one thumb over the other in a repetitive motion. "He's got to be around."

A gentle swish, like the opening of elevator doors came from the oak tree, and the boy stumbled out.

"Here I am, Mom!" he yelled, skipping to her, unharmed and happy.

"Where do you go when you vanish like that?" she asked, fear still in her eyes. I moved closer, staying as silent as possible. Her eyes were the same green-gray as her son's.

The boy fidgeted, scrunching up his little face. "I'm playing with Tuli, Mom. I told you."

The father pointed inside the house. "This imaginary friend thing is ridiculous. This has gone too far. You scared a year of my life away."

I glanced at the trees, sincerely hoping they weren't taking years off this man's life. You never knew.

The mother sighed. "Gideon, you've got to stop disappearing. . . ."

Bam! Bam! Bam! That godforsaken woodpecker jerked me out of my sleep by rat-a-tatting on the telephone pole. I pulled at my clothes which were drenched with sweat.

Had it been a dream, or was it a vision?

The woman had called the boy "Gideon."

Had I just seen my father and grandparents?

Chapter 33

The new insight made me rethink my assumptions and catalogue my questions. If my father had a nymph friend, had traveled to Faerie and had come back, still himself, not a fae child replacement, then he was a changeling who wasn't a changeling.

But my mom had said Trace was the changeling.

The implications made me shake with rage at being duped my whole life.

Only one person had the answers, so I was back to my monumentally stupid plan. This time, I was going in with my eyes wide open and a healthy dose of self-preservation. I was under no illusion that I'd be able to contain a power of such magnitude, but I hoped to summon him so politely that he'd be relatively understanding. Maybe I'd slow him down a little if he was so perturbed at being summoned that I could run away.

I'd tell him I found him "interesting" and see how he liked it.

I rummaged in my hall closet and under my bed, finding items I'd put away as keepsakes from long ago. I stashed them in my backpack and the back of my car, packing them carefully. I also wrote a new note to Kenneth and a letter to Oded. I put Oded's letter within Kenneth's envelope and asked Kenneth to give it to Oded if I didn't return within the week. I figured if I couldn't get back within that time, I was probably dead. I taped it to the outside of the front door.

Mickey was the challenge. How to communicate everything that had happened, everything that I had learned, without raising incapacitating worry? Grabbing my phone, I texted her.

Hey. I typed.

Where have you been?

You know that problem we discussed?

Which one? You have several.

Shoot, that was rude. Correct, but impolite. Good thing she was my sister. I typed again.

Pffft. I mean the main one, not having a trainer.

Yeah . . .

Doing something to address that. It's a little dicey.

Dicey? What do you mean by dicey? Dicey as in dangerous?

I hesitated, not sure how to answer that. She typed back first.

Wait! Is this a "goodbye, in case I get killed," text?

I paused again. That's exactly what this was. I hated to lie, but sometimes dissembling is the better course of action.

No. Don't be silly. ☺ Just touching base. Lots to talk about later.

Okay. Be careful. Love you.

Love you, too. Kiss Ruthie for me.

That done, I closed up the apartment, jogged down the steps, and drove off, never having seen the Longs. I was totally okay with that.

My next stops took me to the grocery store, a hunting and fishing store, and a Wiccan shop that was egalitarian about whether something was Wiccan, fae, or Celtic. I drove through a fast-food joint and had them pack my order to go. By the time I returned to my office, a pale moon hovered in the sky, despite the persistent sunlight.

Rolling up my sleeves, I got to work. I chalked a seven-pointed star, a challenge because it had to be drawn in one smooth motion. It took me seven times to achieve it, which seemed prophetic.

I added a bundle of sage and bay leaves to one point and a bundle of basil, rosemary, and thyme to an opposing point. An eight-inch bone knife, a real deer antler, and a leather pouch filled with tobacco went on three more points. It was the same tobacco brand I'd given Mildread, and she'd liked it, so I stuck with it. On the sixth point, I added a bowl of tumbled river rocks and a cluster of quartz, for harmony. And on the seventh and final point, I added the book with the strange opalescent cover.

I drew a circle around the whole symbol, knowing full well that a binding circle for this summoning was probably for naught, but it made me feel better. I closed my door and changed into brown leather pants, a camouflage T-shirt, and my brown boots. I braided my hair, weaving in strands of baby's breath and added the bow and arrows to complete my outfit.

Hunting, Earth objects, a hint of the wild, and a fae book, plus the Faerie Star. Rolling my shoulders, I focused on my task, blocking out all stray thoughts.

"Oberon—"

Whoosh! And he was there. Just like that. A split second of time and his name. I stumbled back two paces.

Oberon wore full hunting gear. His own quiver, a long knife tucked into a sheath on his right leg, and a greenish-brown cap to hide his auburn hair. His beard hung to his chest in a luxurious waterfall. I wanted to pet it.

The Irish wolfhound was unexpected. He was the tallest, broadest dog I'd ever seen. He reached Oberon's waist, and Oberon, in his full form, was clearly taller than seven feet, since his head almost brushed my eight-foot ceiling.

Oberon bowed. "Rebecca, thank you for the invitation."

"I . . . thought you'd be mad."

Oberon kneeled to examine my offerings. "No, lass. I expected this call." He ran a finger over the deer antler. "This is beautiful. Did ye kill this animal?"

I tugged my ear, embarrassed. Oberon loved the hunt, and I worried he'd think less of me when I told him the truth. I cleared my throat and plunged forward anyway. "No. I didn't kill it. I found it in the woods years ago and kept it. The deer must have shed it."

To my surprise, he smiled.

"Ah. A good gift. An offering from the stag himself." He picked it up, and it disappeared into the ether. "The knife is magnificent. How kind to not present me with cold iron." The knife also vanished.

"I'm glad you like it. It was my father's." I watched for his reaction.

Oberon stilled, pressing his lips together. "Ah," he said again. The knife returned out of the nothingness, and he placed it back on the star's point. "Best you keep it then."

He stroked the wolfhound's head. "Angus says he smells something delicious, and he's wondering if you'd like to share."

It took me a moment to figure out what he meant. "Right," I said, snapping my fingers as I figured it out. I opened my dinner bag and extracted the fries and apple pie. I bent, placed them on the floor and used my foot to push them toward the ginormous canine. Angus lolled his tongue, padded out of the circle, and went to town.

"Is apple pie good for him?" I asked.

Oberon chuckled. "Angus eats what Angus wants."

I watched the Irish wolfhound chomp down and wondered what it would be like to pet him.

"Angus says you may."

"May what?"

"Pet him, o' course."

I quirked my head. "How did you know that I was thinking about that?"

Oberon tsked. "Don't be silly, girl. Everyone wants to pet Angus."

Angus finished his meal and sat, waiting for me. His head almost reached my shoulder. I petted his wiry fur, and he rubbed his head into my hand. I dug my fingers into his beard and scratched. He seemed to enjoy it, leaning in so hard, he almost knocked me over. I used my other hand to rub his back and realized that underneath the top, rough coat, was a soft layer.

Oberon looked on approvingly. "He likes that, lass. Nicely done."

Angus booped my hip and loped back to his master.

Oberon took one stride toward me and settled himself in my chair. So much for that circle. Total fail. I idly wondered what I would have to do to keep him bound. He tapped his foot to get my attention, and I filed that away for another day.

"Pull up yer desk chair, Rebecca."

I did as he asked, rolling it over so we sat face-to-face a few feet apart. I sat on the edge, keeping my back straight to make room for the bow and arrows. Angus turned in a circle three times and then lay down, his massive head over his equally enormous paws.

"Ask what ye want," the fae king said, with a slight bow of his head.

I drummed my fingers on my knee, considering where to start. I decided to start with the most important question.

"Is Trace my father, Gideon?"

"Yes."

I startled. I hadn't expected a simple yes-or-no answer. I'd predicted clever evasions. Falsehoods presented as truth that I'd have to sort through. Instead, the fae king answered with a plain old "yes."

"Why? How?"

He held up a hand. "Yer gettin' ahead of yourself. The men are one and the same."

"Why is he in Faerie?"

The fae king took a big breath and let it out slowly. "Now yer askin' the right questions. Ye read the book?" He pointed a long, elegant finger at the opalescent book still on the floor.

"I did."

"So ye know that summoners, such as yerself, and yer dad can cross planes of existence, something even I cannot do."

"You enter the Slow World all the time."

He dismissed that statement away with a graceful wave of his hand. "That's easy. We have doorways, as ye know. Only summoners can spindrift."

"Spindrift?"

"Travel the walkways between realms. Skim the edges. Yer father calls it spindrifting."

"It's an excellent term. That's what it feels like. Like being blinded by water mist while surfing a thunderstorm."

Oberon sighed, a wistful smile on his face. "I wish I could feel it fer myself."

I wiped my sweaty palms on my T-shirt, astonished I was getting answers.

"Why is my father in Faerie? Why is he also called Trace? Why didn't anyone tell me they were the same person? Why did he *leave?*" I rattled off my most sought-after questions, my most pent-up frustrations, but caught myself with a hiccup before I started crying. My distress was obvious, however. Oberon's eyes told me so, and Angus rose to shove his head under my hand. I petted him automatically. It did make me feel better. Dogs, even fae ones, had the same superpower.

Oberon steepled his fingers, pressing the tips together. "He's in Faerie because that's where Titania wanted him. Me wife is a force of nature, not to be denied. She did it to protect our realm."

"But how does that protect the realm? Is he trapped there? Why didn't he come back to me? Why did he leave in the first place and return under a different name?"

The fae king gave me a kindly smile. "I think, Rebecca, ye need to ask him these questions yerself." He stood and snapped his fingers at my rolling doors, which opened for him on their own. He strode out the door, stopping to look over his shoulder at me.

"Thanks for the visit, and the gifts."

"Wait! Titania isn't happy with me, the Humbees want to kill me, the bridge's stone troll can't be thrilled, and the Death Caps long to burn my mind out. I can't go back to Faerie. I just barely escaped."

He grinned. "What's life without a little adventure?" the fae king said. He jerked his thumb toward the useless chalk circle. "You should give back that book, by the way." He stepped outside, Angus by his side, and I swore I heard a motorcycle vroom off into the night.

I removed the quiver and plopped down on my chair, dumbfounded. I'd expected the fae king to be furious at being summoned, dead set on keeping me out of Faerie, and awash with lies and half-truths.

Instead, he'd been forthright and, dare I say, chipper?

What in all the realms was this about?

I didn't trust him, but it didn't matter. I was going to see my father.

Chapter 34

I'd cleaned up and returned to my apartment for a quick nap and to feed the birds. Kenneth hadn't found my note yet, so I left it there.

Somewhat rested, I assembled my supplies, locked up, and drove to my local gaming store. I also stopped at a gardening center. Outfitted, I searched the park for Pinky and found him lazing under the sun in a bed of late-blooming Black-Eyed Susans.

I plunked down next to him. "Did you know that Black-Eyed Susans are the Maryland state flower?"

"Chatterboxes is what they are," Pinky complained, not bothering to open his eyes. "I can't rest here."

I couldn't hear them, but I took his word for it. "Why don't you move?"

"The Queen Anne's Lace has too many rules. They're stuck on protocol. It's exhausting."

Ooookay.

Suddenly, Pinky shot up to a seated position, sniffing. "Why do you smell like Angus?"

I shouldn't have been surprised he could smell the dog's scent. "I had a talk with the fae king today. Angus came along."

"You spoke to him? Was he following you again? I don't think it is nice for him to do that without your permission."

"I summoned him."

Pinky scratched an itch on his backside. "Why?"

"He had information about my trainer, Trace, who is in Faerie. I traveled there, quite by accident, the other day and saw Trace in the distance. A stone troll guarded the bridge to get to him."

"That bridge goes to an island. I've never been allowed on it."

"Trace is on that island, but here's the other thing. Trace is also my father, Gideon." I laid down in the flowers and thought about my dad. "I don't know why he's there or why he left the first time, or the second time, and I don't know why he didn't tell me who he was."

Pinky lay down next to me, his head cradled in his hands, just as mine was. He shifted toward me so that his elbow touched mine. That was snuggling for Pinky and quite endearing.

"Did the stone troll stop you from crossing the bridge?" he asked.

"Yes." I rolled to face him. "Pinky, I need to tell you something. I got caught in the Nightmarescape and fell into Faerie by accident. I got into a kerfuffle with some Humbees. Your mom saved me."

"She's good in an emergency," was all he said. Then, "I like the word 'kerfuffle,' very much. I shall use it in the future."

I poked him. "Pinky, the point is, your mom is amazing. I'm grateful she was there."

He yawned. "She likes you." He rolled over to face me. "You've been to Faerie twice now. Don't go back."

"Why?"

"You may not get to leave. Three is a magic number. Faerie may decide to keep you."

"The fae king said I should come."

He closed his eyes and rolled to his back again. "Well, that should be okay then. The fae king wouldn't lie, would he?"

He would. Not outright, but he was fae. Trickery was in their DNA. I reviewed my conversation with Oberon in my mind. He said I needed to ask Trace/Gideon myself.

"I have to go, Pinky. I need to talk to my father. He hid his identity from me when he came back as Trace, and then he left again. My mother didn't tell me any of this, and the secrets are destroying me. Without understanding my past, I can't move on."

Pinky stretched his arms over his head, toes pointed. "You smell like buttered popcorn when you talk about your father. It's nice."

"Why did you tell me that?"

"I thought you'd like to know. You still love your dad, even if he left and kept secrets."

"Can you help me get into Faerie through the door at the Winter or Summer Medical Park? Like you do?"

Pinky opened one eye to stare at me. "Even with fae coin you can't get small enough." He started to drift off, his voice becoming a mumble. "You're way too big."

I thought about what Pinky said as he fell asleep, snoring gently. I did love my dad deep in my heart, even though he'd kept so many secrets from me. I was mad at him and my mother, too, but couldn't you love people and still be angry with them at the same time?

Oded's words came back to me. Sometimes we kept secrets because we wanted to protect other people. Because love made us make hard choices. That was why I hadn't told Mickey everything, so I could hardly protest. I'd go to Faerie with an open mind. See what I learned. Maybe, if he'd let me, I'd bring my dad back to carve out a new relationship.

I kissed my pink fairy friend on the cheek. He didn't wake. I left him there among the yellow-and-black flowers, looking like a six-foot newborn babe.

"Keep an eye on him for me, won't you?" I asked the Black-Eyed Susans. I couldn't be certain, but I thought they waved their assent.

Back in my office, I made sure I had all my materials on me. I'd asked the quiver to divide itself into two partitions so I could separate some of the arrows from the others, and it did so. I wore tan utility pants with lots of deep pockets for the other items I needed and slipped the book into an inside pocket of my lightweight travel rain jacket, which had storage for lots of gear. I filled the rest of my jacket pockets with sundry odds and ends, not knowing what I'd need.

My tummy was in knots, and my nerves jangled like a badly played violin. I swallowed hard before sitting in my comfy chair, but once there, I committed. I breathed in and out, sinking further into the trance-like state Oded had taught me, searching for the staircase. I couldn't find it. Just as it came into view, I realized with a start that I'd left the rolling door open, a stupid mistake since my body would be exposed and defenseless.

I tried to claw my way back, horrified at my body's vulnerability, but the spindrift took me under, and I slipped down and away.

The black space opened on a stage, gently lit. I searched the empty theater for the staircase, but it wasn't there. I traversed the stage and noticed a ladder up toward the catwalk and climbed it. Higher I went, higher and higher, even as it twisted in a spiral. I climbed the rickety metal ladder farther than should have been necessary to reach the catwalk, high enough that the air thinned, forcing me to gasp for breath. My already strained nerves rebelled, telling me to retreat, retreat! I gripped the ladder until my knuckles whitened.

Hand over hand, step by step, I scrambled up, following the ladder's coiling path. My palms got sweaty, and I stopped to wipe one off on my pants. My foot slipped, and I swung from the ladder by one arm and one foot, my body flapping like a flag in the darkness. I forced myself not to look down, then pulled myself back and continued to clamber up.

Eventually, somewhere between a minute and a year later, a metal platform appeared, illuminated by a harsh light. I threw myself onto the platform and stared into the brilliance, blinking at the intensity. I pressed myself to my feet, my head pounding with the beginnings of a migraine. Spindrifting wasn't for sissies, I told myself. The realms didn't want people to cross between them. It wasn't supposed to be easy.

Ahead of me, I saw the Supercenter doors. I pushed through them.

"Hello!" said the same cheerful teenager I'd seen last time. "Back so soon?"

"I have to reverse course," I replied. "May I come in?"

"Naturally," she said. "You're a member. Grab a cart."

I did as she asked and proceeded toward the shelves. I passed bins of discount books, children's clothing, and flip-flops. I ignored a man offering cheese samples, complete with toothpicks. I passed the charcoal briquettes, mega boxes of matches, and bundles of firewood. The bright-pink signs advertising a special on family-sized chicken salad didn't move me, nor did the sheet cakes. I wasn't looking for any of those things.

Finally, I found the shelf I required, and I perused it, hoping it still had something I'd noticed last time. I found it between *Rain Check* and *Food for Thought*. I placed the narrow glass test tube in the cart and continued to the checkout counter. The salesclerk seemed surprised to see me.

"What item do you have this time?" she asked, more curious than before.

I showed her, and she clucked her tongue. "That's expensive. How shall you pay for this?"

I extracted a fae gold coin from one of my many pockets. I had five and would now be down to four, but I didn't know what else I would need them for, so this seemed a good use. "Will this do?"

She took it from me and bit into it. "Please hold."

She picked up a telephone receiver and dialed an extension.

"A fae coin," she said into the phone. "It's real." She listened to the response and hung up.

"It is acceptable," she told me. She took the tube, which held only a slip of paper, and passed it over the scanner, which beeped. She handed it back. "Please return the cart before you depart."

I slipped the tube into a pocket meant for mundane things like passports and returned the cart before walking through the exit.

This time the catwalk was made of vines and swung over a raging river. A waterfall to my right fed the river, and its spray drenched my clothes and got in my eyes. My hair was wet and flat against my head in two seconds.

I pushed on, weaving upside down and around, the floor beneath my feet swaying the entire time above the rushing water. I helixed in rotating circles, swinging wildly back and forth as I did so. My stomach threatened to come up into my throat and convinced my heart to follow it. I sternly told them both to stay where they were.

I noticed another walkway intertwining with this one and realized all the walkways were like that. Each had a shadow version that corkscrewed around it. I wondered if they each went one way. One for coming. One for going. It looked almost like. . . .

DNA.

I was walking the DNA, the genetic code that connected the realms.

Before I could decipher what that meant, if anything, I saw the door to Faerie. It looked like an actual door, made of wood. It didn't have a doorknob and when I pushed it, it didn't budge. I knocked.

A tiny slit in the door, so well hidden I never would have found it, slid open and a pale-green eye peeked out.

"Hello," I said to the eye. "I need to get in. Can you please open the door?"

"Becs?"

"Evans?"

"What are you doing here?" we asked each other at the same time.

"I was assigned to this gate," Evans said, his eye staring right at me. "You shouldn't be here. Titania has banned you from all things Faerie! Do you have a death wish?"

"Oberon invited me." I thought it was safe to say his name here. I knew he couldn't spindrift the DNA between the worlds.

"He asked you to come? Said it was alright for you to do so?"

"I have questions, and he said I should ask my father, who's here in Faerie. Come on, Evans, let me in."

Evans slid the peek-a-boo door closed. A series of clunks, crashes, and thuds later, the door opened, and I stepped into Faerie proper.

Bright-green grass carpeted the ground beneath my feet, and sunlight filtered down through oak tree leaves. Evans closed the door behind me, flicking latches closed. He turned to me, face skeptical.

"Do you know where you're going?"

"To the bridge guarded by a stone troll. Can you direct me?"

Evans frowned, his expression a rictus of doubt. "I can tell you the general way. Are you certain Oberon asked you here? Specifically?"

"Yes. Of course. I'm going to stay out of Titania's way, naturally, but I can't talk to my father without being here, can I? I'm prepared for several eventualities." I bit the inside of my cheek. "I think. Look, I don't know, but I've come this far. I can't turn back. Right?"

Evans's pale, drawn face did nothing to reassure me. "Be careful, Becs. Keep your head down and don't dawdle." He turned to grasp a shillelagh and touched the end of it to the ground. A dirt path materialized out of the grass, pushing the blades back until it was wide enough for human feet to follow.

"Neat trick," I said.

"Stay on the path," the elf replied. "Beware the vampire grass."

Chapter 35

Before I could ask him what he meant, Evans and the door disappeared, vanishing as if they'd never existed. The narrow path lay at my feet and everywhere else was greenery. Tall, wide-leaved plants and what I supposed was the terrifyingly named vampire grass.

Trembling, I took my first, uncertain step on the dirt path. Then a second. Nothing happened. Ten more paces and still fine. I decided that I'd follow Evans's directions to the letter, keep my feet on the dirt and move along expeditiously. There was no need to borrow trouble by exploring where I wasn't wanted. I had a mission, and I would stick to it.

I hitched the bow and arrows up on my shoulders, settling in for the walk. I had no idea how long it would take to get to the stone troll and the bridge, and it wouldn't matter, even if I'd done it before. I knew that Faerie could make this as long or short as it wanted. The path worked its way through a grassy lawn that would have looked good in the hoity-toitiest suburbs in Smokey Point. Vibrant, verdant, and peaceful, the entire area was showered in sunshine with only fluffy clouds to break up the blue sky.

I tripped on a tree root that snaked out fast as lightning, even though there were no trees in the vicinity. With a cry, I fell to the ground on my hands and knees and flipped to my side when the root shoved me over. Sharp needles of pain pierced my cheek, the back of my hands, and neck. Any uncovered skin was soon dripping blood as I lay skewered on razor-sharp blades of grass.

The lawn grew lusher and thicker as it absorbed each blood drop, slurping up my life force like a kid with a milkshake.

I pushed myself up, extricating my cheek and neck from the grass needles. Another burst of pain spiked through my body as my palms hit the grass and the blades punctured the soft skin, particularly the webbing between my thumb and index finger. As each individual blade had its fill, another one drilled into my body, taking its turn. I wrenched myself free and rolled back onto the dirt, curling into a tiny ball to avoid encountering anything green. A high chitter undulated across the grassy plain, and I realized the grass was laughing at me.

I could live with the mocking, but I wasn't sure I could survive bleeding my way through Faerie. Too many things were attracted by blood, including pixies both large and small. I sat on the path, dug into a pocket, and pulled out a small first aid kit with antiseptic wipes. I swabbed the puncture wounds, applying pressure until they stopped flowing. I covered the ones on my hand, but my cheek and neck I left alone. I didn't have enough bandages.

I regained my feet but swayed as a dizzy spell washed over me. With an effort, I kept upright and vowed to watch my feet from now on. "I'll be back with a lawnmower one day," I said. "See how you like it then."

The grass rumbled in anger at my threat. Furious at falling into their trap, I warned them again. "Don't fool with me. I have a long memory." The blades rotated as if the grass was turning its back on me. I gave each side of the path the finger and proceeded on.

I was still in the grassy area, painstakingly avoiding the vampire grass when a tiny insect-like thing darted to my face and licked my injured cheek. Another one joined, then another and soon I was swarmed by itsy-bitsy pixies. I batted at them but to no avail, finally ducking and covering my head to deter them. From my curled position I spoke.

"Stop! Humbees, call Queen Clarissa. I have a gift for her."

The Humbees halted in mid-air, buzzing like bees, suspended like hummingbirds. These were specks, smaller than the ones I'd seen in the Slow World. I had to squint to see them at all. I could sure feel them though, as their rough cat tongues swiped the open wounds. I pulled the jacket's hood up and over my face and stayed scrunched down on the ground until a drumbeat announced the arrival of the queen.

Queen Clarissa hovered in front of my face. "What are you doing back here?" she demanded. "Didn't have enough last time? Shall I order these juveniles to partake in their first kill?"

"They're juvenile? Is that why they're so small?"

"Just hatched," she said, hands on her hips, her eyes flashing in ire. "But no less deadly. Their parents are still recovering from withdrawal, thanks to you." She raised an arm high, pointing one long-nailed finger straight up, and the juvenile troops assembled in formation.

"Wait!" I cried. "Rose pollen is terrible for you. I stand by that, but I didn't consider the effects of being cut off suddenly. So I brought something for you to make amends."

She lowered her finger, using her other hand to adjust her crown.

"I'm listening," she intoned.

Slowly, so as not to alarm her, I extracted the test tube I'd just purchased in the warehouse. I presented it to the queen with my hands curled around the bottom and added a minute bow, martial-arts style. She didn't reach for it.

"What is this?" she asked, her tone as sharp as the vampire grass.

"'A Clean Bill of Health.' By accepting it, you should cure your hive."

She eyed me suspiciously, lips pursed, taloned fingers tapping on opposite elbows. "I don't trust you."

"What's the worst that can happen?"

"It's not what you say, and it makes things worse."

The grass rustled and leaned toward us, curious to know how I'd respond. The blades whispered bloodthirsty nothings into the air.

"Shut up, vampire grass. Not one more drop for you. You've had your fill," I said, venom lacing my voice. I wanted to quit this place as soon as possible. Frustrated, I tried one more time to reason with the monarch.

"Queen Clarissa, I promise you by my power as a summoner that I have no ill will toward you. I truly believe this will help."

She glared at me for another second and then snatched the vial out of my hands. She held up a closed fist, and the juvenile Humbees gathered around her, staring at me with a blazing hunger. They were like piranhas eyeing a tasty meal, restrained by their leader's will alone. I held my breath.

Queen Clarissa, slightly mollified but still furious, nodded. "I'll uncork this when I get back to the hive. If it works, we have no more business with you."

"Maybe next time you won't spy on me either. The only reason you're in this mess is because you believed empty promises. Rose pollen is an anathema to your kind, Queen Clarissa. A better queen would know that."

"What do you know about leadership? Nothing. Everything's about you, isn't it? *Where's my father? Where's my trainer? Why did my guardian angel boyfriend leave me?* Please. You have no room to lecture me." With that parting shot, the Humbees lifted as one, a buzzing cloud, and flew away.

"Ye did a good job with that, lassie," said a high-pitched voice. Hums of agreement joined together to create a chorus of accord. I looked down at my knees to find what could only be leprechauns standing in the middle of the vampire grass, totally unaffected.

"Who are you?" I asked.

The lead leprechaun doffed his green, pointy cap and bowed.

"Fiddlesticks, m'lady, and this is my family. We couldn't help but be impressed by your bargaining abilities."

"Gee, that's nice. Appreciated. I hate to be rude, but if you will excuse me, I've some place to be."

Fiddlesticks stroked his long red beard. "See, that's the thing, m'lady. It appears to us, what with this being our patch and all, that a toll is advised."

The other leprechauns blocked my path.

I gritted my teeth, annoyed at the Faerie waystations. Fiddlesticks stuck his pinky in his ear, swished it around, and extracted a glob of earwax, which he promptly ate. I shuddered, totally wigged out.

"What can I do to get you to leave me alone and let me proceed uninterrupted?"

Fiddlesticks grinned and tapped his nose. "Well, m'lady. My nose tells me that you've got riches on your person. Mayhap you may want to share your treasure."

Of course. What else would a leprechaun want?

"If I give you a gold coin, will you not only let me pass but also assist me in avoiding any additional pitfalls from here to the bridge?"

Fiddlesticks twisted his cap in his hands, wringing it like a dishcloth. He looked at me with large puppy eyes. "See, m'lady, I knew you'd catch on! But I think three gold coins seems right for such a large boon."

"Two."

He made a big deal of thinking about it, walking over to confer with his family, muttering under his breath. I waited, impatient.

He returned to stand before me. "We discussed it and agree."

I plucked two gold coins out of my pocket. I held them out but kept them out of his reach. "How do I know I can trust you?"

He grinned. "Ye can't, but a bargain made is a bargain kept. I have a reputation to uphold."

I pointed to one of the other leprechauns. "I want one of you to accompany me all the way there and use your influence to avoid any other fae who might have lofty ideas about killing me or forcing me off the path."

Fiddlesticks paled. "Not one of my young'uns."

"No, of course not. An adult."

"There's no one here besides meself."

"You'll do nicely."

The leprechauns hummed a discordant note, one of worry and concern.

I raised my eyebrows at him. "What are you afraid of?"

Fiddlesticks looked right and left. He lowered his voice, and I had to bend to hear him. "The queen, m'lady."

"I understand that. I've never met her and hope to keep it that way, but if you want your gold coins, you'll have to go with me."

He swallowed hard. "Mayhap we've been hasty."

"Hold on," I said. Digging in my pants pocket, I unearthed a new package of colored chalk I'd brought in case I needed to cast a circle. "What about this? It would make a mighty fine rainbow."

The leprechaun family *ooh'd* and *ahh'd*. The littlest one's eyes grew big and round.

Fiddlesticks eyed me with something that verged on respect. "You drive a hard bargain, but I like that. Done and done. I'll go with you, meself, m'lady."

I dropped the coins into Fiddlesticks's hands. I'd spent three of my five coins, and I had no idea how close I was to my goal.

Fiddlesticks spat into his palm and proffered it to me. Suppressing my disgust, I shook, hoping that leprechaun spit, like dog saliva, had antibacterial properties. His family hummed in approval again, the silvery tinkle of the littlest one rising above the others.

Fiddlesticks beckoned me forward. "This way, m'lady. It's not too far now."

I followed the skipping three-foot-tall man, shaking my head. Vampire grass, Humbees, and leprechauns.

Well, I thought, *better than Titania.*

Chapter 36

We traveled through woods so dark, I could barely see my hand in front of my face.

Even the jovial Fiddlesticks fell silent as we passed into the murk. Heavy, moist fog hung low to the ground, dampening my pants, making them cling to my skin.

Things stirred in the trees and rustled through the underbrush. Ferns lined the path, not grass, and I heard the croak of tree frogs, or whatever passed as tree frogs in this place. I gathered my courage, following the leprechaun, glad for his company. Two gold coins seemed a bargain at that moment.

I thought of everything I knew about his kind, seeking a way to repel the despondency provoked by the shadows.

"Hey Fiddlesticks," I whispered.

"Aye?"

"I'm tall when I'm young and short when I'm old. What am I?"

He snorted softly. "A candle, lass. Ye can do better."

"Okay. What gets wet when drying?"

"My son told me this when he was a wee bairn. A towel, o' course."

"If they're so easy, tell me one."

"If you insist. What can't talk but can reply when spoken to?"

"I don't know. What?"

"An echo, naturally. Mind the path here." He pointed ahead to where the trail narrowed. "The trees are getting uppity, is what they are. Things have a mind of their own in the Gloomweald."

"Well named," I commented, shrinking in on myself so that no part of me brushed even a leaf.

"They're guardians of Faerie's borders. You entered at the western outskirts. We're heading into the heart of Faerie now, and be warned, word will travel that you're here."

A tall birch tree stooped, grazing my head with something that looked like Spanish moss. The moss landed on my arm, and a twig snagged my collar. I jerked free and flung the moss into the ferns. I recoiled as a titter of laughter rang out through the dense forest.

"Let's move faster, Fiddlesticks."

"Aye, m'lady."

We emerged on the other side of the Gloomweald unscathed, but I didn't look forward to traveling through it again and hoped there was another way back.

Assuming I got the chance to return.

The dirt path turned to gravel, and my three-foot friend hopped along, pointing out Faerie sights along the way.

"This is a narrow part, Ms. Rebecca. Mind the water."

"It's ocean on either side."

"Aye, but we don't want to step a single toe in. The Goliathans nurse their young in the ocean to our left, and I never know what's in the coves to our right. Sometimes mermaids, other times, things that rise from the depths and are very, very old. It is best to move quickly and not attract their attention."

I thought back to the giant beast I'd seen breach the water the last time I'd traveled here and agreed wholeheartedly with Fiddlesticks.

"How far to my father?"

Fiddlesticks fished around in his ear again and flung whatever he found onto the path. "Well, we've got to go through the pixies' village and pass by the fairies' land and then we'll get to Gideon's Gaol."

"His jail? He's a captive here?" The thought lightened my heart for it meant he might have wanted to come back to me but couldn't.

"Well, yes. He's been there a long time. That's why the stone troll guards the bridge."

"Who incarcerated him there?"

Fiddlesticks shot me a look that said the answer was obvious.

The fae queen.

My stomach rumbled, reminding me that my body still needed nourishment, even if I wasn't here in a physical way. I dug out a granola bar and chewed it while we walked. No way was I eating anything from Faerie. I sincerely hoped I brought enough for the trip. This was taking longer than I'd expected.

We trudged on, Fiddlesticks never flagging in his good cheer. "Ms. Rebecca, we approach the pixies' land. See how it sparkles!" He clapped his hands.

"It is pretty, but let's walk around it. No need to visit today."

"As you wish."

We circled the pixie village to its north. I marveled at a castle made entirely of rainbows and storm clouds. No wonder the leprechaun liked it. Pixie voices rang out, melodic and beautiful, as the residents went about their business. You would never know these harmonious sounds emanated from blood-drinking "It Girls" who could charm the pants off a priest.

A whirlwind, strong enough to be a tornado blew around us. Fiddlesticks and I were both blinded, and he cried out as meadow flowers and soil flew into his face. I pulled my hood down and covered my eyes, grabbing the leprechaun to cover him with my larger body.

A peal of hysterical laughter pulled my gaze up from the ground as the wind died down. Laurel stood there, hair a wild, staticky halo, eyes bright with fever. "Found you!" she exclaimed and laughed again.

"Laurel?"

The pixie threw her arms out wide. "You did it, Becs! You freed me from the queen."

"That's good, right?" From her behavior, I wasn't sure this had turned out the way I'd wanted.

"It's better than good! Complete and total free rein! No limits on feeding. No geas on my feelings, thoughts, or desires. No constraints at all. I never knew I could feel this free." She leaned into my face, her cheeks reddened with a high blush, and danced in place. "And, it's all thanks to you." She twirled in a circle, rose in the air, spinning, threw her head back, and cackled. "Gotta go. I'm going back to the Slow World and have some *fun*."

"Wait!" I held out an imploring hand. "Don't you think you should calm down a little? Maybe think this through?"

Her face darkened. "Everyone keeps saying that! No! I've got so much energy and so many ideas."

Her voice was too loud, and she spoke at the speed of light. "Don't be upset," I said, trying to mollify her. "I want what's best for you."

She dismissed me with an angry chop of her hand. "I'm not angry or irritable, or any of that, and I'm sick of being told that I am."

"Who's telling you? Your sisters? Don't you want them with you? Don't you trust them? You should bring them along to the Slow World. They'll help you out." I wanted to say they'd keep her from doing stupid things, but I didn't dare.

"I don't need those hangers-on right now." She shimmied. "I want to dance."

"Come on, you need your posse. I mean, who's going to be your wing-women if they're not there? Who's going to stare at me with unbridled loathing?"

She twirled, arms up over her head like a flamenco dancer. "No one. I've got this."

She winked out in a flash of light.

Oh, dear.

Fiddlesticks stared at me. "You unleashed that on your world?" he asked. "Why would you do that?"

I scuffed my toe in the dirt. "I was trying to help her with another problem."

He shook his head. "That sure went sideways."

I sighed, motioning for him to continue leading me. "You can say that again."

"That sure went sideways."

I smacked my palm to my forehead. "I didn't mean . . . oh, never mind. That's a problem for another day." If I survived this, I'd have to deal with Laurel.

We plodded forward, and Fiddlesticks finally tired enough that he ceased his color commentary on the delights and dangers of Faerie. We turned south, and I noticed a door like the one I'd come through. No guard manned the post, and the door appeared unused—I could see the dust from several years had accumulated on the frame and at the bottom.

"Is that another portal into Faerie?" I asked.

"Yes, but it's been dormant for a long time."

"Doesn't it go to the Slow World?"

"I don't know all the rules, Ms. Rebecca, but in theory, yes."

We slipped south without raising any unwanted attention. I ate another granola bar and some dried apricots, drinking water from a thermos. While I'd hated being weighed down by my supplies, I was now glad I had them with me. The sun beat down on us, and I sweated through my clothes but didn't dare take off my jacket. I'd been soaked and was now hot. Steam rose from my body. I was incredibly uncomfortable, but I ignored it, only raising my hood to keep the sun off my head and neck.

The greenery gave way to a beige-and-tan landscape, expansive field of long grasses that looked like wheat. Small animals jumped through the stalks, creating weaving, waving paths I could follow, even when I couldn't see what had made them.

Eventually, conifer trees appeared in the distance, and I knew in my bones that we were getting closer—a fact confirmed by Fiddlesticks, who stopped in his tracks and turned to face me. "I can take you no farther, m'lady. You must proceed on your own. A bargain made and a bargain kept."

He pulled out a mirror from his pants pocket, stared into the glass, whispered a word, and disappeared. Suddenly, now startlingly alone, my courage took a nosedive. I rubbed my hands together. "Okay, Becs. You can do this. Keep going." I took another long pull from my thermos and followed the remaining path to its end.

A stone troll slept in front of the bridge, looking like a mountain controlled by bellows, inflating and deflating in an easy, rhythmic manner. The peaceful scene didn't fool me. That stone troll had thrown me right out of Faerie, right back into my body, no door or spindrifting required. He had powerful magic as well as a powerful body.

I crept closer, sticking to the trees. I'd given some thought on how to get by him without a fight, and maybe he'd go for it, but it would be better if I could sneak in without him noticing.

The stone troll yawned, stretched its massive legs and arms out like a baby waking up from a nap, and sniffed. He lumbered to his feet, and his head topped the trees. He'd grown since I last saw him.

"I smell you, tiny human. Why did you come back?"

Resigned that stealth was out the window, I stepped into the clearing, craning my neck to look up at the giant.

"I need to see Gideon."

"I told you once already that Gideon is off limits. He's there by order of the queen herself. He stays. You go. That's how it works. Simple enough rules that even a stone troll can follow them." He laughed, and the sound grated my ears. It was as if he'd swallowed sandpaper.

"I've come all this way. All I want to do is talk to him."

The stone troll bent at the waist, showing a remarkable amount of hamstring flexibility, and brought his face within ten feet of mine. His visage was so large, I could only focus on his nose or one eye at a time. It simply took up too much of my field of vision.

"Talking, visiting, conversing, or interacting. It's all the same."

Quite a thesaurus, this troll.

"Okay," I said. "Thanks for your consideration."

"That's it?" he said, sounding dissatisfied. "We aren't fighting?"

I lifted my hands, palms up, in a gesture of futility. "What can I say? You're so much bigger than I am. I have no chance of beating you in a physical fight."

The troll plunked to the ground, disgruntled. "I'm bored. Nothing's happened here since your last visit. I thought you'd put up a fuss and I could smash you."

"Geez. Sorry to disappoint."

"Come on," he wheedled. "A few punches. Maybe a kick or two?" He brightened. "You could run, and I'll chase you."

"None of that sounds appealing, no. We're not evenly matched. My whole body is the size of your big toe."

The stone troll crossed his arms with a creaking rasp that skittered down my spine. "Well, then, best be on your way."

I turned to leave and stopped as if an idea had come to me. "We could play marbles."

The troll rumbled. "What is this 'marbles'? Is it a battle?"

"It's a game, a competition where one wins and one loses. Here, let me show you." I withdrew a set of marbles, the ones I'd picked up at my local gaming store, and he held out his palm. I placed them in his hand, and he brought it all the way up to his eyes, opening the pouch with his other hand. Surprisingly dexterous fingers sorted through the tiny fiberglass balls. They were a special kind that had more bounce to them than standard marbles.

"These are pretty. Why is this one bigger than the others?"

"That's how you play the game." I used a fallen branch to draw a circle approximately six feet across. "You hold the big green one. I'll take the blue. They're called tolleys. You flick the tolley at the smaller marbles and try to kick the littles ones out of the circle, while keeping the tolley inside."

I continued, describing the rest of the rules. "Want to play? I challenge you."

"Aw, why not? I can always smash you later."

"Absolutely true," I agreed.

"Who goes first?" he asked.

"This is the fun part. Each of us holds a tolley on our nose and lets it drop to the ground. The player whose tolley is closest to the edge of the circle without going outside of it, goes first."

"Show me," the troll commanded.

I held the big marble to the tip of my nose and let it drop into the circle. It rolled an inch or two and came to a stop about three feet from the center.

I looked up at him. "Your turn."

The bridge's guardian held the marble to the tip of his nose. It was so high up, I could barely see it. Compared to his nose and finger, it was a tiny speck. He let the tolley go, and it landed in the circle, bounded out, high as my waist, and rolled into the thicket of trees. The troll grumbled about it being an unfair game. "Go get it," he said.

"You go get it. It's your marble."

"Fine but sit here. You will stay here?"

"I can stay here."

The troll only needed to take one step to part the trees and find the marble, but while he was distracted, I darted between his legs, hightailing it for the bridge.

"Hey!"

Air swooshed by me as he pivoted on one foot and tried to grab me simultaneously. He got close enough to pull out a few strands of hair. I ducked and kept running, diving for the bridge. As soon as my hand touched it, I curled in, and log-rolled across like a kid down a hill. The troll stuck two fingers in my path, blocking me. With his fingers in front and his body behind me, I was good and stuck. I peeked over the edge at the rushing water and something with huge teeth flipped over, grinning at me from the current.

"You said you'd stay!" the troll bellowed.

"I said I could stay, not that I would," I corrected.

"Either way, Rebecca Naomi Greenblatt, you are done. Time to go back to the Slow World. And this time, stay there." The troll's other hand came down to pinch me and throw me back as he'd done before when he suddenly roared in pain. The fingers blocking my path onto Gideon's Gaol lifted, and I saw a tiny spear sticking out from under the nail, embedded in the nail bed.

My father stood on the other side, a second spear in hand. He wore leather breeches and a tan woven loose-fitting, untucked top under the leather vest.

"Rebecca?"

Chapter 37

I ran to his side and skidded to a stop in front of him, though now that I faced him, I didn't know what to say. Worried that the stone troll would pick me up and fling me back into my body like before, I didn't say anything, just grabbed his hand and pulled him away from the bridge. He allowed it for a few feet but then yanked me to a stop.

"Oh, Becs. What have you done? You've played right into their hands."

"What? I don't understand."

A tinkling, satisfied laugh floated across the bridge, and I turned to see who it was.

Titania. Tall, willowy, and stunningly gorgeous with raven, wavy hair that hit her hips. Even across the bridge, her enormous eyes, flashing green, and tilted up at the corners, pulled me into their depths. If I'd drawn a prototypical elf for a video game, she'd be it. She wore a silver crown dotted with diamonds with a central sapphire the size of an egg.

The queen brought her hands together in a clap of childish joy, amusement in her eyes. "Oh, this is too perfect. Everything has worked to plan."

"What plan?" I asked, too flabbergasted to be scared.

Titania rotated her wrist in a circle, and a gold chair materialized. She settled in it, taking time to arrange her diaphanous blue-and-green dress and cape just so. She held out an arm, and a colorful bird that looked like a small peacock landed on it, ambled up to her shoulder and nuzzled her ear. She stroked it with a finger and then turned her attention back to me, giving me an indulgent smile.

"Why, *my* plan, of course."

"Which was?"

The queen gestured toward me and my father. "To capture you and lock you away with Gideon."

"I'm not following. I traveled here myself."

She held up an index finger. "But who nudged you along?"

I thought about it. Every step, every choice. Had I been manipulated? "I saw you once before, didn't I? In Joey's bar."

"I warned you not to say Oberon's name thrice."

Oberon had been there too, disguised as a handsome elf with a Van Dyke beard. I'd had the death magic in me, and that's when he'd told me to stay "uninterestin'."

"I recall." I pointed to the stone troll who stood sentry behind her. "You can't tell me you manipulated everything. I tricked him. I did that, not you."

The stone troll shook his head, a slow back and forth that made me review my whole journey. I sank to the ground, utterly defeated. Gideon put a hand on my shoulder and squeezed.

"It was too easy, wasn't it? Oberon appearing at my summons. Evans, an elf I knew, at the gate to create the path. A leprechaun to show me the way. Oberon making sure I had the gold coins to pay. A stone troll pretending to be stupid enough to be tricked by a child's game. You're the growling, vicious guard dog, snapping at everyone to draw attention away from Oberon's sneaky long game."

"He and I have the same goal. To protect Faerie." She snapped her jaws. "I bite. He strokes."

The stone troll spoke up. "If it is any comfort, I really wanted to play marbles. I meant it when I said I was bored, but I have to follow the orders of my queen."

Titania stroked his leg. "Indeed, you do."

"All of this to get me here."

"I'd preferred to have you here physically, not an astral projection, but your body is being attended to. With you both here, I don't have to worry about Hell getting a hold of you and using you to ravage Faerie. You're safe here and out of their grasp. Faerie is out of danger."

"Why do you think Faerie is in danger? How could Hell manipulate either of us to get here?"

She scoffed. "I'm not telling you what I think *could* happen. Why give you that information? All I know is that the prophecy refers to the two of you and Hell wants in. My job is to protect Faerie. That's what I'm doing." She lifted one shoulder. "If that inconveniences you, well, too bad."

Gideon broke in. "Why haven't you killed us? Wouldn't that be simpler?"

She pointed a long, elegant finger at my dad. "Excellent question. I've thought this through long and hard. I'm not sure of the ramifications if I killed you altogether. I can see various futures, but the answer to this escapes me. You have connections to Faerie, Gideon, given your friendship with Tuli. You traveled back and forth so many times, you became the changeling that wasn't. And your daughter bore the summoner's mark too. If I kill you, someone else may arise to take your place. Fate abhors a vacuum."

My father closed his eyes as it all sunk in. "By keeping us here and alive, you forestall the prophesy from happening."

"There are other summoners, but no other changelings that aren't changelings who have children."

"Won't my body eventually die?" I asked, seeing a loophole.

"No, my dear. You're in stasis. Your body will stay where you left it, not aging and not moving. To those in your world, you will appear to be in a coma." The queen stood, and the throne vanished. "I shall leave you now. Enjoy your reunion. Take your time telling each other stories. You have eternity to share." She patted the troll again. "Slate shall continue to guard you."

She tossed her arm in the air, and the bird flew off with a squawk.

I didn't miss the disappointed look in Slate's eyes. "Majesty," he said, genuflecting. "You promised that I could return home. I miss the north and my family."

"I've changed my mind, Slate," the queen said, breezy and carefree, knowing her orders would be followed. "You're needed here."

"As you command." Slate responded, agreeing, but his voice was a low, despondent monotone.

The queen gave him a regal nod and flickered out of sight.

I stood there, facing Slate, begging him to let us go with my eyes. He shook his head, bristling with sadness and frustration. He took a moment to snatch up the tolleys and roll them across the bridge to me. I scooped them up and placed them with the other marbles. With a look of regret, Slate turned his back to me, taking up his post once again.

"Come on, Becs," my father said. "We have lots to discuss."

He took my hand. Gideon's home wasn't technically an island. It was connected to the mainland by a narrow stretch that lay directly under the bridge, making it a peninsula. I couldn't see any way that made a difference, though. We were still trapped.

He brought me to a well-kept cottage with flowers outside and a lovely shade tree. A red door stood centered between dark-brown shingles, and the roof sported a chimney. The trees were laden with fruit. "Apples," he noted. "They're delicious."

"How do you eat, besides the apples?"

"Food appears every day. The brownies bring it, and I ignore them as is proper."

"Doesn't eating it mean you can't leave?"

"I don't think so. I can't sense any magic about it. They don't need food to keep me here. I'm already a captive."

"Right." I sank onto a large rock in front of a well-used fire pit.

Gideon placed both hands on his hips. "Look at that. They're two rocks here now. There used to only be one. Guess the peninsula is adapting to your presence."

"Yippee."

My dad kneeled before me and placed an index finger under my chin, lifting my face so he could look me in the eyes. I was instantly transported back years to when he'd done that same thing to me as a child.

"Rebecca, you've done nothing wrong. I shouldn't have said you played into their hands before. Titania is a master of manipulation. Once she set her mind on capturing you, you didn't stand a chance."

"She couldn't manipulate Asher though, could she? How did she know it would fall into place?"

He hugged me, and the feel of his arms around me melted something in my heart that had hardened over the years. I put my head on his shoulder and rested it there for a moment.

He pulled away with a kiss on my forehead and said, "Let's start at the beginning. We'd better compare notes. I'll start and then you can fill in. Above all," he said with a wink, "I'd like to know who this Asher is."

He found a comfortable seat on his rock. "I'm a summoner born, like you." He piled wood on the fire and handed me some twigs to break into kindling.

"It runs in our family, but it is unusual for a parent and child to both have the Kiss. It's one of the things that drew Titania's interest right away." He arranged the logs in a pyramid and indicated I should place the smaller sticks on top.

"I summoned for a living, doing my best to keep the dangers that accompany our profession at bay, but they followed me home."

He added a handful of dry grass on top and dug into his vest pocket for something.

"How?"

He waved my question away. "That's a story for another time." He pulled a flint from his pocket and lit the fire. "It doesn't matter what exactly drove your mom to the brink, but Maya told me I had to leave. That summoning was putting the family in danger."

I barked out a laugh. "Sounds familiar."

He looked up, interested. "Oh?"

"It sounds like me and Mickey."

He wrinkled his nose. "I'm sorry to hear that." He poked the blaze. "Anyway, I stayed away but made sure she had my contact information and knew how to get in touch with me. I sent money home, too." He sat on his rock. "I never stopped loving her. Or you and your sister."

I swallowed the lump in my throat.

He sighed and continued. "When your Kiss came in, your mom was dismayed, to say the least. She contacted me but told me I couldn't tell you who I really was, so I used my childhood nickname, Trace."

"Why Trace?"

"When I was little, I played with a tree nymph named Tuli—"

"I know this! I had a vision about it." I told him what I'd seen.

"I don't know why your magic showed you that. Maybe it was another manipulation of Titania's, but yes. That happened. A lot. I didn't know what it meant that I traveled to Faerie and came home every time. I was just playing with a friend."

I drank water from my thermos, draining it.

"Anyway, I kept disappearing without a. . . ." He rotated his hand and wrist for me to fill in the rest.

"Without a *trace*," I said, finally understanding.

He smiled. "Yup. Drove my parents crazy, and thus, the nickname." He stood and stretched. "Wait here a moment." He walked to his cottage leaving me staring at the fire, letting my mind's tumblers rotate and fall as pieces came together to create a whole canvas.

Gideon returned with bread, jam, and cheese. I swiped a finger through the jam and tasted it. Fig. Delicious. I looked up to see my father raising his eyebrows at me while handing me utensils. "We don't have wolves here, or at least, I haven't met any, but no need to eat like one," he said.

"Still telling me not to eat with my hands? We haven't seen each other in years. Aren't we beyond that?"

"Once a parent, always a parent. And obviously, I have some making up to do."

Embarrassed, I accepted the cutlery and a plate. "I bet there *are* fae wolves."

"Probably."

We ate together, our first shared meal since I was a teenager. When Gideon finished, he placed his plate on the ground and cleared his throat.

"Where was I? Ah. Your Kiss. When it came in, your mom asked me to come home to train you, and I did. You showed so much strength right from the beginning, but you needed control."

"The Death Caps," I said, mournful at the memory.

He nodded. "The Death Caps. There was no good reason they should have targeted you. Again, I can only suspect the fae queen."

I finally asked the question I'd been dreading. "Why did you leave the second time?"

He studied his moccasins. "I didn't mean to, I swear, but I was tricked. A school friend of yours, Derrick was his name? He caught me outside one day and asked me to help him with a magic question. I was intrigued, and worried. He shouldn't have known to approach me, and I fretted about what type of magic he was experimenting with. I wasn't careful, and he got the jump on me. Next thing I knew, I was tied to a chair and he was casting a circle."

My father stared into the distance as he recounted what happened. "He offered me to a demon in exchange for his father."

Dumbfounded, I blinked at him, remembering that when I had followed Derrick to UnderTown, I'd heard Derrick say to his father's wraith that I wouldn't help him if I knew what he'd done. It must have been this. He'd trapped my father.

"This is all. . . ." I couldn't form sentences.

"Unsettling? Confusing? I know. Before the exchange could be made, I managed to escape. He hadn't tied the knots well and I got loose, ran from the room, and when I saw where we were, I headed straight for a door to Faerie that's big enough for humans. You saw it on the way here, I bet."

"I did pass a door, but it looked unused."

"I was probably the last one to use it."

"Anyway, I jumped through the door, knowing he couldn't follow. I fully intended to return home, but Titania was watching and snatched me up as soon as I got here. I've been imprisoned on this peninsula ever since." He wiped his hands on his pants, and with a profound sigh that did more to express his regret and remorse than any words could, he met my gaze.

"I didn't abandon you, my darling. In my heart, I never have."

Chapter 38

I choked up at his words.

"I didn't know how much I needed to hear that."

He bit his lip. "Of course, you did. You were a little girl and you needed your father and your teacher, and I failed at both."

"I understand now, though. Thank you for explaining it to me."

He pinched the bridge of his nose and took a deep breath. "So," he said. "Tell me about your life. Tell me everything I missed."

I brought Gideon up to date, including the struggle of not having a trainer, my apartment above a take-out noodle place, and my pathetic attempts to make a gimlet.

He laughed until I thought he'd fall over. "Wait," he said. "Let me get this straight. You bartend in a fae bar, your boss is half-gnome, you're dating a guardian angel, and one of your best friends is a fairy who forgot how to go small."

I held up a finger. "Don't make fun of Pinky."

He hiccupped. "I'm not," he finally managed to say. "It's just that it's so you. When you were three, you brought home a bird with a broken wing. Do you remember?"

I didn't.

"Well, you did, and we had to find a wild animal rescue that would rehab a robin." He smiled at me. "You've always had a big heart."

He sobered, clearing his throat. "Tell me about your sister."

"Gosh. Where to start?"

"Wherever you like."

I wrinkled my nose, thinking. "Well, unlike me, Mickey went to college and got a degree in psychology. She met her husband, Jonah, in a math class."

He clapped in delight. "She's married?"

"Yup, and you have a granddaughter, Ruthie. She's still a baby."

Gideon brought his hands to his heart, the gesture tugging another string of lost memory. "I hope to meet her one day. I bet your mom spoils her."

I stilled.

"Rebecca?"

I took a deep breath. "Mom died."

"What?" Gideon shot to his feet, only to sag back down. He slowly assumed his former seated position, but now, his shoulders sagged, and he looked like he had aged decades in just a few seconds. He covered his face and moaned.

His cries echoed through the growing dusk, and I gave him some space, waiting in silence, studying the rising moons. They were beautiful and reflected a stunning white light that made it easy to see.

Finally, when his wracking sobs had subsided, I said, "I'm sorry you had to learn this way. She had cancer and fought tooth and nail, but eventually, it took her from us."

Gideon rocked in place, heaving deep hitching breaths. "I always thought I'd make it back to her." His voice grew thick. "I wish I'd been there for her."

"You couldn't. Not your fault."

"Maybe not, but I'm not going to fail again." He cleared his throat and raised his head, a new, determined gleam in his eye.

I frowned. "What do you mean?"

He clenched his fists on his knees. "I mean," he said, leaning forward so I could hear his whisper, "we're going to escape. Grab your things. It's dark enough now. Follow me."

Titania hadn't confiscated anything I'd brought with me. She probably didn't think any of it—including the bow and arrows—was worth her time. I caught my dad by the collar and whispered back. "Why haven't you tried to escape before?"

"The queen told me as long as I stayed here willingly, she'd leave you alone."

"She out-and-out lied?"

"More like intimated. Besides, she manipulated events so you would come on your own. She didn't whisk you off herself. As always, she gave me a technical truth but an overall lie."

"More fae bullshit."

"More fae bullshit," my dad agreed. "Let's go. The forest fae can still reach me here. The trees' roots run deep."

I followed him toward the house, but instead of going in it, we circled around. He knocked on a tree trunk. "Tuli?"

A nymph's face poked out of the trunk. "Gideon? What are you doing? I heard your daughter came here. The news is all over Faerie." Her bright eyes focused on me. "Oh, hi, daughter!"

"Shh, Tuli. We're going to make for the Gloomweald. Will you help us as we discussed?"

Tuli bit her pretty lower lip and glanced behind her, inward into the tree. "Okay, yes, but only if you make it to the Gloomweald. I can't help you get here but once you arrive, I can provide passage through the forest and take you close to the door."

"That's perfect, Tuli, thanks."

"Be careful." The nymph disappeared.

Putting his finger to his lips, my father made his way down a steep hill, and I trailed after him. He led me to a narrow cliff's edge where one false step would plunge me into the water below. We picked our way around the peninsula's circumference, balancing on the rocky lip, like we were tip-toeing a narrow path on the side of the Grand Canyon. I had to walk one foot in front of the other and at one point, pull my quiver around to my front and place my back to the rock, scooting sideways. It actually made it easier that I couldn't see the water below. The unnatural splashes and moans scared me plenty.

My dad touched my shoulder, strong and reassuring. "Come on, Becs. You can do it."

We continued until we'd circled halfway around and emerged under the bridge, basically back where I'd entered, but on the underside. Slate guarded the top side of the bridge just above us. My dad reached up and wiped away webbing, pulling out a fae glowworm. He held it up in front of us where it wiggled, protesting its capture, but its light revealed our escape route.

Under the bridge was a narrow strip of land a few inches wide but deep enough that it descended into the water below. Gideon knelt, shifted to his belly, and inch-wormed his way out onto the tiny land bridge. There was less than a foot between his back and the stone bridge above. The bridge brought us across the water, back to the mainland, but once we got there, we'd have to walk along another steep precipice. I hated this escape route.

Deciding I couldn't worry about the second escarpment yet, I joined my father in scooting across the land bridge on my tummy right beneath the troll. I really, really didn't want to fall into that water. The drop was a long, long way down, and the crushing waves would pull me under and draw me into whatever frenzied, hungry mouths swam below the surface.

I grasped the sides of the land bridge with my palms and knees and scrunched along, centimeter by centimeter. I tried to control my breathing, but my panting echoed in the tight space, and I prayed that

Slate couldn't hear me. The quiver rubbed against the rock, though. I couldn't avoid it.

"Who's that scritch-scratching under my bridge?" the troll boomed.

My dad froze. I froze with him. My heart hammered in my chest.

"Who's there?" Slate's bellow shook the bridge itself.

"Hi, Slate," came a familiar voice. "My name's Pinky."

Pinky? Oh, no. The clever fairy was going to get himself hurt. *Run, Pinky*, I thought. *Don't do this.*

"Who are you and why are you here, fairy?" asked Slate, suspicious.

"My mother told me you've been guarding this bridge for a long time."

"That's true."

"I thought maybe you would like someone to talk to. I don't have many friends."

The troll hesitated but finally admitted, "Company would be nice."

Pinky shuffled around in something crinkly. A bag, maybe?

"Would you like to try this?" he asked.

The stone troll sniffed. "What is it?"

"Something amazing! From the Slow World. It's a caramel-covered apple."

"You go to the Slow World, Pinky?"

"All the time. I'm an arborist. I tend the apple trees, and this is my favorite way to eat the fruit."

I couldn't help it. I smiled. Oh, my wonderful friend.

My father moved again while Pinky kept Slate entertained over our heads with caramel apples and then, candy-coated ones. They crunched and slurped the juicy treats, and Pinky regaled the troll with stories from the Slow World. "They don't know how to fertilize properly in the Slow World," Pinky grumbled. "It's a wonder anything grows."

"I've never been to the Slow World," Slate said.

"It would be hard to hide someone of your size," Pinky commented, in his unjudgmental, earnest manner. "You're way bigger than elephants."

"What's an elephant?"

Pinky described an elephant, even supplying the scientific name and regaled Slate with the differences between Asian and African elephants. Meanwhile, Gideon and I reached the other side. We swung down, and my feet hit another narrow ledge. We balanced, our backs to the cliff wall, and inched west until we left the open ocean behind us and entered the coves. The salt spray differed here, and my father whispered to me that we had to find a way to climb up to normal land or we'd be spotted by selkies.

"Too bad we don't have vodka and grapefruit juice," I whispered back. "They like Salty Dogs."

My dad gave me an odd look. "All the more reason not to be seen. They'd recognize you." He patted the rock with his hands, trying to find a hand hold.

"Becs?" A voice came from up above.

"Who's there?"

"Evans. I told you I was worried. This didn't feel right." Something fell next to me and hit my elbow. "I've kept tabs on you through the trees. Here, grab on." I realized he'd dropped a rope-and-vine ladder.

"Climb up," Evans urged.

"Aren't you going to get in trouble with Titania?"

"Maybe, but that's not the point right now. Hurry up."

My father and I climbed the ladder, and I crumpled to the ground, spent. Evans nudged me with his toe. "No time to rest. Let's go. Your friend said she'd help you through the Gloomweald."

"Evans, I'm concerned," I said, pushing myself to my feet with a groan. "Titania may punish you."

"Don't worry about me. The story of how you got here has spread throughout Faerie, as well as my inadvertent role in it. I don't like being used, and the fae king tricked you, too. He never invited you. He said just enough to make you think he'd done so. They played dirty."

"They're fae royalty." I shrugged one shoulder with dispassion. "That's what they do."

"True." He helped me situate the quiver. "I also felt an imbalance that needed correcting. You warned me about the Death Caps near Joey's place."

"Seriously, you've repaid me."

"You have friends, Becs." The young elf's green eyes glinted in the moonlight. "Okay, hurry along now. I'll get back to my post." He rolled up the ladder and carried it off with him.

"Now what do we do?" I asked my dad.

"This way," came a voice.

"Tuli, oh thank you for coming," my father said.

The slim nymph beckoned to us. She wore a silvery dress that reflected the moonlight. "As Evans said, we must hurry, Gideon."

We followed her, keeping as low as possible until we reached the dark edge of the Gloomweald where the trees stayed preternaturally still.

Tuli knocked on the trunk of a large, old tree. She turned to me and scowled.

"My mother tried to warn you as you passed through the forest earlier, but you shrugged her off."

I thought back, recalling the tree laden with Spanish moss. "I'm sorry. The woods are unnerving to those who don't know them."

"Next time, pay attention to your elders."

Before I could respond, the tree trunk opened wide, and Tuli waved at us. "Enter."

My feet didn't want to move. The thought of being trapped inside a tree froze me to my core.

"Come on, Becs. Tuli won't hurt us." My dad went first, pulling me along with him, and I almost refused, hesitating for a second as I battled my baser instincts but then shuffled in, wary. We were confronted by a maze of tunnels and openings.

"Is this the root system?" I asked.

"Sort of." Tuli pointed toward one of the round entrance points. It reminded me of Tolkien's Hobbit doors. "That's the best way to explain it to a human, I guess."

We dropped to our knees and crawled our way through. On and on we went. The path was sometimes smooth and dry, other times wet and mossy. Tuli never had to crawl. She shrank to a few inches tall and floated along, skimming the floor.

"Here you go." We reached an expansive tunnel that led to a round cut-out in the bark. Tuli opened it, peeked outside, and her demeanor changed from brisk to urgent. "You have to run. Out. Out!"

Gideon hugged Tuli. "Will I see you again?" he asked.

Her eyes teared up. "Probably not, my friend. After this, I'm going to form roots and stay out of the queen's sight." She pushed him out after me. "Now, go!"

We fled for the gate, where Evans stood at his post, his face grim. He pointed at what was coming, but neither of us looked, too scared to see what pursued us.

"Stop them!" a stomach-churning rasp rolled through the Gloomweald. Evans half-heartedly raised his shillelagh, and we halted. We turned, and I stifled a shriek.

A full contingent of Death Caps waited to kill me and my father.

I shook myself out of my reverie and shouted, "Dad! Down!" I reached backward, over my head, and an arrow from the newly partitioned section leaped into my hand. I nocked it and let it fly. I drew again and again, not stopping, and each arrow, excited to finally be used, traveled unerringly toward their targets.

The hit Death Caps screamed in pain, and the sound screeched like metal scraping metal.

"Yes!" my father cried, with a fist pump. "What did you do to them?"

"I dipped the arrows in fungicide before I left."

He gave me a proud look and a thumbs-up. "Good thinking. Keep shooting, but let's walk backwards. See if you can distract them enough that we can make it to the gate."

I kept shooting. One arrow. Then another. The entire first line of Death Caps when down. It was shroomaggeddon.

Until I ran out of fungicide arrows.

The remaining Death Caps attacked, burrowing into my mind and my fears. *You'll never escape. You've doomed yourself and your father, and we'll visit that sweet little baby niece of yours and tell her stories of how her aunt betrayed her. Your brother-in-law was right to fear.*

I shook my head, fighting them. "No. No."

We'll make sure all of Faerie knows that you died with your backs to the entrance, no help in sight, failing, falling, collapsing at our feet.

"Don't listen to them," my dad said, through gritted teeth. He held his hands to his ears.

Anyone that assisted you will suffer the queen's wrath.

Pinky, I thought. *Oh, God. Evans.*

Don't resist. You cannot escape us, either here or in your nightmares. The Death Caps dug into my brain, deeper than ever. *Yield, and the queen will be merciful.*

"Yes, I shall show mercy," said Titania, descending from the swirling sky in a chariot led by flying seahorses, hair floating around her in an electrified nimbus. A flock of miniature peacocks streamed behind her.

"Don't trust her, Becs. Her idea of mercy and yours are totally different," my father ground out, still clenching his jaw against the Death Caps' assault.

Fighting the Death Caps' compulsion to prostrate myself before their ruler, I reached behind me for one more arrow. Shaking, I tried to nock it and failed. The arrow hung uselessly from my hand.

The fae queen rose to her feet, silver lightning crackling around her. "Stop killing my people, Rebecca. I am Faerie, and I protect what is mine."

Titania lifted her hand, and the nearby fae inhaled a collective breath. The trees in the Gloomweald shrunk inward, and the vampire grass curled into tiny green commas.

She didn't shout, but her voice carried in the stillness. "This is my job and my purpose. I. Will. Not. Fail."

I leaped in front of my father to protect him with my body, shouting, "Don't!"

But the queen's ire had reached its breaking point.

She shot a beam of green-flecked silver electricity straight at me.

Time seemed to slow. Evans stood at the gate, just to my left. The Gloomweald to the right. Titania ahead.

Nowhere to run.

I ducked, raising my left arm to protect my head, while grabbing my father with my right and yanking him down with me.

As I did so, a shock of magic sparked to life and ran from my chest down my arm into my left wrist. My leather cuff flared, and the protective symbols burst forth to form a transparent white light with a radius large enough to cover both me and Gideon. As before, the Solar Cross sat at the twelve position, the Star of David occupied the three spot, the Eye of Horus held the six, and the Pentacle, the nine. The Chamsa took the center. Together, they blocked the queen's attack.

Her chariot flew straight up in the air, and she shot down at me from overhead. I shifted my wrist, and the bracelet's disc deflected the assault. The electricity rebounded in the air and struck one of her mounts. The beast bugled and bucked, and Titania had to fight for control.

Gideon studied the distance between us and the gate. "We've got to get there. We can't stay here forever. She'll wait us out."

Titania's chariot raced around us in sweeping, rapid circles. I kept up with her, keeping my lone manner of defense between us and the queen of Faerie, but I tired. This had to end.

"Be ready." I dropped the shield, nocked the arrow, took aim, and shot in the direction of the Faerie monarch. I doubted I could hit her, but I needed to buy us time to flee.

I didn't expect the arrow to fly true.

"No! Becs! You can't kill the queen!" Evans leaped to his feet with supernatural fae speed and grace, somersaulted over our heads, and thrust his body in front of Titania.

The arrow struck him dead center in the back, and he plummeted to the ground.

I'd killed him.

Titania shrieked in fury and sent her chariot downward toward our heads, the seahorses' mouths opened to show multiple rows of gleaming, shark teeth.

I struggled to my feet, grabbed my father's hand, and opened the door. I dragged Gideon through and slammed it behind us. We collapsed on the waiting platform.

I hugged my head to my knees, incapacitated by Evans's death. Maybe he didn't die? Maybe he survived?

But I knew the truth in my heart.

I took in three shuddering breaths and thought I was getting it together enough to spindrift the rest of the way home until my brain fixated on one dominating concern.

Three from Faerie had helped me.

Evans was dead.

Tuli was hiding.

My throat constricted at the next thought.

Where was Pinky?

Chapter 39

"I killed Evans." I scraped my broken nails against the wooden crosswalk. "And I've endangered Pinky." I looked up at my father who stood above me struggling to school his features. "We may have escaped, but the cost was too high."

"Evans helped you but protected his queen, as he had to, as was his duty. As for Pinky, there's nothing you can do for him now. Based on what you've told me, he's surprisingly resilient."

"What if he's not this time? What if he didn't make it out?"

He didn't answer.

I wiped my dripping nose on my shirt and pulled myself to my feet. Gideon twisted his head all around, examining where we were. "This is what it looks like to you when you spindrift? Catwalks?"

I sniffled. "It looks different to you?"

"More like chutes and ladders."

"Mom stopped playing that game with us."

He rubbed the heel of his palm against his chest as if struck. "Ah. Too bad." He huffed a big breath. "Lead on?"

Worried about Pinky, I hustled up, practically running to get home. We jogged along the wooden walkway, paying no attention to the creaks and moans of the wood. It sounded like an old wood rollercoaster at the Jersey shore.

"You sure this will hold up?" my dad asked, clearly uneasy with the odd sounds.

"Has so far."

"Comforting."

The catwalk rose at a steep angle followed by an equally abrupt decline. I slipped and slid the way down and wondered if my dad's remark about chutes and ladders had influenced the spindrift. We both skidded along another slippery slope before hitting a level expanse. We caught our breath and kept going.

The cold feel of metal under my hand told me we were getting close to the entrance to the Slow World. A warm glow gradually illuminated the space, eventually revealing a rising orange-and-pink sun in a clear-blue sky. A sea-salt breeze blew my hair back.

One sharp corkscrew twist later, we exited into the parking lot, and Gideon placed his hands on knees. "I must say," he said with a deep sigh of relief. "I prefer my version."

"I didn't make it up. That's what came to me," I said, as my dad looked around.

"This doesn't look anything like I remember," he said.

"I doubt there were giant warehouse stores then."

"What's a warehouse store?"

"You'll see."

We thumped the automatic door opener and didn't wait for the doors to fully open before charging ahead.

"Welcome back!" said the perky teen. "Oh, and you haven't been here for a long time," she said to my dad.

"Yeah, it's been a bit. This used to look like a grocery store."

"Times change," she chirped. "Go scan in."

I yanked my dad to the desk with the red-vested old man.

"Place your wrist here," he droned, pushing the scanner toward us.

I did.

Gideon did.

As soon as my father waved his wrist over it, red lights flashed overhead, accompanied by a blaring alarm.

"Oh, Mr. Greenblatt, we have a recall notice for you. There seems to be a miscommunication. You're marked as expired."

"Well, clearly, I'm not so fix your records." Gideon snapped. "We've got to get a move on."

"Please stay here while I get a manager."

"Screw that noise," I said. "We don't have time." I looped my arm through my dad's crooked elbow and tugged. We skipped the carts and ran through the store, zipping through the frozen section with its restaurant-sized bags of tater tots, family-sized lasagnas, and mega-bags of fish sticks.

I skipped the aisle with the more esoteric items and dashed toward the cashier who stood with her hands to her mouth and the high eyebrows and wide eyes of surprise. The alarm continued to blare, and when I glanced over my shoulder, I saw several red-vested workers followed, running as fast as they could. I knocked down a full pail and mop, and they skidded and fell in the soapy water, their shouts of surprise bringing other employees into the fray.

Now a mob followed us.

I leaped the turnstile at the check-out aisle, and my father tried to do the same, but he caught his foot. The metal bars rotated, and he got stuck between two of the horizontal rods, unable to move forward or backward. "Go without me, Becs!" he yelled, struggling to wiggle free.

"Don't be ridiculous," I said. "Hang tight."

I jumped a different turnstile, ran into the arcane aisle, and did a quick search for something I'd seen when I'd purchased the Free Rein. It was still there. I flipped open the package and made it back to my dad, who was now surrounded by red-faced, sweaty, middle management.

"A supervisor is on her way," one of them panted at me, holding his hands up.

"Sorry, guys. Need to hurry this up." I turned the cannister upside down and sprinkled the *Get Away Scot Free* on Gideon's head. The turnstile opened, and he extricated himself from their grasp. I plunked down the set of marbles. "As payment. They're a nice set."

One of the managers snatched them off the conveyer belt. "Oooh. Marbles. I haven't played these in ages."

We ran through the doors, and I fell, tumbling head over teakettle. White noise filled my head, and my stomach rose to my throat. Blood trickled into my mouth from a fresh bite of my tongue. I landed hard back in my body, still in my chair in the office. The quiver poked me in the back.

My father lay on the floor next to me, holding his head and whimpering.

We'd made it.

Dizzy and unable to focus, I rotated in my chair so that my feet rested flat on the ground, thinking I needed two aspirin and a week's worth of sleep. A voice said my name, but I was too woozy for it to fully register. I blinked and shook my head, trying to clear it. I gradually became aware of the smell of brimstone clashing with the heavenly scent of birthday cake. That got my attention.

I jolted to my feet.

Chapter 40

In my wildest dreams, I never imagined I'd see what lay before me.

Asher faced off with Valefar. Angel versus demon.

Madame Francesca stared down Gregory Adamos. Medium versus mobster.

I mentally kicked myself.

I never should have left that door open.

My mind went into overdrive, a hyperfocus that allowed me to realize several things at the exact same time.

Valefar was held steadfast by a summoning circle made of rose petals and onyx beads. The only person in the room who would have done that was Madame Francesca. Which meant she'd summoned the demon on her own, after coming here and finding me unresponsive.

I wondered if she knew I was spindrifting or if she found me out cold and just didn't care?

Pushing that aside, I calculated the next thing that must have happened. She'd summoned the demon, and Asher, the angel, had shown up to stop her, protect me, or banish the demon. Or all three.

Why Gregory was here, I couldn't guess, but he glared at the medium, his face cold and furious while the brackets around Francesca's mouth spoke of strained concentration. Francesca had put thought into this circle. The rose petals connected her to Valefar, but then she'd dotted the circle with onyx to strengthen it with a strong protective element. She'd done well, but Valefar was prodding the circle to find a spongy spot.

The demon snarled at Asher, who held out his arms, palms forward in a defensive position. Discs of white light haloed his angelic hands, creating translucent shields in front of his body.

Valefar was no longer transparent and appeared hale, which meant he'd recovered from whatever power loss he'd experienced in Hell. He used that returned power to press against the circle's edges while sparks traveled around the rim. The demon was tricked out in full regalia, horned human head, big lion body, griffin wings. A single angel, slim and in human form, couldn't hold him off. He was too powerful.

I had to help Asher. Sparks meant the circle was weakening.

Madame Francesca's aged face grimaced as she gripped her hands together in tight fists, fighting to maintain the circle.

Gregory Adamos pointed a gun at the demon. "Don't shoot him, boy," Francesca told him through gritted teeth. "The bullet will cross the circle's plane and break it."

Gregory scowled and lowered the gun but didn't put it away.

I'd deal with him later. Right now, the battle of wills between Heaven and Hell took precedence. I watched for an opening to assist my guardian angel but addressed the medium who'd created the circle.

"Madame Francesca! Send Valefar back. Since you made the circle, you need to dismiss him. He's about to break through. Asher is helping . . . but *you* created the circle. You have to end this."

"Not without him releasing his hold on my soul," she snarled. It was a very unladylike sound to come from the normally restrained medium. "Derrick never mentioned my soul as payment. He's in the wrong."

"What?" exclaimed Gregory. "In the wrong? Lady, he's a fucking demon. What did you expect?"

Asher muttered, "Becs," and his pinched face and straining muscles told me he was hanging on by a thread.

I focused on Madame Francesca once again. "Have you given up the tiara?"

She jerked her chin in assent.

I spoke to her like I would talk to a wounded animal or a frightened child, low and calm. "That's great." The medium wasn't thinking straight and needed a lifeline. "This means you've given up his hold on you. You aren't incurring more debt."

Truthfully, I'd already assumed that she had indeed abandoned the garnet because of the wrinkles and crow's feet that had aged her face. Even the skin on her wrists seemed papery and thin.

"Yes," she choked out. "The tiara is locked away where I won't touch it. Nothing, not even returned youth, is worth my soul."

Her waning strength motivated Valefar to push harder. He turned so he could face her and put his back to Asher.

I kept talking to Francesca. "I'm sure we can negotiate this another time. I'll help you." She tossed a skeptical glance my way before returning her focus to Valefar. "No, really, I can help. As a summoner, I can call Valefar back another time when we are less scattered and more controlled."

The medium shook her head. "I want this taken care of now." She straightened her shoulders, digging deep for strength. "The Warlock never mentioned my soul specifically, so the demon must relinquish his claim."

"A small oversight, I assure you," sneered Valefar, "but you're still mine."

I frowned. "I don't think so, Valefar. But that's for another day. Right now, you need to go."

He laughed. "Now it's me who doesn't think so." The invisible barrier shimmered into sight, and a section buckled for a second before becoming firm again.

"Madame Francesca, please dismiss him," I begged. "You can't hold him, and Asher can't do it by himself."

The barrier rippled, wrinkling like an accordion. With an effort, Madame Francesca pushed it back into place.

"Admit it, Valefar," she said. "I don't owe you my soul."

But Valefar wasn't paying her any more attention, and instead, was peering behind me.

The demon blinked his red eyes and reoriented toward me, his tone shifting. "Why, Rebecca Naomi Greenblatt, is that your *father?*" He stopped poking the circle to point at Gideon, his smile toothy and hungry. "You got him back? Titania let him go?" He clapped his paws together. "Oh, you marvelous girl."

"You knew where he was?"

He flicked out a talon. "I know a lot of things."

"It doesn't matter." I stepped in front of my father. "He's no concern of yours."

"Oh, but he is." Valefar snapped two digits on his right paw, like he'd just had a bright idea. "I propose a trade. You give me your dad, and I'll relinquish my claim to Francesca Isabella Pietrov's soul."

"No, Becs. Whatever you do, don't do that," Asher said.

"Of course not."

My father pulled himself to a sitting position, and Asher and I shifted to block him from Valefar's gaze.

"Give up my soul, and she'll discuss the possibility with you," Madame Francesca said.

"No," I said, my voice a whipcrack in the small space. "I most certainly will not. That is not on the table."

"That's too bad," Valefar growled as he shoved against the barrier anew.

The circle bulged, shifted, and bowed. This was it.

Asher dropped his light shields and held out his hands, chanting in Latin. A light formed around his whole body. "Regna terrae, cantate Deo, psallite Domino. . . ."

The demon shuddered. "Shut up, angel! Stop that infernal whining!" He *pushed* Asher with a single, concentrated beam of inky purple power that punctured a hole in the protective circle and struck my guardian angel in the thigh.

Asher flew back and hit the wall. He stood, flexed his arms and shoulders, and translucent wings unfolded from his back. He spoke again, in a language I recognized as Aramaic. Though he spoke the native tongue, the words translated in my head.

"Yahweh will smite you with a great blow, and in his wrath, He will send against you a powerful angel, who will show you no mercy. . . ."

Valefar's mocking laugh boomed through the room. "Are you the powerful angel? You're not an archangel. You're barely out of a cherub's diapers. You think you can take me?"

"I have faith," Asher answered.

"You're nothing but a low-level guardian angel. One who gave in to the pleasures of the flesh." He hissed this last word in delight. "You're a failure."

Asher faltered. The light around him faded, and his wings fluttered out of sight. His hand clenched into a fist, and he turned to me and then back to the demon.

"Don't listen to him, Asher! He's trying to psych you out. That's what demons do. They remind you of your faults and weaken you by making you doubt yourself." I reached out and held Asher's hand. We focused our power, speaking simultaneously.

Asher intoned, "Yahweh will smite you. . . ."

While I said, "Valefar, you have no place on this Earth. You do not walk it. You do not belong to it. You've earned your place in Hell. Return to it!"

Valefar staggered under our combined efforts, screaming in frustration as he flung himself side to side, still trying to break the circle's hold.

"Francesca, now! Send him back," I shouted as a gale wind blew around the room, throwing my belongings all over the place and almost driving each of us off our feet.

"Not until I get what I want," she said between gritted teeth. She held out her arms, clawed fingers taut and strained.

"For God's sake woman, dismiss him!" yelled Gregory, who pulled out the semi-automatic again. "If you do it now, before he escapes, Becs can create a new circle and call him back for you later."

"Gregory, for God's sake, put that damn gun away!" I screamed at him. "Francesca, please dismiss the demon."

"No! Stop telling me what to do!"

Gregory lunged forward, gun out as if he was going to hold it to her head and force her to do as we said. She whirled on Gregory, reached into her pocket, and threw a vial at him.

He shot her, the gun barking twice. The vial fell. Asher dove and caught it before it broke. "A potion," he breathed.

"A distraction," Madame Francesca whispered, holding her side. "Not fatal."

"Gregory! Back the hell off, you moron. . . ." But I trailed off as Madame Francesca dropped to the ground, bleeding from the two bullet wounds in her hip and stomach.

I lost my concentration.

Asher stopped attending to the demon to crouch at Francesca's side.

Gregory backed up, breathing heavily, his hand to his mouth.

And Valefar took advantage.

The circle broke wide open, and a smiling, gleeful Valefar stepped out. He took a single step to Francesca's body and shoved Asher out of the way. Asher rolled backward and scrambled to his feet, but it was too late.

In the time it took Asher to recover, Valefar had leaned over Francesca's body and sucked her escaping soul into his mouth. He turned his head to stare at Asher, Gideon, and me.

"Well now, that's better, don't you think?"

Without thinking, I reached back for an arrow. I let it fly, nocked another, and let that one go too. I sent five arrows at the demon.

Who flicked them all aside like toothpicks.

Gregory raised his gun. I'd gotten a look at it when he'd shot Francesca. It was a Glock 48, compact Slimline, which took ten bullets in a magazine, and he'd already shot two at the poor medium. Gregory shot all eight, straight at Valefar's head, which would be enough against a human foe, but against a demon, it was a peashooter. Valefar easily swatted them away with his big paw, grinning maniacally the whole time.

The reflected bullets had to go somewhere, and when Valefar hit them, they flew off-kilter, zinging around the room. I searched for my father, but he'd already hidden behind my desk. Asher, who'd jumped in front of me, collapsed in a heap.

"Asher? Oh, no." I patted his body and found a bullet lodged in his chest, above his heart.

"Can you die?" I was frantic. "You can't die. Come on, get up. I need you."

Asher took my hand, brought it to his lips, and whispered, "Just doing my job."

I gathered him in my arms and covered his body as the glass partition cracked in a spiderweb of fissures caused by a stray bullet. Valefar roared, and the sound rang through the storage unit, shaking the partition between the two sides. The demon roared again, stomping his back feet, and the already fractured glass shattered completely. He knocked the bottom of the partition out with a single kick, and the entire interior wall collapsed. He pulled the chair on the client's side right out of its bolts, tilting his head back and laughing. With the added room he could roll his shoulders and stretch. He still couldn't open his wings, but he didn't seem to mind.

He had the upper hand, and he knew it.

Gregory reached down to his ankle and extracted a knife. Not that I had any idea what he could do with that but maybe it made him feel better to hold it. I was already incandescent with rage that he'd brought a firearm into my space and that he'd shot Francesca.

Asher lay still in my arms, his eyes closed.

I glanced at my father who was frantically digging in my desk, throwing papers and books as he searched for something. I didn't know what he was looking for, but I couldn't help him. He obviously didn't find it because he moved on to my steamer trunk. Valefar had fixed his eyes on me and giggled like a schoolgirl, drawing my attention back to him.

"I haven't had so much fun in centuries," he said, fangs gleaming as he stretched and yawned again. "All thanks to you, Rebecca. Thanks for arranging this little party and bringing your father back."

"It is time for you to leave." I scooted out from under Asher and pulled his body behind my now shredded chair. Tears threatened, but I didn't have time for them so I wiped my eyes with the back of my hand and drew on my summoner's abilities "Valefar, former duke of Hell, as the bearer of the Kiss. I send you back to the depths from which you've come."

Valefar stutter-stepped and slowed down. He lifted his feet, but it was as if they were stuck in peanut butter. He could move but not well. I pushed more power into it. It took everything I had. I broadened my stance and took a deep breath.

"Valefar, former duke of Hell, you are no longer welcome here. Go back to Hell. You are dismissed!" The dam broke on my tears, and they flowed unhindered. I ignored them, letting them fuel my wrath.

He leaned against my power, refusing the command.

"You didn't ssssummon me," he hissed. "You can't impel me to return."

"I can." I swallowed and dug in my heels. I took another gasping breath and concentrated. "I will. Dad, there's a container with herbs. Rosemary, thyme, sage, and rue. Do you see it?"

"Yes, I see it." My father drew close to my side. "Okay, I've got it. Keep him there. You're doing great."

My father darted in between me and the struggling demon, holding a piece of chalk he'd found in my desk as well as the herbs. "Another minute, sweetheart, hold on!"

He threw the herbs at Valefar, and the demon doubled over in pain. Encouraged, Gideon traced a circle around the angry demon. It was harder than normal because without Asher, Valefar had some wiggle room and he stood broadly on all fours, puffing out his chest and spreading his wings as much as possible. My father had to increase the circumference of the circle to accommodate his size. Then he tossed more herbs at him, and the demon stilled.

"Dad, I don't know how much longer I can do this."

"You can do it."

An arrow poked me in the back, but it didn't hurt. Instead, it loaned me energy, and the welcome boost allowed me to ram more power at Valefar. The lion shivered at the extra intensity and glared at me. He shook his whole body like a dog getting out of a pond after a swim, throwing motes of inky purple magic in all directions.

One hit my father.

Gideon hadn't yet closed the circle all the way and was about two feet short. The mote struck him on the back, and he dropped to the cement. The chalk rolled out of his grasp and as he tried to scramble for it, Valefar struck him with another magical punch. Gideon collapsed, one arm inside the circle.

"Dad!"

Valefar snatched my father by a talon, digging it into his arm. Blood spurted straight up like a fountain and Valefar chortled, lapping it up with glee. He stared right at me as he dragged my dad the rest of the way inside the circle.

He licked his bloody lips. "First a human soul, then an angel, and now your father. You know how to throw a party, Rebecca Naomi Greenblatt."

Valefar and my father disappeared in a downward, smoky circle of energy that dissipated in seconds.

I sank to the floor.

Valefar had kidnapped my father and whisked him off to Hell.

My legs wouldn't hold me, and I stumbled backward until I hit a wall. I sank to the ground, so shocked that I couldn't move.

Humiliation and remorse rolled over me like a frigid wave.

I'd lost my father after just getting him back. Evans had died for this. Pinky and Tuli had put their lives on the line.

And I hadn't been strong enough to keep him. I'd dishonored their sacrifice.

Guilt washed over me and through me, filling my body and my heart. My legs and belly cramped with the shame, and I curled into a fetal position, crying, "No, no, no. . . ."

The cool concrete floor under my cheek couldn't calm the blazing inferno of self-reproach that burned through me leaving nothing but a husk. My brain crackled with static, making rational thought impossible, allowing only one single horrifying realization.

Hell had Gideon.

Which meant Hell had a summoner, the exact circumstance Titania and Oberon had tried to prevent.

And, when I finally opened my eyes, I noticed something else.

Asher was gone, too.

Chapter 41

"Uh, Becs, can you open the door?"

Open the door? When had it closed?

I turned toward Gregory, unable to focus. I blinked at him, trying to hear what he was saying. It was as if I was underwater, and his voice came in bursts of incomprehensible oscillating sound. I concentrated, trying to make sense of it.

"Becs. Please. Open. The door."

The mobster lay sprawled on the floor, blood pooling around his lower leg.

"What happened?" I mumbled.

"Cut by the flying glass. Perrick is on his way, but you need to open the door."

"Who closed it?"

"Asher. To help keep Valefar from escaping."

I hauled myself to my feet and opened the door, moving by muscle memory alone. A big black four-by-four screeched to a halt a minute or two later. I leaned my back against the wall, sank to the floor, and placed my head between my knees. I barely heard Perrick.

"Come on, boss. Let me look at it."

Gregory mumbled something, and Perrick responded with, "We've got to get you to a hospital. You've lost a lot of blood. That's a deep laceration."

"I can walk," Gregory protested.

"Nope. Carrying you."

I turned my head to see what was going on. Gregory lay across Perrick's arms, floppy as a ragdoll, blood still dripping from his leg despite a newly applied bandage. The troll had picked him up like he weighed nothing.

"Becs?" said Perrick, frowning. "I need to get Gregory to the hospital. Are you hurt? Do you need me to come back for you or call someone? An ambulance?"

I managed a weak wave. "Go on. Get him stitched up, but then return for Francesca's body. We need to take care of her. It's the least we can do. After all, your boss killed her. Why did he have a gun?"

"He always carries one when he goes out alone," Perrick said. He took a breath, as if he was going to say something else but didn't. Instead, he carried his boss to the car, and a second later, it zoomed away into the night. I wondered what time it was.

My storage facility/office was officially trashed. The partition had shattered into smithereens. Blood soaked the floor where Gregory had been sitting. A dead woman lay on the floor next to it.

The open, unfinished chalk circle caught my eye. Gideon had almost finished drawing it. Now, three-quarters of the way drawn, it reminded me of an enso, a Japanese symbol. The enso, or Zen circle, is a symbol of enlightenment.

I didn't feel enlightened. I felt defeated. I leaned back against the wall, where I continued to survey the damage.

"Becs?"

"Pinky!"

Pinky stood in the doorway, his wings vibrating in distress. He knelt next to me and put a tentative hand on my shoulder.

"Oh, Pinky, I'm so glad you're okay. I thought Titania might have hurt you."

"No. The king stopped her. He told her I didn't know what I was doing because I'm 'simple.'"

"You did know what you were doing though, didn't you?"

Pinky angled his face downward but cast his eyes upward in a coy gaze. "Did I help?"

"Yes, you did. You really did. That was brave and inventive. You're my hero."

The corners of Pinky's mouth lifted in a shy smile. "I didn't like you being trapped. That's not where you should be. You belong here, with me."

"You also belong in Faerie."

He withdrew his hand. "Yes, and I like to be there too, but you live in the Slow World, and I like knowing where I can find you. It was wrong for the queen to try and keep you there."

I tugged his sleeve. "Please don't take more chances on my behalf, okay? I couldn't bear it if you were hurt." I motioned vaguely at our surroundings. "I've already lost so much."

Pinky took in the blood, the body, and the overall chaos and sat on the ground and rocked, a self-soothing habit I'd come to recognize. After a minute, he ceased rocking and put his back to the wall, focusing on me. "When I imagined you imprisoned, my tummy twisted tight, and I couldn't eat. Is this because we love each other?"

"Yes, Pinky. That's exactly what it is."

"Love sort of hurts."

"It can, but it's kinda great too. Like, how your being here is making me feel better."

He gave me that shy smile again. "I like that."

"Me, too." The details of the last few hours came back to me a crushing wave. "Oh, Pinky. I killed Evans. Asher's gone, maybe forever, and my father. . . ." I couldn't finish.

Pinky hung his head and his wings beat a slow, sad rhythm. "You didn't mean to kill Evans."

"No, I didn't."

"Since he died saving her life, Titania gilded his tree in gold."

"His tree?" I asked, blinking through tears that wouldn't stop. Pinky used his wing to wipe them away. A little of his dust coated my face. He patted my cheek. The move was so maternal, I assumed he was imitating something his mother had done for him.

"When an elf dies, we plant the body in the ground and a tree grows. Titania touched the leaves with gold. It's very pretty."

"That's nice." I sniffled, and he wiped my tears again.

"His family appreciated it."

His family. Oh. Dear. I started crying all over again. All I'd done for the last several days was cry. I was so over it.

Pinky stood up and brushed his hands on his thighs, at a loss for what to do next or how to help me. He went for practical. "You've had quite a kerfuffle. This place is a mess. What do we do first?"

I smiled at his use of "kerfuffle." "Excellent use of the word. Perfectly appropriate."

With a deep sigh, I pushed thoughts of Evans's family to the back of my mind where I knew they'd fester—but that was better than confronting them now. I didn't even know how. How do you deal with the guilt of murdering a friend? What do you say to their family?

"I'm going to wait for Perrick to come get Madame Francesca's body." I rubbed my eyes with the heels of my hands. "Then, I'll go back to my apartment. I don't know what else to do. Do you want to come?"

Pinky shook his head. "No, I'll sleep in the park. Mr. Lincoln will be upset if I'm not there."

The groundskeeper kept a close eye on my fae friend, and I was glad of it.

"Yes, I don't want you to worry Mr. Lincoln."

Pinky touched my cheek again and then walked away. I didn't know how he'd get back to the park, but I trusted he would. In the midst of the wreckage of my life, I at least had him, and he wasn't injured. Thank God.

He wasn't, but what about Asher? I didn't know. My dad? He was probably being tortured, and I didn't know what had happened to Tuli or Slate. I hoped they weren't punished.

I couldn't return to Joey's, not only because I was banished but because I couldn't face her after what I'd done to Evans. I couldn't face the fae.

Besides, Titania was probably on the warpath now. I wasn't safe anywhere, and my friends couldn't help me, even if they wanted to.

No Joey. No bar. No wee ones.

The sadness welled up inside me, and I slumped forward. Much to my chagrin, I started sobbing anew, but once that was done, something else arose.

Fury.

I'd killed Evans but not by choice.

Titania had started all of this by stealing my father. Heaven had made it worse by keeping secrets. Hell had played the long game and won this round.

It was time for me to end it.

Chapter 42

"She threw that vial at me! You heard Asher. He said it was a potion. It would have injured me!" Gregory sat across from me in his living room, clutching his chair's armrests. The room maintained its wealthy, bachelor-chic charm. Lots of leather, glass, and grays, black, and white. It had all the warmth of an iceberg.

"First of all, don't say Asher's name. Second, that vial never hit you. You were never in real danger. You brought a gun to a potion fight, you moron! You killed a woman. I would say your ledger is in the red, but your mother taught us the differently. Your ledger is black. Black and dripping with tar."

He paused mid-sentence. He let out a frustrated grunt. "I didn't mean to kill her."

Yeah, I didn't mean to kill Evans, either. Shit happens.

At least Gregory had ensured that Francesca's body was found by the police and went to the medical examiner, who ruled it an unsolved homicide. When no family came forward, he'd used his resources to anonymously fund a proper burial with a headstone in a local non-denominational cemetery.

I had no such closure with Evans, although I was happy to hear he'd been honored in Faerie.

"Well, you shouldn't have been waving a gun around. You think a gun makes you look tough? It makes you look like an insecure baby with something to prove."

"I carry it for personal protection."

"How'd that work out for you?" I couldn't keep the sarcasm out of my voice.

Gregory's shoulders drooped.

"Why were you there, anyway?" I continued. "You had no reason to be at my office."

"It's ironic. I went to your office to give you some good news and found Francesca summoning Valefar. Asher arrived immediately after. The whole scenario knocked the positive news right out of me."

"And your good judgment."

He didn't say anything but just ran his hands through his hair and sighed.

I gave in. "I could use some good news. What was it?"

He crossed his legs and picked an imaginary piece of dust off his shirt. "Oded's bills are paid."

That was something. It was a relief to know that Oded was out of debt.

"So, what now?" he asked.

I got to business. "Since you have money and I don't, and you owe me for murdering a woman in my place of business, you are going to help out. You will pay to have my office repaired and repainted, plus handle any damages the owners request. You will also pay for my rent at my apartment, make sure someone comes by to feed my birds regularly, and pay for my locker at the Krav Maga studio." I poured myself a drink from a crystal decanter. It looked expensive, whatever it was, and it eased its way down the back of my throat. Brandy. I poured a second.

"Help yourself," Gregory said, his snark returning. "Anything else?"

"Stay on top of Oded's situation. If he needs more treatment, he should get it, and make sure his business isn't bothered by your friends, the Andinos."

"They're not my friends."

"What about Anastasia?"

Gregory, that mobster, killer, loathsome worm, blushed.

I took my third brandy back to my chair and studied him. "You like her?"

"We're not talking about me," he said, with a sniff. He slinked to the liquor cabinet and poured himself a drink too, but whisky on ice. I eyed him.

"Don't form an alliance with that family, Gregory. Don't do it. I see that crazy look in your slitted eyes."

He snorted. "Is that all you want from me, or is there more?"

"There's something else. You will also buy Madame Francesca's shop and keep it maintained until I get back and can go through it."

"Fine." He crossed his arms and peered at me. "Wait? Where are you going to be?"

"I'm going to get my father back."

I slugged back the rest of my brandy.

"I'm going to Hell."

Epilogue

Asher sat cross-legged on the damp earth. Everything he'd done had been for naught. Every warning. Every explanation. Every secret, lie, and deception. Every sin.

He looked to the sky. "What do I do? It happened anyway. I failed."

Motes of light swirled in the navy sky dotted with stars. They spun fast, funneling down toward him in a sharp point until the tip of the cyclone hovered above his hands. He uncurled his fingers, and the motes coalesced into a shining message of three words.

"Go with her."

The message folded in upon itself, first one corner, then the next, until it was just a pinpoint. It glowed like a cigarette in the night and then faded away.

Asher's gut twisted so hard, he doubled over and collapsed to his side. He huffed out a weak breath, unable to move, gripped by the yawning chasm of his disgrace. Lying in a fetal position, he cried, sobs of loss and grief.

Had he lost his wings? Lost his grace?

Angels only went to Hell one way, and they only had one name. Fallen.

The End

Acknowledgment

The first thank-you is to Darin Kennedy, friend, colleague, writer, and beta reader extraordinaire. I'm so lucky to have someone like you in my corner.

I also need to thank Patrick Dugan for reading the first draft, providing feedback, and for supporting me every step of the way. In fact, my whole Secret Library—Darin, Patrick, Leslie Gould, Kristen Gould, and Jim Nettles, are instrumental to me staying positive when pushing words uphill feels too hard.

I'd also like to thank the Thursday Ladies—you know who you are— who force me to sit, butt in chair, fingers on keyboard, and make words. Also, the Authors' Roundtable, Falstaff Authors, and the Cajun Sushi Hamsters. Writing is a lonely business. You make it less so.
I wrote a lot of this book during virtual "write-ins" with The Writing Tribe. You guys have listened to me talk about every aspect of this trilogy and supported me all the way. Thank you. Venessa Giunta, you are a fabulous, and most appreciated, cheerleader.

A huge thank-you to Debra Dixon, and Brenda Chin for believing in this series and making my words better. Thank you to the whole crew at Bell Bridge Books for editing the manuscript so it looks like I know how to use a comma and creating gorgeous covers and internal layouts. Thanks also to John Hartness, who helped me get started down this path.

A special note to my husband who said that it was time to write, to follow the dream. Thank you for your unwavering support.

About the Author

Fae Crossed is J. D. Blackrose's second book in The Summoner's Mark Series. The first is *Demon Kissed*. Previously, she's published *The Soul Wars, The Devil's Been Busy*, and the *Zombie Cosmetologist* novellas through Falstaff Books. She's also published multiple short stories, including "Welcome, Death," in the *Jewish Book of Horror*. She's always lived in her head and is often accused of not listening. To make up for it, she's mastered the art of looking interested.

Follow her: www.slipperywords.com, https://www.facebook.com/JDBlackrose/ and https://twitter.com/JDBlackrose.

Made in the USA
Monee, IL
03 May 2022

95828116R00146